Praise for Angela Jackson-Brown

"Angela Jackson-Brown's reputation for digging deep and going wide at the same time continues to reward readers. Thoughtfully portrayed characters with deep minds and passionate hearts make *The Light Always Breaks* a memorable story that leaps off the page. You can see it, hear it, and feel it in your marrow. Hard and necessary truths are addressed, and as an avid reader of both historical fiction and historical romance, I found this novel struck a refreshing balance between the two. I highly recommend it."

—RHONDA McKNIGHT, AWARD-WINNING AUTHOR OF *UNBREAK MY HEART*

"Jackson-Brown paints a vivid picture of family and community persevering in the pressure cooker of the Deep South. Readers will be drawn to Opal's intelligent and authentic voice, as the book confronts issues of racism, injustice, and white privilege head-on. This is a powerful Own Voices contribution to the historical fiction genre, joining titles such as Alka Joshi's *The Henna Artist* and Kim Michele Richardson's *The Book Woman of Troublesome Creek* in their unflinching look at the past."

—*LIBRARY JOURNAL*, STARRED REVIEW, FOR *WHEN STARS RAIN DOWN*

"*When Stars Rain Down* is so powerful, timely, and compelling that sometimes I found myself holding my breath while reading it. Rarely have I been so attached to characters and felt so transported to a time and place. This is an important and beautifully written must-read of a novel. Opal is a character I will never forget."

—SILAS HOUSE, AUTHOR OF *SOUTHERNMOST*

"All in all, *When Stars Rain Down* is worthy of any reader's attention—especially fans of Southern literature. The writing is eloquent, the story is filled with conflict and tension balanced by warmth and charity, the characters are vivid and well-developed, and the impact is profound. This is the kind of book that will resonate long after the last pages are read."

—SOUTHERN LITERARY REVIEW

"Angela Jackson-Brown is a writer to watch . . . Along the way, [Jackson-Brown] deals with a series of issues: racism, teenage love, the death of our elders. These issues are not just talked through. Jackson-Brown the dramatist presents them in a series of carefully crafted scenes, almost one-act plays. Once in a while, one reads a novel and can already see the film to be made from it."

—DON NOBLE, ALABAMA PUBLIC RADIO, FOR WHEN STARS RAIN DOWN

"In this world there are writers and there are artists. Angela Jackson-Brown is both."

—SEAN DIETRICH (SEAN OF THE SOUTH), AUTHOR
OF THE INCREDIBLE WINSTON BROWNE

"Angela Jackson-Brown interrogates race, love, and family with empathy and style, making her an author you will want to read again and again. This tale of America's tragic past is both compelling and cinematic as the Pruitt and Ketchum families struggle in the mire of racism in the 1930s. It's a moving novel that boldly illuminates the past but also speaks directly to today's politics and the power of faith. You will fall in love with the book's resilient protagonist, Opal. I certainly did."

—CRYSTAL WILKINSON, AUTHOR OF THE BIRDS OF
OPULENCE, FOR WHEN STARS RAIN DOWN

THE
LIGHT
ALWAYS
BREAKS

Also by Angela Jackson-Brown

Fiction

When Stars Rain Down

Drinking from a Bitter Cup

Poetry

House Repairs

THE
LIGHT
ALWAYS
BREAKS

ANGELA
JACKSON-BROWN

HARPER MUSE

Library of Congress Cataloging-in-Publication Data

Names: Jackson-Brown, Angela, 1968- author.
Title: The light always breaks / Angela Jackson-Brown.
Description: [Nashville] : Harper Muse, [2022] | Summary: "In her distinctive Southern literary style, award-winning author Angela Jackson-Brown delivers a moving story of a star-crossed romance and the way love has the power to change everything"-- Provided by publisher.
Identifiers: LCCN 2021061626 (print) | LCCN 2021061627 (ebook) | ISBN 9780785240594 (paperback) | ISBN 9780785240600 (epub) | ISBN 9780785240617
Classification: LCC PS3610.A355526 L54 2022 (print) | LCC PS3610.A355526 (ebook) | DDC 813/.6--dc23
LC record available at https://lccn.loc.gov/2021061626
LC ebook record available at https://lccn.loc.gov/2021061627

Printed in the United States of America

22 23 24 25 26 LSC 5 4 3 2 1

To the ancestors. I feel your spirits always,
especially when I put pen to paper.

"Light breaks where no sun shines."

<small>DYLAN THOMAS</small>

"However long the night, the dawn will break."

<small>AUTHOR UNKNOWN</small>

ONE

Eva

Eva Cardon knelt down to pray the rosary with the beads that used to belong to her maternal grandmother, Bettine Cardon, wishing as she did every morning and evening that she could hear Grandmother Bettine's voice again, calling to her, saying in French, *"Ma belle petite-fille chérie. Le temps des prières."* My beautiful, darling granddaughter. *Time for prayers.* Grandmother Bettine would also say, in perfect French, which she insisted on Eva speaking as well, "The light will always break, Eva. You just have to give it time, and then any sadness left over from the previous day will fade away."

Thankfully, Eva was not feeling any sadness. She was happy to meet this morning head-on because the evening was going to be spectacular. She just knew it. As always, Eva positioned herself in front of the bay window in her bedroom to say her prayers. The sun was just beginning to peek out from between the barren tree limbs, casting eerie shadows throughout her room. It was December, and winter was just starting to make its mark on her beloved city of Washington, D.C., a city she had only lived in since the age of fourteen, but it was the place that had made the greatest impact on her because of the Negro community that consisted of politicians, religious leaders, activists, entertainers, you name it. Just like Harlem, Washington, D.C., was a place Negroes could live and shine, and Eva was learning some of her best lessons while living in D.C.

From the time Eva was a child, early mornings had been her favorite time of the day. She and her grandmother Bettine used to go for long walks through the French Quarter in New Orleans before her grandmother passed away. People would call her Bettine's little twin because Eva looked like a younger version of the Creole woman, from their long, black curly hair to their piercing green eyes and complexions so fair they both could have passed for white, but Grandmother Bettine would correct anyone who mistook them for anything other than Black Creole. "I am Colored," she would say, raising her chin haughtily at anyone who dared to question her ethnicity. "My maman was as black as onyx, and I rue the day I did not inherit her beautiful black complexion." Then she would turn to Eva and exclaim, "Always be proud of who God made you to be. Understood?" It wasn't until Eva was older that she truly understood her grandmother's fervor.

Now, years later, Eva meditated on her grandmother's words. She loved the mornings because she could get quiet with her thoughts and reflect on what challenges she might be facing throughout the day without worrying about being interrupted by her older sister, Frédérique, or her brother-in-law, Pearson, whose house she resided in. Early morning was also a time that was just for her to immerse herself in the rituals that had sustained her through the death of so many people she had loved, like her father, grandmother, and mother. She would alternate between praying in French, which was what her grandmother Bettine taught her to do, and Latin, which she was taught to do in parochial school. She would always say the sign of the cross in Latin, *"In nomine Patris et Filii et Spiritus Sancti.* Amen." But she would pray the rest of her prayers in French.

Eva's sister was no longer a practicing Catholic, but Eva was, in her own way. She didn't regularly attend Mass or confession, but she always, without fail, prayed her rosary in the morning and before she went to bed at night. Although Eva was in a rush to get her morning started, because she had so much to do before the evening, it was as if her grandmother Bettine, a pious, loving woman, was whispering, "*Ralentir, mon cher.*" *Slow down, my dear.* "*En toutes choses nous rendons grâce.*" *In all things we give thanks.*

With those words still in her ears, Eva stopped her rushing around and knelt and prayed the prayers that had been taught to her by her grandmother and the nuns at the parochial schools she had attended in New Orleans and later Harlem, but once she was done praying the rosary, she did not immediately get up. She whispered in a passionate voice, "Please allow tonight to be a success." She was just about to say amen once more, but then she added, "And please do not allow any hurt, harm, or danger to come to those who are out celebrating the New Year, whether at my restaurant or somewhere else. Amen." After that, Eva proceeded with her day, which was the culmination of years of dreaming on her part.

Eva Cardon's restaurant, Chez Geneviève, was going to be closed to the public for a private party she was throwing to celebrate the New Year. She'd opened the restaurant three years ago, and finally, she was at the point where she felt she could do things in a big way. She wanted 1947 to go out with full pomp and circumstance at Chez Geneviève, reminiscent of the New Year's Eve parties her mother used to throw at their brownstone in Harlem just off 147th Street, albeit to a much smaller degree. The guest list for Eva's party read like a Who's Who, thanks in large part to her friends Adam Clayton Powell Jr. and his wife, Hazel Scott. Adam and Hazel had made sure that every famous person they knew and/or had known her equally famous mother, jazz singer Geneviève Cardon, would be present that night.

There were Sammy Davis Jr. and Frank Sinatra sharing martinis with the likes of Jackie Robinson and Dinah Washington. And there were leaders in the Negro community like Howard University professor Alain Locke sharing small talk with local activist Mary Church Terrell.

Eva was awestruck and incredibly humbled by the crowd of high-profile, successful people in both the entertainment industry and politics who had RSVP'd for her huge soiree, but Adam and Hazel had reassured her that this moment wasn't just about her restaurant.

"Eva, my dear," Adam had said on the phone the day before when she had called him to see if he had any last-minute guests to add to the already burgeoning list. "This party of yours is bigger than any of us. The work you have done in the civil rights movement locally has been nothing short of astounding for someone your age. This moment is about showing the white establishment that we are here, and we are not going anywhere." Eva blushed at the compliments Adam was giving her. She didn't feel as if she had done much. Yes, she donated money to various causes, and she offered up her restaurant for planning meetings for voter registration and other causes that appealed to her, but really, she didn't see how her activities had amounted to the praise Adam was offering.

However, once the party started and she looked over the somewhat diverse crowd of attendees, Eva had to concur with Adam's observation that this moment truly was bigger than her. There weren't a lot of white guests who showed up for the party, only those who were brave enough to go to an establishment that was run by not only a woman, but a Negro woman at that. D.C. was a segregated town—as segregated as any Jim Crow South town. This was why this night was so important to her—to so many Negro leaders who had been working to end many of the segregation laws in effect in the city. This was her not-so-subtle way of saying to the individuals who preached segregation that she did not honor those written or unwritten laws. Plus, what police force would dare to storm a party filled with elite white and Negro celebrities like Sinatra and Jackie

Robinson? The optics alone would not go over well, and that had been Adam's goal all along when he first mentioned to her that she should have an integrated party.

"Let's see them tear gas Ethel Waters," Adam had said wryly, "or put handcuffs on Count Basie." Eva knew she was taking a huge risk by throwing this party—a risk that could lead to horrible retributions—but Eva was willing to take that risk. It was in her blood.

She had learned about civil rights at the feet of her mother, and she was not interested in taking the safe or easy way out in life. However, there were many in the Negro community who did not like the idea of her having such a high-profile party with white patrons present. Some of the local business owners had urged her not to move forward with her diverse New Year's Eve celebration. There were more than three hundred Negro-owned businesses on and around U Street in D.C., and most of those businesspeople showed up for a meeting to discuss, among other things, Eva's planned New Year's Eve party.

"How many times do we need to see white mobs coming into our communities with their hatred and violence?" said Hal Conroy, the owner of the upscale Negro restaurant The Phoenix. "Some of y'all weren't around here in 1919, but I was. I remember those four days of rioting like it was yesterday. We don't need to see that level of hatred aimed at us again."

Hal was referring to a riot that involved a Negro man being accused of raping a white woman. The civil unrest did not stop until finally President Wilson sent in federal troops.

Eva watched as various ones in the main sanctuary of her brother-in-law's church, Second Street Baptist, nodded in agreement. She noticed that Pearson was one of them. Eva's sister, Frédérique, had not attended, but Eva knew she would have been on Hal's side. Pearson and Frédérique were constantly urging her to tamp down her activities when it came to activism work in the community, but

Eva was headstrong, so once she made up her mind to host this New Year's Eve celebration, there wasn't much anyone could tell her.

"Eva, we appreciate all that you've done to help support our local young people by giving them jobs and backing various efforts to improve the civil rights of us all in this community, but when you keep challenging these white folks with your integrated parties and such, you put us all at risk," Hal said. "It's one thing for a random white person to come eat at your restaurant out from under the scrutiny of the media, but this event—this highbrow, highly visible event you're wanting to put on—is a direct thumb of your nose at the establishment. Plain and simple."

At that point, Mrs. Mary McLeod Bethune had stood. She was a well-respected educator, humanitarian, and civil rights activist. Mrs. McLeod Bethune had worked closely with Franklin D. Roosevelt and had been responsible for the creation of the Federal Council on Colored Affairs, also known as the Black Cabinet. When she spoke, people listened, both Negro and white, so Eva waited, knowing that the conversation was soon going to come to a close because Mrs. McLeod Bethune had not only offered her support to Eva but also encouraged her to do this and even more.

"I understand your fear," she said to the crowd of business owners and community leaders, "but we're entering into an era where fear is not an acceptable reaction to injustice. Eva is doing more than just 'throwing a party.' She is challenging the unacceptable Jim Crow laws that have no place in modern society, but especially not in our nation's capital. Don't try to stand in the way of progress, because progress has a way of rolling right along with us or without us. Don't be on the wrong side of history. Support this young woman. Don't be a hindrance to her or what she is trying to do."

A few people had clapped as Mrs. McLeod Bethune took her seat, but Eva noticed that many remained stoic and unmoving. Eva knew that it was her time to talk. Her mother had not raised her or

Frédérique to be fearful. Having integrated parties was something Geneviève used to do all the time. So Eva stood and surveyed the crowd, speaking with heartfelt conviction. "I hear your concerns, but the party will go on as planned. I am not trying to ruffle your feathers, and God knows, I am not trying to put anyone in harm's way. I just can't stand idly by while injustice continues to grow in our community. My mother taught me and my sister to never bow or scrape. No matter what, that philosophy has always served us well. I hope to see as many of you who feel comfortable at the New Year's Eve celebration."

As quietly as she had stood, she took her seat as her brother-in-law brought the meeting to a close with a prayer and encouragement for everyone to continue to support one another. Once the meeting was done, Eva turned her attention back toward making her party the best ever.

Coming up with the guest list had been an overwhelming task, even with the help of Adam and Hazel. Eva had spent months working on it. It was a fine dance to bring together the groups of people she chose to invite. Some folks she knew would not come due to her gender and race, and others would opt out because of divorces and friendship breakups, some of which were happening right up until the day before the party. She understood that just having Frank Sinatra present alone would cause her all sorts of headaches. His wife wasn't going to attend the party with him due to her being pregnant, and Frank, ever the playboy, had requested specific women like Ava Gardner and Marilyn Maxwell be present. Eva had purposely "lost" their invitations.

For most people, having such distinguished guests in their midst would have been daunting, but having spent her early years in Harlem, Eva had become quite familiar with a number of important and famous Negroes, as well as quite a few of the influential white celebrities who enjoyed "slumming it" in Harlem. Of all the "in" places one could go to there, like the Cotton Club or the Savoy, most preferred the intimacy of a house party because it lacked the scrutiny and publicity that were often attached to going out to some of the landmark clubs in Harlem.

Eva's mother, Geneviève, or "Viève" as most people called her, threw some of the best get-togethers. Geneviève was a retired blues and jazz singer. She had rivaled some of the greats like Bessie, Ella, and Sarah, but when she met Eva's father, a white, married land-owner in New Orleans, she let go of her dreams of fame to be his kept woman. After he died, she loaded up her family and moved to Harlem, where she said, "Negro folks could breathe out loud and not be afraid."

Everyone loved coming over to Viève's house and dancing the Lindy Hop on her parquet floors, drinking Dom Pérignon, and sipping on gin and tonics while rubbing elbows with the rich and talented. Businessmen, politicians, artists, and performers all loved to hobnob together at Viève's soirees. Eva and Frédérique grew up seeing this type of interaction firsthand.

That is why when Langston Hughes, Representative Adam Clayton Powell Jr., and Thurgood Marshall, to name a few, found out that Viève's little girl had a restaurant in D.C., they were all deter-mined to come out and support it. She had opened the doors three years before when she was only twenty-one, eight years after the sudden death of her mother. Her mother and father had left both Eva and Frédérique a very nice settlement, and Eva invested almost all of her money into Chez Geneviève.

Looking around the room now, she knew she had made good on her investment. Eva had used nearly every dime her parents had left her to buy this building and hire a young Negro interior designer, Calvin Aaron Toussaint, to decorate the place. Calvin had studied in Paris, which was evident by the parquet floors, French chandeliers, textured white walls, gold pendant and sconce lighting, and bone-colored leather banquettes and black-lacquered chairs.

The artwork was a combination of new and old paintings that had once belonged to Eva's mother, many of which were gifts from Eva's father to their mother. However, Eva's favorite paintings were watercolors done by Loïs Mailou Jones. Eva had commissioned her to create some original paintings for the restaurant the previous year, and everyone loved them because of their vibrant colors and abstract shapes. And then the room was filled with every white flower the florists at Lee's Flower Shop could locate.

"*Ce soir a été un triomphe, mère,*" Eva said underneath her breath, trying valiantly to keep the tears from flowing. *Tonight is a triumph, Mother.*

Some of her guests came from as far as Paris and others no farther than across town, but no matter where they came from, they all wanted to be there to witness Eva's success in the nation's capital because as much as some of the neighboring business owners had complained, most of them had shown up. Some because they were nosy and wanted to see what she had planned, and others simply because they wanted to show their support, like Hal, one of her biggest critics. He had kissed her on the cheek and whispered, "I hope you make a liar out of me. I hope this night is all you dreamed of and more, little miss, but more than that, I hope you don't have to pay for your obstinance."

Eva had agreed, and she hoped the same thing. Her thoughts were interrupted by none other than Mr. Paul Robeson, a well-known Negro actor and singer. Paul was not the kind of man to be ignored, so she turned to him with a radiant smile. She hoped it reached her eyes.

"Miss Eva Cardon, you set a fine table," Paul said as he kissed Eva on the cheek while holding a plate piled high with escargot de Bourgogne, Ris de Veau, and candied pork belly. "And I must say, you are the loveliest thing in this room. I can barely keep my eyes on my plate for staring at you."

Eva forced herself to continue smiling. Her face was pained by all of the schmoozing she had done throughout the evening. Eva was tall, standing at a statuesque five nine, but she still had to look up to see Paul, who she guessed was several inches over six feet. Paul Robeson was quite the looker in film, but up close he was almost breathtaking. Way too handsome for any man, and it was clear he knew what sort of effect he had on the ladies. Fortunately, Eva was immune to his advances. She knew his wife, Essie, and had no intention of disrespecting her by responding to Paul's flirtations in spite of the many rumors she had heard that their marriage was in trouble. If the truth be known, what marriage in the world of Hollywood and politics wasn't in trouble? Were it not for her sister and brother-in-law's undying love for each other, she wondered if she would ever believe love was possible.

"Thank you, Mr. Robeson. I'm happy you are enjoying yourself. If you will excuse me," she said, attempting to move around him, but he set his plate on a table and took both of her hands in his.

"Call me Paul. You're acting like this is our first-time meeting," he said. Like so many of the people present, Eva knew Paul Robeson through her mother. "You know you don't have to be so formal with me, Eva. I would enjoy myself more if you would sit and talk to me. I'm beginning to feel like I'm not your favorite guest," he said, flashing her his trademark smile. Clearly Paul Robeson was not dwelling on the fact that at the age of forty-seven, he was old enough to be her father. Eva didn't want to insult him by bringing up that fact, so instead, she chose tact.

"All of my guests are my favorite, Paul. You know that," she said and eased herself out of his grasp. "I'll check back on you later."

Eva had hundreds of guests to appease that night, many with egos just as huge as Mr. Paul Robeson's, so she continued to walk through the throngs of people, thanking each of them for coming out to her New Year's Eve party but not stopping to talk to any one person over a few seconds. She was thankful that all she had to do was be the hostess, unlike when she first opened Chez Geneviève. Back then, she was everything from the greeter to the dishwasher if that was what it took, but she soon realized she couldn't both run the restaurant and operate in the role of head chef too. Plus, her cooking skills were not nearly as strong as her business acumen. Even at such a young age, and with no formal college education, Eva instinctively understood what it took to run a business, and she knew she needed help.

With that in mind, she went back to her childhood home of New Orleans and convinced Chef LeRon du Passe, the head chef at Joseph Broussard's French Quarter establishment, Broussard's Restaurant, to come back with her and help her operate Chez Geneviève. Chef du Passe had been a close friend of her father and mother, and after much persuasion he had agreed to come for a year or two at the most and train her staff in the ways of cooking authentic Cajun and French cuisine.

It was now three years later, and Chef du Passe continued to say, "I shall return to New Orleans next year."

Eva would just smile and dutifully kiss him on his cheeks. She knew that it would take an act of Congress to get Chef du Passe to leave Chez Geneviève. It was as much his baby now as it was hers. Plus, Eva had the good sense to give him free rein over the kitchen and the freedom to go back home to New Orleans and visit his family and friends whenever he wanted. Chef du Passe had gone back to visit home only once. The restaurant kept him busy, and he wasn't ready to turn over the kitchen to any of his protégés, not even for a week.

On the night of the New Year's Eve party, however, it was not the food or the music that caught the attention of every woman and man in the room. It was Eva who had them totally and completely entranced. Eva carried herself like a cross between a Hollywood starlet and a D.C. socialite. She was by far one of the youngest people in the room, but she was able to hold her own among the rich and powerful who graced her establishment that night. And there were many women there to rival her beauty, like Lena Horne and Josephine Baker, who had flown in from Paris to witness Viève's little girl's triumphant night, but none of them came close to stealing her shine.

"Chérie, tu es magnifique!" Josephine exclaimed in an accent that was far more French than American. *Darling, you are magnificent.* "I never thought there would ever be a woman alive to match Viève's beauty and grace, but child, you have. Your mother would be so proud of you tonight," Josephine said, kissing Eva on both cheeks while Josephine's new husband, Jo Bouillon, stood off to the side smiling at both women.

"Thank you," Eva replied, in awe of the older woman who still lit up a room with her very presence. Eva wore a black-and-gold chiffon beaded dress that was reminiscent of the style of clothing Josephine herself had made famous. Eva watched as Josephine glided across the room to a seating area where Langston Hughes was holding court. Eva tried to drink in the sheer magnitude of all that was happening around her, but as always, there was one thing after another that she had to deal with to make sure the night went over flawlessly for everyone in attendance.

One of the waiters rushed up to Eva as the final strains of Duke Ellington's "Mood Indigo" played in the background.

"Miss Eva, we are running low on champagne," the eager young man gushed.

Eva had just recently hired and trained him and several other waiters for the evening, and it was apparent that he was unused to the fast-paced, high-energy atmosphere of Chez Geneviève on a night like this. To be honest, this night was unlike any night Eva had ever experienced, but she knew how to finesse her way through most any situation.

Eva patted his shoulder and smiled. He was only a couple of years younger than she, but she felt decades older. "Don't worry, Lincoln. There is plenty of wine and champagne in the cellar below. I'm sorry no one bothered to tell you. Go get Antoine to help you bring up a few more cases. We should be fine."

Lincoln smiled and attempted an awkward bow and then hurried away in search of the head waiter.

"You are quite the efficient hostess," a deep voice said behind her.

Eva turned and saw a very handsome and debonair-looking white man standing a breath's distance from her, looking at her with a familiarity that almost made her snap something rude at him, but she reminded herself that he was a guest, and she couldn't allow him to get to her any more than any other man in the room.

The unknown man was well over six feet, and he cut quite the figure as he leaned lightly on a walking cane. Eva wasn't sure if the cane was for getting around or for adding to his overall persona. A thick lock of dark curly hair hung down over his left eye in an almost rakish fashion, and he was sipping on a glass of dark liquor, all the while admiring her with his eyes. He reminded Eva of the actor John Payne or perhaps Tyrone Power. He was wearing the standard tuxedo, but nothing was standard about the way he looked in it. Eva could not help but admire how well the suit seemed to mold to his body. Clearly it had been tailor-made for him. Realizing she had been staring at the stranger for quite some time, Eva cleared her throat with embarrassment.

"I-I . . . Do I know you?" she asked, finally settling on something to say.

The man took a sip from his glass and laughed. "No, but I would sure like for us to get to know each other."

Eva blushed. "This is a private party, sir, so if I don't know you, then that means you weren't invited."

He smiled broadly. "Then let me introduce myself so maybe I can get on your A-list. My name is Courtland Hardiman Kingsley IV." He extended a hand, but she ignored it.

"If the name is supposed to mean something to me, it doesn't," she replied.

"Well, I'm no Paul Robeson, but I'm no slouch either," he said and reared back his head and laughed with an abandonment that caused others in the room to look over at them. Just as Eva had decided she was going to find her security so he could throw out this impertinent man who was having so much fun at her expense, Representative Adam Clayton Powell Jr. walked over to them.

"Hey, hey, I see you've met the country boy senator from Georgia, Miss Eva," Adam said, slapping Courtland on the back. "I hope you don't mind me inviting the good senator here to your party. It's not often the House and the Senate get to rub elbows together. Those senators are a snooty bunch," he said with a laugh, then quickly got serious. "Senator Kingsley and I needed to talk some politics, and I thought here would be as good a place as any."

Eva's face turned a dark red as Courtland bowed low and then laughed again as he and Adam walked away together. Eva noticed that he had a slight limp, but it did not detract from his overall aesthetic. She cursed herself for not recognizing Courtland. She had prided herself on knowing most, if not all, of the Washington elites by face if not by name.

Debating over whether or not she should go over and apologize to Courtland for her faux pas, she was once again interrupted by a staff member. One of the waiters had gotten sick and needed to be seen about, so for a time, she forgot about Courtland and their encounter as she got busy putting out fires. It was a quarter until midnight before Eva ran into Courtland again. He was standing by the double doors that led to the balcony overlooking U Street. He halted her with his voice.

"Well, have I made it onto your A-list yet?" he asked.

For the first time that evening, Eva smiled at him. "I'm sorry for before. You startled me, and I behaved rudely."

"All is forgiven. Actually, I am more to blame than you, Miss Cardon. I should have told you from the start that Representative Powell had invited me."

Eva wondered how such an unlikely union of New York's Representative Powell and this "country boy senator" could have occurred.

"You'd be surprised how much Representative Powell and I have in common," he said, almost as if he heard her thoughts.

Eva lifted her brow. "Excuse me?"

"You were wondering how Adam and I became friends."

"Yes. I suppose so," Eva admitted with a slight smile.

"Not all of us Southern senators are bad. We aren't all Georgia crackers below the Mason-Dixon Line," he said, then laughed again as Eva felt herself blush once more.

"You do laugh a lot, Senator Kingsley," she said in a gruff tone.

Courtland took her hand in his. "Why not laugh, Miss Cardon? There is so much to be sad about in this world. Why not laugh when we get those rare moments like we have been given tonight?"

Eva pulled her hand away. "Well, I am glad that I amuse you so much."

Courtland smiled, leaning casually on his cane. "Don't be offended. I love to laugh, and unfortunately, I haven't done a lot of laughing in recent years. The brief interludes that we shared tonight have brought much pleasure to my sad, boring little life."

Eva let out a quick laugh of her own. "Please, Senator Kingsley. I would hardly say your life is sad or boring. From what I can tell, you keep the media hopping with all of your wild escapades."

Courtland tilted his head and looked at her mockingly. "And I thought you didn't know me."

Eva looked away embarrassedly. Although she had been busy

throughout the night, she had made time to question her sister about Courtland. Frédérique, who was always up on D.C. gossip, immediately had choice words to say about Courtland.

"Oh, that one," Frédérique had said in her rich Southern voice.

Somehow the Southern drawl had escaped Eva, who had a more clipped New York sound to her voice. Maybe because she had lived fewer years in the South than Frédérique. Either way, Eva loved the sound of her sister's voice because it reminded her of their mother. Where Eva favored their grandmother, Frédérique was Geneviève through and through—from her light brown complexion to her thick, coarse black hair.

Frédérique continued, speaking softly so as not to be overheard gossiping, "If the papers are to be believed, Senator Kingsley is as wild as they come. They call him and that John F. Kennedy the Rowdy Boys of Washington. Kingsley is the bad boy in the Senate and Kennedy in the House."

Eva had pressed her for more details, but Frédérique had dismissed him as yet another senator from the South whose only concern was to make sure he and his white constituents stayed in power.

"Have you been struck mute, Miss Cardon?" Courtland teased just as someone yelled, "Ten seconds to midnight!"

"I sh-should check that everyone has champagne," she stuttered, but the countdown to 1948 had already begun.

"Five . . . four . . . three . . . two . . . one . . . Happy New Year!" everyone screamed as Duke Ellington and his orchestra began playing "Auld Lang Syne."

Courtland kissed her lightly on her cheek.

"Happy New Year, beautiful lady," he whispered, and then he kissed her again, but this time on the lips. For a few seconds, Eva kissed him back, but then she realized what she was doing and pushed him away, slapping him resoundingly across his face.

"Don't do that," she hissed, looking around to see if anyone had seen them, but everyone seemed engrossed in the act of celebrating the arrival of 1948.

Courtland rubbed his jaw slightly and had the good graces to look apologetic. Eva frowned but was pleased to see that he wasn't a total cad.

"I'm sorry. That was . . . uncalled for and highly inappropriate. I think I have had enough dark liquor for one night. Please, accept my apologies," he said and walked away from her, disappearing into the throngs of people who were back on the dance floor, swaying to Duke Ellington's "Take the 'A' Train."

Instead of going out into the crowd and mingling with her guests, Eva stood rooted in her spot, unsure of what she really felt about that kiss. One thing was for sure, however: this was not how she expected to ring in the New Year. Not at all.

TWO

Eva

The kiss that Eva shared with Courtland on New Year's Eve stayed on her mind long after it ended. Once she got home close to 5:00 a.m. on New Year's Day and was able to go to bed, her dreams were filled with images of Courtland and that kiss. Slapping him was the right thing to do, she acknowledged to herself, but that acknowledgment didn't stop the daydreaming, over and over. Eva couldn't understand what she was feeling, and she felt too embarrassed to bring it up to Frédérique. She and Frédérique talked about a lot of things, but this subject was not one they had discussed beyond the usual, "Do not do anything to embarrass yourself or this family." So Eva tried her best to pack away her emotions as best she could, but out of the blue, the sensuousness of that brief interlude with Courtland would invade her thoughts, much to her dismay.

Eva closed the restaurant for two days after the event, with plans to reopen for business that Saturday. She and Chef du Passe got together on the Friday before she reopened to discuss the menu for the next day and the upcoming week, something that usually excited her, but all Eva could seem to focus on was that kiss. Several times, Chef du Passe touched her arm, causing her to jump.

"*Est-ce que ça va?*" he asked. *Are you okay?*

"*Oui, merci,*" she responded. *Yes. Thank you.* After the second or third time he had to ask her that question, or some form of it, she forced herself to stay in the moment. But as she drove home after her meeting with the chef, her mind returned to the night of the party. Eva tried to stay miffed at Courtland for kissing her like that without even knowing her, but she just couldn't. That kiss awakened something inside of her that she didn't know existed. Just like Eve from the Bible, Eva felt as if for the first time her eyes were opened to things she had never thought about, like attraction to the opposite sex. Oh, she'd had schoolgirl crushes, but nothing happened with them other than a shared giggle with some of the girls at school. But this . . . this felt different. What she was feeling felt very much adult-like.

Times like this, she desperately wished her mother was still alive. When Frédérique spoke of attraction to men, it was always in the context of marriage. As far as Eva knew, Frédérique hadn't shared much more than a peck on the cheek with Pearson before they got married, and she absolutely knew her sister was a virgin on her wedding night. Eva knew a conversation with Frédérique about her current feelings would lead to a lecture that included Scripture and prayers. Lots of prayers.

"Pull yourself together," she chided herself as she pulled her car, a 1946 Super DeLuxe Tudor sedan, in front of the brownstone she shared with her sister and brother-in-law. When she entered the house, she heard the familiar sounds of Frédérique and Pearson cooking dinner together.

"I'm home," she said as she put her coat in the hall closet.

"Good," Frédérique said from the kitchen. "Go wash up and sit down at the table. Dinner will be ready in about five minutes. So happy you made it home."

"Do you need any help?" Eva called back.

"No," Frédérique replied. "Pearson and I have everything under control. You just go and make yourself comfortable."

Eva made her way into the hall bathroom where she quickly washed her hands. She was tired, but she also didn't mind helping out in any way she could. She was grateful that her sister and brother-in-law had taken on the task of raising her after her mother passed away. The last thing she ever wanted to be was a burden, even though she knew both Frédérique and Pearson would insist that she wasn't.

Before turning the corner into the dining room, Eva noticed the newspaper was still sitting on the table in the hallway. She picked it up and went into the formal dining room where Frédérique insisted they take all of their meals. The room was filled with antiques Frédérique had handpicked, as well as artwork that had once belonged to their maternal grandmother. Because they never got the chance to eat a meal with their father growing up, Frédérique was a stickler about family dinners, and she always wanted them to be special, from the food itself to the plates and glasses they used. Frédérique did not believe in saving the "good china" for when they had guests. She always said, "The most special people I can ever have at this table are you and Pearson, so why wouldn't I use my best dishes, linens, and glassware?" Since it was so important to Frédérique to put on an elaborate show at every meal they shared, Eva never balked, although she did tease her sister occasionally about the formality of it all.

As Eva sat down at the table, in spite of herself, she couldn't help but peruse the paper a little closer than usual, just in case there was a mention of the "country boy senator from Georgia." And, as fate would have it, there was an article in *The Washington Post* about Courtland. It pertained to some of the laws concerning the inequities of higher education in the United States. Although Courtland never mentioned Negro people specifically, he was quoted as saying that he felt the present higher education system was not fair to all

American citizens, and he would support any bill that would ensure that everyone got a chance to experience quality education.

A part of Eva wished he would have just come right out and been specific with his words, but she also recognized that with the present racial climate of the country, particularly in states like Georgia where Courtland was from, there was no way he wouldn't be careful about how he introduced new ways of looking at the social ills of the day. Eva was thinking about that and other things concerning Courtland as her sister and brother-in-law placed the food on the table. Once they were settled, Eva brought up what she had just read in the paper about Courtland.

"Senator Kingsley is suggesting some very revolutionary ideas, don't you think?" Eva asked as she passed the roasted duck to Pearson after putting a sliver on her plate. So much of Eva's day was spent tasting food, and by the time she arrived home, the most she would want was a nibble or two, mainly to satisfy Frédérique.

Frédérique eyed her sister with suspicion. "That Georgia senator? What makes you bring him up?"

"Nothing," Eva said quickly. "I was just reading the newspaper earlier and saw something about him wanting to support access to education for everyone."

Frédérique snorted as she put green beans on her plate. "For everyone? Right. We all know everyone doesn't include Negroes."

"Why do we all know that?" Eva pressed. "Perhaps he means exactly what he says."

Pearson chuckled in a loud voice as he put a large helping of roasted duck on his plate. "He's from the South, Eva. That alone tells us he isn't thinking about our people. And anyway, let's just say for the sake of argument he did mean Negroes. How revolutionary is it to suggest the things Negro folks should already be getting in the first place? Warranted, yes; revolutionary, not so much."

Frédérique nodded in agreement as she put a dab of mashed

potatoes beside her green beans. "Pearson's right. It's like Negroes are supposed to stand up and cheer every time a white person throws us a few crumbs. As long as we're still getting strung up in trees in the South and other rural parts of this nation, I don't feel any sense of gratitude for the little bit of good they do for us."

Pearson reached over and patted his wife's hand. Eva knew that Pearson knew the two of them could easily become like oil and water when conversations about race came up. After their father died, Frédérique basically put up a wall between her Black self and her white self. Although, to hear Frédérique tell it, there was no white self; in that regard, she was just like their maternal grandmother, Bettine. If the subject ever came up, Frédérique was quick to say, "I am Negro to the bone." Any and every chance Frédérique could take to deny the white part of her DNA or belittle the white race, she took it. Unlike Eva, who was quite fair skinned, Frédérique, who was much darker, was often teased and ridiculed about her skin color when they were children.

People would refer to Eva as the "pretty one" and Frédérique as the "smart, sensible one." Eva knew it hurt her sister even though she never complained, and she definitely never showed the slightest hint of jealousy over Eva's appearance. But Frédérique did go out of her way to embrace all things Black. A part of Eva wondered if Frédérique had first started dating Pearson because he was so dark skinned. Eva knew her sister loved Pearson with all of her heart, but she also believed Frédérique would not have given him a second look had he been lighter complected.

"I'm not saying we should put white people on a pedestal, Freddie, but I do think we can legitimately respect those few who actually do try to right some of the wrongs that have been done against us," Eva said.

She wasn't sure why she was trying so hard to make her sister like Courtland. If the truth be known, she wasn't even sure if she liked him. Yes, he was very handsome, but other than that, she knew nothing about the man. Well, she knew he was a good kisser, in spite of her slap to his face. She didn't want to imagine what Pearson and Frédérique would say if they knew he had spoken fresh to her and kissed her without her permission. Well, suffice it to say, for all of Pearson's God-love as a Baptist minister, had he seen or even heard about the kiss, he would have been the first to be on the hunt for the country boy senator from Georgia.

Frédérique poured herself a cup of coffee, her drink of choice for every meal. "You go right ahead and respect those folks if you like. I don't have it in me at this time," she said.

Pearson smiled at both women. "My dears, let us pray," he said, reaching for both of their hands. That was Pearson. Whenever it looked like things were about to go left between the two sisters, he always found a way to bring their little family together, which usually involved him saying some type of prayer.

Frédérique was seven years older than Eva, just recently turned thirty-one, but at times the two of them could lock horns like they were children all over again. Pearson chose to deal with their arguments with love and godliness. Eva was thankful Pearson had come into their lives when he did, just weeks after their mother died in her sleep from a heart attack. Pearson, who was ten years older than Frédérique, not only became a husband to Frédérique but also a stand-in father for the then thirteen-year-old Eva. Now, as he sat at the head of the table, looking lovingly from Frédérique to Eva, Eva silently thanked God for this phenomenal man, because without him, she didn't know what their lives would have been like. She listened as Pearson prayed over their meal and for the sisters' peace of mind.

"Lord, bless this family. Bless these two passionate women, who have such strong convictions but who, at the end of the day, love each other. And God, thank you for bringing them both into my life. I can't remember what the world was like before I was blessed with a wonderfully strong wife and a wonderfully strong little sister-daughter. May the food we are about to eat be nourishing to our bodies and minds. Amen."

He kissed Frédérique's hand, and Eva immediately knew the argument was over, although Pearson's next question was just as polarizing, but for a totally different reason.

"Adam called me today, and he mentioned there's going to be a meeting at the restaurant in a few days," Pearson said, carefully loading up his fork with duck and mashed potatoes. "Do you think it's wise to get involved in all of these civil rights activities, one after another?"

"The dust has hardly settled from that party you threw," Frédérique said.

Eva held back a sigh. She was hoping to postpone telling Pearson and Frédérique about the meeting. Adam and Mary McLeod Bethune had asked her if she would be willing to host it, and of course she said yes, but telling her sister and brother-in-law was not something she was anxious to do, so she had put it off. Eva didn't want another argument, but Pearson and Frédérique's approach to protesting was far more passive than hers. Pearson and Frédérique preached patience and waiting on God to move the hearts of racists. Eva didn't believe patience was an effective way to address the social ills of the day, particularly those related to Negro rights.

"Pearson, I know you and sissy worry about me," Eva said. "That's why I didn't say anything, but—"

Frédérique interrupted. "You don't know how much we worry, Eva. You just don't. You are reckless at times, and you are purposely making yourself a target for every racist with an agenda. That party was bad enough, as beautiful as it was, but now you want to join forces with Adam and all of these other folks with a radical agenda? God knows I admire them and their tenacity, but I would be remiss if I didn't say I am scared for your life. Can't you just donate to their causes and stay out of the fray?"

"What would Mother do if she were still here and they asked for her help?" Eva asked softly.

Throughout their childhood, their mother had used her celebrity for groups like the NAACP and the New York City League of Women Voters. No matter what any of them asked, their mother was always eager to support, and she made sure her daughters knew what she was doing and involved them when possible. Eva remembered being a little girl and walking through Harlem with their mother as she talked to people about the importance of voting.

"Yes, Eva, our mother was a trailblazer in a lot of ways, but if I'm to be honest with you, my reasons for wanting you to slow down are purely selfish," Frédérique said softly, looking away as tears rolled down her face. "The thought of losing another person in my life is more than my heart can bear. I'm afraid of what might happen to you if you don't back away from all of this public protesting. We have a comfortable life. You have a wonderful business. Why can't that be enough?"

Eva got up from her chair and walked over to her sister, taking Frédérique's hands in hers. Immediately, Eva knew where a lot of her sister's emotions were stemming from. The week before Christmas, Frédérique had a miscarriage. It was her third. Eva knew her sister tried to be stoic about the miscarriages, always insisting that when God was ready for her and Pearson to have children, he would make it so, but Eva knew the losses were wearing on her. She never wanted to do anything to make things worse for either Frédérique or Pearson, but she had to follow her heart.

"Sissy, I don't ever want to hurt you or make you afraid. I just feel as if this work with Adam and Mrs. McLeod Bethune and the others is part of the purpose God has for me. I might not ever have a husband or family beyond you and Pearson, but this work—fighting for the rights of our people—this feels like my calling."

Pearson cleared his throat and looked at Eva with a smile. "If that is what your convictions tell you, then we will just pray for God's grace over your life. We would never try to stand in the way of what you believe is your purpose, but promise us this: that you will be careful and always let us know what you're doing so we can cover you in prayer."

Frédérique smiled through her tears. "My prayers for you are constant. Just be mindful of what you do. Test every spirit. Sometimes we think we are hearing from God; instead, it is our own desire leading us."

Eva bent and hugged Frédérique, kissing her on the top of her head. "I promise to be mindful at all times. And thank you for understanding—or at least trying to understand."

Later that night, Eva was lying in her bed reading Rudolph Fisher's detective story, *The Conjure-Man Dies*, when she heard a knock at the door.

"Come in," she said, knowing it was Frédérique.

She laid the book down and waited as Frédérique entered the room, already dressed in her nightgown and robe. She came over to the bed and sat beside her sister, taking Eva's hands in hers.

"You know I'm proud of you, right?" Frédérique asked.

"Of course," Eva said with a smile. "You have been my biggest supporter from the day I took my first breath, according to Mother. And I know you worry about me all of the time, and I don't want to contribute more to what you are already feeling, but I just feel like this work with Adam and the others, even more so than the restaurant, is something I have to do."

"I'm trying to understand," Frédérique said, "and when I heard you say you believed what you were doing was according to God's plan, I told myself I needed to trust you more and definitely trust

God. Just continue to listen. That's all I ask. And in spite of what some might think, it is okay to ask God questions. I do it all the time. I'm never accusatory, I just . . . every now and then, say something like, 'Hey, God. Did I hear you right?'"

Eva laughed. "That sounds exactly like you. I will. I promise."

Frédérique kissed Eva's cheek and stood, but then she sat again. "I might be overstepping, but I have been your eyes and ears since before you could walk, and I notice you seem a bit taken by this senator from Georgia. Am I misreading you?"

Eva turned away, feeling her cheeks immediately grow warm. "I just thought his stance on education was good. That's all."

Frédérique smiled. "I know you consider me a prudish Goody Two-shoes, but I know when a woman is feeling something for a man. I saw the light in your eyes the night of the party when you asked me about him, and I saw that same light a little while ago when you brought him up at the table. Your sister sees everything when it comes to you."

"It's nothing," Eva insisted, feeling embarrassed. "I was just asking questions."

Frédérique placed her hand on Eva's shoulder. "I know Pearson and I have sheltered you from boys . . . men. We encouraged you to be a woman business owner, but we never taught you very much about the birds and the bees. The senator from Georgia is a very handsome man, I will give him that, but remind yourself that it could never be anything more than a dalliance, and you deserve more than that. At the end of the day, he is a white man, and you are a Negro woman. Nothing has changed when it comes to relationships between the races. Remember that."

"I understand," Eva said, "but I don't think it is worth mentioning since he was only at the party because of Adam. There is no reason for me to believe I will ever see him again."

"Okay," Frédérique said. "I hope that is true."

Eva watched her sister walk out of the room, then tried to return her attention to her book, but thoughts of Courtland reentered her mind. She knew her sister was right. This white senator from Georgia was the last person she should be thinking about. All she had to do was remind herself of the grief her mother endured and her grandmother before that. Neither woman ever lived to have a love they could have in public like Pearson and Frédérique.

Get him out of your thoughts, she chided herself silently as she gave up trying to read and tried to focus on sleep. *And anyway, just like you told Frédérique, you will probably never see him again.*

It took a while for sleep to find her, but mercifully her dreams were Courtland-free. And by the next day, the crowd was so heavy at the restaurant, she didn't have time to daydream about Courtland or anyone else for that matter. Her staff was so overwhelmed by the lunch crowd that she ended up acting as the hostess, making sure people were seated quickly and that tables were bussed as soon as a group of diners were done. She got so busy that she almost didn't hear the deep, rich baritone voice behind her.

"Good afternoon, Miss Cardon," he said. She turned in time to see Courtland standing with a bouquet of pink and white roses as he leaned on his walking cane, looking extremely dashing.

"Hello, Senator Kingsley," she said, making sure her voice did not show the excitement she was feeling. And anyway, the last time the two of them had seen each other, she had resoundingly slapped him across his face. It would not have made sense for her to suddenly start gushing over seeing him again.

"I wanted to bring you these flowers as an apology for my brutish behavior the other night," he said with an embarrassed look. "I drank more than I should have. That's no excuse, but it is an explanation, and I'm sorry."

Eva took the flowers, feeling a bit embarrassed herself from the attention she was receiving from Courtland as well as many of her patrons whose eyes were fixated on the two of them. Eva stopped one of the waiters and gave the flower arrangement to him.

"Thank you for the flowers," she said to Courtland. "And thank you for your apology."

"You are very gracious. I was hoping I might have lunch here today, but judging from the crowd, that doesn't seem likely," Courtland said, smiling, "which is a great thing. The more customers the better, right?"

She smiled back at him. "Most definitely. The restaurant business can be finicky at times, but I have been blessed. We tend to always have a good crowd." She paused but then decided that since he was so kind to come and apologize and bring her flowers, she would extend kindness to him. "If you don't mind waiting another minute or two, I can seat you at my table," she finally said, maintaining the formality in her voice.

He bowed low. "Thank you, Miss Cardon. I hope you will join me at your table."

"I'm afraid I have much to do," she said.

She would have loved nothing more than to join Courtland for lunch, but if she was truly trying to decrease her attraction to him rather than increase it, she knew she had to keep her distance.

"Come this way," she said, waving away her maître d' as she walked Courtland over to the corner table where she would sometimes sit and observe the goings-on in the restaurant, making sure everyone was happy and content. Other times, she would give that table to important customers who came in to eat.

"I am excited to get the chance to sample more of the restaurant's delicacies," he said, the twinkle back in his eyes, making her unsure if he was referring to the food or her. She blushed and looked away.

"Well, I'm sure our very extensive menu will more than satisfy your taste," she said in a husky voice.

"Any suggestions on what I should order?" Courtland asked.

Eva quickly adopted her hostess voice. "Today the chef has prepared red beans and rice. I think you would like that. The blackened catfish is also tasty. I'll send a waiter over to take your order. And please, order whatever you like. It's on the house," she said and then immediately regretted it. What if he took her kindness the wrong way? Many times, she would give important first-time guests a meal on the house to ensure their loyalty and rapid return, a lesson taught to her by Chef du Passe.

"There is nothing rich people like better than to receive something for free," Chef du Passe had said to her. And he was right. The two of them used to laugh at how the eyes of the rich and famous would light up when she offered them something free, whether it be a free meal or a free bottle of her best champagne.

"You don't have to do that," Courtland said. "I don't mind being a paying guest."

"I do this with all of my preferred customers," she said and almost bit her tongue when she saw the huge grin on Courtland's face.

"I hope you don't have too many preferred customers," he teased.

Feeling her cheeks grow warm, Eva chose to ignore his comment. "Have a nice lunch," she mumbled, then turned and walked with a swiftness to her office.

Once again, she had allowed him to get her all riled up. Determined not to sit and daydream about Courtland, Eva busied herself with the mountain of paperwork on her desk. She employed just a little more than eighty-five people, so keeping up with the payroll and other issues that came up related to having a large staff had her working well into the wee hours most every night. Eva kept promising herself she would hire an assistant, but she never did. She enjoyed having her hands in all parts of her business, and since she was single and not really looking to date, she had the time to focus on her business with a single-mindedness. In fact, she had become so immersed in her work that when someone knocked at the door, she jumped.

"Come in," she said as she stood from her soft leather-back chair, which had been a gift from Frédérique and Pearson when she opened the restaurant.

It was Courtland. He entered the office, leaving the door ajar. "I wanted to thank you for a delicious lunch. Your chef is amazing. How did you happen to find someone of his capabilities here in D.C.? I mean, his cooking tastes so authentic. It was like being in a French Quarter restaurant."

Eva smiled. She always loved telling the story of how she hired Chef du Passe. She walked from around her desk and offered Courtland a seat on the burgundy couch she'd recently purchased. She sat beside him but made certain there was plenty of space between them. She then told him how she lured Chef du Passe from his position at Broussard's.

"You are quite the businessperson, Miss Cardon. Very few women your age would have had the know-how or the drive to venture into something as daunting as opening a brand-new restaurant in a city they weren't even from. Whatever gave you such an idea?" Courtland asked.

"My mother," she said simply. "Mother was the quintessential hostess, so I guess her people skills rubbed off on me. And the other business owners here in and around U Street are very helpful with information. I have relied on quite a few of them whenever I had questions."

"Well, you have definitely made a restaurant your mother would have been proud of," he said. "You are very impressive, Miss Eva Cardon."

Eva gave a shy smile. "I've been very blessed with a wonderful staff. The restaurant practically runs itself," she said.

Courtland shook his head. "I don't believe that. You are clearly the mastermind behind this great operation, Miss Cardon."

"Thank you, but like I said, I am very lucky," she said, feeling uncomfortable with all of the compliments. Humility was something her mother stressed to both her and Frédérique as they were growing up, and Frédérique had continued hammering home the idea that being humble was a trait that would take her further in life than arrogance.

"You are being far too modest. Being business-minded is something to be proud of, and you have every right to be proud. I'm trying to imagine my sisters or my mother running a business," he said, laughing. "They would have had to declare bankruptcy before the end of the first day of business, I'm afraid."

"That's not nice to say," Eva said. "I'm sure they aren't as bad as all that."

"Oh no, Miss Cardon. Trust me when I say I love my mother and sisters, but they can be quite the handful," he insisted. "They are firm believers in the spending of money, not the making of it. When I came home on medical release from the war, the first thing my younger sister, who was twelve at the time, asked me was if I had remembered to stop by Paris to pick up the fineries they had written me about in their letters. Can you believe that? Here I was returning the wounded warrior, and all they could think about was all of those silks and satins I had left behind."

Eva looked at him with concern. "You were hurt during the war? Are you okay?"

Courtland smiled. "I'm fine. It was just a little shrapnel to the leg. No big deal," he said. "My men and I had landed on—hey, are you sure you want to hear these old war stories?"

"Absolutely," Eve said. If the truth be known, he could have been talking about anything. She just wanted to hear his voice. It was mesmerizing. No wonder he was reported to be such a ladies' man. What lady wouldn't be caught up by the sound of his voice, not to mention his good looks? She had read somewhere that he was thirty-five, but he could pass for much younger, even with the walking cane.

"Like I was saying, not long after we landed on Guadalcanal, several of us got separated from the rest of the platoon," he said in a quiet tone. Instantly, he seemed transported to a different place.

"You don't have to talk about this if you don't want to," Eva said in a soft voice. She didn't want him to relive anything that was going to cause him pain.

Courtland shook his head. "It's okay. I don't mind. I get asked to talk about this time of my life fairly regularly. I just haven't really sat down and talked about it one-on-one with anyone in a while. You make talking easy."

"Thank you," Eva replied, blushing. "If you are sure you want to share, then please, continue."

Courtland started talking again. "My men were the best the Army had to offer. We were the first Army unit on Guadalcanal. We came onshore to support the Marines. We joined the 182nd and 132nd Infantry Regiments, forming a new division called the Americal." He paused again. "If at any point you want me to stop, just say so. These war stories can be . . . heavy."

"I'm fine, Courtland. Tell me your story," she prodded. She could sense that he wanted to talk . . . needed to talk.

"Well, several of my men came down with dysentery and were not having an easy go of it; they kept falling behind. Once I realized they were struggling, I sent a couple of other men to rally them up, but then I lost contact with them. I decided I had to go back and locate my men, so I took about a half dozen guys. We found them all deep in enemy territory. They were sick and surrounded—not a good combination."

"My God. You all could have been killed," Eva said, shuddering at the thought.

"You're right about that," he said. "It was so hard to make your way out there. The terrain was dense, and before we knew it, we were outgunned and definitely outmanned. Somehow I managed to get my men out of there, but in the process, I got hit a few times in the leg with shrapnel."

"That's scary to hear, and I'm sure even more scary to live through. You're a hero, Senator Kingsley," she said. One more reason for her to like him, as if she needed more. But at least this reason was less superficial. Courtland wasn't just someone nice to look at. He was a good man—or at least, that was the impression she was getting about him so far.

Courtland gave a wry laugh. "That's not what my father told me. I won't regale you with the colorful language he used, but suffice it to say, he made his point clear to me and half the population of Parsons, Georgia, that I was a fool to the nth degree."

"I imagine you just scared him," Eva said.

"You are quite the diplomat. We need you in Congress. Maybe we could get more done."

This time Eva laughed. "No. I am far happier feeding a member of Congress than I ever would be working with all of you."

"Then that is our loss, Miss Cardon," he said.

"Thank you," she said. "Call me Eva."

He smiled. "And please, call me Courtland. That's enough with the war stories. Tell me about you and your future plans for this magnificent restaurant of yours."

Eva smiled. "I don't know where to begin. When I started Chez Geneviève I had no idea what I was doing. Oh, I did my homework on how to run a restaurant, and so many people have mentored me— like Hal Conroy, the owner of The Phoenix—but this has been a huge undertaking."

"I see a glint in your eye," Courtland said. "You love this, don't you?"

She nodded. "I do. So much so that I'm planning on opening another restaurant."

He looked at her with surprise. "You want to take on opening a second restaurant? Another Chez Geneviève?"

She shook her head, leaning forward, excited to talk about her plans. "No, I plan on opening a less fussy restaurant—more like a diner. I want to be able to have restaurants that serve a myriad of people. My people have so few choices when it comes to dining that I want to give them options—fine dining and/or a restaurant that the local blue-collar workers can take their families to and not have to worry about it being cost prohibitive or too stuffy. I'm still working on the business plan, but when I'm done, I am going to go to the bank and see if I can make this happen."

"I have no doubt you will," Courtland said. Courtland stood, and Eva rose also. "I wish I could stay and talk to you more. Learning about you has truly been an enlightening experience. I don't think I have ever met someone like you, Eva Cardon. You are one in a million."

She blushed again. Receiving compliments of this nature from someone other than her family and friends was a bit unsettling. "It was nice of you to come by today, Courtland . . . Do you have big plans for the weekend? I know you senators love to work hard and—" She stopped, fearful that her teasing had gone too far.

Courtland laughed. "Play harder? Sadly, you are not far off the mark. But this weekend is all about family. I'm taking the train to Parsons, Georgia, later today to attend my father's birthday celebration tomorrow. I probably should have left yesterday, but to be honest, I wanted to avoid as much of the brouhaha leading up to the party as possible."

"But you're one of the Rowdy Boys," Eva said with a smile. "I would think you would be looking forward to this big bash." She was surprised at how comfortable she had gotten with Courtland in such a short period of time. The only other man she had joked with was Pearson, and he didn't count considering he was more like a father to her.

Courtland nodded as if he approved of her teasing. "Look at you with your jokes. In spite of popular belief, I am not as much of a party person as the media would like to think. If the truth be known, I had hoped the party would have been held on Friday night or tonight, just to get it over and done with, but Mother insists that my father's birthday be celebrated on his actual birthday each year, so Sunday it is. My mother and sisters always put on a spectacle. Pops acts as if he hates it, but the old coot would throw a fit if they didn't go all out for his big day."

"That sounds fun. Have a good time," Eva said.

"It will be interesting. Hopefully I will see you again soon, Eva," he said, then walked toward the door. Eva could tell he was working hard not to limp. She wanted to tell him that the limp didn't matter, but she didn't want to embarrass him more.

"That would be nice," she said solemnly, but Courtland grinned.

"Oh, then you can count on it. I will be back," he said, then left.

Eva continued to stand, looking at the door he went out of for a moment, but then she forced herself to return to the work on her desk. As attracted as she was to Courtland, she had work to do, and never in her life had she allowed herself to be distracted by the job at hand. That was true when she was a child in school, and it was definitely true now that she was a business owner.

"No time to be lovestruck," Eva said and dived back into the paperwork, but every now and then her mind would drift and she would once again be thinking about Courtland.

"Dear God, please take this man from my mind," she finally whispered.

Eva thought about her grandmother and mother and wondered if their relationships had started like this . . . innocent banter that led them to make decisions that were still having ripple effects on both her and Frédérique.

"Grandma Bettine . . . Mother . . . if you are listening, please, watch over me. Please." *S'il te plaît.*

THREE

Courtland

"Senator Kingsley, don't forget your briefcase," said a voice from behind.

Courtland turned around with a smile. It was his favorite Pullman porter, Vernon Michaels. Courtland had first met the nineteen-year-old the previous year when Vernon started working the same route as his father, who was also a Pullman porter. Courtland had been impressed by the young man whose ultimate goal was to save up enough money to start school at Howard University in D.C. with the intent of becoming a doctor.

"That's a lofty goal. Do you have the grades to get into Howard?" Courtland had asked the young man when Vernon first brought it up.

"Yes, sir. I never made lower than an A in my life," Vernon had said, lifting his chin slightly. "And I've read through the book *Gray's Anatomy* three or four times. I can do this. I know I can do this."

Courtland could tell the young man was proud, and rightly so. Courtland had been a B student at best, and he had barely made it out of law school before the war took him away, so Courtland stood in awe of Vernon's many achievements.

Ever since then, Courtland would always quiz the young man

on how he was doing and how close he was to his goal of starting college. On this trip, Vernon said he hoped to have enough money saved by the end of the summer to start school in the fall. Courtland made sure to tip Vernon an extra twenty dollars on top of his usual ten-dollar tip before exiting the train.

"Thank you, Vernon," Courtland said, taking the briefcase from the young man who had sprinted up to where Courtland had stopped upon hearing his name.

It was early Sunday morning, and unlike in D.C., it was just cool outside instead of below freezing. Courtland had traveled through the night on the train and had gotten up and dressed in a pair of slacks and a long-sleeved shirt, but judging from the temperature, he would be in short sleeves by midmorning.

"It seems my mind and my body are in two different places."

Courtland had been thinking about Eva most of the night. He had enjoyed their conversation. She was a beautiful woman, but more than that, she was a great conversationalist, and her business acumen fascinated him. He couldn't wait until he got the opportunity to talk to her again.

Vernon laughed. "That's okay, Senator. That's what we porters are here for. Did Mr. George get the rest of your bags?"

"Yes," Courtland said. "And I wish you wouldn't call him by that dreadful name." Courtland knew the practice of all of the Negro Pullman porters using the name "George" so that it would be easy for lazy white folks to remember them. Courtland was grateful that Vernon had felt comfortable, after a bit of probing, telling Courtland his first name.

"I know you don't like it when we go by George, sir, but it does make things easier," Vernon said. "Plus, Mr. George would be mad if I told you his real name. He is real funny about such things."

"Very well then," Courtland said with a sigh. "Rome wasn't built in a day, and neither were the rules of being a Pullman porter, I suppose. You take care, and I'll see you on the train ride home if you happen to be working on Tuesday."

The Congress didn't have anything scheduled for Monday or Tuesday, so he didn't have to rush right back the morning after the party.

"Oh, I'll be working, sir," he said with a huge grin. "You take care, Senator Kingsley, and have a good time at your daddy's birthday party."

"I will do my best," Courtland said, slowly making his way out of the train, his limp a little more pronounced today than normal.

Some days, the leg barely caused him any pain, but during the winter months, he seemed to notice it more and more. As he walked through the train station, he found himself having to stop every so often and rest on his walking cane.

Just as Courtland had thought, the elderly Negro Pullman porter was standing patiently beside Courtland's car with his bags. They had done this dance so much, the porter knew Courtland's car by sight. Courtland had asked his father to get one of the young hired men to bring his car and park it; that way he wouldn't be dependent on anyone picking him up. Courtland's car, a tan 1935 Ford Model 48 Deluxe Phaeton, was a gift to him from his grandfather, Little Jack Parsons, on his sixteenth birthday, a month before the old man died.

"Thank you . . ." Courtland paused. "George."

Courtland knew Vernon was right. This man had withstood all types of indignities, and George was probably the least of them. Courtland had no right to ask him to reveal his name. Courtland hoped the day would come when the practice of calling all of the Negro porters George would become a thing of the past, as well as other equally demeaning practices—from the pittance they received for payment of their services to the horrendous work conditions, sometimes not sleeping for days. For now, the best Courtland could do was make sure he treated the porters with as much respect as he possibly could. Courtland reached into his pocket and gave the elderly man a ten-dollar bill.

The Negro man took the money and placed it in his back pocket. "Thank you, sir."

Courtland waved, but "George" had already started back to the train station. Courtland got into his car and started driving toward home. It was shortly after 10:00 a.m. when he left McDonough, Georgia, and he knew he would arrive just around the time his family was making it home from early morning Mass.

Courtland's mother had wanted him to arrive home on Friday, but he had pushed his return to Parsons all the way up until the last train that would get him home in time for his father's party. Even though Courtland was a constant figure at parties in D.C., he considered those business meetings, albeit on the glamorous side. Those parties gave him a chance to meet with his freshman class of senators from Florida, Alabama, and North Carolina. Most of them were far more conservative than he would ever be, but there were areas that they could agree on, like infrastructure and better benefits for military veterans and their families. When Courtland ran for office, his platform was "The War Is Over. Now What?"

Courtland made promises to his fellow veterans that he wouldn't forget about them once he got to Washington, and that was a promise he intended to keep. So if going to all of those D.C. parties was what it took, he would don a tuxedo every night of the week if he had to. These gatherings in his hometown were not like the parties he went to in D.C. These parties were little more than pageants for every hopeful parent from Hiawassee, Georgia, all the way to Valdosta to attend and try to convince him to take their daughters' hands in marriage. After his time with Eva, Courtland was not in the mood for some mindless prattle with yet another local girl wanting to win over his attention. He planned to spend as much time as possible with his best friend, Jimmy Earl, and Jimmy Earl's wife, his cousin Lori Beth, and avoid the fray if he could. Lori Beth was the daughter of his aunt Lauren, his mother's youngest sister.

Courtland made good time home, and before long he was turning into the driveway leading up to his family's sprawling plantation home. Once he stopped his car in front of the Big House, as most of the Negroes who lived and worked there still called it, he almost reached for his briefcase before exiting his car, but he sighed and left it behind, knowing his mother would scold him resoundingly for bringing work home on this, his father's birthday weekend. So he got out of the car, minus the briefcase, and was just about to take his luggage out of the back when a young Negro boy he didn't recognize came up to him.

"Hello, Mr. Courtland. I'll get your bags," the boy said.

"All right," Courtland said, reaching into the back seat and retrieving his walking cane. "What's your name, son? I don't recognize you, although you look familiar."

The young boy, who was probably not much older than fifteen or sixteen, smiled as he took the bags out of the trunk. "My name is Harper, sir. Harper Jack Parsons."

Courtland laughed and put his hand on the young man's shoulder. "Well, well, well. If it isn't Little Harper. I remember you now. You're one of Miss Easter Lily's great-grands. You're Zeke's son, aren't you?"

Easter Lily was a former slave who used to live and work on the Parsonses' plantation. According to the hushed stories Courtland had heard as a child when he wasn't supposed to be around listening, his grandfather, Little Jack Parsons, had a long, torrid relationship with his family's slave, Easter Lily. From what Courtland heard, even after slavery ended, Little Jack continued seeing Easter Lily until she died. Until this day, many of her children, grandchildren, and great-grandchildren still remained in and around the home she once resided in.

Once, when Courtland was a little boy of about five or six, he was running around, playing with Zeke Parsons, the father of the young man getting his bags, and Courtland innocently asked his daddy if Zeke was his cousin, since he'd heard one of the hired hands say they looked alike. His daddy had nearly beat Courtland within an inch of his life, yelling at Courtland as if he had committed treason. Later, Courtland's mother pulled him aside and sternly told him that questions like that were not questions well-mannered young boys ever, ever asked. It wasn't until many years later that Courtland understood why everyone had reacted the way they did. But it never stopped Courtland from going out of his way to be nice to his Negro relatives. As far as he was concerned, they were kin, no matter how it managed to happen.

"Yes, sir. Easter Lily was my great-grandma, and Zeke Parsons is my pa," the young man said. "Me, Mama, and Daddy are here visiting from Detroit, and your mama asked if we would help out tonight."

Many of the young Negroes of Parsons had left town a few years back, right before the war. Parsons was still struggling to revive itself after the Depression, so many of the Negro and white youth opted to go to bigger cities outside of their rural community in order to find work. Another mission of Courtland's was to help bring industry to their community. Courtland was happy to hear Zeke had come back for a visit.

"Well, you tell your daddy I said hello, and when I come home again, if y'all are still here, he and I need to go fishing," Courtland said of his close childhood friend.

Back when they were young, he and Courtland would rip and run throughout the fields and wooded areas behind the house until Courtland's mother would send someone to find them and tell Courtland to come home.

"I sure will tell him, sir," Harper replied as he walked inside with Courtland.

The house was filled with people decorating it to fit the circus theme his mother had selected for this year's party. Every year for

Nap's birthday, Millicent would choose a theme, and the entire estate would be decorated to the hilt. This year's theme was "Under the Big Top." Millicent had called Courtland several times to tell him about all of the arrangements she and the girls had made. The house and the grounds were to be filled with everything one associates with the circus. There would be clowns and jugglers walking around, and even a man swallowing what would appear to be a sword. Already, Courtland could see the crew setting up an elaborate carousel out back that, by the evening, would be surrounded with all sorts of exotic animals in cages, from a saber-toothed tiger to a bunch of friendly chimpanzees. The circus was just a few towns over, and for a large sum of money, Courtland was sure, they had agreed to bring over a few props and animals. Inside the house there was the huge ballroom that was decorated like the center ring of a circus. This was where the young and old would dance until the wee hours of the morning.

"I'll take your things upstairs, if that's all right with you, Mr. Courtland," Harper said as Courtland continued to marvel at all that his mother and sisters had arranged.

"Yes, that's fine," Courtland said as he looked around, waving at various ones who were hanging up decorations and setting up tables in the formal dining room. Most of them were young people who had grown up on the land. Courtland was trying to decide where the best place would be for him to sequester himself until the party when Mrs. Dulcie Matthews, the housekeeper who had worked for Courtland's family since before he was born, walked into the hallway dressed in a black-and-white maid's uniform with her gray hair pinned up underneath a white cap.

"Courtland," she said with a smile. "You're early. Your mother and the girls aren't back from Mass yet."

"Sorry about that, Mrs. Matthews," Courtland said. "I was trying to time my arrival perfectly. You didn't mention Pops. Did he not go to Mass?"

Mrs. Matthews shook her head as she laughed. "Your father is in one of his moods. He's in there in the office. Would you like for me to bring you both some lunch? Mr. Nap hasn't eaten a bite today."

Courtland's father's name was Courtland Hardiman Kingsley III, but he had been nicknamed "Nap" for Napoleon Bonaparte due to his short stature and his short fuse. The name had stuck, and more people knew him by his nickname than they did his birth name.

Courtland smiled and patted her on the shoulder. "Don't worry, Mrs. Matthews. Let me go in and check on him. I'm sure by the time Mother and the girls arrive, we'll be ready to eat."

Courtland went down the hallway to his father's office where the door was closed. Courtland knocked, and he heard his father gruffly bark for him to come in. Just like Mrs. Matthews had said, Nap was in a mood. He was sitting behind his huge mahogany desk with a fancy party hat stuck sideways on his head while he sucked on an expensive Cuban cigar. Recently, Nap had been forbidden to smoke anymore by old Doc Henry, and even though he had sworn like a sailor about the injustice of it all, he had stopped when the doctor assured him the cigars were not adding any years to his life; in fact, they were most likely subtracting them. So Nap had taken to chewing on them instead as a form of compromise.

"Hey, Pops. What are you doing back here, and why didn't you go to Mass with Mother and the girls? And why do you have that silly hat stuck to your head?"

Courtland knew how important Sunday Mass was to his mother. He felt slightly bad for not arriving in time to attend with them. The older of his two younger sisters, Catherine, had told him, once he returned home from the war, that their mother had attended Mass every single day while he was gone.

"I didn't want to go to Mass, and I am already partied out," Nap said irritably, chewing even harder on his cigar. "Last I checked, I was a grown man who could make his own decisions. We ought to just cancel all of these shenanigans. Your mother has gone way too far and spent way too much of my money."

Courtland laughed. "What are you talking about? You're wrong for skipping Mass. You know how much it means to Mother, and the party hasn't even started yet. What do you mean you are already partied out?'"

"All that noise out there is getting on every one of my nerves, so here I am. They can have the rest of the house, but this one place, this is mine to escape to when all of that estrogen becomes too much to bear," Nap said. "If I had any sense, I would go back with you up to D.C. where a man can find some peace."

Courtland laughed as his father tossed the party hat onto the floor.

"You know you love all of this, Pops," Courtland said, picking up the hat and placing it on his father's desk.

Nap snorted, but then his eyes lit up like those of his youngest daughter, Violet, whenever Courtland came home to visit because she knew she was going to receive some trinket or another from her "favorite brother," as she called him, even though he was, of course, her only brother.

"Well, what have you got for me?" Nap asked with a huge grin.

"I swear, I think my family only tolerates me for the gifts I bring." Courtland reached into the pocket of the coat he had slung over his arm. "Before you open it, however, you must promise to practice moderation. Mother will kill me if she finds out I brought you a bottle of—"

Nap ripped it open and laughed, slapping the top of his desk. "Now this is the kind of present I like," he said, lifting the bottle and whistling. "An 1847 Remy Martin Centaure Napoleon Cognac. Thank you, my son. Share a drink with your old man? I can tell this is going to mellow out my mind."

Courtland laughed. "You aren't going to save it for a special occasion? And don't you think it is a bit too early for you to be drinking cognac?"

Nap let out a loud guffaw as he poured himself and Courtland a drink. "I'm sixty-five years old. Ain't that many more shopping days left for me. And somewhere in the world it's after six o'clock. Let's just say we're skipping time zones."

Courtland laughed and sat in one of the leather chairs in front of his father's desk. The two men quietly drank their cognac, allowing the smoothness of it to wash over them. Courtland had to agree with his father. There was definitely nothing like a good cognac to mellow out the mind.

"I hear you missed breakfast, Pops. We should make our way out there soon so we can have lunch with Mother and the girls," Courtland said after a moment of silence. "And as far as this party goes, you know you love all of this hoopla. You'd be angry if Mother and the girls stopped throwing these bashes for you."

"The heck I like all of this bull crap. I just go along with it to humor the womenfolk. You know how they all three can make a man's life miserable if they don't get their way," Nap said, pouring himself another drink.

"Are you sure you need to drink so much of that?" Courtland asked, regretting for a moment that he hadn't gotten his father a non-alcoholic gift. As much as his father liked to ignore what the doctors said, Courtland, his mother, and his sisters had listened. Nap's heart was not ticking like it used to, and stress, hard liquor, and smoking were three things Doc Henry advised Nap to avoid.

"Heck, boy, I've stopped chasing women, I don't smoke anymore, and your mother has me going to Mass at least once or twice per week. If I give up anything else, there won't be nothing else for me to do but grow some breasts and start wearing flouncy dresses," Nap said in a gruff voice. "I thought I had at least one person on my side in this family."

Courtland sighed. "Alright. Alright. Drink your cognac. I see turning sixty-five didn't do a doggone thing for your disposition."

"Nope. Not a doggone thing," Nap said with a laugh, but he quickly turned serious. "Enough with this kidding around. We've got some things to discuss. I barely get to see you anymore with all of your politicking and carousing. 'Rowdy Boys of Washington?' Really?"

Courtland leaned back in his seat. "The newspapers are always looking for a story. It seems I'm interesting material."

"Courtland, it is time for us to turn up the heat. The senate is well and good, but that's not our final goal. Our final goal is that little white house sitting on Pennsylvania Avenue. That's where the true power resides."

Courtland smiled. He had heard all of this before. So far, Courtland had pretty much allowed Nap to plot out his political career path, although there were times when he truly pushed his father's patience, like when he became involved in hotbed issues like racism against Negroes, particularly in the Southern states.

"Let that Colored mess go, Courtland. For God's sake, they can't even vote," Nap said.

"You mean they aren't allowed to vote in peace," Courtland said, once again feeling angered by the tactics used by some of his fellow politicians in the South.

Between the literacy tests and the poll taxes, it was virtually impossible for a Negro person to "earn" the right to vote. Then, when intimidation practices were factored in, it was truly an uphill battle. Courtland hoped to work to change those details, as he had discussed with Adam, but he acknowledged to himself that it was going to take time.

"Either way you look at the situation, Courtland, you lobbying for their rights is a wasted effort," Nap said. "There ain't enough of them voting for you to jeopardize your career."

In Nap's mind, individuals who could not vote should not be given a second thought when making political choices. In Nap's words, it didn't matter if it was "the Coloreds, children, foreigners, or the infirm." If they couldn't vote, in Nap's opinion, their needs needed to be pushed as far back on the back burner as possible. The only reason Nap encouraged Courtland to go speak to every ladies' organization he could was because white women got the right to vote in 1920. Other than that, Nap would have lumped them in the category of "time leeches."

"Courtland, it's time for you to find a wife," Nap said in a resolute voice, continuing to chomp on his cigar.

"Well, that's a huge shift in the conversation," Courtland said with a groan. "Considering the fact that I'm not seeing anyone, I'm not so sure how I'm supposed to pull that particular rabbit out of the hat."

"For the love of . . . Man, there are dozens of love-starved good girls who will be present at this shindig tonight, ready to respond to your every beck and call. What the heck else are you waiting for?" Nap admonished, standing from his chair and walking around to where his son sat.

Nap Kingsley stood at barely five five, but what he lacked in height he made up for in attitude and disposition. Whatever room Nap Kingsley inhabited, he quickly became the largest thing in it.

"Love is for the simpleminded. What we need is a strategy."

"I hear you, Pops. But as simpleminded as it might seem, I want to love my wife," Courtland said. "I know you haven't always been the most . . . respectful when it comes to Mother, but at the end of the day, don't you love her?"

"For the love of all the saints!" Nap exclaimed, hitting his fist on his desk. "What your mother and I have is irrelevant. We're on a mission to get you the presidency, boy. Is that not adding up inside your head? You've got your entire life to fall in love with your wife. Right now, it's all about strategy. You'll be thirty-six your next birthday. Just years away from the next phase of this operation to get you elected president. We need you married with two and a half children and a dog named Spot by the time you're ready to run. Are you hearing me?"

Courtland nodded, unperturbed by his father's vehemence. "Yes, Pops, I hear you. The whole house hears you. Look, I have been hearing you ever since I returned from the war. I need a wife. I need children. I need a dog and a mansion down the hill from here. I have heard it countless times, but again, the fact remains: I have not found love. Not yet. And until then, you are stuck with me and me alone," he said, just as a mental image of Eva entered his mind.

An impossible image. An image he knew he needed to dispel quickly. A relationship between them was impossible, and he had seen firsthand the type of pain relationships like that could cause. His grandfather's behavior had destroyed Courtland's grandmother, mother, aunts, and uncles, not to mention Easter Lily and her family. But even now, the thought of cutting all ties with Eva made his heart hurt in ways it had never done before, and this was after one kiss and one in-depth conversation.

"Do you hear me, Courtland?" Nap barked, glaring at Courtland as he hit the desk again.

"Yes. I hear you. I need to be married by sunup," Courtland snapped. "Tonight, my only job is to find the girl with the glass slipper so we can live happily ever after in political bliss."

"Now that's what I want to hear. Son," Nap said, softening, "I know this path seems like more sacrifice than reward right now, but I promise you, Courtland, once you raise your right hand to God and solemnly swear to preserve, protect, and defend the Constitution of the United States, this will all feel like a sacrifice that was worth making."

"We'll see," Courtland said. "But until then, can we please go eat lunch?"

"Only if you promise to give some of those young ladies the time of day tonight," Nap said. "You don't have to propose to any of them, but you gotta get yourself in the hunt. Who knows? Your intended might be on her way here as we speak."

Courtland stood and sighed. He was nearly a whole foot taller than his father, but he always felt a bit small next to him. "Okay. I will look for that gal with the glass slipper. Just for you, Pops."

"That's all I can ask," Nap said, tossing his half-chewed cigar on his desk and walking briskly toward the door.

Courtland tried to force himself into feeling some type of excitement, but it was impossible. All he wanted at that point was to be back in the corner office of Eva's restaurant, talking to her and getting to know her better, but he kept telling himself she was not the one.

—

"Son, thank you for helping me and your sisters greet the guests," Courtland's mother said, placing her hand on her son's arm. "Nap is taking his contrariness a bit too far this time."

Courtland kissed his mother's cheek as they watched another car of people drive up to the front door where he, Millicent, and Courtland's two sisters, Catherine and Violet, stood, all decked out in evening attire. Courtland wore the same black tux he had worn to Eva's New Year's Eve party, and his mother and sisters were wearing different varieties of evening gowns in blue—Nap's favorite color.

"Just ignore him, Mother," Courtland said. "This farce he puts on every year is just that. Before long, if he isn't already, Nap Kingsley will be acting as if this entire event was his idea."

Catherine, Courtland's nineteen-year-old sister, said with a laugh, "Father never wants to let anyone know he is appreciative of what they do for him."

Violet, Courtland's sixteen-year-old sister, sniffed and tilted her head slightly. "He always lets me know. Maybe it's because I'm his favorite."

Everyone laughed. Violet had come out of the womb sure of herself. She was at least a head taller than her sister and mother, and where they were ruddier complexioned, Violet was so fair skinned she was almost translucent. And instead of the luscious red hair of her mother and sister, Violet had long black hair that favored her father and brother. She also possessed the same outgoing, fiery personality as Nap and, to a degree, Courtland. He glanced over at his sisters, noticing that both girls were wearing the pearl earrings and necklaces he had given them for Christmas. Both of them were spoiled, and he had contributed to a lot of it, but he loved them beyond words and would do anything to make them happy.

Courtland watched as the line became rather long. It was 7:00 p.m. on a beautiful Georgia night, just cool enough for a light jacket but warm enough that he knew everyone would enjoy themselves out back at the quasi-circus. His mother had gotten Mr. Tote, a local Negro man known for his barbecue skills, and a few other men from Colored Town to come and barbecue a whole goat and pig. Mrs. Matthews had organized the rest of the cooking. As always, the birthday party was going to be a lavish affair. Just as Courtland finished shaking the hand of Doc Henry, he heard a welcome voice that caused him to break out into a full grin.

"Courtland Hardiman Kingsley IV, you old dogface, you," said his good friend Jimmy Earl.

Courtland watched as Jimmy Earl and his wife, Lori Beth, stepped forward. "That's Captain to you, Jimmy Earl Ketchums."

Time had not been good to Jimmy Earl. While they both were fighting in the war, Jimmy Earl's grandmother, Miss Peggy, and his mother, Miss Corrine, had passed away within weeks of each other. Jimmy Earl wasn't even able to come back home for their funerals. Both he and Jimmy Earl were in their midthirties, but Jimmy Earl looked much older. He had lost most of his hair, and fine lines etched his face, but his smile was still the same old Jimmy Earl smile. Jimmy Earl pulled him away from the front door and led him and Lori Beth farther down the hallway so they could talk in private. Courtland limped a bit behind them. He had left his walking cane upstairs and had been too lazy to go retrieve it. He could walk without it, but he didn't feel quite as steady as he did when he had it.

"You ready for this?" Jimmy Earl asked Courtland. "If what is being said is true, there is going to be an auction tonight, and the gal with the lowest IQ wins you as her mate."

"Oh, Jimmy," Lori Beth chided, lightly slapping her husband on his shoulder.

Lori Beth looked the same as always. Flawless skin and fire engine–red hair to rival that of Myrna Loy or Maureen O'Hara. "Don't tease Courtland so. We hardly get him back home as it is. The last thing you need to do is spook him about some of these ninny girls. At this rate, we won't see him for another month of Sundays."

"Don't you worry, sweet cousin. Jimmy Earl is just jealous. Everyone knows that you were the only woman in this entire county who would take pity on him and make him an honest man," Courtland said, ducking as Jimmy Earl swung playfully at him. "And cousin, you are looking quite breathtaking tonight, as usual."

And she was. Lori Beth was wearing a floor-length black velvet evening gown and a white mink stole, which she gave to one of the women who was collecting hats and coats at the door.

"Thank you, Courtland," she said demurely. "It's good to see you as always. We are so proud of you, but it's not the same around here without you."

"I miss all of you too," he said, "but I have to admit I do love D.C. Hey, I expected y'all to come over earlier so we could spend some time together. And, of course, I wanted to see my godsons. Why didn't you bring them?"

Jimmy Earl kissed Lori Beth's cheek. "My lovely wife here couldn't decide which new frock was new enough for her to wear and show off her gorgeous figure in tonight, so I got to see her try on all of them multiple times this morning before Mass. And then, right as we were getting ready to leave for Mass, the twins decided to be sick all over Lori Beth."

"I should be home with them now," she said, worry written all over her face.

"They're fine. Babies throw up all the time, my love," Jimmy Earl said, kissing her cheek once more. "Plus, Beulah Mae is not going to let them out of her sight. And if she thinks we need to come back home, she'll send for us."

Courtland squeezed his cousin's hand. He knew she fretted even more than most mothers when it came to her twin boys. Before she married Jimmy Earl, Lori Beth had married their third cousin, Beauregard Parsons, and had borne him two sons, but the boys had come down with whooping cough at the ages of three and four and died so fast, there wasn't even time enough to call on old Doc Henry. Then, less than a month later, Beau lost his life during the attack on Pearl Harbor. The family didn't think Lori Beth would ever recover from all that pain, but soon after the war ended, she and Jimmy Earl fell in love and got married, and a little over a year later, she gave birth to the twins.

"Lori Beth, listen to Jimmy Earl. For once in his life, he's actually making an ounce of sense," Courtland teased, placing his cousin's arm in the crook of his, while Jimmy Earl did the same on the other side.

"I know you're both right," she said in a hesitant voice.

"We are right. And you and I, my love, are going to enjoy our night out away from those fantastic little baby boys," Jimmy Earl said with a firm voice. "With no fear. Okay?"

"Okay," she said and allowed herself to be led away.

By the time they made it to the ballroom, the floor was already filled with young people dancing. Jimmy Earl and Lori Beth excused themselves and joined the crowd, waltzing and looking totally and completely in love. Courtland watched as his sisters entered the room minutes later, both on the arms of local boys Courtland recognized. He knew Catherine was becoming a tad anxious about dating because her younger sister seemed to garner all of the male attention between the two of them, so he was happy to see she seemed content on the arm of the mayor's son while Violet danced with a boy from McDonough who came from a good Catholic family. Courtland let his mind drift to Eva. What he wouldn't give to have her standing beside him or in his arms on the dance floor.

"Courtland!" he heard his father call out to him.

Courtland turned and saw a smiling Nap standing there with a young woman he had never seen before and an eager-looking older couple he assumed were her parents. Courtland almost cursed, but he planted a huge smile on his face. He didn't want to be rude.

"I would like to introduce you to John and Cynthia Gillibrand and their beautiful daughter, Madeleine. They came all the way from Chattanooga, Tennessee. John and I both attended the University of Georgia at the same time, and through some local contacts, he and I are doing some business together. We thought it would be nice for you children to meet. Madeleine here just graduated from Vassar up in New York. I told her equally beautiful mother that as long as our Southern girls come back home with Southern ways, we have no issue with them getting their education up in Yankee territory."

Courtland just knew the young woman would be embarrassed by such talk, but she laughed right along with Nap and her parents.

Madeleine held out her hand to Courtland. "I am pleased to meet you, Senator Kingsley. I have heard so much about you. All good, I promise," she said, obviously flirting.

Ordinarily, Madeleine would be the kind of woman he would pass the time with during functions like this, but he just wasn't interested in playing the political games his father was trying to orchestrate. Courtland dutifully shook her hand.

"It is very nice meeting all of you," he said, putting the emphasis on the word *all*, "but I just remembered, I have an important phone call I need to make," he said, then turned to leave.

"On a Sunday evening? Can't you make your call tomorrow at a more civilized time?" Nap asked with almost a growl.

"I wish I could wait, Pops, but this is urgent. Senate business. I shall return shortly." He nodded his head once to signify goodbye, then exited the room.

He knew if he turned around he would see a scowl to rival all scowls on his father's face, but at this point he didn't care. He was not interested in being part of this dating merry-go-round his father was determined for him to be on, so he made his way to the back room just across the hall from the kitchen that his mother used as her private office. He had to skirt around the waitstaff, but he knew no one would bother to look for him there. He sat down in his mother's chair and picked up the receiver to the phone, quickly ringing the operator. She came on the line and asked how she could help.

"I would like for you to please find the number for Reverend Dr. Pearson Montgomery in Washington, D.C., and connect me to that line," Courtland said, realizing how impulsive it was for him to call at this time of the night, but much to his surprise and delight, after just a couple of rings, it was Eva who picked up the phone.

"Hello," she said.

Never, in all of his adult life, had just the sound of a woman's voice affected him the way he was being affected now. If Eva didn't say another word, his evening would be complete. Courtland remembered how Jimmy Earl used to behave when he and Lori Beth first started dating. Courtland used to rib his friend about his lovesickness, but if Jimmy Earl felt half of what he was feeling now, after just a couple of interactions with Eva, well, he owed his best friend an apology.

"Hello, Eva. It's Courtland," he said. "I hope you don't mind me calling."

The line went silent for a moment, making him wonder if the connection had been lost, but then she spoke. "I thought you were attending your father's birthday party. Is everything all right?"

He leaned back into the seat, happy to know she was still on the line.

"Everything is fine. If you want to know the truth, I couldn't stop thinking about you."

She went quiet again, and Courtland wondered if he had overstepped his boundaries.

"You shouldn't be on the phone with me," Eva said, but he could hear the breathlessness of her voice. He wondered if he was having the same effect on her that she was having on him.

"I know," he said, "but can you humor me for just a little while before I have to go back out there and face the crowd?"

"Yes," she finally said. "I can do that."

And for the next fifteen or twenty minutes, the two of them chatted about everything from Vernon Michaels, the young porter on the train, to Eva's new menu items the chef was going to debut the next week. To be honest, Courtland just felt good hearing her voice. Eva could have been counting backward or singing "The Star-Spangled Banner" for all he cared. He just wanted to feel close to her for however long he could. Propriety demanded that he return to the party soon, but until then, he listened as she regaled him with anecdotes about her day. She had gone to Mass that morning and had gone out to lunch with some friends from church. He was just about to ask her when he could see her again when his sister Violet knocked on the open door.

"Hold on one minute," Courtland said, putting his hand over the receiver. "What is it, Violet?"

"Your father is fit to be tied," Violet said with an exasperated look. "He sent me to come get you. Will you please come outside and be sociable so he will stop huffing and puffing and scaring all of the cute boys away?"

Courtland sighed and then said to Eva, "I have to go. It seems duty is calling."

Eva laughed. "Have a good time, Courtland. I'm sure there are plenty of beautiful ladies there just dying to dance with one of the Rowdy Boys," she teased. "I'm glad you called."

After they said their goodbyes, Courtland rose from the seat and looked at his sister with a grin and a glint in his eyes. "If you will dance with me for the rest of the evening, I will buy you a dress from that new designer you mentioned last time I was home. What is his name?"

"Christian Dior," she said excitedly, then, ever the negotiator, paused. "I won't do it for one dress, but . . . how about three dresses?"

Courtland threw back his head and laughed, wrapping his arm around his sister's shoulders. "Okay, Miss Kingsley. You drive a hard bargain, but I know when I've met my match. Let's go out there before Nap comes looking for the both of us. God protect us all," he said as he and his sister returned to the party.

Courtland knew he was safe this night because one thing was stronger than his father's desire to see him tangled up with one of the many single women at the party, and that was his sister's love of clothes. Come hell or high water, Violet Kingsley would get those new frocks.

FOUR

Courtland

"Senator, will you work with me on abolishing segregation in the District of Columbia?" Adam Clayton Powell Jr. questioned, his voice elevated.

He had only been in Courtland's office for about ten minutes, but the Baptist preacher in Adam had already reared his head. He was going in on Courtland like he was a fallen sinner on the last night of revival meetings at his church back in Harlem. It was just before lunch on the Tuesday after his father's birthday party, and Adam had stormed in unannounced, once again angry about everything, and Courtland was a good target for him to unload his frustrations on.

Courtland calmly looked at the tall Negro man who stood in front of his desk. He didn't respond. Courtland knew Adam knew the answer to his question before he spoke it. This wasn't the first time they'd had a one-sided conversation. Courtland was a man of his word, and he would only make promises he could keep. Sadly there was nothing Adam was saying that he felt he could touch right now, so he just listened as his friend became more and more agitated.

"What about supporting my efforts to get Negro members of the press admitted into the gallery?" he asked, his booming voice getting louder and louder. "No? That's too much? Well, how about this: Do you see yourself able to support a resolution to allow Negro federal employees the right to eat in the cafeteria?" Adam asked, then paused as if giving Courtland a moment to respond. Courtland didn't, so Adam continued. "Well, okay then. If none of those things tickle your fancy, let's go big. What about a bill to stop the lynching of Negroes?" he barked across Courtland's desk. "What will you stand for, Courtland? Because I truly thought you were more than the country boy senator from Georgia. I thought you were a man of principle—or were my eyes clouded with stardust?"

"Adam, you know I am on your side when it comes to all of those things you mentioned, but we need time to—"

"Time? Time? Man, my people are swinging from trees all the way from Louisiana to well beyond the Mason-Dixon Line. The country is still reeling from that lynching of those young Negroes in Walton County, Georgia, just an hour or so from where you live. You mean to tell me you Dixiecrats can't even get on board to stop lynchings, for God's sake? Are our dead bodies swinging in the poplar trees so entertaining that y'all would rather take photos with our corpses than to vote for a bill that will support our desire to live?"

"You're not being fair, Adam," Courtland said, rising from his chair, gripping his desk in frustration. He hated conversations like this because all they did was put them both in an untenable position. "You know where I come from. I have to be strategic about the moves I make so I don't end up a one-and-done senator. You know how this all works as well as me. Like I was saying, it's going to take time."

"Well, we ain't got no more time to wait, Congressman. Time is the one thing we are fresh out of. So what you gonna do?" Adam said, placing both of his hands on the other side of Courtland's desk, glaring at the younger man furiously. Any other person would be intimidated by Adam, but Courtland had experienced Adam's rage more than once before. He knew the man spoke from a place of justifiable anger. Hell, he was angry too. He just didn't feel like now was the time for him to go rogue in Congress. Not yet. Not until he had made some alliances with fellow senators who would support him on the big-ticket items—hell, the little-ticket items—that Adam was talking about. Rather than continue arguing with Adam, Courtland decided to try another tactic: diversion.

"Have lunch with me. My treat. Maybe we could go over to your friend's restaurant," Courtland said, trying to sound nonchalant, but clearly Adam wasn't buying it for a minute.

He threw back his head and laughed. "Oh, you want to go over to my *friend's* restaurant? Miss Eva Cardon's place? You ain't slick, country boy. Not slick at all."

Courtland looked away, a bit sheepish. "The food there is—"

Adam laughed even louder. "The food? You trying to convince me you want to go over there for the food?"

"The chef—" he started, but Adam waved his hand.

"Let's go to Chez Geneviève, man. Maybe they'll have some gumbo simmering."

Courtland walked around his desk and put his hand on Adam's shoulder. "I'm not trying to be difficult, Adam. I want the same things you want. I just know it—"

"Takes time," Adam finished, sighing loudly, his anger clearly dissipating. "I know, but in the meantime, my people are dying, man. Dying for no other reason than the melanin in our skin. That ain't right, and it's gonna take some of you country boy senators to get behind the work I'm trying to do to make change happen. I can't handle another lynching, Courtland. I just can't."

"I know," Courtland said. He felt the same way. He had closely followed the case Adam had mentioned, talking numerous times with Governor Ellis Arnall, who, at the urging of Courtland, offered a reward of ten thousand dollars to anyone with information about the lynching, but to no avail. President Harry S. Truman had even gotten involved and asked Courtland to be part of the President's Committee on Civil Rights, but Courtland declined. He knew his constituents would not respond nicely to that, and he knew he had a better chance of helping create change if he did it from behind the scenes. Adam would have said Courtland wasn't just behind the scenes, he was in the shadows, something Courtland would not argue with at all.

"Just give me a bit more time to make some power moves that will set us both up for success with the things we are trying to accomplish. I promise you I am working on some things that are going to either revolutionize the country or blow up in my face. Either way, I just need a little more—"

"Time. I get it. Just know that a little is all I've got to give. And Courtland," Adam said, looking at him with a serious face, "don't you go hurting Eva. She's good people. She ain't no plaything."

"I don't know what you're talking about," Courtland said, not quite looking Adam in the eyes.

"Look, man. I am not one to judge. The way me and Hazel got together, well, let's just say I am in no position to be your judge and jury, but Eva is still young, and Washington, D.C., is the half sister of the South. You know this. If anyone got wind that—"

"You have nothing to worry about. I thought you wanted some gumbo," Courtland said, trying very hard to change the subject.

He knew Adam had both his and Eva's best interests at heart; though understandably, Adam was most concerned about the well-being of Eva. Courtland tried to tell himself that he had no ulterior motives for seeing her, but it would be a lie. He had been planning a way to go see her, and Adam was the perfect excuse. Since their phone call on Sunday, his thoughts kept turning to her. Her beauty. Her intelligence. Her . . . everything. He knew he should pull back and listen to Adam. He knew this, and yet he couldn't wait to see her again.

"Ready?" Adam asked, cutting into Courtland's thoughts. "You know what folks will say about you if you keep showing up on U Street? Are you okay with that?"

"Let me worry about my reputation," Courtland said with a smile. "I hear they serve good gumbo at Chez Geneviève."

"Then let's go get that gumbo," Adam said, slapping Courtland on his back.

The two men walked out of Courtland's office, and Courtland told his secretary, Mrs. Martha Nelson, to call down for his car. Courtland didn't splurge on a lot of things, but he hated driving in D.C., so he was happy to spend his money on a driver and a car. Courtland and Adam sat in the chairs across from Mrs. Nelson's desk, chatting and laughing until finally she cleared her throat.

"Your car is ready," she said in a cold voice.

"Thank you, Mrs. Nelson," Courtland said. "I'll be back in a little while. Can I bring you something to eat? We are going to Chez Geneviève. The gumbo there is delicious, I hear."

"No, thank you," she said.

Martha Nelson was old school. She didn't approve of his association with Representative Powell, a fact she reminded him of on more than one occasion. "The company you keep will decide your longevity in this town," she had said one day after Adam left his office.

Courtland had dismissed her concerns, but he knew she was thinking along those same lines as she glared at them both.

"Well then, we shall see you later," Courtland said.

"Be blessed, Mrs. Nelson," Adam said, his voice filling the tight space, causing Mrs. Nelson to jump.

Courtland tried not to look at him for fear of laughing. Mrs. Nelson grunted some reply and went back to her typing.

As Adam and Courtland walked to his car, they passed several members of Congress who served with Courtland. Most of them just ignored him because, Courtland assumed, in their minds he was still a junior senator not worth their energy to engage with, but some of the others . . . Well, they looked at him with disdain, including fellow senator from Georgia, Senator Grisham.

"Good morning, Senator Grisham," Courtland said.

Grisham was a member of the old guard. He had been in the senate for almost as many years as Courtland had been alive.

"Senator," Grisham said, nodding toward Courtland. "How's your father? I'm guessing he's pretty proud having his boy in the senate."

"Yes, sir, I would say that he is," Courtland said. "Sir, let me introduce you to—"

"I know who he is," the senator interrupted in a dry, cold voice. "Tell Nap I said hello. I think I owe him a visit. Need to let him know how his boy is doing in D.C."

Courtland noticed the emphasis on the word *boy*.

"You do that, Senator," Courtland said, getting into the back seat of his Lincoln V-12 Sedan, a gift he had given himself soon after he moved to D.C., although Harold was the only one who drove it. Courtland was used to small-town driving. He was content being chauffeured around by his more than capable driver.

"Be blessed, Senator Grisham," Adam said with a slight bow, then climbed into the car too.

"Brother Harold," Adam said, reaching up to the front seat to shake Courtland's driver's hand, "how is the world treating you?"

"Can't complain, Representative Powell," Harold said with a grin, easing the car into the street.

It only took them about ten minutes to get to Eva's restaurant, and Courtland was trying to curb his excitement. He didn't want to show his friend just how much he wanted to see Eva, although he knew Adam wasn't stupid. He had picked up on their chemistry the night of Eva's party. This would only be their third time seeing each other, but he felt a connection to her that he knew he was going to have to come to terms with at some point. Maybe if he hadn't given her that cognac-induced kiss, he wouldn't be feeling some kind of way about her now. Or maybe if he hadn't gone by her restaurant the other day or called her the other night . . . He didn't know. He just knew he wanted to see her again, if for no other reason than to remind himself that he needed to keep his distance.

Harold pulled the car up to the front of the restaurant, and Courtland and Adam stepped out. Courtland thanked his driver and asked him to be back in an hour. As soon as they exited the car, several people came up to speak to Adam. Courtland just stood aside and observed his friend turn on the charm. It didn't matter if he was talking to a young child, an elderly man, or a beautiful young woman, Adam knew how to make every person feel as if they were the only one. Once he had spoken to each and every person, finally he motioned for Courtland to follow. Shaking his head in awe, Courtland walked behind Adam into the restaurant. Once they were inside, the maître d' rushed up to them, greeting them like old friends.

"Good afternoon, Representative Powell. Senator Kingsley. Welcome back to Chez Geneviève. I will take you to Miss Eva's table. She will be happy to know you both decided to dine with us today," the man said, leading them to Eva's table by the window.

Both men were getting settled when Eva seemed to appear out of nowhere, looking beautiful in an ankle-length, formfitting yellow dress. Her hair was pulled back into a little bun, and her makeup consisted of light pink lipstick. She didn't need makeup, Courtland thought. Both men got up from their chairs, but Eva waved them back down.

"Good afternoon, gentlemen. Welcome back to Chez Geneviève," she said, smiling broadly. "Today, Chef is doing something a little different. He has a degustation menu that consists of smoked yellowtail crudo with citrus and avocado; cold cucumber soup with yogurt and dill; warm salad of chargrilled baby octopus; onglet with red wine shallots; and for dessert, bananas Foster."

"That sounds delicious," Courtland said. He turned to Adam. "Well, what say you, Representative Powell?"

"I say that sounds all highfalutin, but I came here for one thing and one thing only. The—"

"Gumbo," Eva and Courtland finished in unison. All three of them laughed.

"We probably should stick with the gumbo, considering we both have to get back to work," Courtland said.

"Yes, what you described involves a nap after the final course," Adam said. "But if you want to throw in that bananas Foster at the end, you won't hear a complaint out of me."

"Then I will make sure a waiter brings you drinks, gumbo, and some bananas Foster for dessert," she said, turning to leave. As she did, though, Adam reached out for her hand.

"Join us, Miss Eva," Adam said. "We have been discussing politics all morning. It would be nice to have you join us and keep us from falling down that rabbit hole again."

"Adam, you forget," Eva said with a smile. "I can be pretty political myself."

"Touché," Adam said with a grin, "but will you still join us?"

"Please," Courtland said, trying not to sound too eager, but Adam cut him a look. "We would be honored." He gave a quick nod.

"Then I will join you for a bit," she said, motioning to her waiter. Courtland helped her into the chair between Adam and him. After the waiter got through taking their order, for a moment, there was an awkward silence. Courtland was trying not to be too obvious with his admiration of Eva, and Eva was looking nervous, as if she had second thoughts about sitting with the two men.

Adam looked from one to the other, shook his head, then started talking. He asked Eva about the success of her New Year's Eve party, then inquired about her sister and Pearson. Meanwhile, Courtland watched Eva, who was animated when she spoke. She used her hands, and her eyes lit up when she talked about the things she cared about, like her family and her business.

". . . wouldn't you say, Senator?" Adam said.

"I'm sorry. I didn't catch what you said," Courtland replied, a bit sheepish that he had gotten caught with a wandering mind, not to mention a wandering eye.

"No worries, man. Listen, I see someone over on the other side that I need to schmooze with a bit. You kids carry on. Just have them bring my gumbo over to that table," Adam said, pointing, then took off with giant strides, his loud greeting reverberating across the restaurant.

It took Courtland a moment to come to terms with the fact that he was finally alone with Eva. She looked away. He hoped she wasn't still bothered by the kiss they had shared—or actually, the kiss he had taken. He wasn't sure if he should apologize again, but just in case, he did.

"I just want to say once more that I apologize for my behavior the other night," he said. "I assure you, I was not trying to be—"

"It's all right," she said. "You have already apologized. No reason to bring it up again. Let's just say that moment is truly water underneath the proverbial bridge. Okay?"

"Okay," he said, relieved that she was willing to move on. "It's good to see you again, Eva," Courtland finally said, then added, "and talk to you."

She looked back at him and smiled lightly. "It is good to see you, too, Courtland. How was your father's birthday party?"

"Over the top, as usual," he said, then began telling her about all of the circus-themed activities his mother and sisters had arranged. While they were talking, the waiter came back with Courtland's gumbo. He looked at Eva, who refused the bowl the waiter brought to her. "You're not going to eat?" Courtland asked.

She shook her head. "I love the food here, clearly, but I am around it too much to want to eat it every day. I had a salad a little while ago. That was enough."

"Well, I am going to dig in, if that is okay," he said.

"Absolutely," she said. "Bon appétit."

Courtland started eating, and it took all his willpower not to let out a soft moan. This gumbo was delicious—silky with a burst of spices. The shrimp, sausage, and chicken were cooked to perfection, and even though he normally wasn't fond of okra, he actually liked the creaminess it added to the dish.

"My goodness, Eva. No wonder Adam is constantly over here for the gumbo. You could bottle this stuff and sell it for a fortune."

She laughed. "It wouldn't be the same, but thank you. Chef du Passe is truly a wonder in the kitchen. I do pretty good myself, but nothing to his level. I am fortunate he decided to come here and work for me—really, work for the both of us. He owns part of the restaurant. A small part, but enough to keep him tethered to Chez Geneviève."

Courtland nodded approvingly. "Quite smart. You are definitely a shrewd businesswoman."

Yet another reason Courtland felt a pull toward Eva. He had always loved strong women. Women who were not afraid to go toe-to-toe with anyone—male or female.

Eva smiled. "Thank you. I try. This restaurant means the world to me. It is my passion."

"I hope it isn't the only thing you are passionate about," he said, feeling quite pleased with himself for causing a blush to form on her cheeks.

He had wondered if she shared the same feelings he was feeling for her. Seeing her blush in this way made him think that maybe she did. Even if only a little.

"Eva," he said and then stopped. He was torn. He could hear Adam's words: *"Don't you go hurting Eva. She's good people. She ain't no plaything."*

Eva looked at him searchingly but didn't say anything. She waited. Finally, Courtland found the words he wanted to say.

"Eva, I feel like a cad for saying this—and I do mean a first-rate cad—but I can't not say it," he said, then paused. She continued to wait. He started again. "You are a beautiful woman. You are smart and thoughtful, and I . . . I have no right to say this, but—"

"Say what, Courtland?" she asked quietly. She looked at him, her eyes sparkling, her perfect lips looking oh so kissable. It was all Courtland could do to restrain himself. He wanted nothing more than to pull her into his arms, but at the same time, he felt the eyes on them both. He knew that people were wondering what they were saying to each other. He didn't want to do anything to sully Eva's reputation. Both of them had their hands on the table, not touching, but fingers spread out, reaching. He was about to speak, but then the waiter came to the table and began removing his bowl and silverware. He sighed but waited patiently until the young man was done. He didn't want to mess up this moment by rushing. However, he knew what he was about to say would either go over well or sink like a metal plate in the middle of the ocean.

"I want to see you, Eva," he finally said. "These last few weeks I haven't been able to get you off my mind."

She didn't say anything at first; she just looked at him. Finally, she spoke. "I want to say yes, Courtland, but . . ." Her voice trailed off.

"But . . . ," he prompted her gently. "You can tell me anything, even if it is, 'No, Courtland.'"

She smiled sadly. He wanted to reach over and touch her face, but he knew such an action would only bring them unwanted attention, so he sat there and waited.

"Let me tell you a story about my father and mother. Valéry René Arquette was my father's name. My sister and I were not even good enough to bear his last name. He owned land all through Louisiana. Father was Mother's intellectual match. The two of them would sit and debate science and politics and pretty much anything you can imagine. People took Mother to be only a pretty singer, but she was so much more than that, and Father saw that about her," Eva said with a bitter smile.

Again, Courtland wanted to reach over and touch her, but he forced himself not to.

"How did they meet?" Courtland asked.

"Mother was singing at the Cotton Club one night, and Father was in New York on a business trip. When Mother was done with her set, Father was waiting for her backstage," Eva said grimly. "Mother said she never stood a chance. Father was handsome and smart and very engaging."

"How was he as a father?" Courtland asked.

Finally, a smile reached Eva's eyes, albeit a sad one. "He was a phenomenal father when he was around. We didn't get to see him much since . . . well, since he was married with another family, but when he was around, he was doting and loving."

"That had to be difficult for you and your sister," Courtland said. He thought about his grandfather's children with Miss Easter Lily. They always got the crumbs. They never got to be the focus of his grandfather's life. He wondered why this realization just hit him. He instantly felt shame for all of the years he took his grandfather's time and attention for granted. Adam would have said it was just another sign that white folks couldn't see what was right in front of their faces, and in that moment, Courtland would not have argued with him.

"It was difficult for all of us—the not seeing Father on a regular basis—but we made it work," Eva said, and this time a tear did slide down her face, but she quickly wiped it away. "Mother made New Orleans her home base after she and Father became . . . intimate. The good thing about us living in New Orleans where Mother was from was we got to be around Mother's mother, Grandmother Bettine."

"Did you know your father was married to someone else?" he asked.

As painful as he knew it was for her to tell this story, and as uncomfortable as it was for him to hear it, he could tell she needed to tell her truth, similar to how it had been when she gave him the space to talk about the war.

"Frédérique knew. I just knew Father traveled a lot. It wasn't until after he died that I learned the truth," she said. "Up until his death, as far as I knew, all fathers traveled and were away from their families."

Courtland didn't ask her to tell him what happened to her father. He knew. He had done some digging, and he found out that her father was killed by his brother-in-law. According to the newspaper article, Valéry's brother-in-law fought on behalf of the honor of his sister. It didn't mention Eva's mother by name, but it did say a "prominent Negro jazz singer" was the cause of the murder.

"I don't want to hurt you, Eva," Courtland said.

"Then don't," she said softly.

"Eva, I—"

Before he could finish his sentence, Adam returned to the table. A part of Courtland was grateful for the interruption, but the other part of him desperately wanted to figure out what exactly there was between he and Eva. Mild flirtation? The beginnings of . . . dare he say, love? He didn't know, and it frustrated him because if nothing else, he prided himself on his ability to problem solve and think through pretty much any situation.

"Well, country boy, you about ready to head back to the Hill?" Adam asked, looking from Courtland to Eva with curiosity.

"Yes. I suppose we should get back to work," Courtland said, clearing his throat and standing. "It was nice chatting with you, Eva. Take care of yourself."

"You do the same, Senator Kingsley," she said, standing as well. "Thank you both for coming to my restaurant today. I hope your lunches were satisfactory."

"The food was delicious, as always," Adam responded. "Tell Pearson and Frédérique I will see you all this Sunday. I've got my sermon all ready to go."

"That sounds wonderful," Eva said absently. "I'll see you Sunday."

They both watched as she walked away. Courtland wished he would have had time to say more, but really, what more could he say? What promises could he make?

"You're about to do something foolish, aren't you, country boy?" Adam said in a voice low enough for Courtland's ears only.

Courtland slowly nodded in agreement. "Yes. I believe so," he said to his friend as they both walked toward the front of the restaurant. Courtland was looking forward to returning to his office. He had mountains of work to do, and he hoped that somehow, some way, it would take his mind off Eva, even if just for the rest of the afternoon.

FIVE

Eva

The week had gone by quickly, and much to Eva's disappointment, Courtland did not come back by the restaurant or call her at home. At first she thought maybe it was for the best. God knows she couldn't think of a single reason for them to put themselves through the emotional turmoil of a relationship that was destined to fail, but she would not be telling the truth if she didn't acknowledge that she was saddened by the silence. Her sister would be telling her to stop chasing after the impossible. Her mind said the same thing. Now she needed her heart to catch up with her mind.

Courtland was the first man she had ever allowed to get just a little bit close to her in a romantic way, and for him to just disappear without another word, well, it stung. She tried to immerse herself in work, and for a time she was able to do just that. On Friday she met with Albert Cassell, an architect who had designed many of the buildings at Howard University. He was also the head of the architecture department there. He and Eva sat for hours, discussing her plans for the new restaurant she wanted to open in the summer.

"What will you call your restaurant, Eva?" Albert asked, diligently taking notes.

Eva was pleased with the time and attention Mr. Cassell was giving to her dream, and she truly appreciated that he wasn't speaking down to her as if her thoughts and ideas didn't matter. Of course, she also knew he had two daughters he was very proud to boast were students at Cornell University studying architecture. He had no problem with women being in control, and Eva was grateful for that fact because it made working with him so much easier.

Eva smiled broadly. "My plan is to call it Bettine's Diner, after my grandmother."

She had already explained the concept to him—Southern cuisine mixed with Creole. She planned to serve many of the dishes that were already on the menu at Chez Geneviève, such as the gumbo, red beans and rice, jambalaya, and étouffée. But she also planned to include collard greens, fried chicken, and her mother's infamous macaroni and cheese. At Chez Geneviève, she allowed Chef du Passe to take control over most of the menu, giving him the freedom to serve many of the dishes he was classically trained to prepare, but at the diner, she wanted the menu to consist solely of the foods she cherished the most from her childhood, foods she had eaten at the tables of her mother and grandmother. These were meals they had all shared with one another after Sunday Mass or on a Friday night when her mother would have friends over to visit when they lived in Harlem. Eva wanted to give her blue-collar clientele the experience of dining out in a welcoming environment without needing to break the bank to do it.

Eva gave Albert pictures of her mother's kitchen and dining room. "This is the look I'm going for," she said, pointing to one picture in particular.

The room looked like it should be in a country farmhouse instead of a brownstone in Harlem—from the gingham curtains to the overlarge sink and the butcher block island in the middle where she and Frédérique would sit and watch their mother cook. If she was in a teaching mood, they would be dicing vegetables or slicing fruit and cheese to snack on as they waited for the meal to be completed.

"If you looked at the rest of the house, you would not think it was the same place," Eva explained to Albert. "Chez Geneviève represents the sophisticated side of Mother that existed in most of the other rooms in our house, but I want Bettine's Diner to represent our kitchen and dining room, which were modeled after the kitchen and dining room at Grandmother Bettine's house. Every room in Grandma Bettine's house was homey and simple and very country even though she lived in New Orleans on the same street the voodoo priestess Marie Laveau had lived on. Grandmother would always say, 'Fussiness has no place in a home. It needs to be warm and inviting so people will want to return.'"

Albert reassured her he would be able to re-create her childhood memories in the form of a restaurant. Later, the two of them went and toured the building she was interested in buying. It was just two blocks away from Chez Geneviève. The building's structure was sound, but it needed a lot of work in the interior.

After she and Albert finished discussing the plans, Eva returned to Chez Geneviève, her mind once again going back to Courtland. She went to her office and sat staring at her phone. She was tempted several times to call him at his office, but her nerves always got the best of her.

Plus, she knew her sister would have been furious. Frédérique always counseled her about making sure she was a lady at all times. "No man wants to be chased. Rightly or wrongly, they always want to feel like they are the hunter," Frédérique had said one day when they were talking about boys when Eva was still in high school.

Eva had hated that analogy. She didn't want to feel like she was nothing better than some dewy-eyed doe in the forest. Plus, being hunted never turned out well for the prey. But old habits truly did die hard, so she didn't call. The next thing she knew, it was Sunday after church, and she was trying very hard to be sociable with everyone, but all she wanted to do was go to her bedroom and try to figure out how to restore her mind to a place of peace. Eva had forgone Mass this Sunday so she could hear Adam speak at Pearson's church. Afterward, he and Hazel, his wife, had come over for lunch. As expected by Eva, the conversation soon turned to the meeting that was going to take place at her restaurant later that day.

"Adam, I don't want you meeting up with those other rabble-rousers at Eva's restaurant," Pearson said emphatically. "It's too dangerous."

Eva suppressed a groan. It irked her to no end that they were discussing her like she was still a little wet-behind-the-ears child. She despised it when her sister and brother-in-law acted like she wasn't wise enough to make her own decisions. But out of respect, Eva didn't interject in this conversation. She knew Pearson's concerns were coming from a good place. Of course, that didn't stop the sting.

Pearson, a moderate Negro leader, often cautioned his parishioners and his family to be patient and careful when it came to their activism. Pearson had grown up in rural Mississippi and had witnessed his fair share of white violence against Negro agitators for equal justice. Pearson's uncle had been lynched for trying to get the right to vote when Pearson was a small boy, and that had stuck with him. After the lynching, his entire family scattered around the country. Some moved to New York and others moved just outside of Washington, D.C., in Virginia and Maryland. He often spoke about the need for working within the law when it came to change. Sometimes that put him and Adam squarely on the same side. Other times their views were like night and day, and this was one of those times.

"You want to know what scares me worse than a bunch of racist white folks?" Adam asked. "A scared Negro. A scared Negro will get you killed quicker than any racist with a rope in his hands."

Eva's eyes met Hazel's. Hazel shook her head and smiled. She already knew this conversation was about to get truly contentious.

Eva considered interrupting the men but decided against it. Both Adam and Pearson celebrated her independence as a businesswoman, but she doubted either one of them would welcome her voice at this point in their debate.

"Watch yourself, Adam," Pearson warned. "I will not listen to such insulting talk. What you are trying to do is dangerous, and I will not have my sister-in-law involved in any of your tomfoolery. Oh, don't get me wrong, I understand that you are a Negro with a lot of power in this town, but if these white racists turn on my sister-in-law because of her involvement with you and those others, there is nothing you or anyone else can do to stop it."

Again, Eva was about to speak, but she looked at Frédérique, who shook her head, so Eva remained silent, even though she didn't share her brother-in-law's sense of caution. Whenever she was called upon by Adam or some of the members of the American Council on Race Relations or the National Association for the Advancement of Colored People, Eva did what she could, whether that was donating funds to the various groups or providing a safe space for people like Adam or Mary McLeod Bethune to carry out some of their civil rights activities. Fear was not part of Eva's DNA. She didn't know if that was because of her mother's or her father's blood coursing through her veins. Neither one of them was fearful—or so it seemed to Eva when she was young.

One of Eva's greatest memories was going outside to watch a storm with her father. They stood together with their heads thrown back, yelling, "Here we are! We're not afraid!" Ever since, Eva lived her life that way. Unbothered and unafraid.

Adam leaned forward in his chair, a cloud of cigar smoke surrounding his head like a halo. "Being a Negro in these United States of America is dangerous, Reverend Dr. Montgomery. Walking while Negro down U Street here in Washington, D.C., is dangerous. Taking the Greyhound bus from the north to the south is all kinds of dangerous.

Standing in your pulpit at Second Street Baptist Church on a Sunday morning is dangerous, my good friend. But you know this. Tell me a time when it wasn't dangerous to be a Negro in the good ole US of A, and I'll step down from the House of Representatives tomorrow."

"Don't play games with me, Adam," Pearson said, his eyes blazing as Frédérique casually placed her hand on top of his. "Don't try to engage me in your fancy wordplay. I might be a country bumpkin from rural Mississippi, but we played the dozens down there too."

Adam leaned back and laughed just as Hazel placed her hand on his arm. He patted his wife's leg. "See that, Pastor? Hazel and Sister Freddie are trying to tell us to 'slow our row,' like they used to tell our people in the cotton fields of Mississippi, Alabama, and Georgia. I think I must be picking my row a little too fast. Let me slow down a bit and pace myself, so the rest of my Negro brothers and sisters can catch up."

"Gentlemen . . . Hazel . . . Eva . . . would you care for something to drink?" Frédérique asked, rising from her seat beside Pearson.

Eva had to smile at her sister's efforts to cool the waters flowing between Pearson and Adam. Frédérique always had a peacemaking spirit about her. Eva used to get into tiffs with the neighborhood children when she was a girl, especially the boys if they tried to boss her around, and Frédérique would always have some soothing words to calm the situation.

"No thank you, Sister Freddie. I don't think you all will have what I have a taste for right now," Adam said with a deep, throaty laugh.

"I wouldn't mind a glass of water," Hazel said, moving to get up, but Frédérique motioned for her to sit.

"I'll bring water for everyone," Frédérique said, then looked at Eva. "Eva, why don't you give me a hand?"

Eva knew what that meant. Her sister wanted to bend her ear in private about her involvement in the civil rights efforts. Yet again. They had agreed to disagree at one time, but now Eva was sure that

Frédérique was going to hop on Pearson's bandwagon. Sure enough, when they were in the kitchen with the door closed, Frédérique turned toward her sister.

"You have to know how dangerous this is, Eva," Frédérique said. "Negroes are being strung up in trees all over the South for wanting to vote, and in parts of the North it's not much better. This city is a powder keg waiting to explode. The same thing that happened here in 1919 could happen again, except worse. Instead of pushing so hard, so fast, all we have to do is be patient and—"

"Patient!" Eva snapped. "How does being patient when it comes to basic human rights make sense to you and Pearson, Frédérique? I understand the two of you feel the need to protect me, but it's like Adam said—there is no protection for Negroes, and fear is not something you and I were ever taught, so this must be Pearson who planted this seed in you."

"Wait one minute," Frédérique said, but Eva continued as if her sister had not spoken.

"Frédérique, if we don't demand our rights, they will never be given to us freely. White folks have been stringing us along, literally and figuratively, for over eighty years, and we still haven't achieved the freedom we deserve."

"Truman is—"

"Truman is being pushed by Negro leaders," Eva said, trying to be patient with her big sister, but patience was never her strong suit. "Frédérique, if men like Adam and A. Philip Randolph and women like Mary McLeod Bethune were not being a burr in Truman's side, there would be no action on his part. Now, sis, I promise you I will be careful, but I will not promise you that I won't do everything I can to help with the movement that is taking place right here in our own backyard."

Without waiting to hear more, Eva picked up the tray of glasses filled with water, which her sister had just garnished with lemon slices, and carried it into the living room where Hazel was now sitting behind the baby grand piano Frédérique and Pearson had bought for Eva on her sixteenth birthday, proving why she was *the* Hazel Scott, musician extraordinaire. Eva tinkered some with the piano throughout the years, but it never held her attention for long. By the time she was seventeen, she had completely abandoned her piano lessons in order to hone her skills in the kitchen. Frédérique's dream that her sister would one day become the pianist at Second Street Baptist Church soon became a distant memory. Now, as Eva listened to Hazel play a medley of gospel songs, she wished for a second that she had paid a bit more attention to her lessons. The piano never sounded so sweet when she was hunting and pecking out songs.

Both men stood on either side of the piano, their rift with one another apparently over now that Hazel was playing. Eva supposed there was some truth to that William Congreve quote, "Music has charms to soothe a savage breast."

"By and by, Lord, when the morning comes," Adam sang in his rich baritone voice. Eva smiled. She always thought of Adam like an uncle or an older cousin, but she could easily see why the women all swooned at the sound of his voice.

"When all the saints of God are gathering home," Pearson sang, joining in.

They both motioned for Frédérique and Eva, who walked toward them, singing.

"We will tell the story of how we overcome, and we will understand it better by and by," the two sisters sang in perfect harmony. This song was a favorite of theirs, and actually a song Eva could manage to play all the way through on the piano without stopping.

Hazel played a few more flourishes and then stopped abruptly, a broad smile on her face. "I had to find some way to calm these menfolk down after you two left me here all alone with them. It was either see them come to blows or get them warbling behind this piano. I guess you can see which pathway I chose."

"Thank you, dear Hazel. Much appreciated," Frédérique said as Eva gave each person their glass of water. "I would much rather hear some good ole gospel music than a bunch of fussing and arguing anytime. We're all on the same team. We all want what is best for our race. It's just the how do we accomplish it that has everyone stumped. There is no reason for us to fight with each other, especially after that fine sermon you preached today, Adam. 'The Lord Will Not Be Tested.' Deuteronomy 6:15–16. I still have goose bumps. You had the church on its feet."

Hazel stood up, laughing. Eva was so taken by Hazel, who was only a few years older than she was. Hazel seemed so confident and sure of herself at all times. Eva often felt like she was faking her confidence, but Hazel never seemed nervous or out of sorts, even when dealing with a powerhouse like Adam Clayton Powell Jr.

Hazel put her hands on her hips and smiled at Adam. "You mean he had the fine sisters of Second Street Baptist Church on their feet. The brothers were sitting down wishing this ole light-skinned man of mine would hurry up and get himself out of their church so they could have their womenfolk's attention again."

Adam laughed and pulled Hazel close. "I only have eyes for you, my love."

Hazel pulled away, still laughing. "You would tell me just about anything, Reverend Powell." Hazel turned toward everyone with a wry look. "Adam Clayton Powell Jr. could sell ice cubes to an Eskimo, and we all know it."

Everyone laughed, including Adam. One thing about the charismatic preacher turned politician: he didn't mind telling a joke or being the butt of one every now and then. Eva watched the two glance lovingly at each other. They reminded Eva of Pearson and Frédérique; although she knew without a doubt that her brother-in-law truly only had eyes for her sister. Adam was always a bit on the flirtatious side, always aware of the effect he had on the room. Eva supposed that was why he made such a good politician.

"Sweetheart, we need to get home and check on the baby," Hazel said. Their son, Adam Clayton Powell III, who was a year and a half old, was at home with a babysitter. Eva reached over and squeezed her sister's hand. She knew her sister was never envious, but hearing about another person's child always seemed to make her go inward. Frédérique smiled and nodded as if to say, "I'm alright."

Frédérique had learned to hide her pain from an early age, always determined to focus on the needs of others, especially her baby sister. When Eva found out Frédérique had lost this last baby, she had been the one crying, and Frédérique had been the one offering comfort.

Eva debated saying anything further about the meeting at her restaurant, but she felt like she had to reaffirm to Adam and everyone that she was not going to be swayed by her brother-in-law's concerns. She might live in her sister and brother-in-law's house, but she was her own woman.

"I am still determined to have the meeting at the restaurant today," she said as Frédérique groaned. Eva cut her eyes at Frédérique. "I know everyone is worried these days about possible violence, but we have to take a stand, and I am willing to do what I can to support leaders like Adam with whatever they deem fit to do in the name of justice for Negroes in this country."

"Then we will be there this afternoon at four o'clock sharp, Miss Eva. I told everyone if they weren't there by 3:59, I would be exiting the facilities," Adam said, then turned toward Pearson. "Pearson, I promise you we aren't up to anything radical—well, not too radical. We're just trying to work on integrating some of these businesses here in D.C. on a small scale, then helping our Southern brothers and sisters with voter registration."

"Oh, is that all?" Pearson said sarcastically. "Nothing radical at all. Just integrate a few businesses and eradicate racism from the South. Well, y'all should be able to fix that in an hour or so."

"Pearson, I know this is a lot to digest," Adam said to his old friend. "And if I thought we could wait and see, I would sit back and do like it says in Amos, but justice is not going to 'roll down like waters.' If we want it, we have got to demand it. And that starts with the vote. Negroes have got to be able to execute their right to vote if we want to see change happen. Look, I'm scared too. This activism thing is not for the faint of heart, but if those of us with power don't do something with it, we might as well not have it." Adam turned to Eva. "And Miss Eva, if you will have a bowl of that hot gumbo for us to partake of this afternoon, you will have some happy Negroes in your place today."

"You mean I will have a happy Adam Clayton Powell Jr. in my place?" she said with a smile. "I had the chef make a big pot of it last night just for today. And Pearson, you and Freddie are welcome to come with me, if that will make you feel better about everything."

"I have to go back to the church this afternoon and teach a ladies' Bible class, but Pearson, I would feel much better if you went with Eva," Frédérique said.

"I'll be there," Pearson said grimly. Eva knew that look. Pearson would not only be there but also be a very vocal voice of opposition if he thought everyone was getting too carried away. "I'm not happy about any of this, but I will not leave Eva defenseless against your rabble-rousing and your coercive personality, Adam."

"That works for me, Pastor. The more the merrier. See if you can bring a few of those deacons from Second Street with you. We need all hands on deck. See you good people later," Adam said, kissing Frédérique on the cheek and giving Eva a hug.

"Bye, Hazel," Eva said, hugging the woman. "Will you be at the meeting today?"

Hazel stood back, nodded, and winked, then whispered in Eva's ear. "I wouldn't miss it. I'm always up for a bit of rabble-rousing. Oh, I thought you should know . . . a certain senator from Georgia will also be there."

THE LIGHT ALWAYS BREAKS

Eva was startled by the news. She couldn't imagine why Courtland would be making an appearance at their meeting to discuss integration and voter registration.

"Adam invited Senator Kingsley because he believes he is key to pushing forward some of the bills Adam wants to introduce in the House," Hazel said as if she had heard Eva's thoughts. Then she leaned closer, again speaking in a hushed tone. "Adam has kept me informed of the senator's affection for you. Be careful, young one. You're playing with fire. I don't want to see you be the one who gets burned."

Eva nodded and said softly, just loud enough for Hazel's ears, "I haven't heard from him in days. I don't think there's anything to worry about."

Hazel shook her head and laughed. "Your naiveté is showing. I saw how he looked at you at the New Year's Eve party, and I know what Adam has told me. Be careful," she said again.

Then she walked across the room to where Adam was waiting with her coat. The two of them said goodbye once more, and as Pearson and Frédérique went to the door to let them out, Eva began straightening up, taking the glasses and the ashtray to the kitchen. She thought about what Hazel had just told her. Courtland was going to be at her restaurant again. She didn't know what to expect or even how to behave, and she hated this feeling of uncertainty. Eva was washing up everything in the sink when Frédérique entered the room.

"Eva, I . . ." Frédérique stopped and sighed. "Sissy," she started and then stopped.

"What is it, Frédérique?" Eva asked, putting the dish she was washing back into the sudsy water, turning to face her sister.

She could tell by Frédérique's tone that her sister was concerned about something. For a minute she wondered if Frédérique had overheard her conversation with Hazel.

"Eva, I'm sorry for questioning your judgment about this meeting at the restaurant," Frédérique finally said. "You are an adult, and I just treated you like a child. It's hard for me to admit that my little sister is an adult woman. I promise I will be more mindful about how I talk to you. I trust you, and I respect you. I don't ever want you to think otherwise."

Eva sighed, grateful that her sister hadn't overheard her conversation with Hazel. Eva knew how much it took for her sister to make that acknowledgment. Frédérique had been tending to Eva since she was in diapers. Old habits die hard, and ever since their mother died, Frédérique had been particularly protective when it came to her little sister. They were all that they had in the world, other than Pearson.

"You don't have to apologize, Freddie. I know you love me." Eva paused and then asked the question she had been asking for a few months. "Are you okay, sis?"

Neither Pearson nor Eva wanted to bring up the last miscarriage outright, but they both worried to no end about Frédérique.

"I'm fine. You and Pearson mustn't worry," she said, but the pain was still evident in her face. "God will work everything out. I truly believe that."

Eva hugged Frédérique tightly. "One day I hope to become just like you," Eva said in a whisper in her sister's ear. "You embody all that is good in the world."

Frédérique kissed Eva's forehead. Eva was tall, but Frédérique was a couple of inches taller. People used to call them Amazons when they were growing up. Neither girl liked the nickname until their mother explained to them that the Amazons were fierce warriors and hunters who were unintimidated by anyone, including the men.

"You are perfect just the way you are, Eva Cardon. Mother would have been so proud," Frédérique said.

"And Father too?" Eva asked in a soft voice.

Sometimes Eva needed her sister to acknowledge that they did have a father, and although he wasn't around much for them, when he was around, he did everything he could to show them love. She just couldn't despise him the way Frédérique seemed to at times.

Frédérique stiffened but then relaxed, stroking Eva's hair. "And Father too."

Eva recognized how hard it was for Frédérique to speak favorably of their father. Frédérique had a forgiving and loving spirit, but she always took it hard when their father would choose spending time with his white family over them, and she blamed her father for their mother's death because after he died, their mother never seemed to be the same again. Oh, she still laughed and played with them when they were girls, but it never seemed like the smiles reached her eyes.

"Thank you," Eva said.

"I'm going to go get freshened up so I can go teach these ladies thus sayeth the Lord," Frédérique said, deftly moving away from that subject. "I'm sad you won't be there."

Eva smiled. She tried to divide her time between attending the Catholic church and her brother-in-law's church, Second Street Baptist. She knew there were those who would say she was straddling the fence, or she wasn't a serious Catholic or Baptist, for that matter, but she honestly believed that God was everywhere she was at any given time, so she never allowed doubt to creep into her mind when she went from one church to the other.

"In my own way, I would like to believe that I will still be doing the Lord's work," Eva said.

Frédérique nodded and smiled. Eva watched her sister walk away. She continued to wash the dishes, but her thoughts returned to Courtland. What would she say to him? What would he say to her? She had no answers, but she knew one thing. She was anxious to see his face again even though Hazel's words of admonition stayed in her mind: *Be careful.*

SIX

Eva

"Make sure everyone has beverages," she said to Lincoln, one of the two waiters she had asked to come and help this afternoon.

"Yes, ma'am," he said with a nod.

Turning her attention from the behind-the-scenes details, Eva looked around the room at the many Negro leaders, male and female, who had come at Adam's bidding. Adam had spoken to everyone briefly when they arrived, but he soon dispatched the women to one area of the restaurant and the men to the other to discuss how they could best be about the business of making change happen for the Negro population. Eva could tell that the women were not pleased to be segregated from the men's discussion, but Eva knew this was not something that was unusual. As much as the Negro men railed against segregation that was created and supported by white folks, they did not hesitate to carry out their own version of it against their own women—women who often did more work and raised more money to push the agenda of civil rights than the men.

The table full of women were all people Eva admired and wanted so much to be like. There was Ella Baker, Mary McLeod Bethune, Pauli Murray, as well as some local pastors' wives, professors, and young college students from Howard. Eva didn't sit down with them because she wanted to make sure everyone's needs were being met, but she did listen, off and on, to the conversations going on at the two tables. As Eva stood hovering in the background, Mary McLeod Bethune reached out for her. Eva came closer and grasped the older woman's strong, soft hand.

"Thank you for your hospitality, Eva," Mrs. McLeod Bethune said with her usual broad smile that caused her entire face to light up.

She could be an imposing individual, but in moments like these, she always made sure others felt heard and respected. Just as Adam had taken the lead role for the men, she had stepped up as the leader for the women, and no one seemed bothered by her doing so even though every woman present was a shining star in her own right.

As Mrs. McLeod Bethune would sometimes say, "There are no 'big I's' or 'little yous,' just a group of dedicated foot soldiers in the battle for freedom."

Mrs. McLeod Bethune squeezed Eva's hand slightly. "We appreciate you allowing us to meet here. So few of our Negro business owners want to get involved in our civil rights efforts. I understand their trepidation, but we need more folks like you who are willing to step out on faith."

Eva smiled and looked over at Hazel, who nodded and winked.

"Whatever I can do, you all only have to ask," Eva said. "I am here to serve. Now, let me go and check on those menfolk. As much as they think they are in charge, we all know who leads this movement."

All of the women laughed as she made her way over to the other side of the dining room where the men were talking.

Adam, as always, was holding court, but when Eva walked up to the table, all conversation stopped. All of the men rose from their seats. Eva motioned for them to sit, but they remained standing until they were introduced to her by Adam.

"Miss Eva, your phenomenal restaurant outdid itself once more with this delicious gumbo. Please give my regards to Chef du Passe. Am I telling the truth, gentlemen? Wasn't that a delicious afternoon repast?" he asked, and all of the men agreed. "I've been telling these men all about your amazing mother who inspired you to create this gem of a restaurant. Viève was one hell of a woman. This world lost one of the greatest jazz singers ever to live, and that includes Bessie, Ella, and Sarah."

"You better not let Hazel Scott hear you say that. Those would be considered fighting words," Pearson said as the rest of them all laughed, including Adam.

Eva smiled at her brother-in-law. She was happy he had decided to attend. She hoped he would see the importance of the work everyone was doing to try to make the world better for Negroes.

"Touché, Reverend Dr. Pearson," Adam said, grinning. "But as a man of God, I have to let the truth be my guide, and Viève was one of a kind."

Adam and Eva's mother had been close. Throughout her childhood, after they moved to Harlem, he was a continual presence in their home. And knowing Adam Clayton Powell Jr. and his proclivity toward beautiful women, Eva would not have been surprised to find out that he and her mother had been involved in a relationship, even though Eva had no proof. Eva's mother was always private about such things. In fact, Eva had never witnessed her father and mother kiss, let alone sleep together. Whenever their father would be at their home in New Orleans, he and their mother never entered their room until after the girls went to sleep, and when morning came and the girls were up, he would be long gone. They never shared a breakfast with their father. Not once. Eva's reverie was interrupted by Adam's introductions.

"Miss Eva, this gentleman to my left is Dr. Felix Overton. He's a Howard grad. Got his own practice just down the road from here," he said. Eva shook hands with the middle-aged man. Adam continued with the introductions. "This man beside Dr. Overton is none other than A. Philip Randolph, one of the giants in the fight for civil rights for Negroes. Randolph here has been more of a thorn in Truman's posterior than I have ever dared to be."

Eva smiled and nodded at the powerful man, who nodded back. Eva was trying hard not to be starstruck by this table of powerful Negro men. You couldn't be Negro in D.C. and not know the name A. Philip Randolph. Mr. Randolph played politics better than most, and she was constantly seeing his name in the local newspapers.

Finally, after Adam had introduced her to several more of the men, he got to the young man of the group who was sitting at the table. He had been looking at Eva the entire time, smiling and admiring her with total abandonment, and Eva had noticed him too. It would have been hard not to. He was handsome. Very handsome. He had beautiful dark skin and a head full of black curly hair. Even while sitting, he appeared to be a tall man. She tried not to gaze at him too openly, but it was hard to ignore the man's infectious smile. Adam looked from Eva to the young man and grinned.

"Miss Eva, the arrogant young man across the table is an up-and-comer. He's a newly minted lawyer and a Morehouse man. Can't tell them nothing," Adam said, causing the whole table to erupt in laughter. The young man got up and unabashedly came over and extended his hand to Eva.

"Representative Powell is correct. We Morehouse men are confident, so much so that we can do our own introductions. I am Wendell Moss Harrington III. I represent three generations of Morehouse men. I am pleased to make your acquaintance, Miss Cardon," he said, flashing all of his pearly white teeth.

"Don't you mean Miss Eva is pleased to make *your* acquaintance?" Dr. Overton said, causing the table to burst into laughter again.

Wendell didn't seem bothered by the gentle ribbing by his

elders. Eva grasped his hand, which was soft as a woman's. Clearly Mr. Harrington III had never seen a day of hard labor. Even Eva had to pay special attention to her hands since she never saw herself as too good to dig in and do some work in the kitchen, including wash dishes.

"Nice to meet you, Mr. Harrington," Eva said, smiling up at the flirtatious man.

"Please, call me Wendell," he said, returning to his seat.

"Very well, Wendell," Eva said. Then she allowed herself to glance around the table, once again taking in the historic nature of all of these important people being in her restaurant at one time. "You gentlemen seem to be having quite the lively discussion. There is a lot of power sitting here at this table. I'm surprised this room can contain it all, between you all and the women across the way."

Adam laughed. "Less power than you would think. I can't even get Negroes the right to eat in the same dining room as whites on Capitol Hill. Those da . . . sorry, Miss Eva, those white Democrats are determined to drive us back to slavery."

"We're making progress," A. Philip Randolph said with a smile. "Your problem, Powell, is you're too impatient. Rome wasn't built in a day, and neither was Washington, D.C."

"Thank you, sir," Pearson said, his face full of animation. Eva knew her brother-in-law was still feeling salty toward Adam. There wasn't much Adam could say that Pearson would be on board with—at least not today. "Been trying to tell Representative Powell here that for the longest. Patience is what we need, not mindless agitation that will lead to more heartache and heartbreak. I've seen a lynching firsthand. It ain't a pretty sight."

"No one is arguing that Rome was built in a day, gentlemen, but Negroes have been waiting for our time since the signing of the Emancipation Proclamation. If not now, when? We had that brief respite during Reconstruction, and now here we are, right back at square one," Adam said, the anger edging into his voice.

Eva had to agree with Adam. The patience maxim that her brother-in-law preached so fervently was frustrating to her. She knew Pearson meant well, but she worried that his brand of moderation would only lead to more sorrow for Negroes. Many of the white people who wanted to keep Negroes down depended on leaders like Pearson to talk against the very work people like Adam were trying to do. Divide and conquer was their motto. She didn't want to see her brother-in-law and sister on the wrong side of history.

"How are you going to say we are back at square one, Powell, with so many powerful Negroes in this country, many of whom are sitting at this table?" Dr. Overton said. "This is our time. We just have to continue to put pressure on the right people."

"And don't get me wrong," A. Philip Randolph said. "I am as frustrated as anyone that the road to justice has involved so many side roads and back alleys, but I will not be deterred from the mission. We are gaining power, and it won't be long before change truly does happen for the Negro race."

Eva was astounded by what she was hearing. These men—and the women on the other side of the room—were truly the change agents she envisioned who would be the catalysts to end segregation and racism. Or at least that was what she prayed for, but one thing she knew, she was grateful that she had the chance to witness and be part of the revolution she saw happening before her very eyes.

"Having power and being powerful are two different things," Adam said. "Don't ever get the two mixed up."

"And what is the difference between being powerful and having power?" Pearson asked, sitting up slightly in his chair.

Eva waited for the response with an eagerness she was trying to hide. This was the type of conversations her mother, Geneviève, and her friends used to have when they all lived in Harlem. As the champagne and dark liquor would flow back then, so would the conversations between Geneviève, Adam, Jimmy Baldwin, and whomever else happened to be in town. Eva cut her teeth on this type of activism and awareness.

"Man, random Negroes have power, but as a collective? Not so much," Adam said, lighting a cigarette and taking a nice long drag before continuing. Eva smiled to herself. Adam was forever the orator. Always aware of what he said and how he said it. Everyone waited until he continued. "On the other hand, the white race is powerful, and that extends from the richest Rockefeller to the poorest Georgia Cracker, and as long as they got representation in the White House, well, we are fighting an uphill battle. He who controls the money *and* the White House is second only to God."

"President Truman seems to be on board with doing some positive things for Negroes," Eva offered. Adam grunted but Eva continued. She was not easily intimidated, not even by a table full of influential Negro men. "Mr. Randolph, what about the efforts you have made to end discrimination in the military? I read about the Committee Against Jim Crow in Military Service and Training created by you and your committee, and just last month, through your efforts and the efforts of men like Representative Adam Clayton Powell Jr. here, the president signed the executive order to end segregation in the military. Now, I do think the executive order missed the mark in some areas, but it's a nice start. Change is happening on all of your watches."

Pearson looked at his sister-in-law proudly, nodding in affirmation. So did Adam. Both men knew just how wickedly smart Eva was, but it was clear the other men were slightly shocked. Eva laughed at their amazed faces.

"Now surely you all understood that I could read, write, and think for myself," she said. "This business of mine did not grow on a tree. I did this, so it stands to reason I have a mind to go along with everything. You all are looking at me like I just spoke in tongues. Do you need an interpreter—maybe one of the ladies across the room?"

They all laughed, then finally Wendell spoke.

"Yes, we understand that you are quite capable in most things, I would imagine, but Miss Eva, you are not like most women—or at least most women I know." Several of the other men nodded in agreement. Wendell continued talking, looking at her appreciatively. "My mother is one of the smartest women I know, but even she doesn't follow politics. That's just not a trait one associates with women."

"Well, maybe if you menfolk would actually engage in dialogue with your wives, mothers, and sisters, you would find that they are more than just pretty armpieces," she said, folding her arms in front of her. "I believe there are more women like me than any of you can imagine, many of whom are sitting across the room, banished from being part of this conversation. Women with careers that would be just as illustrious as yours if they shared your XY chromosomes."

"Well, young lady, if you are not taken, I have two sons I am looking to marry off. One is a doctor and the other is a lawyer," Dr. Overton said. "Take your pick."

Everyone laughed. Eva didn't. She didn't like being the butt of their joke.

"Miss Eva Cardon, you have the pick of the litter at Dr. Overton's home, but may I also throw my hat into the ring?" Wendell said, looking at her boldly.

He clearly didn't pick up the cues. Eva was not pleased. She did not plan to be any man's possession—ever.

"I kindly thank you for the offer of your sons, Dr. Overton. And . . . well, thank you, too, Mr. Wendell Moss Harrington III. But right now my mind is filled with making my payroll and making sure all of the bellies of you high-class Negro Washingtonians get filled with good New Orleans cuisine. Finding a husband is not on my radar at this particular moment," she said, and they all laughed again. "Now, if you will excuse me, I need to get to my kitchen and make sure everything is in good order. Again, thank you for coming out today."

Eva turned to walk away, but then she looked at the door and saw Courtland enter the restaurant. She didn't know if she was happy to see him or furious with him for daring to ignore her for days without even a single call or visit. Fury seemed to be the overriding emotion she was feeling, especially since he was walking toward her, smiling as if nothing was wrong. She watched as he walked over to the table. Everyone else remained seated except for Adam.

"Gentlemen, this is Senator Courtland Hardiman Kingsley IV, the Democratic senator from Georgia," Adam said. Again, no one moved. Most of the men were looking at Adam like he had lost his mind, but Adam continued talking. "If we truly want change, we have to go to the lion's mouth. We will not get the things we want unless we pull a few of these moderate Democrats into our camp. Senator Kingsley is one of those people."

Eva looked at Courtland, whose expression had not changed. He looked completely comfortable being there even though almost every person was outwardly showing their disgust at his presence.

After a moment of pause, Eva spoke. "Take your seat, Senator Kingsley," she said with a tight voice. "I will have a waiter bring you your food and beverage."

Before he could say anything, she walked away. She needed a moment. She didn't want him to see how much of an effect he had on her. *"Se remettre les idées en place,* Eva Cardon." *Get yourself together.* She prayed she could; otherwise, it was going to be a very long afternoon.

SEVEN

Courtland

As Courtland looked around the table, he was not surprised at all by the cold reception he was receiving. Adam had warned Courtland when he invited the Georgia senator to the meeting that he would not be welcomed by everyone present, but Courtland had still agreed to show up. He was a Southern Democrat who, so far, had not done a whole lot in Congress to prove himself an ally to the Negro race. Courtland acknowledged that fact. Part of him wanted to be the type of ally Adam wanted him to be, but he also knew he had to be careful about the steps he made because, at the end of the day, Courtland had higher aspirations than the senate, but anytime he raised this point with Adam, Adam would call him on his reticence to commit.

"You need to be careful?" Adam had said incredulously the previous week during one of their after-work cocktail hours in Courtland's office. "You, a white male from a prominent, well-to-do family, are telling me that you need to be careful? Is that what I'm hearing?"

"Adam, I—"

"So how about this: You come to Miss Eva's restaurant on Sunday afternoon and have a conversation with the Negro leadership. Tell us to our faces exactly what hill you are willing to die on," Adam had insisted.

Everything within Courtland screamed that going to the meeting was not a good thing for him to do, but he truly believed there had to be a way he could support some of the things Adam was asking for, and tucking tail and running was not his modus operandi. So Courtland accepted the stares from the people at the table with Adam as the older man made the introductions.

Courtland greeted each person by name, making sure he filed that information away in case he met up with any of the gentlemen in the future. Finally, Adam introduced Courtland to the young gentleman who had responded to his arrival with the harshest stare of all.

Courtland extended his hand to Wendell, but Wendell looked at his hand as if it were a snake. Courtland let his hand fall to his side. "Nice to meet you, Wendell. I—"

"We can stop with the niceties, Senator Kingsley," Wendell said, with neither a smile nor a show of enthusiasm over Courtland being in their midst. "As one of your constituents, sir, I have a few questions for you."

"Stand down, Junior," Adam said with a hearty laugh. "Courtland is a good Georgia boy. Don't go getting yourself all worked up. He's on our side—more or less."

Courtland shot a glare at Adam, who only laughed harder. It was clear to Courtland that Adam had set him up. Courtland had known this meeting was not going to be congenial, but he also had not expected an ambush before he could even take his seat. For a brief second, Courtland thought about excusing himself and going off to look for Eva, but the way she had looked at him had not been that friendly either. He briefly wondered why. They hadn't spoken in a few days, but he had been busy with work. He hoped he had not angered her by his silence. His sisters and mother often scolded him for going days without communicating with them, but that was just

Courtland's way. Sometimes he went inward. He made a mental note to pull Eva aside and apologize for his silence.

"It remains to be seen how good the good senator is," Wendell said, clearly spoiling for a fight. "So far, Senator Kingsley has yet to support and/or introduce any substantive legislation that deals with ending the subjugation of our people. Going to a few parties with Negroes and hanging out at Negro restaurants is well and good, but I want to see what the senator is going to do when surrounded by the rank and file of his party."

Adam shook his head, still laughing. "Well, Courtland, are you sure you want to join this table? Junior over there is ready to fight. Are you?"

Courtland smiled in spite of how he was really feeling. As much as he was willing to take pushback from Adam, he was not interested in being the battering ram for some recent college graduate who was clearly hell-bent on shaming him.

"I have never retreated from a fight in my life. I have stared down Nazi soldiers and never blinked once. You know that, Adam. One conversation is not going to break me. Wendell, you have every right to hold my feet to the fire. I work for you. I answer to you."

"Do you, sir?" Wendell asked with a dry smile, cocking his head slightly. "I'm a Negro from the South. The good white folks down there have done everything within their power to suppress and intimidate Negro voters. I wasn't even afforded the opportunity to vote against you. What are you going to do about that, sir?"

It seemed like everyone at the table was holding their collective breath, waiting to see how Courtland would respond. Courtland was holding his breath, too, if the truth be known. The last thing he wanted to do was to lie or to oversell what he thought he could actually do to change things in Georgia as it pertained to his Negro constituents.

Tread lightly, he thought. "Wendell, I will not lie to you. Changing the status quo in Georgia will not be easy, but I promise you this: I will do everything within my power to be more transparent about my actions in the senate. Up until now, my entire thought pattern was I needed to bide my time. I will make a more concerted effort to get into the fight."

Wendell's face was like a storm cloud. He clapped his hands slowly, his voice rising angrily. "Well, that was a lot of nothing, Senator. What is this *more* you plan to do, sir? Specifically, I am a lawyer—newly minted, grant you—but I am still knowledgeable of legalese. Speak plainly, sir. I am sure the entire table would love to hear the details of how you are going to stand up against your Democratic colleagues from the South. I know I would love to hear you speak more on it."

"Junior . . . ," Adam said with a warning tone and a hint of a chuckle. He leaned back in his seat and looked expectantly at Courtland. So did the rest of the men at the table. No one was coming to his defense. Courtland could see that this was going to be a long meal.

Courtland spoke in a calm, modulated voice. "As we speak, I am working on legislation that will lead toward lower taxes. That will help everyone, including Negroes."

"Oh, Senator Kingsley, is that the best you've got?" Wendell asked with a look of derision. "Most Negroes in Georgia are so poor they don't have a pot to piss in or a window to throw it out of. Most of them are already tax exempt because they don't own anything worth taxing, so try again. What about working with Representative Powell here on an anti-lynching bill? Now, legislation like that has teeth. You get behind a bill like that and those Southern boys will know exactly where you stand."

"I agree," A. Philip Randolph said, leaning forward in his chair, looking Courtland squarely in the eyes. "What say you, Senator? Can we get your word that you will support a bill that keeps Negroes from swinging in trees? That seems pretty innocuous to me."

But before Courtland could answer, Eva glided across the room and stopped at their table, placing a bowl of gumbo in front of Courtland, who had never been so happy to be interrupted.

"Are you gentlemen playing nicely with each other?" she asked with a faint smile, looking from one man to the other.

Courtland tried to catch her eye, but she did not settle her glance on anyone, including him.

All of them rose from their seats, but she waved them back down. "As smart as all of you gentlemen are, you are not going to rectify nearly three hundred years of racist ideology in an afternoon. Do you suppose we could take the conversation down to a gentle roar?"

"Very sorry, Miss Cardon. I was just asking the senator here a few questions, but I would never want to get on your bad side. Ever," Wendell said.

Courtland noticed the appreciative look he was giving Eva. The young man's stares did not sit well with Courtland, but he knew there was nothing he could say about it. He had no right to be possessive over Eva, yet the only thing he wanted to do was to slam the young man in his chest for daring to look at her in such a familiar way. Before Eva could respond, Hazel walked over.

"Gentlemen, we ladies believe this is a good time for us all to come together and report on our various thoughts on how to move forward. Good evening, Senator Kingsley," she said with a head nod.

Courtland stood, as did the other men at the table, including Adam. Courtland had only met Hazel a couple of times, but he always liked her. She was the one person on the planet who seemed to be able to keep Adam Clayton Powell Jr. on his toes.

"Hello, Mrs. Powell," he said. "Pleasure seeing you again."

"Same," she said, but her attention was completely on Adam. She whispered something in his ear that caused him to laugh uproariously. Courtland decided to use this moment as a time to excuse himself and hopefully have a word or two with Eva. Courtland moved closer to Eva as the other men scurried to add chairs around the table as the remainder of the women came over.

"Eva, do you mind if I speak to you for a moment in private?" Courtland asked quietly. He watched as a scowl passed across her face, but he didn't allow the look to deter him. "Please," he said. "Just for a moment."

"Fine," she said. "Follow me to my office."

Eva walked briskly across the restaurant toward the back, and Courtland followed her at a slower pace. He had left his walking cane in his car due to vanity, but now he wished he had brought it because his injured leg was even more noticeable. But as he looked around, he saw that no one was paying him any attention. He returned his focus to Eva. As always, she was impeccable from her head to her toes. She had on a black high-necked dress that stopped just below her knees, and her hair was pulled back into a bun. Her attire was conservative, but it didn't camouflage her womanliness at all. If anything, her dress accentuated it. He looked back at the table again, but the other men were so busy making way for the women that they didn't pay him and Eva any attention. When they made it to her office, she left the door open.

"So what is this business you wanted to talk about?" she asked. The warmth in her voice he had been used to was nowhere to be found.

"I need to apologize," he said. "I've been so immersed in new committee work that time got away from me. I should have called. I'm sorry."

Eva looked at Courtland for a moment, but then she spoke coolly. "You don't owe me anything, Courtland, not even a phone call. If that's all—"

"Well," he said, feeling a bit hesitant. "I still wanted to say I was sorry. I still would like to be friends."

"Hmm," she said. "Friends. I suppose one can't have too many friends. Sure, Courtland. Let's you and I be friends."

Although her words seemed open to the idea, her entire demeanor was cold and distant. Courtland wasn't sure what he could say to fix what was wrong between them, so he decided to change the subject.

"Eva, I was hoping to talk to you about something else," he said, barreling forward even though she looked like the last thing she wanted to do at that point was listen to him talk more. "I mentioned to you before the young porter, Vernon Michaels. He's a fine young man, Eva, and all he needs is a chance, and I was hoping you might give him one. I haven't talked to him because I wanted to talk to you first, but I was wondering if you would consider giving him a job when he gets ready to start college. I know he would be a hard worker because he sure works hard on that train."

After he was done speaking, Eva didn't say anything right away. Courtland waited, but the silence was becoming uncomfortable.

"I'll vouch for him," Courtland said, thinking she was unsure about taking on someone she had never met before.

Finally, she spoke. "Why are you doing this, Courtland?"

"Doing what?" he asked, a bit confused about what exactly her question meant.

"Being this champion of Negroes," she said dryly. "I'm trying to figure out your angle. Similar to what others have said, I do not understand this passion for Negroes you seem to have. So I ask again, why are you doing this? You are a Georgia Democrat, and from what I have heard, your family were big-time slave owners. What is it profiting you to do all of this?"

"'For what shall it profit a man if he shall gain the whole world and lose his soul?'" Courtland said, repeating a scripture he had heard often from his mother, but the verse took on a whole new meaning when he actually thought about it in terms of his own life.

Eva gave a dry laugh. "So you are on a religious quest? I see. I can't figure you out, Senator Kingsley. Well, long story short, yes, I am willing to talk to this young man, Vernon Michaels. Not because of you but because of his story."

"Fair enough," Courtland said.

"But I would really like an answer to my question," she said. "Why are you here today? Why are you doing all of this?"

"Adam asked me to," Courtland said simply.

"No, I mean really," she said, sitting in the chair behind her desk, motioning for him to sit, which he did in the chair across from her. "Why are you here, Courtland? Even after only knowing you for a short period of time, I don't think you seem like the kind of man who does things without motivation."

"Eva, you are right to question my motives. I can only imagine what it must look like from your vantage point," he said, leaning forward. "I know I am a product of a South that flourished due to the forced labor of our Negro population . . . still does, for that matter. I have been skirting the question you and others have asked me. The truth of the matter is, I do what I do because of the horrendous guilt I feel. I know I can't undo all that has been done and is being done now, but I am willing to try."

"Are you willing to sacrifice your career in order to stand up for what is right?" Eva asked, her face never looking so serious before in his presence.

Courtland hesitated. He didn't want to rush in and just say the answer he knew Eva wanted to hear. The bottom line was he didn't know if he was willing to sacrifice everything. So far, nothing he had done had inconvenienced or threatened his forward movement in politics or life in general. So far, he had been able to fly under the radar. As much as he would like to say to Eva that he was such a man of principle that if it came down to it, he would sacrifice everything in order to do what was right, but he didn't know for sure. So he told her the truth.

"Every day, I strive to be the best incarnation of myself," he said. "I walk into the halls of Congress, and I acknowledge that the position I hold is one that only a select few will ever hold. I try to make decisions that are good for the many and not just the few, but I have not been tested as of yet. I have not had to put everything on the line. I don't know what I would do if I had to choose between power and principle. I just don't know."

Eva listened intently as he shared with her his honest thoughts. Then she spoke in a careful voice. "Courtland, you and I have not known each other long, so maybe I am overstepping my bounds by saying what I am about to say, but you seem to be a man who believes in fairness and justice. Fighting the good fight isn't popular or even rewarding sometimes, but at some point, we all have to figure out what we are willing to risk losing in order to stand up for what is right—or at least that is how my mother raised me."

Before he could respond, the phone rang. Eva picked it up on the second ring.

"Hello," she said. He watched as her face became ashen.

After a moment, she hung up the phone and jumped up from her chair.

"What is it?" Courtland asked, standing up too.

"The person on the phone said there is a bomb planted in the building. We've got to go," she said, rushing out of the room, with Courtland hurrying as fast as he could behind her.

"We need to exit the building," she said loudly once she reached the table where all of the Negro leadership was sitting. "There is a threat. I need everyone to leave and get as far away from the building as possible. Please hurry, everyone!"

Courtland watched as everyone moved quickly toward the door, not panicking but moving fast. Just as Courtland, Eva, Wendell, and Pearson made it to the door, there was a huge explosion toward the back of the building. Courtland immediately went into military commander mode.

"Let's go!" Courtland ordered, pushing everyone out the door. He was concerned that there might be a second explosion. When they made it outside, everyone who had been at the meeting was standing across the street. Courtland could hear the piercing sounds of police sirens making their way toward them, which he found rather interesting considering the explosion just happened, but he temporarily put that out of his mind.

"Everyone, let's get farther down the block in case another explosion occurs!" he called out, but no one moved.

Then Adam spoke. "You heard Courtland. Let's move down the street a bit. No telling what these racist animals are planning next."

Immediately, the crowd began moving toward the end of the street. Courtland shook his head, but he understood why no one listened to him. Why should they respect his word? Nine times out of ten, whoever planted that explosive device was someone who looked similar to Courtland. Not since the war had Courtland felt so much like the enemy. He hated that feeling, but he was not in any position to fight it. It wasn't long before the police arrived, and Courtland watched as they spread out around the perimeter. The lead officer was talking to Eva and her brother-in-law. Courtland wanted to go over to them, but he felt a hand on his shoulder. It was Adam.

"She won't like it if you intervene," he said. "Let her and Pearson handle things. I'm sure the police will want to talk to all of us eventually. Unless of course you want to sneak away before the press gets here."

"I'm not leaving, Adam," Courtland said. All he wanted to do at this point was go and pull Eva into his arms. He could see how visibly shaken she was.

He watched as Wendell walked over to where she and Pearson were standing beside the officer. Courtland made a move to go to her, but once again Adam stopped him, placing his hand on Courtland's arm.

"Don't let your emotions get the best of you," Adam cautioned, then changed the subject. "What are your thoughts about the police showing up before the explosion even had a chance to reverberate for the final time?"

Courtland nodded in agreement. "I have a feeling your thoughts and mine are the same."

Before they could say any more about the matter, Hazel walked over, and Adam pulled her into a tight hug.

"Are you all right, Hazel Scott?" he asked in a voice so tender, Courtland looked away, feeling as if he were intruding on a private moment.

"I'm fine," he heard her say. "I am thankful things were no worse than they were. This could have been deadly . . . and with so many leaders all in one place . . . this would have been the perfect crime to cripple the movement."

Courtland watched as one of the police officers started walking toward them. When he stopped, he looked at Courtland, ignoring Adam and Hazel completely.

"So, sir, what is your take on all of this?" the officer asked.

He was a large man with an awful red scar on the side of his face. Were it not for his crooked smile, he would have been completely intimidating to the average person. Courtland had seen much worse in his time serving in the military, staring down German soldiers.

"First, sir, you need to introduce yourself and then you need to speak to all three of us," Courtland said, folding his arms in front of him. "Representative Powell and his wife, Mrs. Hazel Scott Powell, were also in the building, and they, too, were witnesses of this horrendous crime."

The officer's smile turned icy. "My name is Lieutenant Stevens. I will be the investigator for this incident."

"It was an attempted assassination," Adam said, equally as cold. "Make sure you get the language correct."

"As of right now," Lieutenant Stevens said, "we don't have evidence that this was anything more than an accident. Perhaps improper kitchen maintenance or poor storage of chemicals. We shall see."

Adam moved closer to the lieutenant, and Courtland placed a restraining hand on Adam's arm. He noticed that Lieutenant Stevens's hand went to his gun holster.

"Easy," Courtland said down low for Adam's ears only. "Lieutenant, I was in the office with Miss Cardon when she received the phone call warning her that there was a bomb in the building."

"I will take that into consideration," Lieutenant Stevens said. "You all have a good day."

Before they could say anything else, Lieutenant Stevens went over to a crowd of police officers. Courtland, Adam, and Hazel all watched as Lieutenant Stevens said something to the group, and they all started laughing loudly.

"This is going to get ugly," Adam said.

"I'm right here with you," Courtland said, thinking about his conversation with Eva. Perhaps the time to choose a side had presented itself to Courtland. Now he had to decide what side of history he wanted to reside on. Eva started walking toward them. When she got there, Hazel went to her and hugged her tightly. When Hazel let go, Eva was standing there with a face full of emotions.

"What did they say?" Adam asked. "I see Pearson is still talking to them. Should I go over?"

Eva nodded. "That might be good. Pearson is fit to be tied. They are insisting this was some huge error on my part or my staff's part. They aren't even entertaining the idea that someone planted explosives."

Adam nodded and began walking over to Pearson and the officers he was still talking to.

"I know my husband," Hazel said with a wry voice. "I better make sure they see Reverend Powell and not the man I know he can become when pushed to the limits." Hazel walked away, leaving Courtland and Eva alone.

"What can I do?" Courtland asked.

Eva looked up at him, her eyes filled with unshed tears.

"I don't know," she said simply. "Nothing like this has ever happened to me before. I want to fight, but all I feel like doing at this point is crying. I don't understand people who would do such things. Is the advancement of the Negro race so intimidating and threatening that white people feel the right to try to destroy us for it?"

"I wish I had answers, Eva," he said, "but I do have an answer to the question you asked me earlier."

She looked at him as one of the tears drifted down her face. Instinctively, he wanted to reach over and brush it away, but he knew she would not be pleased, so he kept his hands to his sides.

"What is that?" she asked as more tears flowed down her beautiful face.

In that moment, if he could find the culprit, it would take all of the heavenly hosts to keep him from throttling the person to death, his anger was so strong.

"I am willing to risk it all to do what is right," he said. "It should not have taken this incident to open my eyes to the fact that I can't do this work that I am doing halfway. Either I'm all in or I'm not. I will fight with you and for you, Eva Cardon."

Eva looked at him, nodded, and then silently walked away. He wanted to go with her, but he knew he needed to give her space to decide what she wanted or needed from him. Courtland decided then and there that he would not let this situation go without doing everything he could to get to the bottom of what happened, and whatever Adam needed him to do, he would do, and let the chips fall wherever they may. Courtland suddenly remembered an old saying his grandpa Little Jack used to say when someone riled him up. "Oh, you done woke up this ole sleeping bear now."

"You will be found," Courtland muttered to himself. "Mark my words. You will be found."

EIGHT

Courtland

The sunlight was not even peeking up over the Potomac when Courtland's driver, Harold, pulled up in front of Courtland's brownstone to take him to work. Usually Courtland got to see the early morning colors painted across the sky—shades of orange, blue, pink, purple, and red. But this morning everything was still dark and cold outside where Courtland had been waiting for his driver. He had not rested well the night before, not being able to get the incident at Eva's restaurant out of his mind or the look of total hurt and fear he saw in her eyes. So finally, at 5:00 a.m., he called Harold and asked him to come take him to work. When Harold arrived, Courtland apologized profusely.

"I'm sorry, Harold," Courtland said, settling himself into the back seat. "I wasn't thinking when I called, and by the time I thought to call you back, you were—"

"It's okay, Senator Kingsley," Harold said, turning around in his seat, looking solemnly at Courtland. "Yesterday was quite a day. I imagine you still have . . . well . . . everything that happened on your mind."

"I'm afraid I do," Courtland said in a grave voice. "Things could have been much worse, but it was bad enough. Mother would say I should be on my way to early morning Mass to give thanks instead of being on my way to work."

"Is that where you would like to go, Senator? To Mass?" Harold asked.

Courtland laughed slightly. "I'm still working on attaining Mother's level of piety. And anyway, I would be way early for morning Mass. I'm sure Mother will say enough prayers today to cover me and all of D.C. No, I'll go to the office and see if I can get something done."

"Are you ready to go now, Senator?" Harold asked.

"Yes," Courtland said, leaning back into the comfortable custom leather seats. He had really splurged with this car because he knew he would be spending a lot of time in it. The drive to the Hill was short, but in the evenings, Courtland was often going from one event to the next. He liked being able to just hop in the car and let Harold maneuver his way through D.C. traffic. Because it was so early, there were very few cars to contend with, so it didn't take long before Harold was pulling up in front of the Russell Building.

Courtland got out of the car and waved one final time. He walked briskly into the building, not wanting to stay in the cold any longer than he had to. When he entered his office, there was not the smell of coffee that usually met his nose every morning. Since he had arrived before Mrs. Nelson, the office was dark. He turned on the lights and continued to walk toward the back where his office was located.

The décor in his office was almost embarrassingly perfect. His mother and sisters had taken it over when he was elected to the senate, and once they were done with this once nondescript space, it looked almost presidential. Sitting prominently in the center of the room was an oak desk that used to be his grandfather's. There was a conference table by the window overlooking the Capitol that his mother ordered from England. And if things weren't already grandiose enough, there were the paintings by Monet and Gustav Klimt hanging on the wall nearest the door. There were also family photos and a corner of the room that his mother said would be reserved for photos of him and his own family someday, but for now she had put a small table with a vase that Mrs. Nelson kept filled with fresh flowers. Anytime someone would come to his office for the first time, Courtland always felt a bit sheepish and apologetic. He was a junior senator, but his office looked like he had been in the senate for decades.

Courtland had a ton of work to do, so he sat down at his desk and began plowing through it. Today's vote was going to be an important one. The discussion was going to revolve around benefits for the dependents of disabled veterans, and that was one of the things Courtland felt the most passionate about. However, it wasn't long before he found himself just as distracted in the office as he was at home. He would get started writing, and then all of a sudden he would think about Eva. The look on her face when she received that call. The sound of the explosion going off as they all ran from the building. And then the tears she shed. All of it was crowding his thoughts, keeping him from accomplishing the tasks at hand.

Courtland looked at the clock. It was just a little after seven o'clock in the morning. He knew she wouldn't be at her restaurant yet, or at least he didn't think she would, but he didn't want to call her at home and risk waking her up or, worse, angering her more, so he forced himself to continue working. Before long Mrs. Nelson arrived. She peeked into his office.

"Good morning, Senator. I did not know you planned on arriving early," she said in an accusatory tone. "Had you told me you were going to get here so soon, I could have adjusted my arrival time."

"It was an impulsive act, Mrs. Nelson," he said. "I couldn't sleep, so I decided to come in early and get some work done. I have some things here for you to type before I leave for the opening session this morning."

Mrs. Nelson walked over to his desk and took the papers. After she left, Courtland threw himself back into his work. Soon it was time for him to walk over to the Capitol.

"I'll see you later today, Mrs. Nelson," Courtland said to his secretary, but she only nodded and continued typing.

It only took him a few minutes to walk over to the Capitol, and from all signs, he wasn't the only senator running late. He nodded at Senator Wagner from New York and Senator Barkley from Kentucky as they all entered the building together. Both men nodded at him as well, but neither slowed their steps.

So far, Courtland was not making very many friends among his colleagues, mainly because he was a junior senator, but also because he wasn't like so many of the other Southern Democrats. He still hadn't done anything majorly divisive in their eyes, but he clearly wasn't coming across as a rank-and-file Democrat either. Courtland thought back to his conversation with Eva the previous day, and his promise to risk it all to do what was right. Well, here he was in the place where that promise mattered the most. He prayed he would have the courage to stand by his convictions.

Once Courtland made his way to his seat, like most days, he looked around in awe, taking in the pageantry of being a member of Congress. The room was full of men. All white. Mostly older. Each of them full of piss and vinegar. Some of them career politicians but others, like him, junior senators trying to make a name for themselves and trying to literally change the world.

Senate Chaplain Reverend James D. Bryden offered the opening prayer: "Help now those who labor here for the good of our people . . . May they have not only strength for their congressional duties, but strength also for responsibility that lies far beyond all assigned duty."

Courtland's mind drifted back to Eva as he stood with his eyes closed, listening to the chaplain drone on and on. Courtland imagined Eva was both stressed and frightened from the bombing of her restaurant the previous day. The one thing he was grateful for was that the damage was minimal. He and Adam had walked to the back of the building after the fire chief deemed it safe to enter, and he saw that whoever planted the explosive device had not gone inside. The most damage was to her back entrance and a storage closet next to the door. Due to the investigation, she might have to close for a day or two, but other than that, no real damage was done to the building. But of course, it wasn't the building that suffered the most. It was Eva. He saw it all over her face yesterday.

All he wanted to do now was bolt out of the chamber and go find Eva and hold her in his arms until she felt safe again, but he didn't want to make things worse for her, so he forced himself to stay and do the job the voters of Georgia elected him to do. The senator who was sitting next to him tugged his jacket. The prayer had stopped, and Courtland was still standing. Courtland sheepishly looked around, but no one was paying him any attention. He was in the second row to the back, and the senators behind him were busy getting their notes together.

Courtland sat and thanked the senator from Connecticut. He nodded. It wasn't long before the proceedings got started with Senator Johnson introducing the bill that was up for discussion that day.

"Mr. President, on behalf of myself and the senator from Arizona, I ask unanimous consent to introduce for appropriate reference a bill providing for the payment of an allowance to the dependents of service-connected disabled veterans," he said.

Courtland took out his notes and began scribbling some thoughts he had concerning the things Senator Johnson was saying. From the first time he had laid eyes on the language of the bill, he knew there were some serious issues that needed to be worked out. He wanted to loosen the definition of dependents to include elderly parents and/ or siblings with disabilities whom the service-connected disabled veteran might be responsible for. He also wanted to make it clear to everyone that this bill included disabled Negro veterans too. As soon as he said that, the floor erupted into chaos.

"Until every white soldier gets his due, the last thing we need to be haggling about is what we can do for the Coloreds!" the other senator from Georgia exclaimed.

There was much back-and-forth, and before Courtland knew it, it was time for the lunch recess. He knew the battle would begin again after lunch.

Courtland hurried back to his office, flying past Mrs. Nelson as she asked him if he wanted her to go pick up his lunch. His mother's voice crept into his head, forcing him to go back to her desk.

"I'm fine, Mrs. Nelson. If you have a pastry from this morning, I will gladly take it and a cup of strong black coffee. If you would like to go take your lunch hour, I will be here and will answer the phone," he said.

"That will not be necessary," she said in a stiff voice. "I always take my lunch at my desk."

She seemed extremely perturbed that he didn't know that about her. Courtland made a mental note to bring Mrs. Nelson a bouquet of flowers the next day to thank her for all that she had done. She was grouchy and quick to pop off if she didn't like something Courtland was doing, but at the end of the day, she was one of the hardest-working secretaries on the Hill.

"Very well. I'll be in my office if you need me," he said, walking away briskly, closing the door firmly behind him.

Courtland sat at his desk and dialed Eva's office number. She picked up on the first ring.

"Hello?" she said, her voice sounding hesitant.

He could hear the tension flow across the telephone line. He wished he could reach through the phone and pull her into his arms. It was hard to believe that one kiss and a couple of conversations had him feeling this strongly for her.

"It's me," he said, his voice gruff with emotion. "Courtland. Are you okay?"

"Yes," she said, but he could hear the tears in her voice.

"I'll be there in ten minutes," he said, but she stopped him.

"Wait. Don't. There are so many people coming in and out," she said. "It wouldn't be wise for you to—"

"I don't care about what is wise," he said, and at that moment he didn't.

He didn't care about Congress, the state of Georgia, his family, or his own political aspirations. All he cared about at this moment was this woman who was now imprinted into his mind like no woman ever before. "I want to see you," he said, stopping short of saying, *I want to hold you and kiss you.*

"I want to see you too," she admitted, although he could hear the reluctance in her voice.

He was glad the anger she had expressed the previous day was not at the forefront of her mind now—or at least it didn't seem to be.

"Now is not a good time for you to come by, Courtland. I have people coming in to fix the damage that was done to my restaurant. I have staff members roaming around, unsure of what to do, and I have to deal with the police who have been coming in and out all day."

"Do they know who did this?" Courtland asked.

"No," she said. "Whoever it was, they were clearly just trying to scare me; otherwise, they wouldn't have called first, and they would have found a way to plant the bomb inside the restaurant rather than at the back door. Plus, I'm still battling with the police over whether or not this was even an attack. In their minds, this could just as easily have been my mistake."

"That's a bunch of bull and they know it," Courtland said. "I am happy to call the chief of police if you want me to."

"Courtland, I read the papers the same as you," she said. "That man is always embroiled in one scandal or another, and never, as far as I can see, has he ever had the best interests of Negroes at the forefront of his mind. He will not be on our side any more than that Lieutenant Stevens."

"There are other people I can involve," he insisted. "The FBI, the CIA, someone."

"Thank you," she said, "but for now I would rather handle things myself. I promise, if there's something I believe you can help me with, I won't hesitate to ask."

Courtland had never felt this helpless before in his life. What he felt right now was beyond just protectiveness. He wanted to erase her fear. He wanted to tell her that although they had only seen each other a few times, he couldn't imagine her not being in his life. He wanted to tell her so many things.

"Do you mind if I call you later? When we're both done with our day?" he asked.

"I don't know," she said so softly he almost didn't hear her. "Nothing has changed, Courtland."

"I just want to talk—make sure you are okay. That's all," Courtland said.

"I feel so stupid," Eva said in a hoarse voice. "Pearson and Freddie tried to tell me I was making a terrible mistake, but I wouldn't listen. People could have died yesterday because I was trying to pretend like I was infallible. I thought nothing or no one could touch me. I thought what was happening down South couldn't happen here. How could I have been so stupid?"

"There's no way you could have known this would happen. There was no reason for you to believe someone would do something so hateful here in D.C."

"I should have known. I should have known that my allowing whites and Negroes to eat together would become an issue. I should have known bringing together some of the most high-profile Negroes in broad daylight would gain attention, but I thought D.C. was different somehow," she said. "Mother used to tell me how Negroes and whites would all be at the Savoy in Harlem, dancing and eating together, and I wanted that same energy and vibe at my restaurant.

Mother used to have the Negro intelligentsia over to discuss race relations and politics, and I thought I could do the same. Freddie and Pearson warned me D.C. was not New York, but I wouldn't listen. I was so full of myself. So arrogant."

"So will you stop allowing mixed crowds at your restaurant like you did New Year's Eve?" he asked. "Will you stop allowing Adam and the others to meet at Chez Geneviève?"

"I don't know," she said, the weariness clear in her voice. "I don't know if I'm brave enough to fight this. Mother would have fought it, but I'm not her. I don't have her strength."

"You are brave. Braver than any woman I know," Courtland said. "Braver than any person I know. Eva Cardon, look at all you have accomplished in such a short period of time. I don't know many people who could do what you are doing. You have every right to feel scared and uncertain right now. Maybe give it a day or two before you make a final decision."

Before Eva could respond, Courtland heard voices on her end, and then Eva excused herself and began talking to someone in the background. The conversation was muffled, but when Eva came back to the phone, he could hear that the tone of her voice had shifted to businesswoman.

"I have to go," she said. "Thank you for calling."

"May I call later?" he asked again.

"Yes. Call me when you're done for the day," she said. "Undoubtedly, I'll still be here working."

Courtland leaned back against his chair, feeling something akin to relief that she had said yes to his request to call. "Take care, Eva. I'll talk to you soon."

Courtland gathered his things, preparing to go back to Congress so he could finish the debate from that morning and try not to think about Eva and how much he wanted to be where she was.

NINE

Eva

"I don't understand you, Eva. Not one little bit," Frédérique said.

Eva turned and saw her sister, who evidently had been standing behind her for some of her conversation with Courtland. The police had only allowed them in an hour or so ago, and everyone was busy cleaning and clearing out debris. Eva knew she should be angry with Frédérique for eavesdropping, but she was too exhausted. This entire twenty-four hours had her struggling to put one foot in front of the other. She was mentally and physically drained. The last thing she wanted to do was argue with Frédérique.

"What don't you understand?" Eva asked wearily.

The desk area she had gotten Pearson to set up for her near the bar was extremely uncomfortable. She missed the solitude of her office, but the work crew needed her out from the back. No damage had been done to her office, but the constant foot traffic and noise would have been too much. Plus, it was easier for the police and others to talk to her if she was in the front of the restaurant. She missed the sense of normalcy she had felt just a little under a day ago. She wanted to put her head on her sister's shoulder and cry, not get into a futile argument over something she didn't even understand yet.

"Chef du Passe said you were going to reopen the restaurant day after tomorrow," Frédérique said. "Why in the world would you do something so foolhardy?"

Eva breathed deeply. At least this conversation was not going to be about Courtland. She was not ready to discuss the growing feelings she was having for that man every time she saw his face or heard his voice. She knew that conversation was going to be long and involved, and today was just not the day to have it.

"Freddie, there is no reason for me to delay opening the restaurant. The front of the house was not even affected by the explosion, and the damage to the back door and the storage room can be repaired fairly easily. Plus, Pearson hired a couple of guards to be here throughout the day and evening, and the police assured me they were not going to stop until they found the people who did this—even if *those people* end up being me," she said wryly. "What more can I do?"

"You could wait a week or two and give the police time to find the people or person who did this," Frédérique said, tugging hard at the belt to her brown tweed dress. "You could not be so impulsive and defiant. That is what got you into this mess in the first place."

Eva looked up at her sister and sighed. She knew Frédérique was just worried about her, but she couldn't deal with her sister's fears and anxieties on top of her own.

"Frédérique, I don't want to argue with you," Eva said, trying to keep the frustration out of her voice. "I have employees whose bills are not going to stop for a couple of weeks. I have customers who can be finicky, and if I don't show them that Chez Geneviève is up and running and back to normal with a quickness, they will take their business elsewhere. I don't have the luxury to wait."

"I could have lost you and Pearson yesterday," Frédérique snapped. "Everybody I love on this planet could have been taken away from me, and instead of you recognizing that fact and practicing caution, you are being reckless—again."

Eva stood and put her hands on her sister's shoulders and said something their mother used to say to them when they would get frustrated as little girls.

"I hear you, Frédérique," Eva said, looking into her sister's eyes, which were full of unshed tears. "I hear every word that you are saying, and I validate your feelings. Right now. In this moment, you are validated and heard."

The tears rolled down Eva's face first. Frédérique took several deep breaths, and then she pulled her sister into an embrace. Eva felt the wetness of her sister's face against hers.

"I can't bear the thought of losing you. Ever," Frédérique said in a choked voice. "I couldn't bear it, Eva. I just couldn't."

"I know," Eva said. "I know yesterday scared you. It scared me, too, but I can't let them win. I just can't. I just realized that fact in this moment. If I stop what I have been doing, they win. They win and everything that we have done to fight against this awful system of oppression was for naught."

"Why do you have to be the one to fight?" Frédérique asked, the exasperation clear in her voice.

"*I heard the voice of the Lord, saying, 'Whom shall I send, and who will go for us?' Then said I, 'Here am I; send me.'* Isaiah 6:8," Eva said softly, brushing away a tear.

For a moment, Frédérique didn't make a sound. Frédérique would argue over a lot of things, but the Scriptures were not one of them.

"I promise you I will not be reckless, but this restaurant means too much to me to give up on it because of the hateful acts of a few. But more than this restaurant, I will not give up on the work I am just now getting started doing to try to make this world a better place for Negroes."

"What about that white politician from Georgia you were on the phone with a few minutes ago? What will you do about him?" Frédérique asked.

Eva felt a catch in her throat. Just as she didn't want to discuss with her sister her plans to reopen the restaurant and resume her activities with Adam and the others, she definitely didn't want to discuss Courtland. The feelings she was feeling for him right now were all too raw, too new. She didn't know what to do with those emotions yet, if ever. Courtland represented everything and everyone she had tried to avoid in her life. Courtland wasn't the first white man to flirt with her. She was used to dealing with the attention of white men as well as Negro men. Before now, she had no problems pushing away their advances. But for some reason, Courtland was different. There was an earnestness about him that attracted her. He wasn't perfect, but he was striving for something akin to perfection, and wasn't that true of all seekers of justice and fairness in the world?

"Frédérique, I don't want to talk about any of this now," Eva said again. "There are things I need to deal with before the restaurant reopens. Let's just call a truce. Okay?"

"You're just like Mother. Stubborn to the core," Frédérique said. "Never thinking about how your actions might affect other people."

"What are you trying to say, Frédérique?" Eva asked, seeing that her sister was spoiling for a fight even though Eva was doing her best not to engage.

Frédérique knew any negative mention of their mother amounted to fighting words to Eva, and Eva was doubly mad that Frédérique would choose this moment to bring her up.

"What I'm trying to say is you are doing whatever you want without thinking about anyone else's feelings. Mother insisted on being with a man who was not available to her, and she never once stopped to think about how her actions might affect you and me. Not once," Frédérique said heatedly.

"I'm not going to participate in this conversation, Freddie. I'm just not. I don't know what has you in this mood, but I'm too overwhelmed and too tired to deal with it," Eva said and walked to the other side of the room where Chef du Passe and Pearson were deep in conversation. This was not the first time Frédérique had dug up old issues and carried them into new ones, but this particular day, Eva was not trying to get into it with her sister.

"Eva!" Frédérique called out, but Eva didn't stop until she was standing next to the two men where it felt safer for her to be. She knew they would not ask the deep questions that her sister was asking. Pearson looked over at her and smiled.

"You okay?" he asked.

She nodded, pushing back her tears. "I'm fine. Thank you both for dealing with the repairmen. What are they saying now about reopening in two days? Are we still on track?"

"The staff is ready to go, Eva," Chef du Passe said with a gentle smile. "They are all here, cleaning up and organizing so we can set up and get everything ready to go. *Ils vous soutiennent.*" *They support you.*

Eva hugged Chef du Passe. *"Ils nous soutiennent."* *They support us.* "Thank you, Chef. I could not do this without you. I could not have done this without either one of you."

Pearson nodded. "You never have to worry about us supporting and loving you. Now, I would be remiss if I didn't ask: Are you sure you want to reopen so soon?"

Eva could feel the anger rise back up inside her chest.

"Don't you start that, too, Pearson," Eva snapped. "I said I was ready." Pearson reached out and placed his hand on her arm.

"I'm not judging you, little sister-daughter. I'm just asking," he said.

"Frédérique said—"

"Go easy on her, Eva," Pearson said in a low voice, looking across the restaurant where his wife stood looking at them. "These last few months have been difficult on Frédérique. Her words might come across harsh, but they are born out of love."

Eva nodded. She knew that Frédérique was still struggling over her recent miscarriage. Eva wanted to be supportive, but at the same time, she just couldn't deal with Frédérique when she became mean-spirited and spoke ill of their mother. Before Eva could say any more, Lieutenant Stevens entered the restaurant. Frédérique immediately walked over and took Eva's hand in hers. Eva looked up at her sister and smiled. One thing about the two of them, they could be fighting mad with each other one minute, and the next minute they'd be each other's fiercest ally. Eva held tight, afraid of what the lieutenant was going to say.

"Good afternoon, Miss Cardon. I have some information for you," Lieutenant Stevens said.

Eva tried not to allow the disdain she was feeling for the man to show on her face. As much as she didn't want to have to deal with him, the fact remained that he was all she had at this point to get to the bottom of what happened.

"What is it, Lieutenant?" Eva asked.

"Well, Miss Cardon, we made an arrest last night, and I wanted you to know about it. It was a young Negro boy from the neighborhood. He confessed to it all."

Eva started shaking her head before the words could completely come from his mouth. "I don't believe it. Like I said yesterday, I do not believe a person from my community would do this. There must be a mistake. And wait . . . Did you say a young Negro boy? How young?"

"Fifteen, ma'am. He—"

Pearson interrupted. "A fifteen-year-old? You are trying to tell us that a fifteen-year-old was able to mastermind a bombing and then have the wherewithal to contact Eva minutes before it exploded? Do you take us to be fools?"

"No, sir," Lieutenant Stevens said calmly but with an unwavering constitution. "The boy confessed. There is no reason to believe he lied."

"Then someone put him up to doing this!" Frédérique interjected, and Eva nodded in agreement. That was the only possible answer if this boy truly was involved.

"No, ma'am. He worked alone," the lieutenant said in a dismissive voice. "When questioned, he said he acted alone. Case closed. I thought you would be pleased."

"Where is he now?" Pearson demanded.

"He is locked up and will remain so until he sees the judge," Lieutenant Stevens said with a smile.

Eva couldn't stand the sight of him, and if she didn't want more information, she would have the security escort him out.

"I want to meet the young man," Eva said resolutely. "Talk to him. This just doesn't make sense to me."

Lieutenant Stevens continued to smile as if he had just delivered the best news ever. "I don't think that would be wise."

"Nonetheless, I would like to meet him," she said.

There was no way Eva was going to stand idly by and allow this young Negro boy to take the rap for something she did not believe he could have or would have done. This was a setup. She knew it with every fiber of her being.

"Miss Cardon, this will all go to trial eventually. There is really no need—"

"And you have him locked up?" Eva interrupted. "He's a child, for God's sake. No, I would like to see him. Right now."

"I will need to talk to my superior officer and make sure that it is acceptable to him," Lieutenant Stevens said.

"You do that," Eva said. "The phone is over there by the bar."

They all watched as he walked over to the other side of the restaurant.

"This is crazy," Eva said in a low voice. "There is no way some young boy from this community had the ability or desire to do such a heinous thing."

"Pearson, you go down there with Eva," Frédérique said, turning to her sister. "I'll stay here with Chef du Passe and make sure the work continues the way it should."

Lieutenant Stevens came back over, not looking pleasant at all. "The chief said you can come talk to him briefly, but I will need to be present."

Eva made long strides toward the door, barely looking at Lieutenant Stevens. "That's fine. As long as my brother-in-law and I get to talk to this young man for ourselves."

Eva and Pearson went out to his car and followed Lieutenant Stevens to the police precinct, which was just a few blocks from her restaurant. Just as they pulled into the parking lot, Pearson turned to Eva.

"Don't let your temper get the best of you. They will punish the boy if we don't keep our cool," Pearson said.

"I understand," Eva said, attempting to open the door, but Pearson restrained her with his hand.

She turned back toward him and waited.

"Eva, honey," he said in a soft voice, "you are not used to having to kowtow to anyone. It's not your fault because that's how your mother raised you, and how your sister and I completed the process, but know this: some of these white police officers are a different breed. They operate under a different code of ethics. There are good ones and bad ones, and until we know what we are dealing with, we must be calm, and we must assume they are not out for our best interest or the boy's. Do you understand, my dear?"

Eva pursed her lips, trying to contain her frustration. "Okay, Pearson. I will acquiesce to you, but if they try to railroad that young boy—"

"Sweetie, the railroading has already happened," he said. "We are just trying to stop any more damage."

Finally, Eva spoke. "I understand. I will be respectful, and I will let you do the talking."

Pearson patted her arm and then got out of the car and came around and opened the door for Eva. Lieutenant Stevens was waiting for them at the door. They went in silently behind him, following him to the interrogation room at the back of the precinct. As they walked through the building, all eyes were on them. There was a sea of white faces, and none of them appeared friendly or happy to see Pearson or Eva. Before they could exchange any conversation, another police officer walked a smallish Negro boy into the room and ordered him to sit. He did not look fifteen, and he did not look like someone who could have planned and executed a bombing. And once Eva got a good look at his face, she saw that it was bruised on the left side, to the point where his eye was nearly closed. Immediately, she knew she, Frédérique, and Pearson were right. There was more to the story than they had been told, and she was determined to get to the bottom of it.

Eva and Pearson went and sat at the table, both facing the boy while the police officers stood by the door, attempting to give the appearance that they were allowing them to have a private conversation.

"What's your name, son?" Pearson asked.

"Simon. Simon Edwards," he said in a soft voice. "You the lawyers?"

"No, we're not the lawyers. My name is Reverend Montgomery, and this is my sister-in-law, Miss Eva Cardon. She is the owner of the restaurant that was bombed," Pearson said in his quietest voice.

Eva could tell he was trying not to alarm the young man.

"I'm sorry," the boy said, looking down at the table.

"Exactly what are you sorry for?" Eva asked quietly. "Did you put the bomb at the back of my restaurant?"

Simon continued to look down at the table.

"Answer her, son," Pearson said softly. "We can't help you if you don't tell us the truth. Did you put a bomb near the back door of Eva's restaurant? A bomb that could have killed her, and me, and a whole host of other people?"

A tear began to roll down Simon's face, but he didn't say anything.

"Who put that bruise on your face?" Eva asked, thankful that her back was to the officers, because if they had seen her face, they would have seen storm clouds and hurricanes brewing. It was all she could do not to scream and yell at them for the lies they had told regarding this child.

"I fell," Simon answered.

"You mean you fell into someone's fist," she said in a steely voice, but then, seeing the crestfallen look on his face, she softened her voice. "You can tell us the truth, Simon. No matter what it is."

"Listen to me, Simon," Pearson said. "We know people—people who can help us fight this—but you have to be brave, and I know that is asking a lot, but I need you to do it anyway. Did you bomb my sister-in-law's restaurant?"

"No, sir," he whispered, "but you can't tell nobody that. Bad things will happen if you do."

"What kind of bad things?" Pearson asked quietly.

"Just bad things," Simon muttered.

"Who put you up to this?" Eva asked, leaning forward, making sure her voice didn't rise a single octave.

Simon looked up at her, tears streaming down his face. Then he spoke in a voice so low that she almost didn't hear him. "Miss Lady, he said he would hurt my little sister."

Eva looked at Lieutenant Stevens to try to determine if he'd heard the young man's words, but he was staring off into space, not looking at their table.

"Who said that to you, Simon?" Pearson whispered. "Was it that white officer across the room?"

"No, sir. It was another white man. I didn't know him. I was in the alley out back of Miss Lady's restaurant, looking for food in the garbage cans the night before the bomb went off, when he came up to me and said he had a job for me to do."

"You were looking for food?" Eva repeated, looking intently at the young boy's face, which was streaked with tears. "You were hungry?"

"Yes, ma'am," he said in a sad voice. "Daddy is out of work and . . . well . . . things have been hard since Mama died. My little sister . . . she's . . . well, she's not well. I was just trying to get us all something to eat for the night. Y'all have good trash."

"Don't ever do that again," Eva said gruffly, the tears threatening to fall down her face. "If you ever need food, you come to me. Do you understand?"

"Yes, ma'am," he said, lowering his head in shame.

It hurt Eva to think that this boy had been outside her restaurant foraging for food for himself and his family. She knew there were poor people in the community, but she didn't know anyone was rummaging around in her garbage cans looking for something to eat. Right then, she vowed she would do more in the community to help those in need. It wasn't enough to open a restaurant. A new restaurant didn't matter if people didn't have money. She would never allow anyone in her neighborhood to go hungry, no matter what it cost her.

"Tell me about this white man who said he had a job for you," Pearson finally said. "Did he give you the bomb to plant outside the back door?"

Simon shook his head profusely. "No, sir. He just said he wanted me to watch the place while he took care of some things. I didn't know he was planting no bomb, but when he got done, he told me if anything bad happened, I was to tell the police I did it or he would kill my sister. Then, not long after the bomb went off at your restaurant, the police picked me up down the road near the school. I was playing baseball with some other boys. They wouldn't even let me go by the house and tell Daddy what was happening."

"How many boys were on the playground with you?" Pearson asked.

"There was five or six of us," Simon said.

"And they knew to come to you out of everybody?" Pearson asked.

Simon nodded. "Yes, sir. They said somebody had seen me hanging around the restaurant. Please don't let them keep me here. I'll do anything you want—just don't let them keep me here," he said, his thin shoulders shaking with grief.

Eva stood. She had heard enough. She raised her voice, trying to keep the tremble out of it, because she was so angry she could hardly speak. "Lieutenant Stevens, I do not wish to press charges, and I would like for this boy to be released."

"I'm afraid that isn't possible," Lieutenant Stevens responded. "He confessed, and—"

"Actually, it is possible," Pearson said, standing up too. "We all know this child was not capable of constructing a bomb like what went off at the back of my sister-in-law's restaurant. This child is being held for something he did not do, and we all know it."

"I will need to go talk to the chief," Lieutenant Stevens stuttered. "The boy did confess and—"

"Was there a parent or someone present to tell him what his rights were?" Pearson asked.

"Everything was done aboveboard," Lieutenant Stevens snarled. "Like I said, I will go talk to the chief."

"You do that, Lieutenant Stevens," Eva said, the anger boiling over, causing her to grip the table. "Does this boy's father know he is here?" Eva turned toward Simon. "Have you talked to your father?"

Simon shook his head. "No, ma'am, I ain't talked to him. We ain't got a phone. We usually use Miss Cotton's phone if we need to call somebody. She lives in the apartment below us."

"Have you contacted this child's father?" Pearson repeated.

"Not to my knowledge," Lieutenant Stevens said. "We still need to—"

"Fix this now, Lieutenant Stevens," Eva ordered.

Pearson reached out and touched her arm to warn her to be calm, but Eva was beside herself with anger. Someone had set this boy up, and the police had not even bothered to make sure his father knew where he was. Once again, Eva wondered if the police themselves were behind this. It wouldn't be the first time the D.C. police had been involved in corrupt behavior toward Negroes in the community. The riot in 1919 had been allowed to go on for days due to police involvement and their very public denial that anything out of the ordinary was taking place. So she knew they had the propensity to stand by while Rome burned right before their eyes.

Eva sat back down beside the young boy and put her arm around his shoulders, pulling him close. "It's okay, Simon. We're going to get you out of here."

"I'm sorry, ma'am. I wouldn't have done nothing like that if'n he hadn't said that about hurting my little sister. She's three years old, and she's slow. Mama died having her," he said. "She can't talk and I . . ." The boy began crying in earnest now.

"It's okay," Eva said, rocking him gently. "I am not angry with you, Simon. You did what any big brother would have done. It's okay."

"I'm going to go talk to this chief and make sure this gets expedited. Don't worry, Simon. We won't leave you here. We promise," Pearson said, exiting the room.

Eva reached inside her purse and took out a handkerchief for Simon to wipe his face. By the time Pearson returned, Simon had composed himself, and he and Eva had worked out an agreement for Simon to come by the restaurant and help clean up. Eva had even promised to pay him a salary so he could help his family with some of their bills.

"The charges have been dropped," Pearson said, and immediately Simon ran to Pearson and hugged him tightly around the waist. Pearson patted Simon on his back. "I made mention that I knew the attorney general, Tom Clark, and I would have him on the phone in minutes if they didn't reopen this case and let this child go."

Eva smiled. Her brother-in-law was never one to call in favors, but she knew that this was one time he would have. She didn't even know he knew the attorney general, but she knew if Pearson said he did, then he did. As always, she was in awe of her brother-in-law and the way he was able to command a room. He wasn't boisterous like Adam Clayton Powell Jr., but he was not easily intimidated either, especially when it came to fighting for underdogs like Simon.

"Thank you. Thank you so much, Reverend," Simon said. "I am so sorry about what happened. I didn't know what to do other than what that white man said I should do."

"It's not over entirely, Simon, but you can go home until everything gets straightened out by the adults," Pearson said. "I will need to talk to your father."

"Yes, sir," Simon said, seeming a bit less excited. Clearly he didn't want to go have a conversation about this with his father.

Eva stood and walked over to her brother-in-law and the boy. "Let's get you home," she said. "Pearson, you can take me back by the restaurant while you talk to Simon's father. Simon, don't forget to tell your father about our deal."

Pearson looked at Eva quizzically. Eva smiled. "I'll let Simon explain it to you and his father."

Pearson escorted them out of the police station, not saying anything to anyone as they passed through the building. Eva looked but didn't see Lieutenant Stevens anywhere. She didn't care. She blamed him for arresting this young man when any fool should have known something wasn't right with his story. It was probably best she didn't see him. When they got outside, Pearson guided Simon to his car.

"Let's get out of here. I am ready to be done with the D.C. police for today," Pearson said as he opened the car door for Eva, who quickly climbed in. The day was getting colder, and she hadn't even worn her heavy coat.

"Thank you," Simon said, getting into the back seat.

"You are welcome, Simon," she said. Before they drove off, Eva happened to glance back at the door of the police station and saw Lieutenant Stevens standing outside, looking at them. Eva stared back at him until he broke the gaze first.

Eva didn't say anything about the staring lieutenant to Pearson, who was busy backing up and pulling the car into the street, but she was determined that, with or without the help of the police, she would find out why someone would try to scare her and would use a frightened child as their vehicle to do it.

"It is going to take more than this to scare me," Eva muttered underneath her breath.

"What did you say, sis?" Pearson asked, looking over at her.

"Nothing," Eva said, looking back as they drove off, Lieutenant Stevens still watching with an ominous expression on his face.

Eva shivered slightly, partly from the cold and partly from the white policeman whose eyes were once again cutting into them. The older man's behavior made Eva even more determined to get down to the bottom of what happened. One way or another.

TEN

Eva

By the time Eva returned to the restaurant, it was getting late in the afternoon. On a typical day, she and the staff would be getting ready for the dinner crowd; instead, she found a crew of cleaners hard at work, deep cleaning the dining area. She could also hear the sounds of saws and drills in the back where her office was located. It was good to see and hear that even though she had been gone, Frédérique and Chef du Passe had made sure the progress did not stop. As soon as she stepped into the main dining area, Frédérique walked over to her.

"Is everything okay?" she asked. "Were you able to get that poor boy released from jail?"

Eva explained all that had happened, only stopping when Frédérique had questions or exclamations over what she was hearing. When Eva got to the end of the story, Frédérique shook her head in disgust.

"Who could be so evil as to try to pin this terrible act of violence on a poor, defenseless child?" Frédérique asked with a look of consternation.

Frédérique was far from naïve, but she often seemed the most wounded by actions such as these. She would read the newspaper and well up with tears, asking the same question over and over: *Who could be so evil?*

If the truth be known, she and Eva both had lived sheltered lives—far removed from the harshness of segregation and racism, partly because of their mother and partly because of Pearson. Eva was only just becoming aware of how awful the world could be.

"Do you think they will let this boy and his family live in peace after all of this?" Frédérique asked.

"I don't know," Eva said, wondering the same thing. In fact, from the moment Pearson, Simon, and she had made it to the car, and she had looked back and seen Lieutenant Stevens staring at them in such a threatening way, she, too, had wondered if Simon and his family would be safe now that he was no longer the prime suspect for the bombing. She wondered if the people who really were responsible for the act would go after him again—would go after all of them again. The idea of Simon or his family being in harm's way was overwhelming. She knew there was one person who might know how to fight back against whomever was responsible for the bombing and the blackmailing.

"I'm going to go and call Adam. No matter what, Simon needs a lawyer, just in case, and I know, based on what he said, his father can't afford one. We might not be able to figure out who did this, but we can put a safeguard in place to keep them from trying to frame Simon again."

"Do you think Simon's father will be open to you providing a lawyer for Simon?" Frédérique asked. "You know how proud men can be."

"We shall see," Eva said and went over to her makeshift office by the bar. She dialed Adam's office phone, and his secretary picked up. Once Eva told her who she was, his secretary sent the call immediately to Adam.

"A fifteen-year-old Negro boy," Adam said in disbelief after Eva told him the whole story. "The convoluted measures these white folks will take to try to slow down our pathway to progress never cease to amaze me."

"So do you agree that Simon needs a lawyer?" Eva asked.

"Oh, most decidedly so," Adam said. "Do you remember the rather cheeky fellow who was at the restaurant yesterday?"

"Yes," Eva said dryly. "Who could forget Wendell Moss Harrington III? You think he would be a good choice to help Simon and his family?"

"Absolutely," Adam said. "Don't let his arrogance throw you. Wendell is a good young man with a lot of aspirations. He has been laboring hard on voter registration and has taken on a generous number of cases pro bono. He blusters and brags, but at the core of him is a deeply caring young man who is going to make a difference in this world."

"Then please, ask him to call me as soon as he can. If Wendell is up for it, I will see if Mr. Edwards can come over to the restaurant and talk with him about Simon's situation. I don't want us to wait around for the other shoe to drop. I don't trust those policemen. At all."

"There are some good ones, but they tend to stay quiet with their heads down," Adam said, "which, of course, does us no good. How good is one really if they won't speak out for justice? I'll give him your number. Knowing Wendell, he'll call you immediately."

"Thank you, Adam," Eva said. "I appreciate everything you have done and are doing. I'm sorry that you all got mixed up in this drama."

"Miss Eva," Adam said, "this incident is bigger than you and me. Don't internalize any of this. We are all fighting the same enemy, and the enemy knows we have him against the ropes. They only come for you when they are scared of what you represent."

Eva thanked Adam and then hung up, but before she could get up and go tell Frédérique what Adam said, the phone rang again.

She picked it up on the second ring. She noticed that Frédérique was looking at her intently.

"Hello," she said.

"Hi," the voice on the other end of the phone said.

It was Courtland. She had forgotten that he had said he would call her back. It seemed like she had lived a lifetime since talking to him last.

"Hi," she said. She looked at Frédérique and smiled, trying to look normal.

"How have things been for you today?" Courtland asked. "Did the police find out anything more concerning the bombing of your property?"

"Actually, yes," Eva said, and she began to tell him about the situation involving the young boy Simon. When she was done talking, there was complete silence. For a moment, Eva wondered if they had lost their connection.

"Are you still there?" she finally asked.

"Yes, I'm still here," he said in what sounded like a careful voice. "I was just mulling over what you said about the boy. This is getting uglier and uglier by the moment. Are you sure you don't want me to get involved? I could call . . ."

"Of course I'm sure," Eva snapped. "You act as if I am incapable of handling my business."

"Eva, I'm sorry," Courtland said before Eva could hang up the phone. "I didn't mean to make you angry, and I definitely wasn't trying to imply that you can't handle your business. Clearly you can. I was just offering to help. That's all."

Eva took a deep breath. She wasn't angry with Courtland, but at this moment, he was the easiest person to take her frustrations out on. "I'm sorry. I'm just on edge right now. I didn't mean to snap at you that way. I do understand you are only trying to be helpful. Listen, I need to go. I have a million and one things to do before I reopen. Thank you for offering to help. In spite of how I sounded, I do appreciate your kindness," she said.

"I understand," he said. "I'll talk to you later."

Eva gently hung up the phone once she heard the *click* on the other end. She was about to get up when the phone rang again. She quickly picked up the receiver, wondering if maybe Courtland was calling her back. "Hello?"

"Hello, Eva. This is Wendell," the deep voice on the other end of the phone said.

"Wendell," Eva said. "Thank you for calling. I wasn't expecting to hear from you so soon."

"Adam called and said you needed me," he said. "That's all I needed to hear."

"Well, it's not really me," she said, ignoring the flirtatiousness in Wendell's voice. Making the transition from talking to Courtland to now talking to Wendell was dizzying, to put it mildly. Both men were formidable in their own way, and both men were extremely attractive. It was all so confusing. She had gone from barely noticing men at all to now having two on her radar. *Stay focused*, she thought. "Did Adam tell you about Simon?"

"He did," Wendell said, the playfulness gone. "Do you think you can arrange for me to meet the young man and his father?"

"I can try to—" Eva stopped and looked across the room where she heard voices.

Coming through the door were Pearson, Simon, and a thin-looking man holding a little girl of about two or three. "Well, it looks like Simon and his family are here. I will talk to them and get back in touch with you."

"I can come over there now, if you like," he said.

Eva did not miss the suggestiveness in his voice. It was clear to her that his desire to come over had as much to do with her as it did with helping Simon and his family.

"No," she said quickly. "Let me talk to them first. I don't know how the father will take any of this. Leave me your number, and I will call you back."

"Gladly," Wendell said, causing Eva to groan and Wendell to laugh. "I'm teasing you, Eva Cardon. I understand this is business, but I would be remiss if I didn't flirt with you just a little. You talk to the father and let me know what you find out," he said, then gave her his home and office number. "You can call me anytime you like. For any reason."

"Goodbye, Wendell Moss Harrington III," Eva said with a laugh and gently hung up the phone. She stood as everyone came over to where she was.

"Eva," Pearson said, "this is Mr. Edwards, Simon's father, and Simon's little sister, Daisy. Mr. Edwards wanted to come and thank you personally for helping to deal with the situation with the police."

"Hello, Mr. Edwards," Eva said, extending her hand, which he took and gently shook. He was a tall man whose frailty was almost too painful to look at because Eva could immediately tell he was not naturally so. She wondered just how many meals he and the children had missed. Glancing from him, to Simon, to Daisy, she saw they all looked beaten down by life. Mr. Edwards had a cut underneath his right eye, and when he took off his hat, his hair was a wooly mess. Both of the children looked a bit unkempt as well. The little girl's hair didn't look like it had been combed in a month of Sundays, and Simon's hair was just as messy as his father's. Instantly, Eva felt sympathy for all of them.

"Hello, Miss Cardon. I'm so sorry to bother you this fine afternoon, but I wanted to come by and tell you thank you, face-to-face," he said, squeezing his hat tightly, almost like someone would if they were wringing out the wash. "You don't have to call me no Mr. Edwards. Everybody calls me Johnny Mac."

"Very well, Johnny Mac, and you must call me Eva," she said, then turned her attention to Simon, who was looking down at the floor. "Are you feeling better now, Simon, now that you are back with your father and sister?"

He grunted something nondescript, and his father popped him on his butt. Hard. Eva tried not to grimace, but she felt the sting—almost as if she had been the one to receive the blow.

"You answer this kind lady like you got some sense," his father ordered.

"Yes, sir," Simon said in a low voice. "Yes, ma'am, Miss Lady. I'm very happy to be back home."

"That's good," Eva said. She wanted to reach over and pull him into an embrace, but she knew that would probably embarrass him. So instead, she decided to address what she felt was a need for everyone. "Have you all eaten?" she asked.

"No, ma'am," Simon quickly said, but his father cuffed him.

Eva winced. She hated seeing him hit Simon over something as simple as the boy being hungry. She tried not to judge Johnny Mac, but she could not see a single reason for him to hit the boy like that. Eva's mother had never believed in spanking, so she and Frédérique had never gotten a lick from a switch or a swat of the hand, even when Eva would be a bit cheeky. Her mother would always patiently explain how she had erred, and before long, Eva would be crying like a repentant sinner at church. Eva never thought too much about having children, but she knew if she did, she would never lay a finger on them.

"Johnny Mac, why don't you all go sit at the table by the window, and I will go to the back and see if my chef has something he can put together for us all. If the truth be known, I am a bit hungry myself, and I would hate to have to eat alone," she said, choosing her words carefully.

"I believe I could eat something too," Frédérique said quickly, giving Eva a look that let her know they were thinking along the same lines. "Let's go have a seat while Eva gets everything taken care of with Chef du Passe."

"We're not dressed to eat at a fancy place like this, Miss Eva," Johnny Mac said, but she could hear him wavering. "We just wanted to come by and tell you thank you. We can leave you and your family to your meal."

"Nonsense. There is no one here but us," she said. "And we would be honored to have you and the children eat supper with us."

"My sister-in-law is telling you the truth. We would be honored to break bread with you," Pearson said. "Let's go over to her table and await what I can promise you will be a scrumptious meal. Chef du Passe is a master in the kitchen."

"Very well," Johnny Mac said. "Thank you for your hospitality."

Eva walked past the bar to the door of the kitchen where Chef du Passe was getting ready for the reopening in a couple of days.

"Do you suppose you could pull something together for us to eat?" she asked. "There's Pearson, Frédérique, Johnny Mac, Simon, the little girl Daisy, and me."

"Of course, *ma chérie*. I will make you *croûte savoyarde* and a bowl of tomato bisque," he said. "It will only take me a few minutes."

Eva stood on her tiptoes and kissed the chef on the cheek. "*Merci, mon ami.* And only you could turn a grilled cheese sandwich with tomato soup into something elevated. You might want to just do a simple version of it for the children. I don't know if they will like the added French flourishes."

"Very well," Chef du Passe said with a smile. "Although when you girls were young, you had quite elevated palates. You loved it when I made your food with . . . *s'épanouit.*" *Flourishes.*

"Frédérique and I were ahead of our time when it came to our palates," she said with a huge grin. "You'll bring it out?"

"*Tout à fait,*" he said. *Absolutely.*

"*Merci,*" she said and went back out to where everyone was sitting. Pearson, Johnny Mac, and Simon rose when she entered the room.

"Everything is set. The chef will have our food in just a

moment," she said. "Is there something specific that you think the baby might like?"

Johnny Mac looked down at his daughter, who had her head pressed against his chest, drool rolling down her chin.

He shook his head sadly. "No, ma'am. She'll be fine. She's not much of an eater."

"She likes crackers," Simon chimed in.

His father gave him a glare but did not cuff him this time. Eva was grateful for that. She didn't think she could stay silent again if Johnny Mac struck Simon.

Eva stood and went to the bar where she knew there was a stash of crackers. She opened a package of Lance saltines, and brought them back to the table, giving one to Daisy, whose hands were already outstretched. She began drooling on the cracker, sucking it loudly.

Eva turned back to Johnny Mac and Simon. "I'm happy you all came by today, and Simon, I am especially happy to see you again. Did you tell your father about our agreement?"

Johnny Mac nodded. "Yes, ma'am, he did, and I wanted to thank you myself. You didn't have to do what you did to get this boy out of jail. I just wanted you to know that his mo—his mother and I didn't raise him this way. She and I didn't have any family to raise us the right way, but we did our best to make sure Simon was a good boy. We were going to do the same with . . . We were going to do the same with the baby girl, too, but, well . . ." His voice trailed off.

Frédérique reached over and patted Johnny Mac on his arm. "We understand, Johnny Mac. But please, don't be angry with Simon. From what we gather, he was just trying to protect his little sister. That is honorable."

Johnny Mac scowled at his son. "That's no excuse, ma'am. We don't hurt somebody else in order to save ourselves. Isn't that right, Simon?"

Simon nodded. "Yes, sir."

"I'm so sorry my boy had any part in this awful thing," Johnny Mac said, looking pained. Then he turned toward Eva. "I just wanted to check with you and see when you wanted him to start working, and ma'am, you don't owe him a single penny. He told me you said something about him making a bit of money. He don't deserve that kind of favor from you."

Before Eva could reply, Chef du Passe brought them their food. He had also included a cheesecake from the freezer.

As soon as the food was on the table, Simon began reaching, but his father slapped his hand. "Say grace, boy. Show these good people you have some kind of home training."

"Thank you, Lord, for this food and the hands that prepared it. And please bless my daddy, my sister, Miss Lady, and her kinfolk. Amen."

They all looked up at the same time, and Eva noticed a tear slide down Johnny Mac's face. Eva decided not to embarrass the man by acknowledging the emotion. She was realizing more and more that all of Johnny Mac's gruffness and abrasiveness stemmed from fear and anxiety about his condition and that of his children. She couldn't imagine a life like Johnny Mac's. Even with all of the loss she and Frédérique had experienced, they had never been without a roof over their heads or warm food in their bellies. The very fact that she, a Negro woman, was able to open up a restaurant like Chez Geneviève was proof that even though she was Negro like Johnny Mac, the two of them were like night and day.

Eva glanced over at her sister, but Frédérique's eyes were fixed on Daisy. Eva watched as Frédérique reached over and patted Daisy on the side of her thin little face. Finally, Frédérique spoke.

"Mr. Edwards, I'm not very hungry. I would love to hold Daisy while you eat," she said in a hesitant voice, almost as if she feared being rebuked.

Eva noticed Pearson was looking at his wife with the most

tender expression she had ever seen. It was so full of love. Eva was grateful that her sister had a love like Pearson's.

"Oh, ma'am, she might dirty up your fine clothes," Johnny Mac said, "and she's a little skittish with other people."

Frédérique reached toward Daisy and cooed softly. "Sweet girl, will you come to me?"

The little girl looked at her for a moment, but then, to the obvious surprise of her father and brother, she reached out to be picked up. Frédérique took Daisy from her father and pulled her close.

"Miss Frédérique, I've never seen her take to someone this quick," Johnny Mac said. "When she first started staying with her babysitter, Miss Haynes, a lady who lives in the building we do, she cried for days on end. She just started warming up to Miss Haynes, but now I've got to be looking for someone else to keep her. Miss Haynes is getting feeble . . . She can't handle a child like Daisy no more."

Eva caught her sister's eye. She knew that an idea was forming; she could see it all over her sister's face. It was almost as if she could hear the words inside Frédérique's mind. She was going to offer to help with Daisy. And as Eva glanced over at her brother-in-law, she knew he would say yes.

Eva watched her sister glance at the little girl with all of the love she had been holding in her heart for all of the babies she had lost. In that moment, everything that had happened that week that was bad was all worth it to see her sister's joy. She prayed that when the conversation about keeping Daisy did come up, Johnny Mac would be receptive to her sister's kindness. Eva felt herself smile for the first time since before the bombing occurred. Their grandmother always used to say, when something bad would happen, *"Des cendres, quelque chose de bien peut sortir." Out of the ashes, something good can come.* This was definitely one of those "out of the ashes" moments.

ELEVEN

Courtland

After Courtland got through talking with Eva, he had to run to a committee meeting in the Capitol. The discussion had been about an infrastructure bill, and even though there was partisan support among Courtland and the senators from Maine, Colorado, Alabama, and Indiana, the discussion became heated at times. Each senator was jockeying for position for their home state, trying to make sure that they walked off with either the lion's share of the funding or, at the very least, not a smaller piece of the pie than any of the others. It took a while for them to come to an agreement, but at about four in the evening, resolution was made. Before anyone could start arguing again, Courtland dismissed himself and went back to his office. He had an event to go to that night, and he just wanted to go home and rest first. But before he could even sit down, Mrs. Nelson knocked on his door.

"Come in," he said.

She stepped into the room. "Sir, it's your friend Mr. Ketchums. Sir, I'm sorry, but—"

Courtland snatched up the phone and barked, "Jimmy Earl,

what's wrong?" He was terrified that something had happened to the twins or Lori Beth.

"It's your daddy," Jimmy Earl said, not mincing any words. "He had a stroke while out riding with Violet. Some of the hands got him back to the house, and Doc Henry was able to stabilize him."

"Why am I just now getting called?" Courtland snapped. "How long ago was this?"

"Not long, Courtland," Jimmy Earl said. "Your daddy himself insisted no one call you. He started feeling better, and we all thought he was going to be okay, but then he started jumbling up his words. We brought him to Emory University Hospital here in Atlanta. Go to the airport, Courtland. Buddy Candler has a private plane waiting to fly you to Atlanta. I'll meet you at the airport."

Buddy and his family were longtime family friends. They once owned the Coca-Cola Company until they sold it in 1919 for a reported twenty-five million. They had hosted three or four events in Courtland's honor when he ran for office. Buddy was quite eccentric and suffered from bouts of depression, but there was nothing he wouldn't do for his friend Nap.

"What are the doctors saying?" Courtland asked.

"Doc Henry said he felt good about Mr. Kingsley's chances, but he also said you needed to get here quickly. So head to the airport, and I'll see you when you arrive. Don't worry about your mother or your sisters. I will personally take care of them until you can get here," Jimmy Earl said.

Courtland nodded, trying not to allow his mind to go to a dark place. "I'll be there as quickly as I can. Tell Mother and the girls I said not to worry."

Courtland gathered up a few files and threw them into his briefcase. He looked up and saw Mrs. Nelson was still standing there, waiting for his orders.

"I have meetings that need to be postponed. You have them all in my appointment book."

"Don't worry about anything, Senator Kingsley," she said calmly. "I will let the appropriate people know that you had a family emergency."

"Thank you, Mrs. Nelson. Would you mind calling Representative Powell and telling him what's going on? I was supposed to have a meeting with him later this week, and I don't think it's in the appointment book. I doubt I'll be back in time."

Mrs. Nelson screwed up her face but then nodded. "Yes, sir. Anyone else?"

Courtland thought for a minute about having Mrs. Nelson call Eva, but he really didn't want her that deep into his business. The phone rang, and Mrs. Nelson quickly picked it up, said a few words, and then hung up almost as quickly.

"Your car is downstairs, Senator. I will be praying for you and your family," Mrs. Nelson said in a quiet voice.

"Thank you," he said and gripped her hand, squeezing it slightly. He exited the office right after giving her a few more instructions for taking care of things while he was gone. His main concern was for her to notify Senator Gurney, who was the chair of the Senate Armed Services Committee, of what was going on. The two of them were supposed to meet this week to discuss him possibly becoming a member of that committee.

When Courtland got downstairs, his driver, Harold, was already standing by the passenger side with the door open.

"So sorry to hear about Mr. Kingsley, sir," he said. "Would you like to go by your house and pick up some things for the trip?"

"No, thank you," Courtland said, climbing into the back seat. "Anything I need I either have at my parents' home or can buy when I get to Atlanta. I just want to get to the airport."

"Yes, sir," Harold said and quickly got back into the car and carefully took off toward Washington National Airport. The drive was only about ten or fifteen minutes, depending on the traffic, and right then, traffic was light, so before Courtland could overthink things too much, Harold was pulling up to the airport.

"Thank you, Harold," Courtland said. "I'll let you know when I will be returning so you can pick me up."

"Yes, sir. You fly safe," Harold said.

Courtland exited the car and walked as briskly as he could into the airport where he was met by a security agent.

"Good afternoon, Senator Kingsley," he said. "My name is Steve, and I will be taking you to your awaiting plane. The pilot is ready for takeoff. He is just waiting for you, sir."

"Thank you," Courtland said and followed Steve to the plane. When they got there, the pilot came out and introduced himself.

"Good afternoon, sir. My name is Lonnie, and I will be your pilot. If you are ready, we will take off soon," Lonnie said. They were flying in a nicely decorated Lockheed L-12. Even as tall as Courtland was, he didn't feel cramped or stuffed in like he had in other small planes. Courtland wasn't fond of flying, but he felt like if he focused on work, he could make it through the flight okay. He also had to remind himself that this wasn't like when he had to fly in planes when he was in the military.

Different time, different planes, he thought over and over.

"Thank you, Lonnie. Whenever you are ready," Courtland said, settling himself into one of the comfortable leather seats in the eight-passenger plane. Beside the seat was a bar, and Courtland poured himself a glass of scotch. He needed it. He couldn't relax knowing that his father was not in good health and his mother and sisters were having to deal with things on their own. Yes, he knew Jimmy Earl was there with them, but it wasn't the same thing.

Within a few minutes, Lonnie had them in the air. Courtland

tried to keep his mind occupied during the flight by reading over some of his notes from the day's congressional activities. He didn't want to think about Nap not making it. He and the old man were at odds over a lot of things, but the idea of losing his father was something he couldn't fathom.

"You better hang on, old man," he muttered.

Although the flight seemed to go on forever, about two and a half hours later, Lonnie made the announcement over the loudspeaker that he was getting ready to land. Courtland clicked on his seatbelt and sat back as the plane banked and then made its descent. Once the plane was safely on the ground, Courtland thanked Lonnie for a smooth ride, slipped the man a nice-size tip, and then exited with his briefcase, making his way into the airport terminal. It was already dark outside, and although it wasn't as cold in Georgia as it was in D.C., it was still a brisk evening. Standing at the end of the walkway was Jimmy Earl.

Jimmy Earl walked over to Courtland and gave him a huge hug.

"How's Pops?" Courtland asked, pulling out of the hug so he could see his best friend's face. One thing he and Jimmy Earl had always promised was not to lie to each other.

"Mr. Nap is holding his own," Jimmy Earl said, taking Courtland's briefcase as they both began walking through the airport to the parking lot outside.

Neither one of them paid attention to the onlookers, mainly women, admiring the tall, thin redhead and the dashingly handsome senator.

"Your daddy is weak, and his words are a bit garbled, but he's still spewing the same old piss and vinegar. The doctor is just trying to keep him quiet, which is no easy feat with your daddy, but Dr. Mason thinks with some rest, Mr. Kingsley should be okay."

Courtland smiled, relieved by the promising words. "That's Nap Kingsley for you, king of the bounce-back. How are Mother and the girls?"

"Scared. But happy that you're coming home to take charge of them and your daddy," Jimmy Earl said as he led Courtland toward his car, a 1946 Packard Clipper that Jimmy Earl babied nearly as much as Courtland did his cars. Both men never found a car they didn't like, one of the many things they had in common.

"Not so sure about me taking charge of Pops, but I'll be happy to get those three womenfolk in my arms. This is a lot for them to have to deal with," Courtland said as they climbed inside Jimmy Earl's car.

Since it was late in the day, the crowds were at a minimum. Most of the flights at the airport were early flights. It didn't take long for them to get on the road. It was about a forty-five- to fifty-minute drive from the airport to the hospital, so Courtland decided to tell Jimmy Earl about Eva. Courtland had kept the details about his feelings for Eva to himself, and he needed someone to talk to about them. But as soon as the words came out of his mouth, he regretted speaking.

"She's Negro?" Jimmy Earl repeated, almost swerving the car.

"Yes, she's Negro. And yes, I do understand the complexities of the situation," Courtland said.

Of course Jimmy Earl wouldn't understand, and he could kick himself for thinking otherwise.

"Well, if you understand the complexities of the situation, Courtland, why are you seeing her?" Jimmy Earl asked gruffly.

Courtland knew that common sense would dictate that he leave Eva alone, but he couldn't. He just couldn't, and he didn't have any better response than that. She mentally stimulated him in ways he did not quite understand himself. And he couldn't just walk away. Not now.

"We've only kissed once, and I've only talked to her a few times," Courtland said. "Look, I understand this is complicated, but I can't just walk away from her. Not yet. Not until—"

"Not until you screw up her mind and yours completely?" Jimmy Earl said in a heated voice. "You're being foolish, Courtland. You remember the feelings I thought I had for . . . well . . . Opal, back in the day?" Jimmy Earl said, and as Courtland looked over at his friend, he saw the pained expression on Jimmy Earl's face.

That was a topic the two of them had not discussed in years. It was just too painful for Jimmy Earl. His feelings for Opal had started the summer of the worst racial incident ever to happen in Parsons, Georgia, to Courtland's knowledge. It was the summer of 1936. The year of the worst drought to hit the country and the last year of the annual Founders' Day celebration. Racial tension had been high all summer, and on top of that, Jimmy Earl had told him several times that he had feelings—strong feelings—for Opal, his family's seventeen-year-old housekeeper. Unfortunately, violence broke out at the Founders' Day picnic, and Jimmy Earl's father, Earl Ketchums, shot and killed Opal's grandmother, Birdie Pruitt, who was also a housekeeper for Jimmy Earl's family. Nothing was able to heal the rift that grew between Opal and Jimmy Earl. Jimmy Earl said Opal would see him coming in one direction, and she would turn around and go in the other. Jimmy Earl had tried everything to make up for what his daddy did, including testify against his own daddy in court, but his and Opal's friendship, if you wanted to call it that, was never the same again, and Jimmy Earl was never the same. Courtland knew Jimmy Earl loved Lori Beth with all of his heart, but there was always a sadness about his eyes that Courtland knew had something to do with loss of innocence and love unrequited.

"Look, man. My situation is different," Courtland said in a quiet voice. "Y'all were kids, and the circumstances were . . . awful. Back then, our hormones were raging, and we didn't know left, right, up, or down. This is different."

"Not that different, Courtland," Jimmy Earl said. "There might be a day someday when a relationship between the two races can be possible. This ain't that day. If you care about this woman, don't put her through the heartbreak. My heart never healed from the pain my family put Opal and her family through, and I know for certain her heart never healed either. And when it comes to me fancying myself in love with her . . . well, I was wrong. I had no right to feel that way about her or to ever come close to kissing her like I did."

"Why, because society says so?" Courtland asked bitterly. "Because the Jim Crow South dictates it?"

"Yes, Courtland. Because society says so," Jimmy Earl said. "We didn't make these rules, but we sure better follow them. Find you a good white woman who can help you become the leader you want to become. Find a woman who is good and kind like your mama and your sisters and my sweet Lori Beth. Forget about this Negro woman . . . for both of your sakes."

Courtland didn't reply at first. He knew Jimmy Earl was making sense, but he wasn't ready to listen to his own inner voice or the well-intended words of his best friend.

Jimmy Earl must have picked up on his friend's mood because he didn't say anything else to him about Eva for the remainder of their drive to Emory. They made small talk about his and Lori Beth's twins who were growing like weeds, and anything else that wasn't too heavy to chat over.

Once they made it to the hospital, Courtland's attention turned to his mother, sisters, and Nap. When Courtland entered his father's luxury hospital suite, both of his sisters ran to him, and he gathered both crying girls into his arms. His mother remained seated by a sleeping Nap, her hand gripping his tightly, but her eyes met Courtland's and he could see the relief shining from them.

"I'm here now," Courtland said, kissing both girls on the forehead and then hugging them tighter. "Don't you worry none about your daddy. He's a tough one. He'll pull through this. You girls just watch."

Courtland led the girls back to their seats by their mother, then knelt in front of her, kissing her free hand. "How are you holding up, Mother?"

She nodded with a smile, but tears streamed down her face. Normally, Millicent Parsons Kingsley was the most put-together woman ever. She never left her bedroom without being perfectly coiffed, dressed, and made up, but this afternoon, she looked unlike Courtland had ever witnessed before, including when her daddy, Little Jack Parsons, passed away. His mother's bun was slightly unraveled, and her face looked splotched with tears. She was dressed in some nice-looking frock, but it was terribly wrinkled. The only one in the room who looked at peace was Nap, who was sleeping soundly, a light snore escaping from his parted lips. Courtland got up and bent and kissed his father's forehead. He noticed that Nap's mouth was slightly twisted.

"I would like to speak to his doctor," Courtland said, looking at his father's left hand, which was curled under on top of the covers. Courtland touched his father's hand, and it moved slightly, but Nap continued to sleep.

"Dr. Mason said he would be back to check on Nap in about an hour," she said. "Are you hungry, son? I can get them to bring you something to eat."

"I'm good, Mother," Courtland said, looking back at the door where Jimmy Earl stood giving them privacy but still being ever watchful. Ever kind. His best friend since first grade. "Mother, I need to go make a phone call. I won't be gone long. Jimmy Earl will stay with you."

His mother nodded and smiled. "I know you are busy with things that are important. Don't worry. Everything is fine here."

"Hurry back, brother," his sister Violet said, sounding much younger than sixteen.

"I'll be right back," he promised. "I just need to make a quick call, and then I'll be all yours."

She jumped up and ran into her brother's arms again. "It's just," she whispered, "as long as you're here, he won't . . ."

She couldn't finish her words, but he knew what she meant. Violet had always thought Courtland could move heaven and earth, and now she thought his mere presence would be all that was needed to keep their father from taking a turn for the worse.

"Oh, Vi," he said, hugging her tightly. "I will be just down the hallway using the phone. I won't be gone long. I promise. You can come stand by the door and watch me if you'd like."

"She will do no such thing," his mother said, motioning for Violet to come sit beside her. "Let your brother conduct his business. We will be fine. Go make your phone call, sweetheart."

Courtland nodded, feeling guilty that his phone call had nothing to do with business and everything to do with Eva. He had to hear her voice. He needed to hear her almost as much as his mother and sisters needed him to be with them in Atlanta. Courtland made sure not to meet Jimmy Earl's eyes as he made his way toward the door, but he could feel his friend staring as he exited the room. Courtland hurried down the hallway to the nurses' station and asked if there was a room where he could make a private phone call.

"Yes, sir. Right this way," the nurse said, escorting him to an office just behind the nurses' station. Courtland closed the door, went to the desk, and began dialing the phone number to Eva's office. She picked up on one ring. It was after 8:30 p.m. He was surprised she was still there.

"Hello?" she said quickly.

"It's me," he replied. "Courtland. I didn't want to leave you wondering where I was or why I wasn't coming by. I'm back home. My father had a stroke, and I wasn't sure when I would be able to see you again face-to-face."

"Oh, Courtland," she said. "I'm so sorry. How is he doing now?"

"He's resting," Courtland answered. "The doctor thinks he will pull through—or at least that's what I've been told so far."

"I will pray the rosary for you and your family every day," she said. "I know how close you said you all were."

"That we are. And thank you for your prayers. They are much appreciated," Courtland said, thinking about how his little sister clung to him, terrified at the idea of him even leaving the room. He knew he needed to cut this conversation short, but he wanted to talk to Eva as long as he could. "I wasn't sure if you would still be at work. How are things there now? I hope you aren't there alone."

"Things have quieted down here considerably," she said in a soft voice. "And no, I am definitely not alone. There is a guard my brother-in-law hired standing just a few feet away, and he is menacing—like a one-man army. I think he is a former soldier. The cleaning crew just finished straightening up in the back, so I should be able to reopen the day after tomorrow."

"Do you think that's wise?" he asked hesitantly. He didn't want to aggravate her again now that they were talking civilly to each other once more.

"I can't shut down forever. This restaurant is my heart. I won't allow someone to scare me away from it. I'll just be smarter next time," she said, the defiance clear in her voice. He imagined that she had been arguing this point most of the day.

"I understand," he said, determined not to add himself to the list of people questioning her choice to reopen so soon. "So I guess I should get back to my father. I'll probably be here for the rest of the week at least. I'd like to call and check on you, if that's okay?"

"I would like that," she said, the softness returning to her voice.

"Then I'll talk to you tomorrow," he said, and after she said okay, they both bid each other good night.

Courtland walked back to his father's room and saw that his father was awake.

"He hasn't been awake long. The nurse just brought him some

broth to drink," Jimmy Earl said, looking on from a chair in the corner of the room.

Nap was propped up in his bed wearing a burgundy robe while Courtland's mother continued to sit and hold his hand, stroking it. Courtland's sister Catherine was feeding him the broth one spoonful at a time, and Violet was positioned by Nap's feet with her head on his bed looking up at him. Courtland hurried over to them, resting his hand on top of his father's shoulder.

"Pops, you sure know how to scare a man," Courtland said.

"Didn't mean to do that," Nap said, his voice slurred. "Went and had a stupid stroke."

"That's what I hear," Courtland said, "but we are going to get you better and back home before you know it."

"You didn't need to come," his father said, trying to carefully enunciate his words. "I'm fine. You have a job to do. Congress waits for no one."

"I know you are fine, Pops, but I needed to see it for myself. I won't stay long. Promise," Courtland said. "Just long enough for me to make sure you, Mother, and the girls are all right."

"That sounds like a plan to me, son," Nap said, sounding old and worn out for the first time in Courtland's life. Courtland watched as Nap closed his eyes, breathing deeply, signaling that once again he had drifted off to sleep.

"He should eat," Catherine said, looking panicked. "The nurse said he needed to drink all of this broth so he can get strong again."

"Don't fret, Cat," Courtland said. "Rest is probably what his body needs even more than that broth. Why don't you three go take a walk and get out of this room for a bit? Jimmy Earl and I will stay with him, and if he wakes up again, I'll make sure he eats the broth."

All three of them started to fuss, but Courtland was insistent, and finally they agreed to go and stretch their legs.

"We'll be right outside the door," his mother said. Before leaving, she bent and kissed Nap on his cheek and whispered something in his ear. He smiled in his sleep, and after smoothing down his sleeve once more, she and the girls stepped out, leaving Courtland alone in the room with Nap and Jimmy Earl. At first there was silence as Courtland continued to look at his sleeping father, but finally, Jimmy Earl spoke.

"You called her," he said. His voice wasn't accusatory. Just knowing.

Courtland didn't respond. What could he say?

"You're making a hard bed for yourself, Courtland," Jimmy Earl said.

Courtland turned to look at his friend. "I expect you're right," he said, then turned back toward Nap. There was nothing more he could say. He agreed with his friend, but at this moment, that was all he could do, and listen to the long, deep breaths of his father and the faint sound of the ticking clock on the wall over the chair where his mother had sat.

TWELVE

Courtland

"Is there anybody in this house besides me?" Nap roared from his office, which had temporarily been set up for him as a bedroom since he was still having trouble walking up stairs.

Mrs. Matthews, the housekeeper, was making her way back to Nap's makeshift room for what seemed like the hundredth time. Courtland's mother had already worn herself out and was resting in her bedroom. As usual, the girls were nowhere to be found. Once they realized their daddy was going to be alright, they found ways to be scarce when he started barking orders. Nap's doctor had released him from the hospital the previous day, and ever since, he had been a total monster toward everyone.

"I've got it, Mrs. Matthews," Courtland said to the elderly woman as he rose from his seat in the sitting room outside of his father's office. He was trying to get some reading done on an upcoming senate hearing concerning tax cuts, but every time he would get immersed in the reading, Nap would yell out for something or other, ranging from food to house slippers, even though he had not left the room since they brought him home.

"Are you sure, Courtland?" she asked. "He's been in a bad mood all morning. You might not want to go in there."

"Well, he can just get out of his bad mood," Courtland grumbled. "You and Mother have worn a path in this carpet going back and forth to take care of his every whim. Let me have a crack at the old coot."

Mrs. Matthews laughed. "Don't you mess around and get on his bad side."

"Every day I have to deal with old coots in the Congress. I reckon I can handle one old coot in this house," Courtland said as he walked to his father's partially closed door. He opened the door just as Nap was yelling again.

"My God, Pops," Courtland said, entering the room. "What in the world is wrong now?"

"Where's your mother?" Nap barked, his face red from yelling, his voice still slurred.

"Upstairs resting. What you should be doing," Courtland said, walking to the hospital bed they had brought for him to sleep in.

"What about Dulcie? Where is she?" Nap insisted.

"Mrs. Matthews has plenty to do without running in here every five minutes. Now what can I do for you, Pops?" Courtland asked, modulating his voice like he was talking to a petulant child.

"Her name is Dulcie," Nap grumbled, frowning at Courtland, but Courtland was used to that look from Nap. He was not his mother or his sisters. Nap's testy disposition did not affect him at all.

"I know what her name is, but that has nothing to do with why you keep yelling for someone every few minutes. What can I do for you, Pops?" Courtland asked again.

"It's hot in here," Nap finally said, clearly grasping for something to complain about.

Courtland reached over and picked up the blanket that was covering Nap and folded it, throwing it on the chair beside his bed.

"Better?" Courtland asked.

"Don't be flip," Nap said. "And put it at the foot of the bed in case I get chilled. This room is not fit for someone who is standing at death's door. It's just a matter of time before I have another stroke. That's what that doctor told me."

Courtland took the blanket and placed it at the foot of his father's bed, then sat down in the chair beside him. Even though Nap was being difficult, Courtland was pleased that his father was alert and sounding more like his old self.

"Pops, you are a lot of things, but standing or lying at death's door would not be it. You've had a stroke, but if you work hard, you can recover from some of the side effects. And the doctor spoke to me extensively before you left the hospital," Courtland said, "and not once did he say you would have another stroke."

"I know what I heard," Nap said, then changed the subject. "Courtland, I need to talk to you about something."

"What is it, Pops?" Courtland asked, concerned about his father's serious tone.

As much as Courtland tried to be reassuring, he knew that his father's condition was serious and Nap could have another stroke, this time fatal, but he didn't want Nap worrying about it.

"Son, I want you to run for the presidency this year. I want you to take on Truman," Nap said, taking the time to pronounce every word carefully.

It hurt Courtland's heart to hear his giant of a father struggle so hard to speak. But when he heard what his father had to say, he wondered for a moment if the old man had lost his senses. Surely his father was not saying what he thought he heard.

Courtland tried to smile, but his father's lopsided face was completely stoic. "Well, you don't start at the bottom when it comes to your requests, do you? Good grief, Pops. The presidency? This is not what we have been planning. That's years down the line."

"I don't have years, Courtland," his father snapped. "I might not even make it to November for the election. I want to see you run, and I need you to do it now, son."

"Pops, this makes no sense. I can't beat Truman. I'm just getting my feet wet in politics. In four to eight more years, I—"

"In four to eight more years, I'll be fertilizing your mama's daisies out back," Nap said. "And don't try to sell me some song and dance that I'll get better. Listen to me. I might sound slow in the head, but I'm not. There ain't no getting better with this. You know it, and I know it."

"I know no such thing, Pops. I'm not God, and neither are you. Instead of you trying to throw me into the presidential pool, we just need to focus on you getting better. It's just not feasible for me to run against Truman, and if you weren't feeling so dang awful, you would see that too," Courtland said, getting up from his seat and pacing. "I'm not ready to run. No one is going to trust a thirty-six-year-old to take on the presidency."

"Listen, boy," Nap said, hitting the covers with his good hand. "I've been thinking about this since even before this stroke foolishness. Yes, you are young, but you're a war hero, and that will look good to voters."

"So is Truman," Courtland said. "His military record during the Great War is impeccable."

"Be that as it may, he didn't get a Purple Heart like you did, and his military days are far behind him. Nobody remembers his achievements from thirty years ago, and his stance on the Coloreds is not going to fly here in the South. I'm already hearing rumblings that the convention is going to be a total fiasco. He won't get the nomination, Courtland," Nap said, "and if he does, he'll rip the party apart. No, this isn't just an old dying man's wish for his son. If you get in the race now, you've got a damn good chance of beating him. A damn good chance."

"Pops, it would be political suicide to try to take on the incumbent. This isn't the right time. I'm making some great strides in the senate. We just have to be patient," Courtland said, trying to reason with his father, but he could tell by the look on Nap's face that he wasn't hearing a thing Courtland was saying.

"So you're not going to honor your father's dying wish?" he asked.

"Why don't we just wait until you aren't feeling so poorly to talk about this more thoroughly?" Courtland said, trying to reason with Nap.

"There's nothing we need to talk about that I am not fit to discuss right now," Nap said, but Courtland could tell that his father's voice was weakening.

He didn't want to upset Nap any more than he already was, but Courtland just could not wrap his mind around what his father was saying. The last thing he wanted to do was to announce his bid for presidency based on his father's fear of dying. It just didn't make sense, and he knew—or at least, he hoped—after Nap had a few days to come to himself, he would see the rationale behind Courtland's logic. Before either man could say anything else, Courtland's mother and Jimmy Earl entered the room. Courtland stood as his mother got closer, offering her his chair.

Millicent rushed over to her husband and kissed his forehead, sitting in the chair beside him. Once again, she was back to being impeccably dressed and coiffed, looking more like the mother he had grown up seeing.

"I'm sorry I was gone so long, darling. I meant to take a short nap, and next thing I knew it was hours. Look who came to see you today, Nap. Jimmy Earl."

"I recognize Jimmy Earl," Nap said in a testy voice. "I haven't lost all my faculties."

Millicent stroked Nap's head. "Nap, you look tired. Courtland, did you wear your father out?" she asked, looking at her son with disapproval. "He looks positively peaked. Maybe we should call Doc Henry to come check on him."

"I'm fine," Nap mumbled, "but I could do for some sleep, I suppose. That's what old folks do. We eat, we sleep, and we—"

"Nap," Millicent interrupted. "Don't be crass, darling."

"Mr. Nap, I just wanted to come by and check on you before heading back home," Jimmy Earl said as he approached Nap's bed.

The old man reached out his good hand and shook Jimmy Earl's.

"You're a good man," Nap said in a slow, hoarse voice. "You've been a good addition to this family. Now, I need you to talk some sense into my boy's head. He'll listen to you. He listens to you better than he does me, so you talk to him, Jimmy."

"What is your father talking about?" Millicent asked, looking from Courtland to Nap. "You two weren't arguing while I was sleeping, were you?"

"Don't worry yourself about anything. This is men's business," Nap said. "Jimmy, do what I said."

"Yes, sir, Mr. Nap," Jimmy Earl said, eyeing Courtland, who just shook his head slightly and mouthed, "Tell you later."

"You walk out with Jimmy, Courtland," Nap ordered, his eyes already closed. "I'm going to try to get some sleep."

"All right, Pops," Courtland said, then bent down and kissed his mother's cheek. "I'll be back shortly, Mother."

"All right. We'll be here," she said. "And Jimmy, you drive careful and tell Lori Beth we said hello. I worry about you children so much in your fast cars."

Both Jimmy Earl and Courtland grinned at Millicent's words. No matter how old they got, she would always view them as the young, gangly boys they used to be as opposed to the grown men they were now—one married and the father of twin boys and the other a highly decorated war veteran and a United States senator. Jimmy Earl kissed Millicent on the cheek, too, and promised to drive carefully. The two men walked out of Nap's office, and immediately Courtland began telling his friend about his father's desire for him to run for the presidency.

"This upcoming term?" Jimmy Earl questioned, sounding incredulous as they walked into the foyer and outside where they stood on the porch. "Against Truman?"

"I know. The old man is scared out of his mind, Jimmy Earl, and now he wants me to give him something to live for, I guess," Courtland said, "but I can't run now. It wouldn't be a smart move on my part."

"I agree the timing seems off," Jimmy Earl said. "I mean, you had a plan to run after serving in the senate for a few more terms, but what if your father is right? What if you could beat Truman?"

"Come on, Jimmy Earl, not you too," Courtland said as they began making their way down the stairs. "I won't have the party on my side, Jimmy Earl. They are going to back Truman. That's just the truth of the matter."

Jimmy Earl reached out and halted his friend from going any farther. "Look, Courtland . . . I agree, this is not the pathway you had in mind, but man, Truman is struggling right now. The Southern Democrats are not pleased with the stances he's taking on civil rights and the labor unions. Not to mention, we lost both the House and the Senate under his leadership. There are a lot of reasons to think maybe Mr. Nap is right. Maybe this is your time."

"Look, if the truth be known, Truman and I aren't that far apart in our political ideologies. I don't know if the South is any more prepared for someone like me than they are for Truman," Courtland said.

Jimmy Earl shook his head. "You can't change the way things are overnight. You know where I stand on those issues, but you have to think logically and time yourself. That's what has Truman up against the ropes, moving too damn fast for his own good."

"A friend of mine warned me about moving too slowly,"

Courtland said. "Now you're accusing me of moving too fast. I just don't know about any of this, Jimmy Earl."

"Well, let me make things clear. I think you can beat Truman, the more I think about it. I truly do," Jimmy Earl said, a huge grin on his face. "And now that women have the right to vote, that ugly mug of yours will send them running to the polls. Hell, you won't even need to have a platform. You just have to grin in their faces like you used to do in college. Half of the female population at the University of Georgia would have followed you to Hades and back."

Courtland continued down the stairs leading to Jimmy Earl's car, which was parked out front. "You're sounding about as daft as my father. And here I thought I could rely on you to make sense of this situation with me, Jimmy Earl."

"There is never going to be a perfect time for you to throw your hat into the ring. Sometimes you've just got to rely on serendipity."

"That's not how I operate, and you know it," Courtland said, stopping to face his friend. "I have to know that when I do run for the presidency, *if* I run for the presidency, it is the right time. Now just feels rushed and based off of an old man's whimsy."

Jimmy Earl reached over and put his hand on his friend's arm. "At the end of the day, you have to do what makes sense to you. But if I were you, I wouldn't discount your daddy's idea of you running just because he's saying it while ill. Nap Kingsley is the most brilliant mind I know, other than yours. If he sees a way for you to win, then I would venture to say there is a path to the White House for you right now. That's all I'm saying."

Courtland didn't respond. His mind was so filled with various thoughts that he didn't know which way was up at this particular moment. Were his father and best friend correct in their assessment? Could he run for president now and actually have a fighting chance? Courtland didn't know. He had gone from feeling pretty certain about his desire to wait to now wondering if waiting would only lead toward his missing out on the best opportunity he was going to get to be elected president.

"You know Lori Beth and I will work our butts off to help you get elected, just like we did when you ran for the senate," Jimmy Earl said, clapping Courtland on the back. "You won't be in this alone."

Courtland put his arm around Jimmy Earl's shoulder, walking with him toward his car. "I know. That's not the issue. It's just me wrapping my brain around all of this. That's all."

Jimmy Earl turned and stared at Courtland with a serious look on his face, lowering his voice to a whisper, even though no one was around. "You know if you do this, you can't have a relationship with her. This won't work with her in the picture."

Obviously, Courtland didn't need Jimmy Earl to go into greater detail. He knew what his friend was talking about, and he knew that Jimmy Earl was correct. If Courtland did decide to run, he couldn't have any blemishes on his record or any relationships that his Southern constituents would consider unfit or inappropriate.

"I know," Courtland said in a quiet voice. There wasn't much else he could say.

"Well, you let me know what you decide about everything before you head back up the road to D.C.," Jimmy Earl said. "I'll support you however you need."

The two friends grasped hands and shook.

"President," Courtland mumbled underneath his breath as Jimmy Earl drove away. "President Courtland Hardiman Kingsley IV."

Courtland shook his head and walked back inside. He knew it was a crazy thought, but he couldn't help but allow it to simmer for a moment.

THIRTEEN

Eva

Eva had never seen so many people trying to get into her restaurant at the same time. The day before, she and the staff had spent all morning and afternoon preparing for the opening, not knowing if anyone would take a chance to come back after the bombing incident. But looking at the people wrapped around the corner of the building brought tears to Eva's eyes. She stood at the door, greeting everyone as they came inside.

"We will get you seated just as quickly as we can," she reassured each person, squeezing each and every hand as they went by. Eva pulled one of her waiters to her. "Go and take cups of coffee out to the people waiting. No charge."

"Yes, ma'am," he said and hurried off to do her bidding.

Eva barely noticed him leaving she was so busy smiling and speaking to every single customer as they filed into the room. She had a banquet room that she seldom used, and an hour ago she got some of the waitstaff to open it up, so the wait time was only fifteen or twenty minutes tops. Eva had become so engrossed in her efforts to make sure all of her guests were comfortable, she didn't notice Wendell sliding up beside her.

"Hello, pretty lady," a voice said in her left ear. She turned quickly.

"Wendell," she said with a smile. "I didn't see you arrive. How long have you been here?"

"Not long," he said with a smile so perfect, he belonged in the pages of a magazine.

He was wearing a three-piece, gray-striped suit with a gold pocket watch, a matching gray coat, and a wool fedora. And Lord, did he smell amazing—woodsy with a hint of something else, maybe lavender. Either way, Eva had to watch herself because Wendell was dangerous . . . not in an evil way, but definitely in a distracting way. He looked like old money, and he was. The perfect catch. The kind of man she should be gravitating toward. Eva motioned for one of her hostesses to come take her place at the door.

"Would you like to join me at my table?" she asked, knowing her gesture might be misinterpreted by Wendell, but then again, why shouldn't she flirt with the handsome, single bachelor? Her mind drifted to Courtland for a second, but she pushed those thoughts away.

"Absolutely," he said, offering her his arm. She hesitated for a moment but then allowed him to escort her to her table in the corner by the window. She knew all eyes were following them as they walked across the room. They did make quite a handsome pair. Eva was wearing a formfitting, gray-blue wool suit with a matching pencil skirt, and her hair was pinned up in her signature chignon. She wore pearls and a pair of gray flats. They were comfortable, and she didn't need the added inches, standing at a statuesque five nine.

Once they were seated, neither of them said anything right away. The waiter came over and took Wendell's order. Today's special was shrimp remoulade, creole turtle soup, and filet mignon au poivre.

"I'll take what you just said," he said to the waiter, smiling broadly from him to Eva. "All of that."

"Yes, sir," the waiter replied. "Would you care for something, Miss Eva?"

"A glass of sparkling water," she said. "Oh, and please take Mr. Harrington's hat and coat and check them at the front." The young man took Wendell's things, bowed, and then went off to take care of their order.

"How do you keep your figure working around such amazing food?" Wendell asked.

"Everything in moderation," she said.

When Eva was working, it was hard for her to drum up an appetite. Oh, she would taste food because she had to, but that was about all she did. Taste. Probably the reason she was at her all-time thinnest, and she didn't have many pounds to concede in the first place.

"How are you doing, Eva?" Wendell asked.

"Fine. Couldn't be better actually," she said. She still couldn't get over the fact that the place was packed at lunch during a workweek. Her brother-in-law would say, "Look at God." "I am floored by the support I am being shown," she said. "I did not expect this type of turnout."

"It's phenomenal seeing so many people here," Wendell said with a nod. "But I will confess, I was surprised to see you reopen so soon after the . . . well . . . the incident. Weren't you frightened?" he asked, leaning closer, looking at her intently, as if he didn't want to miss a word. Eva was not one to blink in the face of anything or anyone, but she was finding it hard to sit still with Wendell's intensity aimed completely and totally toward her. But she finally found her voice.

"I am not easy to frighten, and anyway, this restaurant is my baby," she said with pride—and she was proud of her accomplishments. This restaurant was a testament to all that her mother had taught her. She would never allow anything or anyone to deter her from her goals.

"You have made a remarkable comeback," he said, looking at her, his eyes glowing with appreciation. "You are an incredible woman, Miss Eva Cardon."

"Thank you," she said, finding him easy to talk to in spite of his over-the-top flirtations. "Where are you practicing law, Wendell? I don't recall you saying on Sunday."

"Bomont and Goody. Have you heard of them?" he asked, smiling because he had to know that she and every Negro in D.C. knew the names Bomont and Goody. They were right up there with Attorneys Charles Hamilton Houston and Wendell P. Gardner Sr. Another Wendell, but one who had already made his first and last name famous.

"Yes, I believe I am familiar with those names," she said, teasing him, but he was so intent on bragging that he missed her sardonic tone.

Normally his level of arrogance would have already turned her away from him, but she found his confidence level engaging.

"I'm a new associate, but I expect before long to have my name included on the list. Bomont, Goody, and Harrington has a nice ring to it, don't you think?" he asked, clearly relaying a dream that he had voiced before, probably to some adoring female.

"Oh yes, Attorney Harrington. Quite impressive," she said, just as the waiter brought Wendell his food. *"Bon appetit,"* she said with a smile.

She watched as he carefully cut up his filet mignon. He took a bite and closed his eyes. "My God from Zion. This is good."

She laughed. "I don't ever recall getting that reaction, but I will relay the sentiments to the chef."

After he ate a few more bites, he paused, looking at her intently. "So do you have any information to share with me about the young man you mentioned the other day?" he asked.

"Actually, yes," she said. "I spoke to Simon's father, and he is open to meeting with you. They don't have a phone, but Simon will be working here this afternoon after he finishes school. I will make sure he takes your number with him. They have a neighbor who allows them to make local calls."

"That sounds good to me. I will look forward to hearing from them. We can't be too careful in situations like these. Since we don't know who was responsible for this act of cowardice, we have to treat everyone like a suspect," Wendell said, taking another bite of food.

"Unfortunately, that is true," Eva said, shivering slightly at the thought.

She still couldn't get that awful Lieutenant Stevens out of her mind. She didn't know if he was responsible for the incident or had knowledge of who was, but he definitely was not an ally. That she knew for certain.

"Are you okay?" Wendell asked, putting down his knife and fork.

She tried to smile. "Yes. I put on a good front, but this did overwhelm me."

Wendell reached over and took her hand. "You don't have to put on a front with me, Eva. Ever."

She smiled, slowly taking her hand back. "Thank you. It is nice to have a friend."

Wendell threw back his head and laughed. "Oh Lord. When a woman calls you a friend, you know your chances with her are nil to none."

Eva felt embarrassed. "I didn't mean it like that." She was still learning the fine art of talking with a member of the opposite sex who wasn't a part of her family or an employee. Flirting did not come naturally to her.

"Oh," he said, turning his head to the side, smiling at her. "So I do have a chance? Is that what you're saying?"

Eva looked down at the table as Wendell continued to laugh.

"You are so easy to rattle," Wendell said. "Are you like this with everyone or just me?"

"How is your food?" she asked, looking him straight in the eye. She was not going to let Wendell get the best of her. He continued to laugh for a moment and then he stopped, his expression more serious.

"Did I tell you that I had met your brother-in-law before?" he asked, changing the subject.

"No, you didn't," she said, happy to be on a subject that didn't involve her.

"I had the good fortune to hear him preach several years ago. He was in Atlanta at my home church, Wheat Street Baptist, where Reverend William Holmes Borders Sr. is the pastor. I remember him being quite the orator. I will need to come visit you all. Being new to town, I haven't quite found a church home yet."

"You should definitely come visit. My brother-in-law and sister are doing a powerful ministry at Second Street," Eva said. "They've done a lot to reach out to a younger segment of the Negro population here in D.C. Seems like there is something going on there all of the time."

"Will I find you there?" he asked, clearly flirting again.

Eva blushed. "Sometimes. I am a practicing Catholic—most of the time. My grandmother was Catholic, and my mother was a lapsed Catholic who made sure my sister and I were always at Mass. However, I do go to my brother-in-law's church quite often. As my sister says, God can find us wherever we are."

"Amen to that," Wendell said. He looked at her for a minute before speaking, and then he reached for her hand again. "Eva, would you be open to me coming by and escorting you to church this Sunday?"

Eva was unsure of what to say or do. She liked Wendell. He was smart and handsome, and someone who didn't always take himself seriously. She was attracted to him. She just didn't know what to do. Courtland kept coming to her mind, but she kept saying to herself: *Off limits. He is off limits.*

"I would love to attend church with you this Sunday," she said, and she meant it.

She gave him her address, and a minute or two later he stood, prepared to leave. He reached into his pocket for his wallet, but she shook her head.

"Consider the meal my treat," she said, rising from her seat as well, holding herself at her full height.

"Thank you. I could stay here talking to you all day, Eva," he said, "but I have a case I need to be working on. If you speak to Simon's father, please urge him to call me soon. I will do what I can for them."

"Thank you, Wendell," she said with a genuine smile.

He took her hand and kissed it lightly. "You have a good day, Eva Cardon," he said and made his way through the restaurant and out the door.

"Looks like I did good," said a voice from behind, causing Eva to jump. It was Adam.

"I have no clue what you are talking about," she said as he threw back his head and laughed.

"Young lady, I am not that old. I could feel those sparks between the two of you," he said. "Wendell is good people. Arrogant, but he's got his head on straight. A woman could do worse."

She knew he was talking about Courtland. She would be lying if she said Wendell Moss Harrington III didn't intrigue her just a bit, but so did Courtland, in a different way. It was all so confusing.

"He's high maintenance, but any man worth your time is going to be that way, Eva," Adam said, interrupting her thoughts. "Don't let this restaurant be all that you focus on. A restaurant can't keep you warm at night, and it won't be there when you need someone to love on."

Eva's cheeks got warm for the second time that day. She was not used to such frank conversation, least of all with a man like Adam. "I will take that into consideration," she said, just as one of her waiters came up.

"Excuse me," he said to Eva. "You have a phone call, Miss Cardon."

Eva smiled, happy for the interruption. "We must talk again soon. Thank you for coming by today. And thank you for encouraging so many others to come. I know you had your hand in this."

Adam feigned a surprised look. "Me? I had no hand in this. Oh, I might have called one or two people, but this is all you, Miss Eva. The people love you and your delicious food. You set quite the table, young miss," he said, giving her a quick hug and then making his way toward the door, pausing to speak to this one and that. Eva thanked the waiter for coming for her and then went to her makeshift office by the bar.

"Hello," she said into the receiver.

"Hello, Miss Eva Cardon," the deep, rich, masculine voice said on the other end of the line.

Suddenly, just hearing Courtland's voice, Eva knew with all certainty that she had gotten herself into a fine mess. She had agreed to go to church with Wendell, yet the sound of Courtland's voice made her heart beat in triple time.

Oh what tangled webs we weave, she thought as she tried to settle her nerves so she could have a coherent conversation with this infuriating man who both intrigued her and caused her to question everything she and Frédérique had been taught by their mother.

Don't be me. It is okay to love a man, but do not allow yourself to be consumed by him.

I'm trying, Mother, she thought. *I'm trying.*

FOURTEEN

Eva

"Eva, are you there?" Courtland asked.

Eva hesitated before answering. She was trying to get her bearings. This attraction to the opposite sex was all so new and confusing to her. She had never been allowed or allowed herself to be caught up with the flirtations of men. In the past, she took their attention with a grain of salt, but suddenly, these two men had her twisted up on the inside. Finally, she spoke.

"Yes, I'm here," she said, trying not to be so excited about hearing from him, but failing miserably. She felt guilty for going straight from interacting with Wendell, even accepting a date of sorts to attend church, to talking with another man who had captured her interest.

"I was worried that we got disconnected," he said. "How did the reopening go?"

"Oh, Courtland," she said, unable to keep the excitement out of her voice. "It was fantastic. Crowds were gathered around the building, trying to get in. I have never seen so many people waiting to enter my restaurant. It was so exhilarating. Still is, if the truth be known. People are still crowding in."

"That is wonderful, Eva," Courtland said. "You deserve this

moment and then some. My fondest wish for you is that the crowds will continue to be constant."

"Thank you," Eva said. This world . . . this world of food and business was exhilarating to her. Where her sister daydreamed about babies and growing old with her husband, Eva's thoughts were always about the restaurant business and how she could grow it into something unforgettable to her patrons. "This business of mine is my dream. My only dream, really."

"What about love and marriage?" Courtland asked. "Do you ever think about giving up the restaurant to settle down?"

"Do you ever think about giving up your career to settle down?" she snapped. "Why is it everyone thinks a woman can only have two things on her mind at one time? Babies and husbands. Believe it or not, some of us have different dreams."

"I'm sorry, Eva," he said quickly. "I seem to regularly put my foot into my mouth when we have conversations. Of course you don't have to think about those things. You are absolutely right. It is unfair that women are expected to give up on their hopes and dreams in order to support the hopes and dreams of some man. I stand corrected."

Eva sighed. She didn't mean to snap at him so, but this was a sore subject for her. "I'm sorry, Courtland. I didn't mean to bark at you. To answer your question, I don't know how love and marriage fit into the equation of my life. I truly don't. But I figure if it is meant to be, it will happen. In the meantime, I will focus on working."

"You mentioned a while back that you were going to open a second restaurant. Are you going to sell this restaurant and focus on the new one?" he asked.

Eva smiled because she could tell he was trying to change the subject and return them to less volatile ground.

"No," she said. "This is still my restaurant if for no other reason than it bears my mother's name, so I will continue to give this place my attention, but it is now at the point where I can start thinking about other business ventures."

"Besides the restaurant business?" he asked.

"Maybe. Adam is always pushing me to invest my money in things other than the restaurant, especially now that it is turning a profit."

"Like what?" he asked.

"Stocks and bonds, I guess," she said. "Land maybe. I don't know. That isn't really my forté, but I do want to leave a legacy behind when I am long gone. There are a lot of causes I feel strongly about, like the NAACP and the United Negro College Fund. I would leave my money to them if something should happen to me and I had no heirs at the time."

"You truly are a wonder, Eva," he said. "I listen to you talk, and it is almost like listening to a woman two or three times your age."

"Thank you," she said softly. Once again, she was feeling embarrassed. She decided to change the subject. "How is your father? Is he doing better?"

"Yes, he is, actually. Thank you for asking," Courtland said, but then, before she could hear the rest of what he was saying, several of Eva's guests were leaving, and they all came over to hug her and congratulate her on the reopening of the restaurant. One of the patrons was Mrs. Mary McLeod Bethune.

"Hold on one minute," she said to Courtland.

There was no way she was going to ask Mrs. McLeod Bethune to wait. She laid the phone down on the desk and stood to give her a hug.

"Thank you so much for coming today. It means a lot to me," Eva said.

"Of course, dear," she said. "I am so pleased that you did not allow that distraction over the weekend to keep you from reopening your fine restaurant. Not many Negro women have their own business, especially a thriving business like yours. We must keep you going, and I was honored to come by today with a few of my friends."

"Thank you, Mrs. McLeod Bethune. I am always grateful to be in your midst and to do whatever I can to help any cause you are associated with," Eva said.

She so admired the work Mrs. McLeod Bethune did throughout the country, and especially the work she did here in D.C. Not many Negro women got to sit down with one sitting president, and Mrs. McLeod Bethune had experienced the pleasure of having the ear of two presidents—Roosevelt and Truman. And then there was the work she did to promote women's rights. Eva had helped her with voting registration, even allowing Mrs. McLeod Bethune and other women volunteers to sign up women voters at her restaurant.

"You must come over to my home next week for a meeting with some of the women who were present at Sunday's event here at your restaurant," she said, placing her hand on Eva's arm. "Powell and the rest like to believe they are the beginning and the end of our civil rights movement, but I don't mind reminding them when the occasion arises about the relationship I had with President Roosevelt and now have with President Truman. These Negro men will never acknowledge the power that we Negro women possess, so it is our duty to remind them of it from time to time, not to be boastful, but simply to let them know that there is no them without us."

Eva smiled. "Yes, ma'am. And I would be honored to come to your meeting."

"Wonderful," she said. "I will send you a formal invitation. You take care and keep the faith, my dear. You make us all proud."

Before she could go back to her conversation with Courtland, one of her waiters came to her with a question. Once she got him on the right track, she turned her attention back to the call. "I'm sorry, Courtland. It's a madhouse here today. What were you saying?

I thought you said something about running for something. Is your senate seat up already?"

"No," he said. "In the last few days since my father has regained the ability to communicate properly, he has been trying to convince me that I should run for president."

Eva was silent for a moment. She wasn't entirely sure what to say at first. "President? Against Truman? Now?"

"Hearing you say the words like that makes me wonder why I even bothered to listen to my partially cognizant father," he said wryly.

"No," she said quickly. "I didn't mean it like that. It's just you are so young, Courtland, and you have only been in the senate for a little over a year. It just seems a bit rushed. I know you could do the job. It's convincing others who don't know you yet."

She hoped her frankness didn't offend him. The one thing Eva had learned about politics by living in D.C. was that it was a game of the highest-level chess ever, and one wrong move could ruin a person's chances of ever recovering.

"I'm not offended," he said. "You're right. From a logical standpoint, entering the race for the presidency now makes no sense, but at the same time, other than volunteering to go fight in the war, I have followed the path Nap Kingsley laid out for me my entire life," Courtland said. "I went to the college of his choice. I joined his fraternity, Delta Kappa Epsilon. I majored in law like he wanted. I spent a summer clerking for his friend, Hatton Lovejoy, even though I wanted to focus on tax law. From the first moment I understood that Nap's rules were the only rules that mattered, I have obeyed him. Period. So even though my logical mind says this is ridiculous, because Nap Kingsley wants me to run, I am seriously considering it."

"You know you don't have to do this if you don't want to, Courtland," Eva said quietly. "You are no longer his little boy or his teenaged son. You are a fully grown man who can make his own decisions. Don't let your father or anyone pressure you into doing something you don't think is wise."

"That simple, huh?" he said.

Eva smiled. "Yes, Courtland. That simple."

"How did someone as young as you get to be so wise?" he asked.

"I don't know, Courtland," she said, leaning back in her seat. "I don't know everything, but I do know that every time I have followed my heart instead of someone else's, I have had no regrets. Regret comes when we try to honor the desires of everybody else at the expense of our own desire. After Father died and then Mother, I decided, even as a young girl, that I was going to live my life the way I wanted to live it, and I was going to follow my own pathway. Sometimes it gets me into trouble. Most times not."

"I would like to see you when I return on Friday," he said abruptly. "I know it's not wise, but I—"

"It's not wise," she interrupted. "You are about to embark on a path that few men ever embark on. Your every move will be under scrutiny. Seeing me will involve us sneaking around and hiding in the shadows. I don't want to be in the shadows. Not even to see you."

Courtland didn't say anything at first. Finally, he spoke. "You're right. You deserve much more than I can offer. Asking you to sneak around and see me is unfair. I'm sorry, Eva."

"I am too," she said with regret, "but I wish you well. I hope that whatever you decide, it will work out the way you want it to."

"Are we allowed to be friends?" he asked quickly. "Just chat sometimes? I value your opinion, and I would hate to lose all contact with you."

"I don't know. I—"

"Say yes. Just to friendship. Say yes," he said.

Eva could hear the raw emotion in Courtland's voice. She knew this was not a good decision. They should just end all contact and move on with their lives, but she couldn't imagine not hearing his voice again, so she acquiesced, praying her decision would not lead to greater heartbreak.

"Yes," she said. "We can be friends. Mother used to say one can never have too many friends."

"Good," he said, the relief evident in his voice. "I'll talk to you when I return to D.C. I truly am happy that you had a good reopening today."

"Thank you, Courtland. And you travel safely," she said.

They both said goodbye, and Eva sat holding the phone for a moment, hanging it up quickly when she saw her sister coming around the partition. Frédérique's face was bursting with excitement.

"Eva, you are not going to believe this," Frédérique said, coming over to stand in front of her sister's desk. "I mean, I can't believe this myself."

"What?" Eva asked. "What has happened? And sit before you fall."

Frédérique took the seat beside her sister's desk, and Eva waited with expectation to find out what had her sister so worked up. She didn't seem sad, but she didn't exactly seem happy either. For a moment, she wondered if Frédérique was pregnant again. Part of her hoped, but the other part of her worried that if her sister was expecting, this pregnancy might end up like all of the others.

"Well, you know Daisy stayed with me yesterday while Johnny Mac went out looking for a job," Frédérique said.

"Of course," Eva said, anxious for her sister to get to the point, but she knew not to rush Frédérique when she was telling a story or sharing information. Frédérique had always been a meticulous story-teller, and that often meant a five-minute story might end up taking half an hour.

The previous day had been a great one for Frédérique. By the time Eva had gotten home the night before, her sister had been gushing over how good the day had been with Daisy and how much she hoped Johnny Mac would let her keep Daisy regularly.

"This morning, after you left for work and before Pearson took off to go to the church and meet with the trustees about something or another, Johnny Mac stopped by," she said.

"Well," Eva said, "don't leave me in suspense. What did he say? Let me guess, your trial day was so amazing that he is going to officially let you babysit Daisy while he works. Am I right?"

Frédérique shook her head. "Johnny Mac's cousin called him last night about working with the railroad as a Pullman porter. Johnny Mac knew he couldn't take care of the children and work on the railroad, too, so he called his wife's sister in Virginia and asked her about taking in the children, but she said she would only take Simon, not Daisy. He said he called a few more people, but no one wanted Daisy."

"That's awful," Eva said, feeling sad for the little girl.

"Yes, it is awful," Frédérique said as the tears lapped underneath her chin. "My first instinct was to say, 'How heartless,' but we shouldn't judge. Who knows his in-laws' circumstances? They might be as poor as Johnny Mac."

"Very true. So, sissy, what did he say next?" Eva asked, trying to imagine where this story was going.

"Johnny Mac asked us if we would be willing to watch Daisy until he could make other arrangements," Frédérique said. "He said he would never find a job like this again, and if we would just give him a few days, then maybe he could find someone who would take her."

"Oh, honey, what a sad, sad story," Eva asked. "The very idea that he was so desperate that he would come to total strangers asking for help."

Moments like this, Eva had to work hard not to question God's judgment. Sometimes it felt as if there were perpetual rain clouds over the heads of the most vulnerable members of society like Johnny Mac and his family.

Frédérique nodded. "Eva, it was the saddest thing ever to see this poor man so in need of friends. He started sweating and tearing up and apologizing for being so presumptuous to ask something so huge, but before I could say anything, Pearson said, 'Unless you truly do find someone you would prefer to keep Daisy, you don't have to look any further than my wife and me, Brother Johnny Mac. We will take care of Daisy and love her for as long as you need us to.'"

Large tears began to slide down Eva's face. Daisy had so many needs, and he had to know that she was going to take up every free second that Frédérique had, but as always, he put everyone else's needs ahead of his own.

"What did Johnny Mac say after that?" Eva asked, handing her sister a napkin from her desk. By this time, both of them were shedding tears.

Frédérique dabbed at her eyes and then continued to share the news. "Sissy, Johnny Mac and I both started crying at the same time. There is paperwork to be drawn up so we can make certain decisions about her well-being when he is not around, but come Sunday, Johnny Mac will bring her to me. I don't know for how long, but before Johnny Mac left, he said he wanted her to have a mother, and the way the two of us took to each other, he couldn't think of anyone better than me. Can you believe it?"

Eva got up and pulled her sister into her arms. "Of course I can believe it. You are the most incredible, nurturing, loving woman I know. It is no surprise to me that Johnny Mac wants you to help take care of his daughter."

"Oh, sissy," Frédérique said. "This situation is so tragic, and I worry so much about how this will affect Simon. That boy was willing to sacrifice everything to take care of his sister. I just don't know how he will fare being separated from her. Pearson and I even offered to take Simon, too, but Johnny Mac said that was too much, and he wouldn't even entertain the thought."

Eva stepped back from the embrace so she could look her sister in the face. "He will hurt, but knowing Simon the very little time I have, he will eventually come to the conclusion that Daisy staying with us is for the best. And Virginia isn't far away. He can always visit."

Frédérique nodded. "Pearson said the exact same words. He said this was God's will, and we should be rejoicing that this sweet angel will be in our care, but it is hard to feel joyous knowing that so much sorrow is going to come from Daisy living with us."

"Sorrow mixed with happiness," Eva said, taking her sister's hand in hers. "I think you and I have some shopping to do. We have a little girl coming home to us."

"Oh Eva," Frédérique said, the first glimpse of a smile crossing her face. "It's happening. It's really happening."

Eva hugged her sister again, praying silently that things would work out for the good and her sister wouldn't find herself once again with an open heart and empty arms.

FIFTEEN

Courtland

The train ride back to D.C. was uneventful, unless one considered the scenery Courtland was so used to seeing as he traveled from Parsons to D.C. At this point in his trips back and forth between the two cities, he barely gave the countryside a cursory glance anymore. Georgia's winter landscape of barren fields that would soon be planted with tobacco and soybeans raced by Courtland's window unnoticed by him, not to mention the Blue Ridge Mountains and the coastal plains of South Carolina as well as the stark, hilly countryside of the Appalachian Mountains of North Carolina and Virginia. The first time Courtland made this trip, his eyes were glued to the scenery. It was still just as breathtaking, but now that he had become a fixture on this train and on this route, he stayed focused on whatever work happened to be in his briefcase.

Courtland sat in his passenger car by himself, and other than one of the porters checking in on him periodically, he was alone the entire time, exactly how he liked it, because that meant he could get work done, and his plate was pretty full as he prepared for the upcoming hearing on tax cuts, something his constituents desperately needed.

Most of the white dirt farmers in and around Parsons had never recovered from the Great Depression, turning to factory jobs or selling off their farms and moving to the larger cities like Atlanta or Savannah. Many of the Negro farmers who had been showing progress by buying and farming their own land had ended up selling it off or losing their land and working as sharecroppers for some of the local white farmers who were still in business. Two steps forward and many steps back was what many of his constituents were experiencing, and Courtland was determined to be their mouthpiece in Congress. It was the whole reason he had agreed to run in the first place. Courtland recognized his station in life and how it had afforded him so many opportunities that were not common in his part of the country, so he took his job as Congressman seriously. Before leaving this morning, he and Nap had argued something fierce about Courtland's behavior in Washington. Word had gotten back to Nap that Courtland was "acting friendly" with a Negro from New York. At first, Courtland wondered if his father was referring to Eva, but it didn't take long for Courtland to realize Nap was referring to Adam. The argument went on way too long, and nothing got resolved between them, causing Courtland to leave his parents' home feeling angry and disgruntled. Courtland understood that his political choices would always cause conflict between him and his father. But that didn't mean he liked it. He was used to being the "good son" who never disobeyed his parents. But his friendship with Adam and his commitment to change were nonnegotiable. By the time the train made it to D.C., Courtland had let go of some of his frustration with his father. He knew, at the end of the day, Nap wanted the best for him, even if his methods were unorthodox.

Vernon Michaels, the young Negro porter, stopped and checked on Courtland as he was preparing to exit the train.

"Good evening, Senator Kingsley," Vernon said. "I trust that your trip was satisfactory."

"Thank you, Vernon. It was. Smooth and uneventful. Just like I like my train rides. How is your father doing?" Courtland asked.

"He's doing fine, sir," Vernon said. "He's spending some time down home in Lewisville, Arkansas, with my mother. She has been sick, so he wanted to see how she was doing for himself. I could have taken some time off, but I need to work every chance I get so I can continue to save every penny for school."

Courtland reached into his pocket and took out a card, handing it to the young man. "Vernon, once you're done with this trip, come by my office so I can help you get yourself into school. I believe you have waited long enough, and I think the good folks of Lewisville have waited long enough for their doctor. I don't want you to become an old man still talking about going to Howard."

For a while, Courtland had been thinking about helping Vernon get into school sooner rather than later. He admired the young man, and Courtland knew that the longer Vernon waited, the more likely he wouldn't go to school, especially if something happened to his mother or his father. Vernon had a houseful of siblings, and Courtland knew there was nothing Vernon wouldn't do for them, including give up on his dream of becoming a doctor.

"Senator Kingsley, do you mean that?" the young man asked, taking the card and wiping a tear from his eye. "But you barely know me. Why would you do something so kind?"

"Being kind is the least we can do for each other," Courtland said, patting the young man on his back. "Do you think you can get everything wrapped up here by Monday? I will make some calls and see if we can get you an appointment with Admissions. Who knows, maybe you can get into school sooner than the fall."

"Yes, sir, Senator Kingsley," Vernon said with excitement. "I'll be done with this run on Sunday. I can be at your office first thing Monday morning, sir. Senator Kingsley, I don't even know how to thank you. I have dreamed of becoming a doctor my entire life. I knew it would happen someday, but I had no idea it would happen so soon. Thank you for blessing me so."

Courtland nodded with embarrassment. The accolades Vernon was bestowing upon him were a bit overwhelming. Courtland usually liked to do things in secret. That way, he could see the effects of his good deeds without actually having to deal with the fanfare.

"Good man, Vernon. Then I'll see you on Monday. You and I will take a drive over to Howard. After that, I have a friend I would like for you to meet. She has a restaurant and has said she is happy to hire you as a waiter."

"You are far too kind, sir, but I appreciate every bit of it," Vernon said.

"Good enough. Now help me get out of here. I have a party to get to," Courtland said, although he wasn't exactly looking forward to going. It was just one of the many obligations one had to fulfill if one was interested in politics in a serious manner. The schmoozing was almost as important as the actual legislating.

Vernon picked up Courtland's bags and carried them out of the train.

"Senator Kingsley, I just want to thank you again for this amazing opportunity. I promise I won't make you out to be a liar for vouching for me," Vernon said, removing his hat and bowing toward Courtland, who reached out and patted the young man on his shoulder.

"Thank me by becoming one of the top doctors in this nation and proving to everybody that good medicine can be performed by a Negro as well as a white man. Do that, and you will have definitely not made a liar out of me," Courtland said with a smile as they continued walking toward Courtland's car. His driver, Harold, got out of the car and opened the trunk so Vernon could put the bags inside.

"I get to the office by seven thirty in the morning. I expect you to already be there waiting for me."

"Yes, sir," Vernon said and bowed once more and then ran off, dodging people who were exiting the train. His exuberance was evident in every step he took. Courtland was glad he had extended this opportunity to Vernon. He was determined to help the young man however he could, including helping him with his tuition. For a moment he thought about Eva's words: *Why are you doing this? Being the champion for Negroes.* He understood how what he was doing might look like to some, but Vernon was a special young man, and if he could pull strings to give Vernon a better opportunity, he didn't care what others thought. Courtland tossed his walking cane into the back of the car and climbed inside.

"How is your father doing, Senator?" Harold asked as he pulled out of the station and began the drive toward 35th Street where Courtland's house was located. It was a twenty-minute drive there from Union Station. Courtland had bought the home soon after he was elected to Congress. He had wanted a showplace, somewhere he could have parties and invite local dignitaries. His mother and father had agreed that he needed a house in D.C., so Courtland used some of the money his grandfather had left him to buy his D.C. home. Once he had found just the right house, he got his mother and sisters to decorate it, and when they were done doing their magic, the house was a sight to behold. Four bedrooms and four baths with a huge great room and an office just off the entrance. The kitchen was magnificent but seldom used except for when he needed to heat up a pot of coffee. It was a lot of house, but when his family came to visit, it was nice having space for them to spread out. He had hosted a few large gatherings of some of his colleagues, and all of the parties had gone off nicely.

"He's doing much better," Courtland said. "Thank you for asking. How has your week been?"

"Busy, sir," he said. "I ended up hiring two more mechanics. No one seems to know how to drive in snow and ice, so we've been doing quite a bit of business this week."

"Well, I am very pleased that you know your way around a car, snow or no snow," Courtland said as Harold deftly made his way through the evening traffic.

It was a cold night. Clouds were forming but stars were still peeking out, looking like tiny diamonds scattered around the sky. Having traveled all over the world now, Courtland had to admit that he liked D.C. best of all. Something about the sunset over the Potomac, something about the row houses that lined the streets, something about being in the city where the major decisions about the country were being made appealed to him. Courtland couldn't imagine living anywhere else.

"Senator Kingsley, are you still planning on going to the party you mentioned earlier today on the phone?" Harold asked.

Courtland sighed. "I suppose so. To be honest, all I want to do is go and fall into my bed, but I guess there is no rest for the weary. At least not tonight. I won't be out late."

"Yes, sir," Harold said. "I will make sure I am close by so when you are ready to leave, you won't have to wait long."

Harold took a slight right onto Dumbarton Bridge from 23rd Street. They were getting near to his house. All Courtland wanted to do was go home, eat something, and go to bed. Instead, he needed to go out and hobnob with the local elites in D.C. Marjorie Post Davies and her husband, Joseph, were hosting a gathering at their house, and he had begged off of several other events Marjorie had invited him to in the past. He couldn't beg off again. She was too influential, and there would be a houseful of important people in attendance whom he would need on his side if he did decide to follow Nap's dream for him to run for the presidency this year. Courtland's mind drifted to Eva. He wished . . . No . . . he had no right to wish anything. Things were as they were with Eva, and no amount of wishing on his part would change things.

Harold made a quick turn onto Q Street and then a right onto 35th. Then they were sitting in front of his lavish home, which stood empty and alone. For a moment, Courtland didn't move. He didn't want to go to this party, but he also didn't want to be alone all night in his house.

"Are you ready to get out, sir?" Harold asked after a moment.

"Yes, I suppose so," Courtland said. "I'll just run upstairs and get dressed and be ready to go in about an hour. Do you want to come up and wait?"

"No, sir. I'll help you get your bags inside, but I'll wait out here until you're ready to go," Harold said. Courtland had invited Harold into his house several times, but unless he needed Harold to do something for him, the Negro man always declined. Harold believed in keeping their relationship on a strictly business level. Courtland understood. Throughout his childhood, his father and mother had stressed the need for him to keep a firm line between himself and the Negroes who lived on their plantation.

"It just makes things easier if we all stay in our place," his mother had said in her gentle way.

His father was far less gentle. "If you lay down with dogs, you wake up with fleas," Nap had snapped at him one day. "If you ain't careful, you'll have a bunch of mixed-race mongrels running around here like your grandpa Little Jack."

Courtland had hated both of their takes on how he should conduct himself, but he understood—begrudgingly. He especially understood it when he witnessed the great loss his friend Jimmy Earl experienced when he and his childhood friend, Opal Pruitt, lost their connection. It seemed this chasm between the races was insurmountable. He hoped with Vernon's generation that something would shift and change.

"Very well," Courtland said to Harold. "If I'm going, I'd better get busy," Courtland said and exited his car. Harold went to the trunk and retrieved Courtland's bags and carried them inside, leaving immediately to go back and sit in the car.

Courtland tried not to think about Eva, but he couldn't help but think how much better the night would be if she were on his arm.

You took on the German army, but you are too much of a coward to take on a racist world that would dare to look down on someone as exceptional as Eva, he thought.

For the first time in a long time, Courtland was disgusted with himself, but at this point, he wasn't sure what to do to change it. As Jimmy Earl said, they didn't create this world. That may be so, but they were definitely benefiting from it, and that made Courtland even more frustrated. But there was no time for him to ponder all of that. He had a party to attend.

SIXTEEN

Courtland

When Courtland arrived a little before 8:00 p.m. at Tregaron, the illustrious estate of Ambassador Joseph E. Davies and his wife, socialite Marjorie Post Davies, the party was already in progress. The mansion was a two-story brick building in the Georgian style named after Davies's father's ancestral home in Wales. The mansion overlooked D.C. to the south and the suburb of Cleveland Park on the north side. Just before one reached the main entrance, the north vista opened out to the wooded area surrounding the mansion. It was truly a sight to see. Cars lined the road, and people were still filing into the house for what was surely going to be yet another party of the century thrown by Marjorie. Courtland had met the Davieses at another event when Courtland first arrived in D.C. Marjorie had cornered him and insisted that he come to her next soiree. That was over a year ago.

"Come back for me within an hour or so," Courtland said to Harold from the back of his car. "I'm sure I will be partied out by then."

"Yes, sir," Harold said. "I'll be waiting for you right here."

Courtland got out of the car and headed toward the main

entrance of the house when he saw Jack Kennedy get out of a car, along with his sister Eunice. Courtland and Eunice had dated a couple of times, but both decided they made much better friends than suitors. Eunice was always good for some laughs though. Courtland's mother, Millicent, and Mrs. Rose Kennedy, her good friend, had been heartbroken when Courtland and Eunice didn't seem to connect with each other, but Eunice was quick to say she had a brother for life in Courtland, and that was better than a boyfriend or husband any day.

Jack looked over at Courtland and smiled, throwing up his hand to wave. Courtland could tell that Jack wasn't any more excited to see him than Courtland was to see Jack. Their paths crossed frequently due to politics, but Courtland didn't think Jack took his career very seriously.

"Senator Kingsley," he said. "Good to see you." Jack was not a fashion plate. His clothes always looked a size or two too big for him, and they were always a bit crumpled and wrinkled. Jack was wearing a tuxedo, but it did not have the pristine look that Courtland's did.

"Good to see you, Representative Kennedy," Courtland said. "And Eunice, you are looking lovely as ever." He went over and kissed her on the cheek, but she laughed and swatted his arm playfully. She was wearing a modest hunter-green evening gown with a Peter Pan collar. She looked relaxed and stately as always.

"Aww, cut it out, Kingsley. The politicking doesn't begin until you enter through yonder doors. Remember you used to call me EuNicorn? Be that Courtland. Not this stuffy, D.C.-savvy guy you're pretending to be," she said, then whispered in Courtland's ear, "I saw your underbelly, Kingsley. Don't lose that vulnerable part of yourself; it's what makes you human."

"I hear you," Courtland said. The three of them all laughed and walked toward the entrance together where Mrs. Davies was standing. The smile on her face became even more pronounced when she saw the three of them.

"Well, I declare. A Kingsley and two Kennedys all on the same night," she said with a laugh. "My party just became interesting. How did I get lucky enough to get you young people to grace me with your presence?"

Jack Kennedy kissed her on her cheek and spoke with that New England drawl of his that had all of the ladies, regardless of their age, swooning at his every word.

Eunice took the older lady's hands in hers. "We are the lucky ones, Mrs. Davies. Your soirees are always the talk of the town."

"You are very kind." the older woman said. "But don't you worry. There are plenty of young people here for you all to socialize with, including my daughter, Dina, and her husband, Stanley. Courtland, I think Stanley has about as many medals as you do from the war."

"Your son-in-law was quite the pilot, so I heard, and very deserving of every medal he has received," Courtland said diplomatically.

"Mrs. Davies, I think I see someone we know over there. We'll see you later," Eunice said, taking her brother and Courtland by the arm, leading them away. When they were out of earshot from Mrs. Davies, Eunice whispered loudly, "Let's go find food and libations, boys."

The three of them went inside where the majority of the party-goers were already drinking, eating, and dancing. A live band was finishing some Benny Goodman tune, only to follow up with music by Artie Shaw. Eunice directed her brother and Courtland to the food table, which was filled with every delicacy one could imagine. Negro men in white tuxes were helping to get people through the food line quickly. Before long, the three of them had found a room toward the back of the house that was relatively quiet and easy for conversation to take place. The room was elaborate in its décor, filled with Victorian and eighteenth-century artwork and furniture. Eunice and Courtland sat on the long, velvet-covered couch, and Jack stretched out in a dark walnut Victorian lounge chair. Courtland and Jack had piled their plates high with roast beef, mashed potatoes with gravy, mixed vegetables, and anything else they could fit on it.

Eunice, on the other hand, had a plate with a dab of this and a dab of that, but she quickly pushed her plate aside, instead plopping down on the couch with a Cuban cigar, which she promptly lit.

"You're not eating?" Courtland asked with a slight smile.

"Nope. Going to enjoy this cigar and the company. So, Courtland, we heard about your father," she said. "Is Mr. Nap feeling better?"

Courtland gratefully took a bite of roast beef. "Yes, he is doing much better. Before I left, he was already back to barking out orders to everyone."

"Bless him," Eunice said with a smile. "I know Mother spoke to Mrs. Millicent the other day. You all let us know if there is anything we can do."

"I will," Courtland said, but then he turned his attention to Jack. "So, Jack, when are you going to join me over in the senate?" Courtland asked, causing Eunice to groan.

"And here we go," she said, shaking her head. "You boys can't go five minutes without talking shop."

Courtland grinned. Although he and Jack Kennedy were not close friends, they did like egging each other along when the opportunity arose.

"Considering how rough things are going over there in the senate, I might just stay put for a while," Jack said, leaning back in his seat, stretching out his long legs. Courtland knew the stretching was as much about Jack's back issues as it was about him simply getting comfortable. Courtland could relate because his leg had been bothering him since he made it home from his trip to Parsons.

"We do have some work to do over on my side of the hill, but things are coming along," Courtland said. "We are making some headway, in spite of what you and others might think. Now, I have noticed that you have been away a good deal. Has D.C. lost its luster for you already? Are you sure you aren't working on another campaign? Governor of Massachusetts maybe?"

Jack laughed, wagging his finger at Courtland. "I will never tell a tale until I have to. I am still young and still weighing all of my options. My life is a vast and endless pool before me. I have no reason to feel rushed to do anything politically. What about you? Are you getting antsy for more power?"

Before Courtland could respond, a young woman in a very stylish sleeveless, winter-white evening gown entered the room.

"Oh, excuse me," she said, although it was clear she had no qualms about being in this room. "I didn't know anyone was in here. Should I leave?" Both Courtland and Jack stood, Courtland a bit quicker than Jack.

"You need not leave," Courtland said, eyeing the woman curiously. She seemed familiar to him, but he couldn't quite place her. "Come and join us. I assume you were trying to get away from the social aspects of this party the same as we were. Consider this the young curmudgeons' room."

She laughed and walked over to one of the chairs across from Courtland. "Thank you for the invitation. I gladly accept."

"And what is your name?" Jack asked, looking at the young woman appreciatively as he and Courtland took their seats again.

"My name is Madeleine Gillibrand. Courtland, I met you at your father's birthday party," she said, "but we didn't get much of a chance to talk."

"Yes," Courtland said sheepishly, suddenly recognizing the young woman he had expertly avoided all night at his father's party. "Nice to see you again."

"Same," she said, crossing her legs seductively as she continued to make eye contact with Courtland.

Not to be outdone, Jack Kennedy turned on the New England charm. "So what brings you to D.C.? This is a long ways from Georgia."

"I work here in the congressional office of Senator Stewart

from Tennessee. I am secretary to his secretary. He and my father are friends, so this opportunity availed itself, and I took advantage of it. Before that, I was a struggling actress. I was an extra in *George Washington Slept Here* on Broadway when I met Dina Merrill, Mrs. Davies's daughter. Dina and I became fast friends, and she has pulled me along from one social event to another ever since. I think she is hoping to find me a husband. Between my friends and my family, everyone seems to think I need that little gold band around my finger as soon as possible."

"That is quite the story. Nice to meet you, Madeleine," Eunice said, taking a long puff from her cigar. "I am—"

Madeleine threw back her head and laughed heartily. "Oh, I know who you are. I know who all of you are, so you can save your introductions. You three are extremely memorable and notable, Miss Eunice Kennedy, and I think they refer to Jack and Courtland as the Rowdy Boys of Washington."

Eunice laughed too. "Yes, that is us. In the flesh."

"So you aren't interested in getting married someday?" Courtland asked with mild curiosity. The beautiful blonde was quite intriguing, Courtland had to admit. He could tell Miss Madeleine Gillibrand was the kind of woman who got what she wanted when she wanted it.

"No, I am not opposed to getting married, but when I do, he will have to be the most powerful man in town," she said.

"The most powerful man in town? You mean this town?" Eunice repeated. "You are referring to the president of the United States? That man?"

"I like it here in D.C., but I have my sights set on one particular address, so the man I marry will have to be either on his way there or already in residence," she said.

Everyone laughed except for Madeleine. Courtland noticed a determined look on the young woman's face. He couldn't believe she truly thought it would be that easy for her to will herself into living at 1600 Pennsylvania Avenue.

"So you see yourself as the First Lady of the United States?" Eunice asked with an incredulous look. "You do know that role is not an elected position? The odds are not in your favor of accomplishing that particular *coup d'état*, dear one."

"Listen, I already know what being a wealthy man's wife looks like just from my parents' relationship alone. If I wanted, I could have the pick of the litter back in Tennessee, but that is not what I want." Madeleine smiled as if she were speaking to individuals who were a tad bit slow.

Courtland was greatly amused by the conversation. If nothing else, Madeleine Gillibrand was a confident woman who clearly had a plan in mind for her ascension to the throne.

"And what, exactly, is it you want besides snagging the next president of the United States?" Courtland asked with a bemused look.

Madeleine held herself straight and postured in her chair. "I want a powerful man—a man so powerful that kings and international dignitaries acquiesce to his ideas and thoughts. That is the kind of man I plan to marry when the time is right." She looked from Courtland to Jack, causing both men to laugh.

Courtland didn't mind a woman who knew what she wanted, but he wasn't exactly sure what he thought about this young woman. Madeleine was definitely an original.

For the rest of the evening, Courtland sat back and watched Jack Kennedy flirt ridiculously with Madeleine, who responded nicely to his suggestive double entendres, but she never took his bait completely.

"I think we are boring Courtland to death with this line of conversation," Eunice said, reaching over and grabbing Courtland's hand. "My brother can be somewhat of a one note."

Courtland laughed. "I'm fine, and the conversation is fine too.

I just need a breath of cool D.C. air. I'll return in a bit," he said and excused himself and went outside. Madeleine was a beautiful woman, but she was not the kind he wanted in his life, so he was more than happy to leave her to Jack, who never met a woman he didn't want to wax poetic with. Before Courtland had time to breathe in the coldness of the night, he was approached by Edward T. Folliard, a reporter he recognized from *The Washington Post*.

"Senator Kingsley, would you like to make a statement about a bombing that occurred approximately a week or so ago at a Negro eating establishment where you were reported to have been present when it occurred?" Folliard asked.

Folliard was well known in D.C. He had covered leaders from Calvin Coolidge to the current president and was well known for his hard-hitting journalistic style. Just a couple of years ago, Folliard had done a story about a hate group from Atlanta called the Columbians that had garnered much attention and caused a great deal of embarrassment for local Georgia politicians who couldn't seem to control the group or its leaders. Courtland knew the bombing incident at Eva's restaurant would appeal to Folliard, who had already won a Pulitzer for his journalistic work, and clearly he was seeking another. This story involving Courtland, a well-known senator from Georgia; Eva, a prominent Negro businesswoman; and a whole cadre of powerful Negro men and women like Adam Clayton Powell Jr. and Mary McLeod Bethune was filled with just the type of intrigue that would keep Folliard nosing around until he found what he was looking for.

"Mr. Folliard," Courtland said with a tight smile. "You should know that I will not talk about an ongoing investigation. I have no comment."

Courtland tried to move around Folliard, but the older man stood firm. Short of pushing Folliard out of the way, Courtland was trapped.

"Surely you can answer a few questions, Senator," Folliard said coolly. "This story isn't going to go away, sir, so either get in front of it or get mowed down by it. Your choice."

"What story?" Courtland asked. "A Negro business had an incident. If you have any questions, Mr. Folliard, you should take them to the police. I have nothing more to say about any of it. Now, if you don't mind, sir, I would like to go back into the party."

Folliard moved out of Courtland's way, but he stopped him cold with his words.

"Rumor has it that the police may have played a role in the entire incident," Folliard said. Courtland turned around.

"Rumor?" Courtland repeated. "I thought you were a top-notch reporter. I didn't think Pulitzer Prize winners relied on rumor to write their stories."

"Rumor also has it that some powerful people are trying to shut down the civil rights movement that is taking place throughout this country," Folliard said, clearly ignoring Courtland's slight. "Some say these Negro leaders are becoming too big for their britches, so some very powerful white men are willing to do whatever they have to to shut this down, including bombing Negro businesses, churches, and homes."

Courtland knew he had to tread lightly on this subject. "Again, this has nothing to do with me. If you have information of the magnitude you are suggesting, you should contact the FBI or the attorney general. I'm just a lowly junior senator. I can't help you."

"Well, let's go at this from a different angle. On Sunday, you were in attendance at a meeting that had many of the nation's movers and shakers in the Negro community present also, correct?" Folliard asked.

"What would be your point?" Courtland asked in a measured voice.

"Well, your presence at the meeting would imply you support their cause," Folliard said. "Is that true, sir?"

"I have no comment," Courtland said, starting to walk away again.

"I am close to figuring out who all of these powerful men are who are trying to shut down civil rights in places like Georgia, Mississippi, and Alabama, specifically, and now I guess I can add Washington, D.C., to that illustrious list. I will come up with those names, but already, one name seems to keep making its way onto my list," Folliard said.

"Is that so?" Courtland asked, but already he had a sense of foreboding.

"Courtland Hardiman Kingsley III, otherwise known as Nap Kingsley, your father. His name keeps coming up when I dig deep into some of the most violent acts that have been happening in the state of Georgia," Folliard said. "Lynchings. Beatings. Bombings. You name it. I don't have anything airtight yet, but all roads seem to lead back to your father and his cronies. I can't say if he was involved in this bombing, but it wouldn't surprise me. Of course, one wouldn't think he would do something that could harm his son, but then, maybe he didn't know you would be at that meeting. I wonder what his thoughts would be about your involvement with the civil rights movement."

Courtland came back to Folliard and stood menacingly over the man who, to his credit, did not flinch. "Be careful, Mr. Folliard. Be careful with your words and your accusations."

"Oh, I am careful, Senator Kingsley," Folliard said in a calm voice. "I do not throw out idle comments, and I always check my sources. Your father is very meticulous about his actions, but here of late, some of his words have been problematic, to put it mildly."

"My father is recovering from a stroke, Mr. Folliard," Courtland said. "He is no threat to anyone but himself thanks to those damn cigars and whiskey. Like a lot of Southern people of a particular age, he says things, but that's it. Talk. Nothing more, nothing less. Are we understood?"

Folliard put his pencil and paper into the pocket of his jacket. "Oh yes. We are understood, Senator Kingsley, and my sympathies go out to you and your family. Hopefully my investigation won't cause any additional stress to your father's already weakened state."

"Good evening, Mr. Folliard," Courtland said and walked back into the house. He was ready to leave and get home and call his father to figure out what if anything was true about the reporter's words.

Courtland looked at his watch. It was approximately ten o'clock, much later than he had intended to stay. He went and found the hostess, Mrs. Davies, to say his goodbyes, but then he ran into Madeleine.

"Hello again, Senator Kingsley," she said. "I thought I must have scared you off with my forthcomingness."

"No," he said, doing his best to remain polite. "I just figured you were more likely to make it to the White House on the arm of Jack Kennedy than me. You two will be a match made in political heaven."

"Oh, one never knows," she said, placing her hand gently on his arm. "Good evening, Senator."

"Good evening, Madeleine."

Courtland lightly kissed Madeleine's hand and then walked briskly toward the front door. He was determined to get home in time to call his father. He did not want to believe the insinuation of the reporter, but he also knew better than to dismiss the claims without first asking. When Courtland got outside, Harold was waiting for him in front of the mansion. The drive home was quick, and once they arrived, Courtland said good night to Harold and hurried into the house. He went to his office, sat at his desk, and dialed his parents' number. After a few rings, Dulcie Matthews picked up.

"Kingsley residence," she said.

"Hello, Mrs. Matthews," he said. "Is Pops still awake?"

"I don't know, Courtland," she said. "I'll go check."

Courtland began massaging his knee while he waited.

"Courtland," his father said, his voice slightly slurred still, but strong, "what's going on? I figured you would be partying it up all night tonight. No one there piqued your interest?"

"Pops," Courtland said, ignoring his father's words, "tonight I was approached by a reporter who seems to think you might be up to some dirty business. Do you have any clue what I am talking about?"

"Can't say that I do," Nap said, but Courtland could hear the guarded tone of his voice.

"This reporter seems to think you and some other men might be involved in some illegal behavior against Negroes. Bombings, to be exact. Are you sure you don't know what I'm talking about?"

"What evidence did this reporter give you?" Nap asked in a tight voice.

"Nothing," Courtland admitted. "He mentioned your name, but he did not offer me any type of evidence."

"Then that's the end of that," Nap said in a decisive voice. "Son, I am rather tired. Give me a call tomorrow or the next day."

Before Courtland could say any more, his father hung up the phone.

"We will finish this conversation, Nap Kingsley," Courtland said. "I promise you that."

But then Courtland realized he had another call to make. Eva. He couldn't leave her defenseless if this information were true. Courtland dialed her home number, and after several rings, Pearson picked up the phone.

"Hello," he said, sounding sleepy.

"Pearson, this is Courtland," he said.

"Why are you calling my home so late, Senator Kingsley?" Pearson asked.

"I need to talk to Eva about some information I was told by a reporter," Courtland said. "But let me start by telling you first." After Courtland was done telling him everything he knew, Pearson went quiet and then he finally spoke.

"She will want to hear it from you," Pearson said. Then after a long pause he added, "If your father or anyone else threatens a member of my family, I might forget for a moment that I am a man of the cloth."

"I understand," Courtland said, and he did. He would be feeling the same way if someone called him with similar news concerning the women in his life. Courtland waited until he heard Eva's voice.

"Hello, Courtland," she said. "Is everything alright?"

"Eva, there is something I need to talk to you about—something I found out concerning the explosion," he said.

"What did you find out?" she asked.

He could hear the hesitancy in her voice. He wished to God he could spare her this news, but he knew there was no way around it. She had to know what he knew.

"I saw a reporter tonight at a party. He approached me, saying he had some information I needed to know. Eva, he knew I was at the restaurant on the day of the explosion," Courtland said.

"Go on," she said slowly as if she was bracing herself for the worst, and of course the worst parts were yet to come.

"The reporter didn't know—or at least he didn't reveal to me— exactly who was involved in the explosion, but he said it was related to the civil rights activities that were going on that day," Courtland said. "The reporter also said that some members of the police were most likely involved."

"Oh *mon Dieu*," she whispered loudly. *Oh my God.* He could hear the trembling in her voice. "Pearson and Frédérique tried to warn me."

Courtland felt terrible for revealing this information to her over the phone. He wished desperately that he was where she was so he could take her into his arms.

"I'm sorry, Eva," Courtland said, not knowing what else to say.

"I knew that awful Lieutenant Stevens was up to no good. I

knew it," she said in a whisper as if she were talking to herself. "Is that all he said?"

"No," Courtland said, taking a deep breath, and then he told her the rest as it pertained to his father. "Eva, I don't want to believe my father had anything to do with this or any of the incidents that have taken place in the South."

Eva snorted. "You can't believe what you are saying. Every racist who ever lived was someone's father, son, husband, nephew, cousin. They didn't just spring up out of the earth. I get that you want to think the best of your father. God knows I have made enough excuses for my own, but at some point we have to acknowledge their weaknesses and their frailties, if not to others, at least to ourselves."

Courtland started to further defend Nap, but he knew he couldn't absolutely convince anyone that Nap was innocent. "I don't know what else to say, Eva."

Eva was silent for a few moments. "Thank you for calling me, Courtland. I know it couldn't have been easy for you to share these details. I truly do appreciate your honesty and your candor. This is a lot to digest. I need to go. Please, if you learn anything else, call me."

"I will," he said. "Eva, I'm sorry, and I need you to know I will not stop until I get to the bottom of all of this."

"Be careful what you promise, Courtland," she said, her voice sounding tired and sad. "Good night."

Courtland gently hung up the phone. His office was dark, and there wasn't a single star shining through the trees. It was eerie outside, matching perfectly how Courtland was feeling on the inside.

SEVENTEEN

Eva

Eva awakened the next morning with a start. She sat straight up in her bed, sweat pouring down her face even though she was cold and shivering. She was disoriented at first, trying to remember what could have caused her to awaken feeling so uneasy, and then she remembered—the phone call from Courtland. Now she remembered her dreams too. All night she had been running from Lieutenant Stevens and a group of white faceless men. They were chasing her in the woods, and she could hear dogs barking and howling behind her. She didn't have on any shoes, and the clothes she wore were threadbare. The rocks, sticks, and briars were making every step excruciating, and the night air was so cold she could feel her teeth chattering, but she knew she couldn't slow down. She tried to scream for help, but no sound would come out of her mouth. Eva was thankful to finally be awake. She slipped out of the bed and went to her prayer window, not even bothering to put on her robe and house slippers. She didn't immediately reach for her rosary like normal; instead, she prayed from her heart, as her sister called it, in the language of her grandmother Bettine.

"*Cher dieu, j'ai peur. Aidez-moi, s'il vous plaît,*" she said as tears streamed down her face. *Dear God, I am afraid. Please help me.*

Eva was not used to feeling weak or helpless, but that was how she was feeling now. Somehow these men filled with hatred were targeting her and so many people she cared about. And on top of that, one of the men might be Courtland's father. She couldn't wrap her brain around that, so her prayers centered around asking God to remove her fear and grant her inner peace. Eventually, tradition called out to her, and Eva reached for her rosary and began the familiar prayers.

Usually she found peace when she prayed the rosary, but peace seemed to be evasive this morning. She decided she would go to Saturday morning Mass at St. Augustine, the church she regularly attended if she didn't join her sister and brother-in-law at their church. She looked at the clock by her bed and saw that she only had half an hour to get ready and get out the door. She hurriedly showered and changed into her favorite chocolate-brown wool dress.

Once she was done primping, Eva hurried outside, both to get out of the cold and to quickly get to her car so she could make it to Mass on time. It only took a few minutes for her to get to St. Augustine. Before she got out of the car, she carefully placed her veil over her head. She saw several people she knew, but she didn't feel up to having a conversation, so she waved at them and hurried into the building. Normally she sat near the front, but today she sat down in the back corner near the door.

When the service started, she tried to immerse herself in what was being said and done, but her mind continued to be crowded with the conversation she had with Courtland the previous night. She felt unshed tears threatening to fall and a wail forming inside her chest so strong that she had to catch her breath to stop it from coming out. Just when she thought she might run out of the church, someone slipped into the pew beside her and pulled her into a strong embrace. Her blurred eyes were able to make out the calm and ethereal face of Sister Gloria Therese.

Sister Gloria Therese was a beautiful, dark-skinned woman of Haitian descent. Eva first met Sister Gloria Therese when she was a student at St. Augustine Catholic Church and Sister Gloria Therese was her Latin teacher. She and Eva had spoken often about her life and her religious journey, when, for a brief period of time, Eva had thought about entering into the sisterhood, but conversations with Sister Therese had helped her come to the conclusion that becoming a nun was not the path for her.

"I will pray for you and with you," Sister Gloria Therese said softly in her ear. Eva nodded. After the service was over, the two women hugged.

"No matter what you are going through, dear one, find solace in God, for he will always carry you to a place where troubles cease to exist. God's grace will always suffice," Sister Gloria Therese said, kissing Eva on both cheeks and then making her way through the crowd. Eva exited the building before she was forced to come face-to-face with those she knew. By the time she got home, she was feeling decidedly better. As soon as she entered the house, Frédérique called out to her from the kitchen.

"Breakfast will be ready in a minute!" she said.

"Thank you, sissy!" Eva called back, smiling at the familiarity of it all. No matter what the circumstances, Frédérique believed in her own rituals of feeding the spirit and the body.

Eva removed her veil and put it and her coat in the closet, went and washed her hands in the guest bathroom, and then walked into the kitchen where her sister was placing fried ham onto a platter. She was already dressed for the day, but she had on an apron that covered her from her neck down to her knees. Eva saw that Frédérique had also made oatmeal, boiled eggs, and homemade biscuits. Eva hadn't thought she was hungry before, but she couldn't wait until she could begin eating.

"Where's Pearson?" Eva asked just as her brother-in-law entered the room, dressed casually in black slacks and a black long-sleeved shirt.

"My nose led me right here," he said, first kissing Frédérique on her cheek and then Eva. "How are my two favorite girls who are soon to become three?"

Frédérique smiled, but there was a hint of sadness to her eyes. "I'm fine. I spoke to Johnny Mac this morning. He was asking me what things he needed to get for Daisy. I told him there was no rush, and if he wanted to send us something later, he could. Bless his heart, I thought he would cry again. That poor man has shed more tears over that child than any person should have to."

Pearson hugged his wife. "Thank you for preserving his dignity. There is no greater sorrow for a man than to feel like he can't take care of his family."

"Eva, Johnny Mac also wanted me to apologize to you about Simon not being able to work at the restaurant," Frédérique said. "I told him that we all were grateful that Simon was going to be going to a good home and he shouldn't think twice about the work arrangement."

Eva picked up the platter of ham and the bowl of boiled eggs and started walking toward the dining room. "No reason for them to feel bad about that at all. If the truth be told, I was just trying to come up with a way for Simon to help his family and have access to food he could take home."

Once they were seated and had said grace, Eva decided to share an idea.

"Pearson . . . Frédérique . . . I have a thought I wanted to share with you," Eva said. Both of them looked at her expectantly, so she continued. "I want to start giving away the leftover food at the end of the evening, and I wondered if you would be okay if my staff dropped it off at Second Street for people to pick up. My staff can stay there and make sure it gets handed out to the people. I would do it at St. Augustine, but I know the community primarily goes to Second Street and would probably feel more comfortable picking up meals from there. What do you think?"

Eva looked at Pearson as tears started to stream down his face. "You are such a good soul," he said, reaching over and taking her hand. "I know that your grandmother, mother, and father would be so proud of the woman you have become, Eva. We would be honored to help you with this mission, and I know there will be some very appreciative people in the community."

They continued to talk about how to make everything work, and Eva was so excited she wanted to get started immediately. She called the restaurant and spoke to Chef du Passe. He assured her he would put together a team to deliver the food at the end of the day. She offered to come by before she and Frédérique went shopping, but he insisted she enjoy her day with Frédérique.

When she was done with the phone call, she turned to Frédérique, who was standing beside her. "Are you ready to go buy out some stores?"

Frédérique nodded. "I have been waiting my entire life for this moment. Let's go," she said, and the two sisters left arm in arm to go buy out the stores for their newest family member, Daisy.

EIGHTEEN

Eva

Eva lay quietly in her bed, waiting for the alarm clock to go off at 6:00 a.m. She knew she was minutes away from the bells chiming, but she was tired. She and Frédérique had shopped until late in the afternoon and then had stayed up until the wee hours of the morning preparing the bedroom for Daisy. Pearson had all of the painting done when they arrived home, and shortly after that, the furniture was delivered. The room was filled with pinks and yellows, from the walls to the curtains to the little rug in front of Daisy's bed. The room was most definitely fit for a little princess, exactly what Frédérique wanted.

They had experienced a bit of a scare right as they walked into the house the previous night. Pearson was on the phone with Daisy's father, Johnny Mac, who called and said he didn't know if he was making the right decision by leaving Daisy with them. He said he didn't want anyone to think he was just throwing his daughter away, and he also said Simon, her brother, was taking it extra hard that they were leaving Daisy behind. Eva had worried that everything was going to fall apart. She didn't say this to Frédérique, and after Frédérique and Pearson were able to talk to Johnny Mac, Eva was relieved to hear that they were going to move forward with allowing

Daisy to stay, so Eva and Frédérique began decorating in earnest. Around ten or so, the phone rang again, and this time it was for Eva. It was Wendell.

"I just wanted to make sure we were still on for tomorrow," Wendell said, sounding not quite as confident as he normally did. For some reason, his hesitancy made her feel better about agreeing to go to church and later out to lunch with him. She did not like a braggadocious person or someone so stuck on themselves that they forgot to think about others. She liked that Wendell had spoken to the police about Simon's case and made sure it was okay for him to move to Virginia, so she was willing to leave herself open to the possibility of seeing Wendell. She remembered what Adam had said about the restaurant not being a person who would love her back.

"Yes," she had said. "We are still on for tomorrow. And we don't have to go out to eat, Wendell. My sister always makes a huge Sunday dinner. You are welcome to come here and eat."

"No," Wendell said, the confidence returning to his voice. "I would rather take you out and have you all to myself."

"Very well," she had said.

Now, with morning approaching, she wondered if she should have insisted on eating with Pearson and Frédérique. Did she really want that much alone time with the young attorney? Before she could talk herself out of it one way or another, she heard a knock at the door.

"Eva, are you up?"

It was Frédérique, of course. Sunday morning was their time to get caught up on each other's lives. Eva would share any news she had heard from customers or her staff about the things that were happening on U Street—from who was playing at Club Bali on a Saturday night to what Negro leaders were planning next in the community. Frédérique would talk about church politics and her women's ministry.

So Eva was pleased to hear her sister at the door. She had

wondered if Frédérique would be too sleepy or too excited over Daisy to come in for her sister session, as they called it.

"Come in, Freddie," Eva said as she sat up in bed.

Frédérique walked into the room, still wearing her robe. It almost felt like when they were children, when Frédérique would leave her room and come to Eva's and climb into the bed. Eva put her arms around her sister, hugging her tightly. "Are you excited?"

Frédérique smiled, her eyes brimming with tears. "Very. I could hardly sleep at all last night. Pearson and I finally got up an hour ago and just talked and talked about what it was going to mean to have a little girl in the house."

"She has already taken to you and Pearson," Eva said, and it was true.

Eva had gotten home early from the restaurant the other night, and she had watched how her sister and Daisy had bonded in the short time they had spent together. Daisy would make small grunts of approval whenever Frédérique would give her kisses.

"But sis, she is going to be a lot of work. You don't know whether she is going to develop beyond where she is now. There are so many unknowns."

Eva didn't want to sound like sour grapes, but she also didn't want her sister to enter into this situation blindly. She had been all for them watching Daisy during the week, but this new decision that happened so quickly—to basically adopt the child, taking on all of her mental and physical issues—it was a lot.

"I know there are a lot of unknowns, but it doesn't matter to me," Frédérique said. "I truly believe God put her in our lives for a purpose. Just look at how quickly everything happened. What are the chances of us meeting this beautiful family in need at the beginning of last week, and now, the beginning of this week, we have a child to love and help? With or without issues, I will love her just as much as if she was a child with no special problems."

"What time is Johnny Mac bringing her over?" Eva asked, trying to see the silver lining that Frédérique was determined to focus on.

"In about an hour," Frédérique said, getting up from the bed. "I need to go make breakfast and get ready for church. I want them to have a nice, relaxing meal before they get on the road to Richmond. I was telling Pearson with Richmond being so close to us—only two hours away—there's no reason we can't take Daisy to see Simon or have Simon come visit for a weekend. This can work for everyone concerned. Daisy can have the best of all possible worlds."

"Absolutely," Eva said with a smile, even though in her heart she was still very unsure of how all of this was going to work out.

"What are you going to wear today?" Frédérique asked.

"My burgundy suit that we bought in New York last year," she said.

It was a Lilli Ann velvet jacket and skirt with fur on the collar and the sleeves. Until now, she had not found a good reason to wear it.

"You are going to knock that young man off his feet," Frédérique said, smiling broadly. "Are you nervous?"

Eva nodded. "A little bit. Okay, a lot. I know how to run a business all day long, but I am not one hundred percent sure how to date, and you, Mother, and Pearson are to blame. You encouraged me to be independent, but you didn't teach me how to be social with men."

Frédérique laughed. "We didn't teach you because we didn't want you to be social with men."

Eva laughed along with her sister. "Well, be that as it may, I am a bit socially awkward when it comes to knowing how to behave around the other sex."

"Just be yourself, darling," Frédérique said. "That is all you ever have to do. And if, for some reason, being yourself is not enough for some man, then you don't want any part of him."

"Thank you for your advice," Eva said. "Freddie, I know you don't want me to talk about Courtland, and maybe it is in poor taste to bring him up now that I am committed to going out with another man, but I can't get him off my mind, even with everything he told me about the bombing and his father. He just keeps invading my thoughts. Am I terrible?"

Frédérique sat back down on the bed. "Of course not. You can't help your feelings, Eva. You can only help how you act on those feelings. You already know how this particular story will end. Why put yourself through that heartbreak? I know Mother is a sore subject between us, but use what she went through as a cautionary tale. Think about it: We have a whole family out there we don't even know, and they don't want to know about us. Why put yourself and any future children you might have in that position?"

Eva nodded in agreement. She knew everything her sister was saying made sense, and goodness knows she had spent enough sleepless nights wondering about her father's other daughters and son, whom they only knew about from the death notice in *The Times-Picayune*. After their mother died and they were going through her things, they found the cutout article from the obituary section of the newspaper. It read: *Valéry René Arquette leaves to mourn his wife, Béatrice LeBlanc Arquette, and their three daughters, Calixte, 17; Céline, 14; Claudette, 12; and a son, Valéry René Arquette III, 6.*

Eva had cried for hours because their names weren't in the notice, but Frédérique had only gotten increasingly angry.

"Why cry for someone who didn't care enough about us to make sure such slights didn't happen?" she had snapped at Eva, but then had turned right around and gathered her crying sister into her arms, rocking her and promising her that things would be better eventually.

Now Frédérique was pretty much repeating the same message. She reached out and stroked Eva's hair. "Don't go down that road, sweetheart. All it will do is cause you heartbreak."

Eva nodded. As much as she loved her mother and father, their choices cost Eva and her sister more than anyone would ever know, including their parents. But she just couldn't get Courtland out of her mind. They had only seen each other a handful of times and spoken on the phone, but those moments meant so much to her, and she couldn't figure out exactly why. Did he remind her of her father? Was she doomed to repeat her mother's past? Eva didn't know the answer. She just knew she was confused and torn, and she didn't know what to do about it. She was shocked she hadn't worn her rosary down to powder, she had prayed so much for God to remove her attraction to Courtland. If the truth be known, she was lonely. She wanted the affections of a man, but not a man whose own father might have tried to kill her or others like her.

"Thank you, Freddie," Eva said, reaching over and hugging her sister. "You don't always tell me what I want to hear, but you are always honest, and for that I thank you."

"You're welcome," Frédérique said. "I better go cook. You are going to have a wonderful time with Wendell. And if you don't, let Pearson know and he will give that young man a piece of his mind."

Eva smiled. "So true. I'll be down shortly." Eva watched as her sister walked out of the room. For a moment, Eva allowed her head to fall back on her pillow as she looked toward her window where the sun was starting to rise over the treetops.

Eva was glad she had gone to Mass yesterday. She would miss it today. She loved Pearson and his sermons, but the impromptu nature of Baptist worship just didn't appeal to her. Although she and Wendell hadn't really discussed her religion much, she wondered what his family would think about him dating a practicing Catholic.

When Frédérique met and fell in love with Pearson, the Baptist church was a novelty to both of them. Frédérique took to it immediately, loving the more demonstrative worship—the fervent, unrehearsed prayers; the soulful singing; and the interactive nature of worship—but Eva loved the pageantry and the ritual of the Catholic church. Unlike her sister, who had joined the Baptist church and gotten baptized, Eva had held back. Neither Pearson nor Frédérique had questioned her about it. They both believed religion was a personal journey each person needed to take on their own.

Eva got up and knelt in front of her window facing the backyard, the sun's rays streaming through the window, touching her face almost as if they were the fingertips of God. She made the sign of the cross and began saying the Apostles' Creed in French, just like her grandmother had taught both her and Frédérique.

"*Je crois en Dieu, le Père tout puissant, créateur du ciel et de la terre. Et en Jésus-Christ, son Fils unique, notre Seigneur,*" she said softly. *I believe in God, the Father almighty, Creator of heaven and earth. And in Jesus Christ, His only Son, our Lord.*

Once Eva finished saying the rosary, she got up and got dressed. She spent a little extra time with her makeup, so when she finally did make it downstairs, Simon, Johnny Mac, and Daisy were sitting in the living room with Pearson and Frédérique.

Simon, Johnny Mac, and Pearson stood when she walked into the room. She noticed Simon was holding his sister, and all three of them were dressed in what were probably their best clothes. Frédérique and Pearson were sitting together on the couch, and Eva could tell that Frédérique's nerves were shot. Everyone looked uncomfortable. Eva knew this day was not going to be easy, but she didn't know it would be this bad. Simon's eyes were shining with tears, and Johnny Mac looked like he just wanted to grab his children and run. Daisy was the only one who seemed relatively happy. She was gurgling and sucking on her fingers.

"Good morning, everyone," Eva said.

"Good morning, Miss Eva," Johnny Mac said quietly.

She could hear the sadness in his voice. The pain she heard made her want to go and hug him, but she didn't think that would be appropriate. The last thing she wanted to do was embarrass him.

Simon didn't even respond. He just held his sister tighter,

causing her to squirm. Eva decided to take matters into her own hands. "Simon, why don't you and I go make the coffee for the adults and Ovaltine for you and Daisy? Do you think you could let my sister hold Daisy while you help me with the beverages?"

A huge tear rolled down Simon's face, but he looked over at Frédérique and quietly went to her and handed her Daisy. Eva led the teenager into the kitchen. She didn't want to embarrass him by acknowledging his tears, so she pointed him toward the Ovaltine while she made a pot of coffee. For a time they worked in silence, when finally Simon spoke, his voice choked with emotion.

"She likes to suck on a cracker before she goes to sleep at night," Simon said, "and she likes to drink a glass of water first thing in the morning before she eats anything."

Eva turned and faced the young man. "I'll make sure my sister knows to give Daisy a cracker every single night, and first thing in the morning, one of us will make sure she gets a glass of water. I promise."

Simon wiped his face with the back of his hand. "She doesn't like being in a dark room. She sleeps with the light on. If you turn the light off, she'll start yelling, and it will be hard to calm her down."

"I will tell Frédérique," Eva said solemnly. "She will never be in a dark room. I promise. I know this is hard, Simon."

"No, you don't know," he said, shaking his head. "I lost my mama, and now I'm losing my sister. You don't know what that feels like."

Eva went over to Simon and put her hands on his shoulders. "I know what it is like to lose someone you love, Simon. I lost both of my parents when I was younger than you, and I thought I would never get over the pain of not seeing them, but I did. I survived, and you will survive this too. You just have to keep telling yourself that this situation is different than your mother dying. You and Daisy will only be two hours apart. You will be able to come see her here, and Frédérique and Pearson will take her to where you are. Daisy will always know that you are her big brother. That will never change."

Simon looked at Eva and nodded. This time she did pull him into her arms and give him a hug. They stood there for a moment, and then Eva gently pushed him so she could look him in the eyes again. "You are the strongest young person I have ever met. I know you will get through this. Now let's go eat some of that good breakfast my sister prepared."

Eva carried the pot of coffee, and Simon carried the two glasses of Ovaltine. Eva looked at her sister, who had Daisy sitting on her lap. Frédérique was looking like she was in heaven. The sight of her sister holding Daisy made Eva's heart sing inside. Simon and Eva sat, and Pearson said a quick prayer. Eva noticed Simon looked less stressed than he had looked before, although Johnny Mac still looked longingly at his daughter, but Eva knew he would honor their agreement.

"Johnny Mac or Simon, would you like to hold Daisy?" Frédérique asked.

Eva knew the last thing her sister wanted to do was let Daisy out of her reach, but she also knew if Johnny Mac suddenly said he couldn't let his little girl go, Frédérique would acquiesce. That was just the kind of person she was. Eva watched as both Johnny Mac and Simon shook their heads, and Simon was the one who bravely spoke.

"She needs to get used to you doing the holding," Simon said.

"That's right," Johnny Mac said hoarsely, looking over at his son with pride. "She gotta know you is her . . . her . . . her stand-in ma now."

Eva decided to excuse herself. She wanted to give them all some privacy, and she was feeling like an extra wheel. Pearson, Johnny Mac, and Simon all rose to their feet.

"Miss Eva, I just want to thank you again for everything," Johnny Mac said. "You and your family have been a blessing to mine."

"We are all family now," Eva said, and this time she did give Johnny Mac and Simon hugs. Once Eva got back upstairs, she dressed in the outfit she had put out to wear the night before, then took out her Bible and began reading. When about an hour had passed, she heard a knock at her door.

"Come in," she said, and Frédérique walked in carrying Daisy. "Have Simon and Johnny Mac left?"

"Yes, they have," Frédérique said. "I was expecting tears, but both men were stoic and told Daisy they would see her in a few weeks. She cooed and then burped, which made everyone laugh."

Eva smiled. "That's wonderful. I'm so happy."

"Sweetheart, Wendell is downstairs," Frédérique said.

Eva noticed that Frédérique had tidied up Daisy's hair and had put her in a long-sleeved pink cotton dress that was similar in shade to the pink wool suit Frédérique was wearing. They definitely looked like they belonged to each other.

"I'll be right down," Eva said, dabbing a bit of Chanel No. 5 on her wrists. "I am so happy to see you so happy, sissy."

"Thank you," Frédérique said. "God definitely works in mysterious ways. I'll see you downstairs," she said and left with the babbling little girl.

Eva checked herself once more in the mirror and then exited her room. As she walked down the stairs, Wendell, who was standing by the door with Pearson, looked up and smiled.

"Good morning," he said.

"Good morning," she said, smiling back at him.

As usual, Wendell was dressed to perfection. He was wearing a dark blue suit with a matching coat and hat.

Eva looked over at her brother-in-law. "Pearson, I'm surprised you are still here."

"Today I am going to be a guest at Second Street so I can sit with my wife and Daisy," he said. "Brother Talbert is going to deliver the message. We are about to leave now," he said as Frédérique walked into the foyer. "Looks like we can all leave together."

Pearson guided Wendell over to the coat closet where they

retrieved the women's coats. Wendell helped Eva into her fur, and then they walked together to his car, a 1946 Cadillac Series 62 convertible, he told her. "My parents gave me this car when I graduated from Morehouse."

"What a nice graduation gift," she said, settling back into the comfortable seat.

Second Street was only a few blocks away from their house, and Eva and Wendell chatted the whole way there. He was curious about Daisy and how she ended up with Frédérique and Pearson. Eva quickly filled him in on the story.

"All of this happened within a week's time?" he asked incredulously.

"Yes," Eva said. "It's hard to believe that just last Sunday someone bombed my restaurant, and now, well, so much has happened in such a short time."

When they pulled up to the church, the parking lot was filled with people. Wendell got out and opened the door for her. Eva could feel the curious eyes on her and Wendell. She waved at various ones as they walked toward the entrance to the church.

Eva did her best to stay focused on the sermon, but she couldn't help but glance every so often at Wendell. He was handsome. And he was smart and driven, everything she knew she should want in a man. But she also feared what a man like Wendell would want from her if they did continue with a relationship. Men like Wendell wanted dedicated wives and mothers for their children—women who were willing to give up everything so their men could shine. Eva couldn't see herself doing that for anyone. Maybe that was why Courtland was so appealing. She absolutely knew he would never make those demands because a true relationship between them was taboo. Off limits. Impossible. Maybe choosing an impossible man was in her blood.

"Eva, are you okay?" she heard Wendell ask.

He was looking at her curiously. She wondered how long she had been lost in thought. The service was over, and people were beginning to stand and mingle. There was a long line of people trying to get to Pearson and Frédérique. Everyone at the church knew how much they both had wanted children, and they all wanted to see Daisy. Eva hoped they didn't spook the child, but she could see from where she and Wendell were sitting that Daisy was content in Frédérique's arms.

"Yes, I'm fine," she said, looking up at Wendell and smiling.

"Are you ready to go to lunch?" he asked.

"Mm-hmm," she said. "Let me go say goodbye to my sister."

It took Eva a moment to get through the crowd, but finally she was able to get to Frédérique's side.

"We're leaving," Eva said in her sister's ear.

Frédérique looked up at Eva and smiled. "Have a good time. And really . . . have a good time, sis."

Eva nodded. "I will. See you when I get home."

Wendell was talking to one of the deacons when she walked up to them. He looked down at her. "Are you ready?"

She nodded. "Yes," she said as he helped her with her coat. He took her by her arm and guided her back outside to the parking lot to his car. It was beginning to snow. He opened the door and helped her inside, and then he hurried to his side of the car and got in.

"It looks like we might get some heavy snow today," he said.

"It sure does," she said, and then she placed her hand on his arm. "Wendell, before we leave, there is something I need to tell you."

"Okay," he said, looking at her intently.

"Wendell, I am not like most women," she started.

He laughed. "Of course you're not. That's why I—"

"No, please, let me finish," she said. "When I say I am not like most women, I mean I don't have the same aspirations as a lot of women. Getting married sounds nice, but only if it can be on my terms. I love running my restaurant, and I don't plan on giving it up when I get married—if I get married. In fact, I plan on opening more restaurants, and that means a lot of my time and energy will go toward them, not a spouse . . . not children. I like children, but I have no interest in becoming a mother anytime soon. If ever. That is a lot for anyone to process, but especially a man like you. I just don't want to mislead you."

For a moment, Wendell didn't say anything, and Eva didn't rush him. She watched as people streamed out of the church, hurrying to their cars to get out of the snow, which was coming down at a steady pace. She saw her brother-in-law and sister walking out of the church with Daisy in Pearson's arms.

Finally, Wendell spoke. "Eva, what you are saying is a lot to process, but this is our first time going out together. I promise I would never ask you to give up everything on my behalf. That would be selfish on my part. All I am after right now is your amazing company for lunch. Is that alright?"

That was not the response she was expecting Wendell to give. At all.

"Okay," she said with a broad smile. "Let's go to lunch then."

She settled back into her seat as Wendell carefully backed up and proceeded to exit the parking lot.

～

For the second time in two days, Eva found herself at Hal's restaurant, The Phoenix. She and Frédérique had eaten lunch there after they were done shopping for things for Daisy. Unlike Eva, Hal kept his restaurant open seven days a week. When she arrived, as always, Hal was at the door greeting guests. His eyes lit up when he saw her.

"Well, what did I do to deserve the honor of having Miss Eva

Cardon at my restaurant two days in a row? God truly must be looking out for me," he said with a smile. "And who is this young fellow you have with you?"

Eva shook her head and laughed. "Mr. Hal Conroy, I would like to introduce you to Wendell Moss Harrington III."

The two men said hello and shook hands, and Hal told his *maître d'* he would escort Eva and Wendell to their seats.

"I am so pleased you two chose my restaurant for your . . . outing," he said and winked at Eva. She blushed, which she knew was his mission. Hal could give her the business when he didn't agree with her on something, but most times he took great joy in teasing her. "If you will allow me to order for you . . ."

"That would be fine with me," Wendell said and looked at Eva. She nodded.

"Then I will have my waiter bring you today's special, which is *Escargot à la Bourguignonne, Salade Niçoise,* and *Ratatouille,*" he said with a smile, as if he already knew they were going to love the food.

Unlike her sister, Eva was far more of a risk taker when it came to food. Eva looked at Wendell, and he looked pleased as well.

After Hal finished taking their order, he briskly walked away. Eva noticed he was talking animatedly with one of the waiters. Probably giving him their order so Hal could go back to greeting his guests.

"So, Eva, I have been thinking about what you said," Wendell began, his face serious.

"Yes," Eva prompted, although she thought she knew where the conversation was going.

"I have only seen marriage work in one way," he said, "and Eva, I am not going to lie. I grew up in a family where the women took care of the home and the children and the men worked. I have watched my grandmother, mother, aunts, and sisters fade into the background in order for the men in their lives to shine in the foreground. I thought I wanted that—until I met you."

Eva was shocked by his words. She truly expected him to say, "Nice knowing you, but . . ." She wasn't sure how to respond. If Frédérique had overheard Wendell, she would have already been contacting the wedding dressmaker with Eva's measurements.

"Wendell, I just don't know. My plate is very full," she said. "I know what you are saying now, but I also know the novelty of a relationship can wear off soon. I see all that my sister does for her husband. Frédérique is not *just* Frédérique anymore. She is Mrs. Reverend Dr. Pearson Montgomery."

"Is that so awful?" Wendell asked.

Eva shook her head. "No. No, it isn't awful at all, but it is a restrictive lifestyle that I am not interested in right now, possibly never, and the last thing I want to do is stand before God and make promises I can't keep."

"Well, we aren't at the point of making promises to each other. However, if we want this to work, we can figure it out," he said in a determined voice right as the waiter brought them their first course. Both of them thanked the waiter, but after he left, neither of them started eating. "Eva, may I ask you a question?"

"Yes," she said. "Of course."

Wendell nodded, drummed his fingers on the table for a moment, then leaned back slightly in his chair. Eva imagined this was exactly Wendell's posture when he was about to cross-examine a witness. "Eva, are you and that white senator involved with each other?"

Eva was shocked by the question. To her knowledge, Wendell had only seen her and Courtland interact the day of the bombing. "No, we are not involved," she said carefully.

Wendell nodded, but this time he leaned forward. "Eva, do you have feelings for Senator Kingsley?"

Eva was not one to play cat-and-mouse games, so she answered the question honestly. "There is an attraction—on both of our parts, I would say—but that is all, and that is all there ever could be."

Wendell laughed bitterly. "So are we sure this conversation was about you having the ability to work and possibly not have children, or was it about the fact that you are in love with a white man?"

"I am not in love with anyone," Eva snapped, but as quickly as the words came out of her mouth, she wondered if she was being honest with Wendell. More importantly, she wondered if she was being honest with herself.

Wendell smiled and began eating his escargot. "Listen, to each her own. I am not judging you. I am just trying to figure out where I stand with you. I am not the kind of man to chase a woman, Eva. I only want to be in a relationship with someone who wants the same thing. Everything else, I figure, is negotiable."

For a moment, Eva didn't say anything, and neither did Wendell. She wanted to truly process what he'd just said. The thought of eating was gone for her, but Wendell seemed very content eating his food and waiting for her to gather her thoughts. Finally, she spoke.

She took a deep breath. "Wendell, I really like you a lot, but . . ."

Wendell put down his fork. "Don't finish the thought after the 'but,'" he said quickly. Then he laughed. "It's okay. You need to figure things out, and maybe that includes getting this unattainable white man out of your system. Do what you need to do. I can't promise you I'll be waiting, but I will be rooting for you."

Eva felt terrible. This was not how she wanted their date to go. She knew now she shouldn't have said yes. Wendell reached over and took her hand.

"Don't beat yourself up over this," Wendell said. "If the truth be known, I probably needed to get punched in the gut. I have spent most of my life getting exactly what I wanted when I wanted it. This is my time to see what it feels like not to. Now either you eat your food or I will, because this is good."

Eva smiled, and before long the awkwardness wore off, and they were both chatting like old friends. Once they were done eating and

Wendell drove her home, they sat in silence. She turned to him, placing her hand on his arm.

"Wendell, I know you think my hesitation with you is about Courtland," she said, using his name for the first time, "but it's not. Not really. It's about me figuring out who I am and what I want out of life."

Wendell nodded. "I hope you find out what it is you are trying to find," he said. "Just know that sometimes what we are looking for is right underneath our noses." He picked up her hand and kissed it lightly. "Now let me get you into your home before I start begging like a toddler for you to give me another chance."

Before she could respond, Wendell hopped out of the car and opened her door. Snow was still lightly falling. He escorted her to the front door of the house, kissed her cheek, and hurried back out to his car before she could say anything else.

Eva went inside, and Frédérique was standing on the other side of the door holding Daisy, waiting for Eva to come in.

"Hey, sissy," she said with a huge smile. "How was your . . ."

"Oh, Freddie," Eva said and went and laid her head on her sister's shoulder.

Daisy reached over and patted Eva's head. Eva looked up and smiled through her tears. "Hey there, pumpkin. Your almost Auntie Eva has made a fine mess of things."

"Come," Frédérique said and guided Eva into the parlor where Eva sat and told her sister everything.

NINETEEN

Courtland

"Take us to Chez Geneviève, Harold. We should have time," Courtland said to his driver.

Courtland wanted to take Vernon Michaels, the young Negro porter, over to meet Eva so that he could get started working and saving money.

"Yes, sir, Senator Kingsley," Harold said and drove off slowly, making sure not to hit any of the students moving to and from classes on the Howard campus where Courtland and Vernon Michaels had just finished visiting.

"Well, Vernon, what are your thoughts about Howard University?" Courtland asked once they were leaving the campus. Vernon was sitting up front with Harold, but he twisted around excitedly and faced Courtland, looking like a giddy child at Christmas.

"Senator Kingsley, that place and those people are nothing short of amazing," Vernon said, his eyes flashing with excitement, making Courtland happy once again that he had taken the young man underneath his wings. "I can't believe that many smart Negroes are all housed together in one place. It's like nothing I've ever seen before, and now I'm going to be one of them."

Courtland knew Vernon would fall for the Howard campus, but he had no idea the fall would be this hard. Vernon had hung on every word President Johnson uttered, to the point of taking notes whenever President Johnson would say something the young man deemed memorable, which was just about every other sentence. President Johnson regaled the young man with all sorts of stories about Howard University and its illustrious graduates like Thomas Wyatt Turner, Thurgood Marshall, Dr. Harry Penn, and so many more that finally, Courtland interrupted with a laugh.

"President Johnson, you had this young man sold on Howard when you greeted him at the door," Courtland said.

All three of them laughed, President Johnson loudest of all in his big, booming preacher's voice.

"They pay me well to speak nicely about this little piece of heaven near the Potomac, Senator Kingsley," President Johnson said, leaning back in his leather chair. "I don't want to cheat young Mr. Michaels out of the full measure of the Howard introduction."

"Well, I can't imagine the young man being any more enamored than he already is with your fine institution, but by all means, President Johnson, don't let me stop you, and I apologize for the interruption," Courtland said with a grin, and with that, President Johnson continued, pausing only when he saw Vernon was burning with a question or comment.

"Sir, I know I have missed the cut to enter school this semester, but . . ."

"And who says you have missed the cut?" President Johnson asked, leaning forward. "Are you a quick study?"

"Yes, sir," Vernon said, nodding rapidly. "I have read the book *Gray's Anatomy* more than once, and you could quiz me on any parts of it. I have a copy of it in my briefcase, and—"

President Johnson held up his hand and laughed. "That won't be necessary, son. I spoke to your teachers this morning back at the

Colored Training School where you attended, and they all spoke highly of you. I also spoke to your mother and your father, and they said you were a good son. That's all the endorsement I will need for now, along with Senator Kingsley's word that he will help you find employment so you can offset any money you might end up owing. So don't worry about proving to me that you are ready for Howard University. Perhaps I should ask the question: Is Howard University ready for you?"

"Oh, sir, you just don't know what that means to me," Vernon said.

"I believe I know. Now, you are a few weeks behind your classmates, but if you are willing to do the work, I see no reason for you to wait until the fall semester," President Johnson said, leaning back in his seat again.

Vernon looked from President Johnson to Courtland and then back at President Johnson, the grin on his face so wide, Courtland was surprised the young man's face didn't split open. "Oh, sir, I appreciate this kindness. I promise to make both you and Senator Kingsley proud of your decision to support me in this manner."

From there, things moved quickly. President Johnson had his assistant phone over to the registrar's office to get Vernon into some classes, and after that, it was a whirlwind tour of the campus, including the dorm where Vernon would be staying. By the time they left, Vernon had his dorm key, his class schedule—Composition, General Chemistry I, Human Anatomy, and French—and a sweatshirt that read *Howard University*. When it came time to pay tuition at the registrar's office, Courtland stepped forward and wrote a check. Before Vernon could protest, Courtland laid his hand on Vernon's shoulder.

"You will pay me back," Courtland said firmly. "But for now, I want you to focus on your first semester as a college student and putting some money away for a rainy day. Going to college will be like nothing you have ever experienced before. Before today, you were a big fish in a small pond. Now you are swimming in the ocean."

"I just can't thank you enough, Senator Kingsley," Vernon said for what seemed like the hundredth time that morning, tears threatening to fall. "I promise I will—"

Courtland laughed. "I know. Make me proud. I don't doubt for a moment that you will, young man."

Courtland got out of the car and led Vernon into the restaurant. It was bustling with activity and crowded wall-to-wall with people waiting to be seated. When they got to the maître d', he smiled at Courtland and Vernon apologetically.

"I am so sorry, Senator Kingsley, sir, but we will not have a table for at least a half hour or so. Even Miss Eva's table is filled with guests. But if you are willing to wait, I can . . ."

Before Courtland could respond, Eva walked toward them. "Hello, Senator Kingsley. This must be Vernon Michaels," she said. "Pleased to meet you."

She extended her hand to Vernon, and Courtland watched with a bit of a smile as Vernon took her hand and shook it, looking up at her as if he had just encountered a celestial being. It was quite clear that the young man was taken by Eva. Understandably so. She was looking like a vision, as always. Courtland could not help but take in every single detail. She was wearing a powder-blue silk dress that hugged her slender frame, and her hair was loose, hanging down the middle of her back in soft waves. He had never seen her wear her hair any way but pinned up. He had to admit she was even more breathtaking than usual.

"Nice to meet you, Miss Cardon," he said. "I am grateful for this opportunity to come speak to you about a job."

"The senator spoke very highly of you. I would love to talk to you further about working here for me. Would you like to accompany me to my office so I can ask you a few questions?" she asked.

Vernon nodded. "Yes, ma'am. I would be honored."

"So they finished repairing everything in the back of the restaurant?" Courtland asked.

"Yes," she said. "The men worked around the clock to get everything back in order. It is better than ever. It just goes to show that it takes more than a few ruffians to stop this show." She turned to Vernon. "Are you ready?"

"Yes, ma'am," he said.

Eva turned toward the maître d'. "Find a table for the senator." That was all she said, and then she walked away. Courtland stifled a laugh as the maître d' quickly led Courtland to a table in the back of the restaurant. Eva was a quiet general who never had to raise her voice to be heard. Courtland loved that about her. Before long a waiter came and took his order. Courtland ordered the étouffée, and as he sat waiting for his food to arrive, he noticed Lieutenant Stevens.

Courtland watched as he spoke to the maître d', then his eyes settled on Courtland, who was struck by the look of derision on the man's face. But as quickly as he looked at Courtland, he turned his face back to the maître d'. Courtland watched with interest as the lieutenant followed the maître d' to the back of the building where Eva's office was located. Seconds later, the maître d' came back to the front of the restaurant. For some reason, red flags went off in Courtland's mind, and without a second thought, he got up and made his way to Eva's office.

"Self-sabotage!" he heard Eva exclaim. "That is the most ridiculous thing I have ever heard. Why would I bomb my own building?"

Courtland stood by the door but didn't go in. He didn't want Eva to think he was trying to usurp her authority. He just didn't trust Lieutenant Stevens, especially after what Mr. Folliard had told him. As a former soldier, Courtland had learned how to judge people by a simple look into their eyes or observance of their body language. He had seen enough in the eyes and the posture of this policeman to know he was potentially a dangerous man, so Courtland made the decision to stand there in case Eva needed him to intervene.

"People burn down their properties all of the time. Everybody is trying to make an easy nickel these days," Lieutenant Stevens said with a snide tone.

The way he was speaking to Eva was enough for Courtland to want to storm in and shove the guy into the wall, but he stayed put.

"Insurance scam is big business, and since we have not had any other leads but the boy, you and all of your friends who were here that day are prime suspects."

"I can assure you that neither I nor anyone I know had anything to do with that explosion. Someone planted explosives outside the back door of this building, Lieutenant Stevens, and you need to do your job and figure out who really was responsible for this crime. You are wasting my time and yours with these wild-goose chases."

"You'd better watch yourself, Miss Cardon. Things like this have a tendency to happen again. Maybe you should mind the company you keep," Lieutenant Stevens said, the threat in his voice so clear that Courtland pulled open the door and stepped inside, feigning a look of surprise.

"Oh, Miss Cardon, I didn't know you were busy," he said as the lieutenant backed away from his menacing stance over Eva, who, to her credit, did not seem unnerved by him at all, though she had every right to be rattled. The lieutenant had just issued a threat. It wasn't even a thinly veiled threat. Courtland was still fighting the urge to ram Lieutenant Stevens against the wall.

"Senator Kingsley, thank you for stopping by," she said. "Officer Stevens was just leaving."

Courtland smirked inwardly at Eva's verbal dismissal of the lieutenant's rank. Looking at the storm cloud on the man's face, he could tell she had riled him.

"We will leave the investigation open for now, but I will have additional questions for you soon," he said, turning on his heels and then stopping abruptly. "You were here on the day of the incident, weren't you, Senator?"

"Yes, I was here," Courtland said. "You and I spoke, remember? If you have questions for me, call my office and make an appointment. I also think it wise that you not come back here without calling first, especially if you are making these bogus claims against Miss Cardon. She has the right to have an attorney present if you are going to be questioning her on an official basis."

Lieutenant Stevens cut a menacing look at Courtland, but Courtland was nonplussed.

"Perhaps I should call my brother-in-law so he can get in touch with the attorney general," Eva said. "If your department is struggling this hard to get to the bottom of what happened here, then maybe it is time to call in a higher power."

"I will be in touch with both of you real soon," he said as he exited the room, slamming the door behind him.

Courtland watched as Eva grabbed the corner of her desk as if she needed it to keep from falling.

"Are you okay?" he asked. Eva nodded but didn't say anything. Courtland went to her and took her shaking hands in his. "Are you okay?" he repeated.

Eva shook her head as tears began to fall down her face. Courtland let out a groan and then pulled her close, whispering to her over and over, "You're okay. You're okay. You're okay."

"What if the police are involved, Courtland?" she finally choked out. "How do I protect myself, my family, my friends, and my customers from the very people who are supposed to protect us? And what about your father? What if he is mixed up in all of this? It's too much. All of this is too much."

"I'll get to the bottom of this, Eva," he said, rubbing her back. "I swear to you I will find out who was responsible for this, and I don't care if it was a bum on the street, the chief of police, or . . . or my father. I will figure this out. I promise you that."

Eva stepped aside so she was no longer in Courtland's arms. "This isn't your responsibility."

Courtland wanted nothing more than to pull her back into his arms, but he didn't. He respected the space she put between them. "I'm your friend, Eva—or at least I hope I am. If this worries you and frightens you, then as your friend, I can't turn my back on all of this."

"Thank you," she said, looking at him with what appeared to be the same longing he felt. *Take a step*, he willed her in his mind. *Just take one step, and I'll do the rest.*

"Courtland," Eva said in a husky voice as she moved toward him. That was all the encouragement he needed. Courtland reached over and lightly pressed his lips to hers. Her lips were so smooth. This kiss was different from the last one. That kiss was all fire. This one was more smoldering. More electric. More familiar. He began probing her mouth with his tongue. Gently. She stiffened slightly, probably from the shock that kissing could involve such intimate exploration. He had to remind himself that she was so young and so naive, but soon she relaxed, seeming to enjoy the moment they were sharing.

"Eva," he said, his voice hoarse with passion, "you are so beautiful."

"I'm afraid, Courtland. We should stop," she said.

"If you want to stop, I will stop," he managed to say, pulling his mouth from hers reluctantly. Stopping was the last thing he wanted to do, but he was resolved to do only what she felt comfortable doing.

"I-I-I don't want to stop. I'm just afraid. I've never kissed anyone before you. Ever," she said.

Courtland smiled. "Such a beautiful contradiction in terms you are, Eva Cardon. You are a tough businesswoman by day, but still an innocent girl."

"You're mocking me," she said. Courtland kissed her on her forehead.

"No, I'm not," Courtland said, moving back a few steps so that he wouldn't end up kissing her even more. "Where is Vernon? I should probably get him back to the school."

"He is meeting with Chef du Passe in the kitchen," she said. "They should be done by now. I'll walk you out."

Just before she could walk around him, he lightly placed his hand on her arm. "Go for a drive with me tomorrow. Last November I purchased a 1947 Kurtis-Omohundro Comet. Since I don't drive that much in D.C., I have barely broken her in. I finish my work in the senate at noon tomorrow. Go driving with me. Just to talk. I won't even stop the car so I can kiss your beautiful lips."

For a moment, Eva just looked at Courtland. Almost as if she was trying to read his thoughts. He wouldn't be honest if he said he didn't want to hold her in his arms again and kiss her, but the drive, the drive would give him a chance to be alone with her and talk and listen, and that was enough for the time being . . . until he could figure out what to do next.

"Yes," she said in a voice so quiet he wasn't sure he heard her correctly.

"Did you say yes?" he asked, unable to keep the excitement out of his voice.

"I said yes," she said, not quite meeting his eyes.

Courtland lifted her chin so she was looking at him eye to eye. "A drive. That's all. Just a drive."

"Okay," she said softly.

"Then let's go find Vernon Michaels so I can go back to work and earn my paycheck," he said. He motioned for her to lead the way.

She glanced back at him briefly, a soft smile on her face, but then he watched as she squared her shoulders and once again became Eva Cardon, businesswoman.

"You are one amazing woman," Courtland said underneath his breath, smiling as his thoughts turned to the next day and their getaway, even if only for a few hours.

TWENTY

Courtland

For the first time in a long while, Courtland drove himself to work. When he told Harold the night before that he would not need his services the next day, the older man had grinned.

"I wondered when you were going to take the Comet out and see what she could do," he said. "You be careful, Senator. Driving in D.C. ain't nothing like driving in Parsons, Georgia."

Courtland had laughed. "You underestimate me, Harold. I have driven on the Champs-Élysées in Paris, not to mention in Scotland and Cornwall and all parts in between. I just don't like to drive. I never said I couldn't drive."

"Yes, sir," Harold said. "Well, either way, enjoy your ride. She is a beauty."

Courtland thanked Harold, but he was less concerned about his car and how it handled on the road than about whether Eva would follow through with their arrangement. He hesitated calling it a date, but whatever it was, he was looking forward to it. Once he got to work, he sat and began writing responses to letters he had received from constituents all over Georgia. They ranged from congratulatory letters telling him to keep up the good work, to the occasional "What in the Hades are you doing up there in Washington?" notes from folks who thought he was a tad too liberal for their tastes.

The phone rang, causing him to become mildly irritated when his secretary, Mrs. Nelson, didn't pick it up. He had a meeting in an hour with the members of the Senate Armed Services Committee, and the last thing he needed was to get bogged down in some mindless phone call.

"Mrs. Nelson!" he called out. No response. "Mrs. Nelson, the phone!" he called out again, but there was still no reply. He ripped the phone from its cradle. "Yes!" he barked.

"Senator Kingsley, did I call you at a bad time? This is Edward Folliard," he said.

It was the reporter from *The Washington Post*. Courtland had reached out to his office the day before after he left Eva's restaurant, but they said he was out covering a story.

"Mr. Folliard," Courtland said. "Thank you for calling me back. I wanted to touch base with you on a few things you said the other day concerning the . . . situation at Chez Geneviève."

"You mean the bombing, Senator? That situation?" the man asked in a wry tone.

"Yes," Courtland said. "I would like to talk to you about the bombing. Do you suppose you could come over for a few minutes?"

"Sure," he said. "I'm actually calling you from the Capitol. I'll walk over."

"Thanks," Courtland said and hung up.

He did not want to have this conversation on the phone. The idea that someone might be wiretapping his phone or the phone of whomever he was speaking to always entered his mind. He didn't want to take any chances with this discussion, especially since his father's name came up the last time he and Folliard spoke.

True to his word, Edward Folliard was soon being escorted

into his office by Mrs. Nelson, who had been out of the office on an errand when Folliard called.

"Hold all calls," Courtland said to her. "Mr. Folliard, would you care for any coffee or sweets? I know Mrs. Nelson probably has something good to eat up front."

"No, thank you," he said. "I just ate a little while ago, and I have filled my caffeine quota for the morning."

"Very well," Courtland said. "Thank you, Mrs. Nelson. That will be all."

She nodded and exited the room, closing the door softly behind her. Courtland offered Folliard a seat, which he took, and Courtland made his way to his chair on the other side of the desk.

"Sir, I won't beat around the bush," Courtland said. "When we talked before, I must admit, you caught me off guard, especially the reference to my father, but I need to know more about what you were discussing, particularly the part about the police involvement."

"Senator, this investigation of mine is still in its infancy stage," he said. "But I can say this with all certainty: that explosion was a warning. I've been digging trying to find who the ringleaders are, but whoever they are, they are cagey and good at covering their tracks. If Miss Cardon is a friend of yours, you might want to warn her that her current activities and the company she is keeping are not sitting well with certain people."

"Is she in danger?" Courtland asked, not caring at this point what Folliard thought of his question.

"Yes," Folliard said simply. "She is in danger, but so is anyone who is involved in civil rights for Negroes, and if you aren't careful, sir, that will also include you."

"Are there specific policemen involved in all of this?" Courtland asked, ignoring the last part of what Folliard had to say. "If you give me names, I can do something about this."

Folliard shook his head. "Do you not think there are people

higher up than you who already know what is going on? President Truman is a good man, and he is fighting a valiant fight, but even he must be careful because there are many who want to silence him and his agenda for the Negroes."

"Then what should Miss Cardon do?" Courtland asked, the frustration clear in his voice.

"There are only two choices really," Folliard said. "She can continue doing what she is doing, but she puts herself and her family in danger, or she can give up on all of her civil rights activities and maybe, just maybe, she will be left alone. But at this point, there might not be any way to put Pandora back into the box. Miss Cardon should prepare herself for the worst, because things like this have a tendency to happen again."

Folliard's words had a chilling effect on Courtland because they were the same words Lieutenant Stevens had said to Eva the day before. Courtland knew he would need to tread lightly with this information. Eva was not the type of woman to take direction from him—or anyone, for that matter. Telling her to curtail her involvement with Adam and others who were fighting for justice for Negroes was not going to go over easy.

"What about my father?" Courtland asked. "You mentioned his name before. How is he connected to all of this?"

"As far as your father is concerned, I have nothing solid at this point, but I won't stop digging," Folliard said, standing. "Nap Kingsley is well known for his anti-integration rhetoric. He and the now-deceased governor of Georgia, Eugene Talmadge, were big-time friends. I think your father held at least two or three fundraisers in Talmadge's honor."

"There's no crime in that," Courtland said. He was still struggling with the notion his father was somehow entangled in everything that was going on. "Those circles of power run deep in the South. People put money and energy into the candidates who they believe will best support their agendas. My father's association with Talmadge is no indication that he supported everything Talmadge said or did."

"Every single person in Georgia knew Talmadge had ties to the Ku Klux Klan, and your father had ties to Talmadge and several well-known Klansmen . . . birds of a feather, or so they say," Folliard said, crossing his arms in front of his chest.

"As I said to you before, my father is an old man who is behind the times. That's not a news story. Half of Georgia thinks the way my father thinks," Courtland said.

"Maybe," Folliard said, "but half of Georgia doesn't have the financial ability to back up their hate. I just follow the bread crumbs, Senator. Wherever they take me, that's where I go. You have a good day, sir, and don't bother seeing me out."

Courtland watched the reporter leave, but he didn't have time to sit and ponder their conversation. Secretary of State Marshall and Defense Secretary Forrestal were going to make an appearance before the Senate Armed Services Committee and discuss President Truman's request for the draft and universal military training. Courtland supported Truman's plan.

Courtland left his office and gave Mrs. Nelson some handwritten letters he wanted her to type. Others he wanted to stay handwritten, so he simply asked her to mail those. Then he made the walk over to the Capitol building. In the meeting room, Senator Gurney soon called the meeting to order.

The discussion was heated at times, and no resolution was reached that day, but by lunchtime Courtland left the meeting feeling somewhat satisfied that resolution would be made eventually.

When Courtland got outside, he went directly from the Capitol building to his car. He had told Mrs. Nelson he would not be back in the office until the next day. He didn't want to take any chances that he might get waylaid by work. He pulled his coat close. It had gotten colder. Much colder. The sky was dreary. Snow clouds were gathering, but the weather report on the radio had said earlier to expect only light snow, and not until after midnight, so Courtland wasn't worried about going for a drive with Eva out in the country. But as always, he made sure his car was equipped with warm blankets, water, and a few cans of Campbell's soup and Chef Boyardee Beef Ravioli, something he ate a lot of during the war. His father's favorite expression used to be, "Keep your rifle loaded so that when the battle starts, you aren't running around hunting for bullets." He meant that both literally and figuratively.

It didn't take long for him to reach U Street, but to his surprise he saw Eva a block away from her restaurant. He pulled up to where she was standing, and before he could get out and open the door for her, she hopped inside.

"What are you doing down here?" he asked, but then he looked at her face. She was trying to be discreet, and here he was in the most indiscreet car there was, with its shiny red paint job and all.

"I was . . ." She stopped. He placed his hand on hers.

"I know," he said. "I'm sorry." And he was. This was not how he wanted things to be between them. He wanted to be able to shout from the rooftops that he was seeing the most beautiful woman in the world . . . the most intellectually savvy woman in the world . . . the woman of his dreams. Instead, they were forced to cater to the prejudices of a group of people whose opinions neither one of them should have to entertain. Courtland watched as a frown began to form on her face.

Eva turned and looked at Courtland with an imploring look. "What are we doing, Senator Kingsley? What in the world are we doing? I'm lying to my family. I'm sneaking around like I'm some criminal. What are we doing?"

Courtland put his hand lightly on Eva's shoulder. "Right now, we aren't doing anything. And if this is too much, I can leave. Just let me know what you want."

Leaving was the last thing Courtland wanted to do, but if that was what Eva wanted, he would.

"I don't know what I want you to do," she said. "I just hate this. I hate that the first man I fall for is someone I am not free to get to know. This would be so much easier if you were a good-looking Negro senator instead of the country boy senator from Georgia."

Courtland removed his hand. "I understand. I wish I could change things, too, Eva. I wish a lot of things, but one thing I don't wish is . . . I don't wish you to be anyone other than who you are. Eva, we are just two friends going on a drive in the countryside of Maryland. That's all. I just want your friendship. Okay?"

Finally, Eva nodded. "Okay."

Courtland smiled a broad smile. "Good. Then let's go."

"My goodness. This car is something else," she said, looking around admiringly at the sporty red two-seater. "What kind of car did you say this was?"

"It's a 1947 Kurtis-Omohundro Comet. Only one of two made, and I got the second one. This baby will reach a speed of 105 on the wide-open road," he said, then laughed at her expression. "I will keep it at a nice leisurely speed. Eva, you might as well know, I have a bit of a car addiction. Here in D.C., I have the car Harold drives and this pretty girl. Back home, I have two more cars—a Ford Deluxe Coupe and a Lincoln Continental."

Eva laughed. "Yes, I would call that an addiction." She looked around nervously. "Do you think we are being too careless, Courtland? What if someone sees us?" she asked.

He watched as she slipped on a pair of dark sunglasses with thick plastic frames that framed her face perfectly.

"I don't think anyone is paying us any attention," he said in a calm voice. The streets were pretty quiet in spite of it being the lunch hour. "We'll be careful, Eva. I promise."

"Where are we going?" she asked, still glancing around as they drove away from her neighborhood and away from the heart of D.C.

"About ten miles north of Baltimore. Beautiful farmland. I thought we might stop and take a walk or, if it's too cold for you, just sit in the car and be together," he said, making his way down Minnesota Avenue.

His thoughts went to his conversation with Folliard earlier. He told Eva everything Folliard said.

"So I'm supposed to give up fighting for my basic human rights and the basic human rights of other Negroes just because some white men with hate issues have it out for me?" she asked, her voice rising with each word she spoke.

"I'm just telling you what Folliard said," Courtland said, glancing over at her briefly. "You have every right to be angry, Eva. I don't have any answers. All I know is I don't want to see something bad happen to you or someone you love."

"This is why we fight, Courtland," she said. "These awful people are the reason we do what we do, and I'm just getting started. I haven't been in the fight as long as the others, but this I do know: I have the luxury of being a well-to-do Negro woman. Right now, a hired guard is at my restaurant, and if need be, I can hire other guards to protect my family. But what about those Negro families like Simon and his father, Johnny Mac? Who is going to protect them? If people like myself and Adam and the others don't stand up for them, no one will."

"But you could die," Courtland implored. "These people are not playing around, Eva."

"Do you think I don't know that?" Eva cried. "Do you think I'm oblivious to that fact? Yes, I could die, but Negroes are dying every single day, Courtland. Right there in your own state two years ago, four Negroes were lynched by a white mob. Whether I get involved or not, Negroes are dying every single day, but if you truly care about me or Adam or Vernon Michaels, then do something, Courtland."

Courtland was trying not to get frustrated, but he wasn't sure what he could do beyond what he was doing. He and Adam had had this conversation often, and like he said to Adam, patience was the key . . . making incremental steps was the key. He said this to Eva, and she groaned loudly.

"Oh, for goodness' sake, Courtland. Stop," she said. "Just stop with this 'we've got to take it slow' mentality. That's the politician talking. I want to talk to the man that I . . . I want to talk to the man who paid for a young Negro boy's college education."

"Vernon told you?" Courtland asked, looking over at Eva.

"Yes," she said. "And that is wonderful—beyond wonderful—but it's not enough. You are a United States senator, and so far you have tiptoed around policies that could literally change the landscape of the country. You say you are considering running for president, but what type of president would you be if you are too scared now to stand up for simple things like anti-lynching laws?"

"Eva," Courtland started, but then he stopped.

She was right. Everything she was saying were things Adam had said to him. He was about to respond, but then he noticed that the snow was beginning to fall, and it was coming down in sheets. For a moment, he wondered if the weatherman got things wrong. It wasn't impossible to drive through, but he feared that if he kept going, things might get worse.

"Oh my. I didn't think the snow was supposed to start until late tonight or early tomorrow," she said as Courtland eased the car over to the side of the road.

"I know. I thought the same thing," he said. "I think we should turn around. We haven't gone far. We are only about sixteen miles away from D.C. I'm sorry. This wasn't much of an outing."

"It's okay," she said. "I suppose the weather angels were looking out for you. Now you are safe from our conversation."

Courtland did a quick U-turn and got them going back in the direction of D.C. "Eva, I don't want to avoid our conversation. The things you said were things I needed to hear. I promised you before that I would do better, and I haven't. I have allowed myself to do acts of kindness for Vernon and others in an attempt to absolve myself from having to do the big things. I wouldn't have admitted that an hour ago—heck, maybe not even five minutes ago. But I can't stand back and let others fight this battle. I went thousands of miles across the sea to fight for the freedom of Jewish citizens in Germany. I should be able to fight for the freedom of Negro citizens in this country. Otherwise, I am nothing but a highly medaled hypocrite."

"Thank you," Eva said. "I appreciate you listening. I know what I am charging you to do isn't easy. Pearson shared a quote by the philosopher John Stuart Mills the other night at dinner, and it stuck with me. Mills said, 'Bad men need nothing more to compass their ends than that good men should look on and do nothing.'"

"I will have to borrow that quote," Courtland said. "Maybe I should get it put on a plaque and hang it in my office to remind me of what I should be doing."

As the snow came down harder, Courtland breathed a sigh of relief when he saw that he was only about five miles away from the city center, but once he got into the city, the bottom dropped out of the sky, and the snow seemed to be coming down in large piles. He felt like he could make it to his home, which was only a block away, but he wasn't sure if he could get beyond that. Eva's house was about twenty minutes away from his house under normal circumstances. He didn't see any way for him to get her home until the snow let up some.

"Eva," he said, "I need to tell you something."

"What?" she asked.

"We're going to have to stop," he said.

"What do you mean?" she asked.

"I mean it's getting to be too dangerous for us to drive," he said. "My home is just down this street. We need to stop."

"Are you . . ."

Before Eva could finish, Courtland felt the car begin to spin out of control. To Eva's credit, she didn't scream; she just held on to the seat. The wind was fierce at this point, and his car did not stand a chance. He tried to remember everything he knew about driving in snow and ice. Don't slam on the brakes. In fact, don't touch the brakes, just hold on to the steering wheel and steer into the slide until he was able to gain control.

"Hold on," he said as he managed to bring the car to a stop without hitting anything or anyone. He was grateful that the street was free of cars and people. "There's my home over there," he said. "Once this slows down, I'll get you home."

"Courtland, I don't know about this," she said, and he could hear her anxiety but at this point, there was nothing he could do except park the car.

"It's going to be okay," he said, turning to look at her. "We're just getting out of this blizzard."

"Blizzard?" she said.

"Blizzard," he repeated. "Let's hurry inside while we can still get out of the car."

Courtland opened his door, and the wind was blowing so hard he could barely see. He didn't want to be the one to tell Eva, but this snow did not look as if it were going to stop anytime soon.

TWENTY-ONE

Eva

Courtland held on to Eva as they walked toward his house, the wind whipping them around like they were one of Daisy's little rag dolls, and the snow was piling up so quickly that Eva worried it could be days before they got dug out, assuming they even made it to the door. It was so windy that it was impossible to talk, which was good because all Eva wanted to say was, "Take me home." She couldn't believe she went from going on an innocent drive in the country to going to a man's house unchaperoned. She knew Frédérique and Pearson would be fit to be tied if they knew where she was, and Pearson would be on the road coming to get her, blizzard or no blizzard.

It's going to be okay, she said to herself. *It's going to be okay.*

Finally, in what felt like an hour but was only a minute, they made it to the front door. Courtland inserted the key, and the wind pushed them inside. Courtland closed the door, and Eva welcomed the warmth of the house that met them.

"Are you okay?" he asked.

No, I'm not okay, she screamed inside her head. *How can I be okay? You and I are here alone, and my family is probably worried to death, so no,*

I am not okay. But she didn't say those words. Instead, she looked at Courtland and nodded. "Yes, I'm fine, but I need to use your phone and let my sister know that I am safe. She will worry. And then I need to call my restaurant. I know Chef du Passe has everything under control, but I just need to make sure."

"That's fine," Courtland said. He pointed to a room just off the entrance. "My office is in there. You can use the phone. Here, let me take your coat."

Eva shrugged out of the coat and then went into his office. It was immaculate. It hardly looked like it was in use at all. Eva went and sat down at the mahogany desk. She felt dwarfed in the room even though she wasn't a tiny woman. This was definitely a man's space, from the dark paneling on the walls to the deep-brown bookshelves and the dark maple hardwood floors. The artwork was of sailboats and children fishing in a pond. In the far corner of the room near the fireplace, there was a deer head on the wall. She made sure she didn't look in that direction because she found the sensitive eyes of the deceased animal a bit too much. She knew she was wasting time. She didn't want to make the phone call, but she knew the longer she waited the more Frédérique would worry, so she dialed their home number. Frédérique picked up on the first ring.

"Hello, sissy," Eva said. She knew she sounded like she was about five years old instead of a confident adult woman who didn't have to answer to anyone.

"Oh my God!" Frédérique exclaimed. "Oh my God, where are you? We have been beside ourselves with worry. I called the restaurant, and all Chef du Passe would tell me was you had business you had to take care of, and he was sure you were okay. Where are you, honey? Are you stranded somewhere?"

"I'm sorry. This storm just came out of nowhere," Eva said. "I didn't mean to worry you. I just got to a safe place a minute ago."

"Where are you?" Frédérique asked again. "Pearson is in the other room with Daisy, but he can come get you."

"No," Eva said. "I'm fine. There is no reason for him to get out in this mess. I'm safe. I'm warm. Everything is fine."

For a moment Frédérique was silent. Then she spoke again. Quietly. Calmly. "Eva, I'm going to ask you one more time. Where are you?"

"I-I-I'm at Courtland's house," she stuttered, taking in a deep breath and releasing it slowly.

"The senator?" Frédérique exploded. "You're at the house of that white senator from Georgia? Oh, Eva, how could you? Is this why you pushed Wendell away?"

"This has nothing to do with Wendell. We didn't plan to be at his house," Eva said softly, hoping her quiet tone would cause Frédérique to calm down. It didn't.

"I can't do this with you, too, Eva," Frédérique said in an almost wail. "First Mother and now you. It's too much. Think about me if you can't think about yourself."

"This is not the same, Freddie," Eva said, even though she knew there was a kernel of truth in Frédérique's words. She just didn't want to believe it. She knew that a relationship between her and Courtland would not end nicely, just like her parents' relationship didn't, but she couldn't help herself.

She felt something for Courtland that she was not ready to walk away from just yet, and she thought to herself, *Maybe the storm is a sign. Maybe we are meant to be, even if only for a brief period of time.* Even though she allowed these thoughts, some part of her wondered if what she longed for was a lie, a half-truth designed to make her feel justified for staying here at Courtland's house instead of braving the blizzard in an effort to put distance between her and him? She didn't know.

"How is it not the same, Eva? He is a rich white man from the

South just like Father. How do you see this relationship becoming anything other than what Mother and Father had, which was nothing?" Frédérique spat out, the bitterness still evident in every syllable she spoke. "Father gave us nothing but the crumbs, and Mother was miserable. Is that what you want for yourself?"

"Of course I don't want to be miserable, Freddie, but I can't just walk away," Eva said. "I just know he makes me feel . . ."

"Carnal desire," Frédérique said. "That is all this is. Wendell is a good young man, and he likes you, and given time, I know he will be on bended knee asking for your hand in marriage. Why turn your back on the possibility of a respectable relationship with a bright young Negro man for this . . . this . . . nothing, Eva?"

Eva put her head into her hand. "I don't know. I'm sorry. As soon as this storm is over, I will be home."

Frédérique sighed, and for a moment there was silence. Finally, she spoke. "Save something for yourself, Eva. Don't give him all of you like Mother did with Father. Keep something that he can't touch."

A tear rolled down Eva's face. "I will. I'm sorry. I don't ever want to disappoint you or make you not love me."

Frédérique chuckled bitterly. "I could no more not love you than I could not love breathing. You and I are a package deal, remember? I will always be your big sister, and I will always be here to pick up the pieces. That is what I do. Now, tell me the phone number and address of where you are. As soon as this storm lets up, Pearson will come get you."

Eva nodded and then gave her sister the information she asked for.

"Pray for me?" Eva asked.

"Without ceasing," Frédérique said, and then Eva heard her gently place the phone back on the receiver.

Eva put her forehead onto the desk and allowed the tears to flow down her face, her shoulders wracked with the grief she felt over the situation she had allowed herself to get into. She almost didn't hear the knock at the door. She sat up, wiped away the tears, and cleared her throat.

"Yes," she said, her voice sounding hoarse even to her ears.

"Are you okay in there?" Courtland said from the other side of the door.

"Yes," she replied. "I'll be out in just a minute. I just got off the phone with my sister. I need to call my restaurant." She reached for a tissue and dabbed at her eyes.

"Okay," he said. "When you're done, come straight down the hallway to your left. I will be in the parlor."

"That's fine," she said. The second call was much easier. Chef du Passe answered the phone and reassured her that everything was fine at the restaurant. He had closed early when he realized the storm was going to get bad, and he had sent all of the staff home. He was going to stay there in one of the back rooms where there was a comfortable sleeper sofa for just such an emergency.

"Are you okay, *chéri*?" he asked. "You do not sound like my Eva. You are not in danger, are you?"

"No, Chef. I'm not in danger. Not really," she said, although it all depended on how one defined the word *danger*. "I am fearful that I am drawn to a path that is not going to be good for me, but I don't know how to stop myself from careening wildly down this road. I wish I could be more like Frédérique."

"*Chéri*, you are brilliant in all ways possible," he said. "Trust your instincts. They have not betrayed you as of yet. And sometimes we have to meander about on the road we should not be on before we can appreciate the road we were intended to travel. Your sister is a wonderful young woman, but so are you. *Tu es différente de* Frédérique, *et la différence est une bonne chose.*" You are different from Frédérique, and different is a good thing.

"*Merci*," she said, her voice husky from the tears. "I will check back with you tomorrow."

"I will be here," he said, then hung up the phone. Eva placed the phone back on its cradle, stood, and smoothed her skirt with both of her hands. Then she felt her hair, making sure there were no flyaways, but it was still neatly pulled back and pinned into a bun at the nape of her neck. She had brought her purse with her, so she grabbed it and made her way out of the office and down the hallway where Courtland had directed her. When she got to the parlor, she found him sitting in front of the fireplace in a wingback chair with his feet on a matching black leather ottoman. He stood when she walked into the room.

"I know I seem to ask you if you are all right the entire time we are together, but here I go again. Are you all right?" he asked.

"I'm not going to be able to go home tonight, am I?" she asked. She had glanced toward the window, and all she could see was whiteness. She couldn't make out a single tree or house. Just a wall of white.

"No, you won't be able to go home tonight," he said. "The radio is comparing this storm to the blizzard of 1922. The weather reporter says we are currently getting a half inch of snow per hour, just like the '22 blizzard. It doesn't look good out there at all."

Eva went and sat down on the couch. She tried to concentrate on the flickering flames in the fireplace.

"How long did that snowstorm last?" she finally asked.

Courtland joined her on the couch. He turned toward her, but he did not reach out to touch her. She was grateful for that. The last thing she needed was Courtland's hands or, worse, his lips on her.

"Three days of nonstop snowing," he said. "I'm sorry. Listen, no one predicted this storm. It was supposed to bypass us. They only thought we would get a light dusting at best."

"What am I going to do?" she asked. "I can't stay here."

"I'm afraid you don't have a choice. There is no way for you to safely go home tonight. Possibly not even tomorrow or the day after that," he said. "But I have four bedrooms, Eva. You can sleep in any one of them, and I believe my sister Violet, who is built similarly to you, has a closet full of clothes and sleepwear in one of the rooms."

Eva nodded. "Thank you, Courtland. I'm sorry for being such a big baby. It's just, my sister is not happy with me, and my brother-in-law is most decidedly disappointed as well. This is just a lot."

This time Courtland did reach over and take Eva's hand in his. She didn't pull away, so he continued to hold it. "You're not being a baby. You have every reason to feel awkward and uncomfortable with this situation. You're a classy woman, Eva, and I want you to know that I will not try to make you feel any more uncomfortable than you already are. I apologize. I should have paid closer attention to the clouds in the sky when we were out driving."

"It's not your fault," she said with a sigh. "You didn't know."

"Are you hungry?" Courtland asked. "There's food in the kitchen. It's not cooked, but the cupboards are not bare. Hester Mae, wife of my driver, Harold, comes over twice per week and cleans and cooks things. She was coming over to cook today, so there is only uncooked food in the refrigerator. But the good news is, we won't starve."

Eva jumped up. "Well, I can't control this storm, but I can cook. Direct me to your kitchen, Senator."

Courtland stood. "Follow me. I am never one to say no to a good home-cooked meal."

Eva followed him down the hallway. The walls were filled with photos of family, Eva assumed. The house was truly a showplace. Antiques were everywhere, and along with the family photos, there were paintings that Eva recognized by artists like Edvard Munch and Salvador Dalí.

"Your artwork is phenomenal," she said, slowing down as she admired the paintings.

"This is all my mother and sisters," he said. "I admire the art, but I wouldn't know an original Salvador Dalí from a copy. Mother can spot a fraud a mile away, so I leave it to her to invest my money into pieces like these."

They rounded the corner, and Courtland's kitchen nearly took Eva's breath. The kitchen was huge, and Eva could imagine the parties that got catered in this space.

"A Roper Town and Country Triple Baking Oven," she said with a smile, gliding her hand over the magnificent showpiece. "Now this is better than any old Salvador Dalí." She went to the refrigerator and found a whole chicken, along with some carrots, garlic, bacon, and onions. She looked at Courtland. "I assume you have red wine and brandy?"

Courtland smiled. "Absolutely."

"Then I will make you the best coq au vin you have ever eaten," she said, smiling back at him. Romance and love were all foreign to Eva, but cooking . . . That was her wheelhouse.

"May I help?" he asked.

She shook her head. "No. I can handle it."

"Then I will get you your red wine and brandy, and while you cook, I will go look and see which room Violet used last. You can stay there," he said. "I think she may have also left some toiletries in the adjoining bathroom."

"Thank you," Eva said, but she was already busying herself getting her ingredients together.

She was also pleased that she found the ingredients to make them a quick bread. Baking was not her strong suit, but Chef du Passe had taught her this recipe, and now her family requested it regularly.

"Here's the brandy and the wine," he said, putting it on the marble countertop. The kitchen was decorated in dark blue and white.

"Thank you," she said as she expertly broke down the chicken.

"You're good," Courtland said.

Eva looked up at him and smiled. "Thank you," she said. "I have been fortunate to learn from one of the best chefs D.C. has to offer. Do you have an apron somewhere?"

"I think I saw Hester Mae put one in the closet over there. Let me look," he said.

Eva had found a large bowl, and she placed the chicken inside of it. She barely noticed Courtland as he came up behind her.

"Do you mind if I put the apron on for you?" he asked politely.

"Not at all," she said as he lifted the white apron over her neck and then tied it around her waist. "This is a great kitchen, Courtland."

"It was a mess when I first bought the place, but by the time the decorator got done—with Mother's input, of course—it has far exceeded anything I will ever need in a kitchen," he said. "I count it a win if I can figure out how to make a decent cup of coffee."

Eva laughed. "Cooking isn't as difficult as you might think. Oh, I mean, of course there are certain techniques that require special knowledge on the part of the person cooking, but what I'm doing now is low-level French cooking. It sounds far fancier than it really is."

"Well, I trust you explicitly, and unless you have something else you need me to do, I will leave you to your cooking," he said.

"I should be done in about an hour and a half, so take your time," she said and turned back to her ingredients. She didn't even notice when Courtland left the room, she was so intent on what she was doing. She poured the wine and the brandy over the chicken. While the chicken was marinating, she quickly mixed up her bread and got it into the oven. She seasoned the chicken with salt and pepper, then began searing it. It wasn't long before the smells in the kitchen had her feeling hungry. She realized she hadn't eaten at all today. Normally she at least ate breakfast every morning because her sister insisted on it, but Daisy had been out of sorts this morning, so Eva had left without so much as a cup of coffee in her system. By the time she got to work, she had to deal with a wayward employee.

She began to deftly chop the onions and carrots, which she

planned to add to the pot once the chicken was done searing. She went to the pantry and found a can of Campania tomato paste and a bag of rice. She grabbed both and went back to the stove.

Before long, she had the coq au vin, the rice, and the bread all done. She looked up just in time to see Courtland walk into the room dressed in a pair of dark slacks and a white shirt. His hair was still damp, and there was a faint hint of a beard darkening his face. Eva averted her eyes so as not to be caught staring.

"It smells good in here," he said.

"Thank you," she said, feeling a bit out of sorts now that she didn't have the distraction of cooking. "Everything is ready. Would you mind helping me get the food to the table?"

"You go sit, and I will bring everything over," he said. "You have done more than enough. This is a feast."

Eva smiled as she took off her apron and draped it over the corner of the counter. She left the kitchen and went to the dining room. She saw the plates and silverware neatly organized on the buffet table. The napkins had been washed and ironed. Eva quickly set the table and had it ready by the time Courtland brought the food in, including a Beaujolais and a carafe of water.

"Ready?" he asked.

"Ready," she said and took her seat across from Courtland. "Do you pray before you eat?"

Courtland smiled. "Not as regular as my mother would like, but if you don't mind a prayer from my youth, here we go. *Bless us, O Lord, and these, thy gifts, which we are about to receive from thy bounty. Through Christ our Lord. Amen,*" he said. Both he and Eva made the sign of the cross, and Courtland looked at her with surprise. "You know, I remember you saying when I called you about Pops being sick that you would pray the rosary, but it slipped my mind that you are Catholic too."

"Yes," she said, placing the napkin on her lap. "My sister and I were raised Catholic. Both of our parents were Catholic, although

Mother was a seasonal Catholic. Most of what I learned was from my maternal grandmother. When Frédérique married Pearson, a Baptist minister, we sort of left the Catholic church, but I returned to my faith as I got older."

Courtland nodded as he put food on a plate and passed it to her. Then he did the same with his own plate. "I haven't been the best Catholic since the war. I saw things over there that made having faith difficult."

"I would think the miracle of surviving the war would have strengthened your faith, not diminished it," she said.

Courtland nodded and took a bite of the coq au vin. "My goodness, Eva. This is delicious. What did you season this with? Hopes and dreams?"

She laughed. "You're funny. No, I did not season it with hopes and dreams. Just a few things you had in the kitchen. Nothing special."

"Well, to answer your assessment, yes, I suppose surviving the war is a miracle, and maybe my faith should have been strengthened, but it wasn't," he said. "Seeing people I had trained with lose limbs—or worse, die in the thick of battle—was overwhelming, and faith didn't have room in all of that for me. I'm still working through it, but I know if my mother had just witnessed you getting me to say grace, she would have started praying her rosary on the spot."

Eva shook her head sadly. "I doubt very seriously your mother would be any too pleased to know you were entertaining me in the house I'm sure she was decorating for your someday family."

"You're probably right," he admitted. "But tonight she is not here, and you are, and I would say a hundred Hail Marys in thanks for you being right where you are."

Eva didn't know what to say, so she took a bite of her food.

"I've made you uncomfortable," he said.

She looked up and smiled. "This situation makes me uncomfortable."

"Then let's talk about something else," he said.

"That's fine with me," she said, and the two of them began to talk about everything but the elephant in the room, and Eva began to feel comfortable, maybe too comfortable. In that moment, she was not concerned about the blizzard that was raging outside. She was focused on the here and now and the sound of Courtland's voice.

TWENTY-TWO

Eva

Eva couldn't sleep. She had been tossing and turning, and now, a few minutes after midnight, she was still wide awake. For someone who had never even kissed a man before Courtland, she was shocked at the level of intensity she was feeling every time she thought about him. It was overwhelming and not exactly a welcome emotion. Eva was used to being aloof when it came to men. It wasn't that she was not attracted to them, it was just that she didn't want to allow any man to turn her attention from her goal, which was to grow her restaurant business. That was her first priority. And if the truth be known, she never learned the fine art of flirting. Partly because of how she was raised by her mother, then later her sister, Frédérique. Both women had been extra careful about Eva's upbringing, making sure she didn't become like some of the spoiled girls she went to school with, who were often shallow and arrogant.

"You are beautiful, Eva," her sister had said to her when she became a teenager, "just like Mama. But you don't want to be known for your looks. Looks fade, but a kind heart and a brilliant mind can last you a lifetime."

Eva had taken those words to heart, and anytime someone

complimented her about her looks, especially a man, she always pushed their words away in her mind, knowing that their attention was based on something superficial. But Courtland seemed different. He wanted to know about her work, and he valued her opinion about things. That appealed to her. Eva twisted and turned in the bed for a few more minutes; finally, though, she gave up the fight and got up.

There was a bookshelf near the wall by the door, so she went over and tried to be inspired by something on it, but nothing tickled her fancy. Not *Little Women,* which she had read in high school and had actually liked. Not *Pride and Prejudice,* which she hadn't liked very much at all. Not *Jane Eyre,* which she found to be even stuffier than *Pride and Prejudice.* Eva continued to scan the shelves, but nothing appealed to her. The last book she had read was *Passing* by Nella Larsen, a book about a light-skinned Negro woman passing for white. She and Frédérique had discussed it for days. Eva had hated it. As a light-skinned Negro woman, much lighter than her sister, she already battled with her own feelings about her looks and how she was perceived. She never wanted to pass for anything other than who she was, a Negro. When Eva was a little girl, she would go outside and play in the sun all day, trying to turn her skin the same beautiful shade of brown as her big sister's.

Their mother would fuss at her, telling her she would get heatstroke if she wasn't careful, but Eva didn't care. She just wanted to be sunbaked and beautiful like Frédérique. Nella Larsen's book put her into a negative space for days afterward, even though Frédérique called it a cautionary tale and nothing more.

"Clearly this book is showing us that it is our responsibility to always know who we are, sissy, and that is a proud Negro woman," Frédérique had said. "You could never be like the woman in this book."

And yet, here she was—not trying to be white but definitely not appreciating the fact that a wonderfully handsome and talented Negro man wanted to date her, and all she could think about was Courtland.

Pushing those thoughts as far back as she could into the recesses of her mind, Eva continued to peruse the bookshelf. She assumed all of these books belonged to one or both of Courtland's sisters. They didn't seem to be the kind of books she would imagine him sitting down to read. She reached for one of the books that had an interesting-looking cover. It was called *Tristram Shandy*. Eva considered herself well read, but she had never read this book before. She didn't even know the author—Laurence Sterne. She opened the first page and read: *I wish either my father or my mother, or indeed both of them, as they were in duty both equally bound to it, had minded what they were about when they begot me.*

She stopped reading. That was a little too close to home, so she put the book back on the shelf. The last thing she wanted to think about right then was her mother and father's relationship.

She contemplated getting back into bed, but she knew she was wide awake at this point, and all she would do was stare at the ceiling. Often when she couldn't sleep at home, she would just get up and do some paperwork, whether that be making payroll or plotting out menu suggestions for the upcoming week. But she didn't feel like trying to focus on work, and besides, she had forgotten her briefcase at the restaurant.

"Maybe if I just go and make myself some warm milk," she mumbled to herself.

Eva went to the closet and found a long pink robe, put it on, and cinched the belt tightly. She slipped her feet into the house shoes she had found in one of the drawers earlier. Then she made her way into the dark hallway. She didn't even look toward Courtland's room before going down the stairs. She didn't want to tempt herself because all she wanted to do was go to his room and slip into the bed beside him. She felt awful for having such thoughts. Instinctively, she began praying. She didn't have her rosary with her—it was back home in her bedroom—but she prayed the prayers nonetheless.

"*Je vous salue Marie pleine de grâce, le Seigneur est avec vous,*" she said in a whisper. *Hail Mary, full of grace, the Lord is with thee . . .* She continued to repeat the words as she walked down the hallway. Eva's thoughts turned to her mother.

Once, when Eva was a little girl, she had asked her mother why her daddy had never married her, and Geneviève had looked at Eva sadly and said, "Women like me are not the marrying kind for men like your father. Make sure you don't turn out like me. Do better than me." Eva had never forgotten that conversation. The grief that her mother clearly felt stayed with Eva long past Geneviève's death. Eva had promised herself never to get into a similar situation, and lo and behold, here she was. She imagined her mother's disapproving eyes looking down on her.

Once Eva made it to the kitchen, she turned on the light and was startled to find Courtland sitting at the table in the corner of the kitchen drinking a glass of dark liquor that she assumed was bourbon. He looked at her with a tired face.

"You couldn't sleep either?" he asked.

He was wearing a robe over his pajamas. She tried not to stare. Although he was slightly disheveled, he still caused her breath to catch in her throat.

"I'm sorry. I didn't know you were in here," she said. She turned to leave. She didn't trust herself to stay, but Courtland halted her with his voice.

"Don't go," he said. "Come sit with me. Come have a glass of wine, or bourbon, or water. Whatever your fancy. Just don't walk away."

Eva looked back at Courtland. She was torn. She wanted to stay, but she also knew the smart decision would be to go back to the bedroom and try to sleep. Perhaps an even smarter decision would be to go somewhere and pray until the sun came up.

"Please," he said. "Just sit with me."

"I was going to warm myself some milk," she said. "I'll just do that." She went to the refrigerator and took out the bottle of milk.

"I hope it's still good to drink," he said, taking a large sip from his glass, still watching her. Eva shivered. The power of his stare was a lot to take in.

"I'm sure it's fine," she said, reaching into the cabinet next to the stove and taking out a pan. She poured some of the milk into it and then turned on the burner. There was nothing more to do besides watch it boil, so she reluctantly joined Courtland at the table.

"Have you slept at all?" she asked.

Courtland reached out and took her left hand in his. "I haven't slept a wink. I'm still tired, but I can't stop thinking about—"

"Don't," she said. "Don't." She pulled her hand away. "Is it still snowing outside?"

He nodded. "Still coming down in sheets. I'm sorry."

Eva got up from the table and went back to the stove. The milk was just warm enough, so she turned it off, reached into the cabinet for a mug, and poured the milk into it. She sipped the warm beverage. It felt good going down her throat. She suddenly felt bitterly cold from the inside out. She was about to turn when she felt Courtland's strong arms around her waist and his lips against her neck. She stiffened at first, but then she melted into his arms, a groan escaping her lips.

"Courtland," she said, her voice ravaged by the passion she was feeling. Unsteadily, she placed the cup of warm milk on the counter and turned to face him. She could smell the heady scent of bourbon on his breath. "I should go back to bed."

"I know," he said, but he lowered his mouth to hers and kissed her again. She soon found herself in his arms, kissing with a hunger she had never experienced in her life. She couldn't imagine ever feeling this level of want for another human. Courtland stopped kissing Eva abruptly, and before she knew what was happening, he was carrying her to the couch in the parlor. If his leg was bothering him, he didn't show it because he moved with a quickness. He sat down with her in his lap, his arms around her waist. She wanted to pull away, but she couldn't.

"I know this makes no sense, Eva. I know I should figure out how to get you home to your family where you can be safe and sound, even in the midst of a blizzard, but I have to believe that the heavens conspired against us or for us for this moment. This moment. I know we can't promise anything more than this, but Eva Cardon, I want . . . I . . ."

"Courtland, I am battling the same questions you are, and it scares me," Eva confessed. "Even though my mother had both me and my sister out of wedlock, I was raised a good Catholic girl. You are the first man I have ever kissed. I don't understand what I am feeling, and it scares me."

"This scares me, too, Eva," he said. "I have lived a very carefully constructed life thus far. I won't lie to you, there have been women in my life, but they were diversions. I know that sounds awful. It sounds awful to my ears."

Eva tried to take in all that Courtland was saying. It was painful for her to think of him sharing this type of intimacy with other women. It was even more painful for her to know that it had gone further than kissing, and it had meant nothing to him. That was not a part of Courtland Eva wanted to think about.

"Did I just ruin the moment?" he asked, looking at her with a tenderness that was almost too powerful for her to bear. She looked away, but he tilted her head back toward his.

"Eva, I have seen a lot in my life, and I have experienced things no human should experience," he said, easing her onto the couch so that they were facing each other. "I fought in a war that I didn't know I would return from, and when there was another warm body to offer me comfort during the night, I took it. I don't regret that part of it at all. My only regret is that somewhere along the way, I may have hurt another human who was looking for something more than one night."

"I do understand some things," Eva said carefully. "I know my life experiences don't measure up to what you have gone through, but I guess I can see how being away from home and having to fight every day to live would make your choices different. I don't think less of you, Courtland. If anything, I think more of you for telling me the truth."

She watched as he took a deep sigh. He reached for her hand and cradled it.

"Before you, I only thought about pleasing my father," Courtland said, stroking her face. "My father has always been the compass that has guided me, but now I just don't know anymore what I want from life. Except for you. I want you, Eva."

"I don't think I would fit the vision your family, specifically your father, has in mind for you," Eva said with sadness.

She understood what men like Courtland's father would think about her. It was the same thing her father thought about her mother. It took Eva being in this moment to come to that realization. Her father had loved them in his own way, Eva had no doubt, but he never believed they were worthy to see the light of day—to come outside of the shadows.

"I'm sorry," Courtland said, looking at her with a sadness that matched her own. "I know I have no right to ask anything of you, Eva. I have no moral high ground to stand on. I am a product of a society that invalidates someone as talented and smart as you for no other reason than the color of your skin. I know this, and I hate it, but I have no clue how to change it."

Eva smiled, trying to swallow back the tears that were threatening to fall. "We didn't create this world we live in, Courtland. It was already this way when we both got here. I know it must have sounded like I expect you to right all of the wrongs your people are doing and have done to my people, but I don't."

"Maybe you should," he said quietly. "Maybe you should hold me and every white person breathing right now responsible for this.

Maybe we should hold ourselves responsible for the hatred and the prejudice even if we aren't the ones meting it out. We're still benefiting from it—this system of racial injustice and hatred. Our mutual friend, Adam Clayton Powell Jr., is one of the most brilliant men I know, and what is he spending his time doing? Trying to get a resolution to allow Negro federal employees the right to eat in the cafeteria. He can't focus his attention on large, substantive measures in the House because he's got to worry about where he and his Negro colleagues get their lunches and where they go to the bathroom."

"Then what are you going to do about it, Courtland?" she asked.

Courtland got up from the couch and walked over to the window. Eva watched but didn't move. Her instinct was to go to him, hug him, and tell him that he didn't need to worry about all of this, but maybe he was right. Maybe he needed to wrestle with the things she and other Negroes wrestled with all of the time. So she sat and waited patiently. Finally, he turned back around.

"I want to be a change agent, Eva," he said, walking back toward her, his limp more pronounced now. "When I was stationed overseas during the war, I remember some of the Negro pilots came to the officers' club one night. I sat and watched while two of the white officers ordered them to leave. This was hours after those same Negro pilots had flown interference for us, making sure not a single one of our lives was lost in battle, and all they wanted to do was come have a celebratory drink with us. Like equals. Like men who were fighting on the same side."

"And what did you do?" Eva asked, seeing the turmoil play out on his face. She hated making him relive that night, but she also recognized that he needed to own up to his part in that evening's outcome, no matter how big or small.

"I did nothing," he said. "I sat and nursed my drink, and I pretended like the conflict going on right in front of me had nothing to do with me. Maybe I wouldn't have been able to stop my white counterparts from escorting those Negro men out of the officers' club, but what haunts me on a regular basis is I'll never know because I never tried."

"You can't change that night, Courtland," she said, getting up and standing in front of him, putting her hands on his shoulders. "But you can change what you do in the here and now. You can stand up for Adam and the other Negro politicians. You can support bills that come through your chambers that are fair and just, and you can fight for their right to eat in the same dining hall as you. That, you can do."

Courtland pulled Eva into his arms, holding her tightly. "Your wisdom floors me at times, Eva Cardon," he said, then slowly released her from his embrace, allowing his hands to fall by his sides. "You should go to bed now."

Eva realized Courtland was giving her a way out. He was giving her the power to escape what had seemed inevitable just a few minutes ago, when both of them were being driven by their passion. She knew she should take him up on his offer to end the sexual tension that was lingering in the air, but in that moment, Eva made a decision. She wanted this night. She wanted to have the memory of this night for the rest of her life, and she wasn't going to allow herself to feel guilty for it. This moment was for her—her gift to herself—and she was going to give herself freely to this moment.

"I want to be with you, Courtland," she said. "I want to have tonight. I don't care about tomorrow. I just want to have tonight."

Courtland looked down at her with a quizzical look, as if he were searching for the untruth in what she was saying. "We can't undo this once we cross that line, Eva. I don't want you to wake up with regret."

"I won't," she said in a firm voice. "But more than that, I don't want to live with a lifetime of regrets wondering what could have been."

Courtland kissed Eva's face gently all over. "I won't hurt you."

"Yes, you will," she said as the tears rolled down her face. "And

I will hurt you, but somehow, even knowing that, I can't walk away. So let's just not think about the hurting for now."

Courtland pulled Eva close and held her tight. For a time, that was how they stayed. Eva tried not to think too many steps ahead of the moment. She promised herself that if she gave in to what she was feeling tonight, she would find a way to walk away from Courtland. She had to if she wanted to preserve her sanity. Determined to follow through with what she was feeling, Eva reached out to Courtland.

"I'm not afraid. I want this," she said.

"You are the most incredible woman ever," he said. "I wish . . ."

Eva put her finger on his lips. "No regrets. No wishes. Just tonight."

They held hands as they walked out of the parlor and out to the hallway to the stairs. Once they got to the door leading to her bedroom, Courtland turned and looked at her intently.

"Are you sure?" he asked.

Eva smiled. "Yes. I'm scared because this is new to me, but I want this, and I have no qualms about this moment, Courtland, so no more questions. I promise not to be a crying mess in a few minutes. I am making an adult decision. So please don't worry that I will ruin the moment by losing my nerve."

Courtland kissed her. "You couldn't ruin this moment if you wanted to," he said and quietly led her down the hallway to his room. Before he opened the door, he looked at her one more time. "Are you sure?"

"Yes," she said. "I have never been surer of anything."

He opened the door and led her inside, closing the door behind them. Eva didn't know what she would feel like in the morning, but right then, in that moment, everything felt right, and that was enough for her.

TWENTY-THREE

Courtland

Courtland awoke with a start. He reached over and realized Eva was no longer in the bed. He shivered and then stretched, working out the kinks in his body. He peered over at the clock on the wall and saw that it was a little after seven. He didn't want to get up, but more than he wanted to stay in bed, he wanted to see where Eva was. He wanted to make sure she was okay. Their night together had been amazing—everything he hoped it would be—but he needed to make sure she felt the same way.

He went and showered and then dressed in a pair of slacks and a casual two-toned shirt. Once he opened the door to his bedroom, he knew where Eva was because the smell of bacon frying filled the air. He followed his nose to the kitchen. When he got there, Eva was dressed in a cream-colored pair of wide, flowing pleated pants and a teal men's-style shirt. He remembered his sister Violet wearing it once. Eva's hair was pulled back into a ponytail. She looked as young as his sister, but there was also a womanliness about her curves.

"What a vision of loveliness you are," he said, walking up behind her. "You didn't have to cook breakfast. I'm not handy in the kitchen, but I make a mean fried egg sandwich."

Eva smiled. "That's okay. I didn't do anything complicated. Eggs, toast, and bacon. Everything is ready. I thought we could just eat at the kitchen table. Oh, I need to put the coffee on. I totally forgot. Breakfast is always Frédérique's domain."

"Sounds good to me," he said. "You go sit, and I'll make a pot of coffee and bring the food over. How do you like your coffee?"

"Black is good," she said. "My mother always drank her coffee black. It's funny the little things I do just because she once did it."

Courtland kissed Eva on her cheek. "Your mother would be so proud of you."

Eva shook her head. "I don't know if she would be proud of me right now, but yes, I think, overall, she would be happy with how I have turned out."

"How are you feeling this morning?" he asked.

She smiled, but there was a sadness to it. "I'm okay. I thought I might wake up feeling terrible about my choice, but . . . well . . . last night was incredible. I'm not going to allow my mind to go deeper than that."

Courtland was about to respond, and then the phone rang. He went over and picked it up.

"Hello . . . Yes, she is right here. Good morning," he said, but Frédérique did not respond to his greeting. He tried to hand the phone to Eva, but she didn't reach for it.

"Do you mind if I take the call in your office?" she asked.

"Of course I don't mind," he said. "I'll hang up as soon as you are on the line."

He watched as Eva walked away. He noticed how she squared her shoulders as she walked. He hoped the conversation between her and her sister didn't end up being contentious. Once he heard her voice on the other end, he placed the phone back into its cradle. Courtland busied himself setting the table and making the coffee. By the time he was done, Eva was coming back into the room. She didn't seem upset, but he could tell that the phone call wasn't exactly easy for her either.

"How did it go?" he asked.

She smiled at him absently. "As well as expected. Thankfully, she has Daisy to take some of her attention."

"I'm sorry," Courtland said, and he was. "I should have been stronger. I shouldn't have put you in this position."

Eva went to Courtland and put her arms around his waist. "You didn't put me in any position that I didn't want to be in. Courtland, I might be young, but I am not a child. I am a grown woman, and I have grown-woman feelings and thoughts. I wanted last night as much as you did. There are no victims here. I went into this situation with my eyes fully open. I have no regrets. Not one."

Courtland kissed her. "You say that now, but what about tomorrow or the next day?"

"Then I will deal with it tomorrow or the next day, but until then, can we just not dwell on the aftereffects of our actions? Please?" she asked, and in answer, Courtland kissed her soundly on her lips, but then he stopped abruptly.

"If we keep on like this, we won't be eating breakfast," he said with a slight laugh.

"Well, we better stop because I am quite hungry," she said and went to the table and sat while he poured her coffee and fixed her plate.

Just like they did the previous night, they said grace, then Eva took a sip of the coffee. She looked up at him and smiled. "This is quite good. See, you are handier in the kitchen than you give yourself credit for."

Courtland laughed. "It's coffee. Any hack can learn to make good coffee, and I was the resident coffee maker back during the war. You can't be a good soldier if you don't know how to make the grounds taste good. Some days it was so cold and rainy that coffee was all we had to keep the Hawk away."

Courtland watched as Eva picked up the newspaper.

"That's an old newspaper," he said. "I usually take them to the office. Not sure how this one got left behind."

"I read *The Washington Post* every day, but somehow I missed this paper," she said, flipping to the back. "It's talking about the turmoil in the Democratic Party. Rumblings of a split. Maybe this is the time for you to run."

"Running for the presidency now just doesn't feel like the right move," he said.

"Talk to the people you trust, like Adam. One thing's for sure, he will tell you the unvarnished truth," she said, and they both laughed. "I don't know if this is your year to run, Courtland, but I do believe in you, and I think you would make a very good leader for this country. Just don't let your father pressure you into running too soon. Be as strategic as you always have. You'll know when it is the right time to run."

Courtland and Eva ate in silence, both deep in their thoughts. Courtland poured himself a second cup of coffee.

"More coffee?" he asked.

"No, I'm good," she said. "It looks like it has stopped snowing."

He looked toward the window, and for the first time in hours, he could see something besides whiteness outside the window. He could see a bit of blue beyond the snow-covered trees in front of his brownstone. He got up and went to the huge picture window on the other side of the kitchen table.

"It's going to take a day or two for everyone to dig themselves out from under this," he said.

"Then I guess we better find a way to amuse ourselves," Eva said, coming up behind Courtland. She laid her head against his back.

"What do you have in mind?" Courtland asked, turning so that he faced her. He saw a mischievous look on her face.

"Well . . . I thought we might play a game," she said in a breathy voice.

He leaned down and kissed her. "What game do you have in mind?"

"Chess," she said with a laugh. "I saw your chessboard in the den. I assume you play?"

"Oh, Miss Cardon," he said, laughing with her. "You don't want to go down this road. Many have tried and failed. Maybe we should start you off with something simple. Backgammon maybe, although I am pretty good at that game too. How about checkers?"

Eva shook her head, still laughing, still looking so beautiful. "Nope. I want to play chess. I might surprise you. I'll clean up, and you get a fire in the fireplace. Then we will see who the best chess player in the land is."

For a moment, Courtland's mind turned to the war. So many amazing chess players had lost their lives. Courtland had been an avid player throughout high school and college, even playing on the collegiate chess team, so it was with great sorrow when he learned of the death of so many of the world's greatest players. Courtland didn't think another sport had been so desecrated by the war—the chess world lost men like Izaak Appel, Mikhail Platov, Lazar Zalkind, and the list went on and on. The effects that war had and continued to have on society baffled Courtland's mind at times. He wondered whether there would ever be a time when world leaders could work out their differences somewhere other than the battlefield.

"Are you okay?" Eva asked, placing her hand on his arm.

Courtland looked down at her and smiled, stroking her face.

"Yes," he said. "Sometimes that bloody war takes me out of the moment at the strangest times. I'm fine."

"We can talk if you want to, if that would make it better," she said.

He shook his head. "You are not going to get out of a chess

whooping that easily. We have tasks to complete, my lady, before I can give you a resounding thrashing on the board."

Eva laughed and went toward the kitchen while Courtland went to the den and began stacking wood inside the fireplace. In a matter of minutes he had a fire going and had set up the chessboard on the ottoman. Eva came into the room with two mugs of hot chocolate, one of which she gave to Courtland.

"Ready?" she asked, sitting limberly on the floor. "Am I white or black?"

Courtland grinned. "You are whomever you want to be on the board."

She nodded decisively. "Then I shall be white," she said and made her first move. It did not take long for Courtland to realize Eva was more than an average player.

"Edward Lasker," he muttered. "You've studied the moves of Edward Lasker, haven't you, you little sneak?"

Eva threw back her head and laughed. "Father said I needed to learn from the greatest, so when I was a little girl, he gave me the books *Chess Strategy* and *Chess and Checkers: The Way to Mastership*. I also read *Chess Review* on a regular basis."

"Is there anything you don't do?" Courtland asked as Eva took one of his rooks. He shook his head, trying to figure out how he could stop the bleeding.

She winked and smiled. "I'm sure there is. Let me ponder that for a minute."

Two hours later, Courtland somehow got himself out of the mess he had allowed himself to get into, and he squeaked by with a win.

"Checkmate," he finally said.

Eva jumped to her feet and clapped.

"That was phenomenal," she said. "Other than Father, you are the best player I have ever played against. Pearson used to play me, but he gave up because I always beat him. Frédérique doesn't even like to play checkers. I'm going to go heat up the leftovers from yesterday, but I expect a rematch after we get done eating."

"You've got it," Courtland said, watching her walk back toward the kitchen. *I don't want this to end*, he thought. The feeling washed over him like a flood of water. What he and Eva had shared the night before was something he had never experienced. What kind of fool would he be if he turned his back on what they had shared? Before he lost his nerve, he called out to her.

"Eva," he said. He got up and went into the kitchen where she was arranging the food on the counter, humming a tune, looking as content and happy as he was feeling. Evidently, she didn't hear him. He called to her again. "Eva."

She stopped what she was doing. "Is everything okay?"

"Put that down," he said.

She looked at him quizzically, but she put the bowl she had in her hand on the counter. He took her into his arms and kissed her on her lips with the hunger of a man who just realized he had met the person he wanted to spend the rest of his life loving.

"What brought that on?" she asked breathlessly when he finally stopped kissing her.

"Eva, last night . . . what we shared . . . It was amazing," he said.

"Yes. It was. Better than I ever could have imagined."

"I don't want what we shared to end," he said.

"It was magical, but this can't continue between us, and you know that. Your life does not allow for someone like me, and my life does not allow for someone like you. Maybe fifty years from now the world will accept a you and a me together, but let's not fool ourselves into believing that time is now."

"I'll walk away from all of this," Courtland said, surprised to hear the words come out of his mouth, but as soon as they did, he knew that he meant them. "I'll walk away from it all. I don't want to lose what we have."

Eva shook her head. "What do we have, Courtland? One night of make-believe? There's nothing to walk away from."

"I love you, Eva," he said.

There. He said it. Yes, his feelings for her had grown at an unbelievable rate, but one thing he did know was his feelings for her were real. It didn't matter if they had known each other for a lifetime or for a few weeks. He loved her, and he prayed she loved him back.

He watched as tears began streaming down her face. He blotted them with his thumb.

"It doesn't matter what we feel. It's what they feel," she said, pointing toward the outside. "Find someone society deems appropriate for you to love, Courtland, and then you go and be the best politician you can be. Change the world for the next generation. It's too late for ours."

"Why do we have to give up on something we both feel?" he insisted. Now that he had said his thoughts out loud, he couldn't imagine letting the idea go. But then he had a thought. "Do you not love me? Do you not even have the rumblings of love?"

Eva looked away, but he turned her face back toward him. "Please, tell me what you feel. If it's just me feeling this way, then I won't pressure you, but if you do love me or think you can, why won't you entertain the idea of there being an us?"

"Courtland, I would like to tell you about my mother and father," she said. "Is that okay?"

He wanted to say no, that he wanted to discuss them and only them, but he knew she had a point to make, and like it or not, he needed to listen to it. He nodded, and she took him by the hand and led him to the table. When they were both sitting, she began her story.

"When my father met my mother, he was married and already the father of at least two or three children. He immediately wanted to set Mother up with a house and have her commit to a relationship that was similar to the Plaçage agreements of the past where wealthy white men created separate families with Negro women—primarily light-skinned Negro women. Mother said no. Emphatically," Eva said, "but Father had a way of persuading people to do just the opposite of what they wanted, so it wasn't long before Mother was seeing Father on a regular basis. Finally, she made the commitment to move back to New Orleans where both she and Father were from. She didn't allow him to set her up with a home. She bought her own from the money she had made singing. And then she got pregnant with Frédérique."

"I'm sorry," he said. "I'm sorry for the anguish your mother had to have experienced. But what I am suggesting is nothing like that. I want to marry you, Eva. I want you to be my wife, and I am willing to do anything to make that happen."

"I can't live that life," Eva said. "Last night was amazing, Courtland. I know I should feel terrible for what we did, and who knows, in a few days I might be at confession pouring out my soul about our actions, but right now, I just want to stay in the present."

"We could leave the country," he said, grasping at straws. "There are countries where we could—"

"I'm not running away for love," Eva said simply. Courtland could see that she was in pain, too, but she also was resolute. "I have my family, my business, my life. I don't want to sacrifice everything for love. My mother did it, and all it did was bring her a lifetime of heartbreak. I won't do that. I won't be her. I just won't."

"Why does it have to be a lifetime of heartbreak?" he asked. "I am willing to give up my political career and find other ways to do the things we talked about."

"Courtland, if you give up your political career, the clout you currently have will evaporate," she said, the exasperation clear on her face. "You know this. You know if there is a you and a me, every good thing you could do will cease to be a possibility. You can do more good in the world without me in your life. And likewise, I can do more good if I follow the path I am on."

"I'm not going to give up," Courtland said. "I'm not going to give up on us without a fight."

Eva smiled sadly. "Then it will be a fight you lose, Senator. Don't pursue this with me. And I know it might seem like this is all about you being a white man and me being a Negro, but there is more to it than that. I don't want to give up on my dreams and aspirations, not even for love. I didn't realize that about myself until recently, but I love my life, and if that means I don't get to have a spouse in it, then I can live with that."

Courtland began to see Eva in ways he hadn't before. She was an exceptional woman. He knew if he continued to push now, he would wind up pushing her out of his life completely, so he kissed her again.

"Let's get our food warmed up so we can quickly eat and I can quickly get back to beating you in chess," he said, trying to ignore the impulse to continue the previous conversation.

Eva smiled. "That sounds good," she said, and that was what they did for the remainder of the day. They ate, they played chess, and they kissed and held each other like it was their last time, which, more than likely, Courtland conceded, it would be.

Courtland remembered studying the research of Sigmund Freud in college. Freud had said, "Isn't what we mean by 'falling in love' a kind of sickness . . . ?" He and Jimmy Earl, who had been in the same psychology class, had laughed at the notion, but now here he was, feeling as if his world was on a course of destruction, and he had no clue how to stop it.

TWENTY-FOUR

Courtland

Courtland and Eva had gotten into the habit of staying up late, talking, playing chess, and, of course, making love, so it was midmorning on the third day when they were both awakened by the sound of the snowplows. It wasn't long afterward that Pearson called to let Eva know he would be by to pick her up within the hour.

Courtland watched as she silently slid out of the bed and went into his bathroom to shower. He wanted to join her, something he had done the previous morning, but Eva seemed a bit detached after the call with Pearson, so he gave her the space he thought she needed. Instead, he went downstairs and started a pot of coffee. Unlike the previous two days when they both awakened ravenous, Courtland didn't have an appetite. It wasn't long before Eva joined him in the kitchen, wearing the same clothes she had been wearing when he picked her up the other day, which seemed eons ago.

"Would you like breakfast?" he asked. "I can't cook as well as you, but . . ."

Eva shook her head. "I'm not hungry," she said, "but I wouldn't mind a cup of coffee."

He went to the cabinet and got two mugs. He poured hers black and then handed it to her. He watched as she took small sips from her mug. He felt as if he was drinking her in, imprinting memories for when she wouldn't be in his home. He hated thinking about what it would feel like when she was no longer here. He was struggling not to start praying for another snowstorm.

"Eva, before you leave, I wanted to ask you if anything has changed," he said.

He knew he was grasping at straws, but he couldn't stop himself from at least trying one more time to convince her that the two of them could work.

She looked at him with sad eyes. "No. Nothing has changed."

"But what if—"

"There is no what if," she said with a slight smile. "Courtland, we might be happy for a time. A few months . . . a few years . . . but after that, we both would begin to resent each other because of the things we would have to give up just to make a relationship work."

Courtland shook his head. "I would never resent us, Eva. I love you. I don't know how else to say it or prove it to you."

"It's not enough," she said simply.

Before he could say anything else, the doorbell rang.

"That's Pearson," she said. "I need to go."

He could see the relief she was feeling all over her face.

"Eva, wait," he said, but she moved around him to retrieve her purse from the counter, then turned back around so she was facing him.

She hesitated, then went to him and put her arms around his waist.

"Thank you," she said, looking intently into his eyes.

He stroked her face, and she closed her eyes for a moment before she continued speaking. "Thank you for these last three days. They have been amazing. I will never forget what you and I shared. And, Courtland, I need you to know that I love you too. Feeling these emotions has scared me to no end, but I didn't want you to think the feeling wasn't mutual."

"Then I don't understand why—"

"I've got to go," she interrupted.

"I'll walk away from all of this," Courtland said, repeating his words from the other day. "I'll walk away from it all."

The doorbell rang again.

"I've got to go," she said, reaching up to kiss him again. Then she walked with a purpose toward the front door.

Courtland fought the urge to follow her. He knew she just wanted to get away, and he didn't want to make her departure any more painful than it was.

He could almost hear his father calling him a lightweight for allowing a woman—any woman—to cause him to become this begging, whining man. When Courtland heard the front door close, he sat at the kitchen table and drank his coffee, thinking back over the last few days . . . wishing there were words he could have spoken to change the outcome. After sitting for several minutes, he got up with the intentions of working on senate business when the telephone rang.

"Hello," he said.

"Son, it's me," Nap said, sounding more and more like himself again. His words were still slurred in places, but he was much easier to understand. Courtland was grateful for that. "I've got some news to share with you."

Courtland did not want to hear any news from Nap right then. "Pops, this isn't a good time. How about we talk later?" Courtland asked.

"No," Nap said. "This is important. You'll never guess who came to see me the other day."

"Pops, please," he said, wanting to hang up, but the idea of disrespecting his father in that way kept him on the phone. No matter what, Nap Kingsley was his father, and he had internalized the rule of honoring one's father and mother. It had been instilled in him from before he could even say his first words. "This isn't a good—"

"Strom Thurmond," Nap said quickly. "Strom Thurmond came by the house to talk to me about your future in the party."

"Strom Thurmond? The governor of South Carolina?" Courtland asked. He was confused.

Why would Strom Thurmond make a trip to Georgia to see his father about him? It didn't make any sense to him at all. And anyway, Courtland didn't care for Strom Thurmond. At all. He considered him an arrogant man who would do anything for power. Courtland had met him a time or two, and from what he gleaned from their encounter, Thurmond was all about Thurmond. He didn't mind changing his morality to suit the circumstances. The older man was more than willing to shift his point of view to match the point of view of those who could write the biggest checks for his campaign. It wouldn't surprise Courtland to hear Thurmond was wrapped up in whatever mess his father was mixed up in.

"The very same," Nap said. "And what he came to talk to me about is going to rattle your cage, son."

The idea of Thurmond making a special trip to see his father about him left him with an uneasy feeling.

"Okay, Pops, I give. What did he want?" Courtland asked.

"He was fishing to see if you might want to be his running mate," Nap said.

"Running mate? For what?" Courtland asked. Nothing his father was saying was making any sense. This felt like some elaborate puzzle where half of the pieces were missing.

"Listen, son. There are some rumblings going on in the Democratic Party. Folks are not happy with Truman after he presented that civil rights package for the Coloreds, and as a result, based on what Strom had to say, there might be a third party forming, and he might be its presidential nominee," Nap said. "And he is considering you for his running mate, if some things can be negotiated. That's why he came to talk to me first. To see if I thought you might be willing to adjust a few things rhetorically."

Courtland shook his head. This was the craziest thing he had heard in a long time. "And at no time did you think to tell him this was a conversation he needed to have with me? And exactly what is it that he wants me to 'adjust rhetorically'?"

"Son, this all happened so quickly," Nap said. "And as far as the adjustment to your rhetoric goes, Strom wants you to stand down on some of your positions on Coloreds' rights, and he wants you to distance yourself from these Colored leaders like Adam Clayton Powell Jr. Something I've been telling you for the longest."

"I am who I am, and you know this," Courtland said, "and I'm not sure if I will be in politics much longer."

"Rubbish. You are not leaving politics because, at the end of the day, you are a Kingsley first and a politician second. Everything other than that is up for negotiation," Nap said. "This is about power, son. And you can spout all of the bleeding-heart liberal claptrap that you want, but I know deep down inside, you want power as much as I want it for you. Maybe even more."

"I haven't heard anything about a third party," Courtland said suspiciously. "This sounds like some elaborate hoax. Either you or Strom have gotten your facts messed up. And weren't you just saying you wanted me to run? Now you want me to be someone else's running mate for a party that doesn't even exist?"

If Courtland wasn't so disgruntled with this conversation, he would laugh at the hilarity of it all. There was no way this conversation was real. In fact, he wondered if Nap had dreamed it all up. A few days after his stroke, Nap had been talking out of his mind, referencing people who had long died as being his visitors. Courtland wondered if Nap had experienced another stroke. He was about to ask his father to put his mother, Millicent, on the phone, but Nap started talking again.

"Son, this is no hoax. And yes, I know I said you should run, but the more that I think about it, the more this route for you makes sense," Nap said. "Running on the ticket with Strom gives you a chance to get your feet wet, but as the second man on the ticket, even if things don't pan out, that's Strom's loss, not yours."

"Pops, I am not interested in splitting the party," Courtland said. "Like it or not, Truman is going to get the Democratic nomination at the convention, and with or without the Southern Democrats, he will win. Or worse, the Republican nominee wins because the Democrats have split the vote. This won't work."

Courtland was ready to be done with this conversation, but of course, Nap was like an old hound dog with a bone. He was not going to let this conversation end until he was ready for it to end.

"Courtland, the Southern Democrats are fed up, and if the Southern Democrats break free of the party, there goes the party. The rest will follow, I promise you. Strom knows he needs someone like you—someone who is charismatic, has a strong foothold in the senate, and has an impeccable military career. Just talk to him, Courtland."

"There's nothing to talk about," Courtland said. "I am not interested in being on some splinter group ticket, and like I said, I am not sure if I will stay in politics. There are other things more important to me."

"Nothing is more important than this!" Nap roared into the phone. "Courtland, you need to listen to me on this one thing. You have got to stop seeing that Colored woman. Do you hear?"

Courtland was silent for a moment. How did his father know about him and Eva?

"What are you talking about?" Courtland asked.

"You know what I'm talking about," his father said, his voice gruff. "It's one thing to have a dalliance or two with one of them, but a relationship is out of the question. You can't afford to be traipsing all over D.C. seeing that woman. It's been kept out of the news so far, but it's just a matter of time before folks down here in Georgia get wind of it, and if they do, you will be a one-and-done senator. And at that point, you can forget about the presidency or anything else related to politics. Cut ties with that woman now, son."

Courtland wanted to slam the phone down, but he needed to know what his father knew and how he knew it.

"How do you know about Eva and me?" Courtland asked.

"I know everything about you, son," Nap said, his voice as chilly as the outside of Courtland's home. "Do you honestly think I would leave you to your own volition up there in Washington? I have eyes and ears everywhere."

"My personal life is my business, Pops. Call off your goons, and remember, I am my own man. I make decisions on my own. I have to go," Courtland said and gently hung up the phone. Courtland knew only one thing to do. He had to go home and confront his father face-to-face, because if there was any chance Nap was involved in the violence that had happened to Eva's restaurant, he wanted to see Nap Kingsley for himself. He would deal with the Strom Thurmond situation later.

TWENTY-FIVE

Eva

"You okay?" Pearson asked, looking over at Eva as they drove toward home.

The first few minutes of their drive, he didn't say anything. Pearson was always good about respecting boundaries and giving her space, but he would also go out of his way to be protective of her. So even though she just wanted to sink into the seat and allow the sadness to wash over her, she knew she had to respond.

"I'm okay," she said, but she wasn't. She had thought she would be able to just take things in stride . . . enjoy the moment and not allow the guilt to enter into her psyche, but that was not the case. She wanted to sink into the earth when she saw the love in her brother-in-law's eyes. No judgment; just brotherly concern.

"Eva, no matter what we do in life, we always have a way to get forgiveness," Pearson said. "We just have to ask."

Eva nodded. She wasn't ready for a sermon. She just wanted to get home and get into her bed and try to process all that had happened. Maybe *ashamed* was too strong a word for what she was feeling. No, the better word would be *disappointed*. She was disappointed that she hadn't fought her feelings harder. She wished she had protected her heart more. She wished she hadn't allowed herself to be so vulnerable with Courtland. She had gone from never being kissed to making love in a matter of weeks. She was not an impulsive person, but Courtland had somehow made her feel things she had never felt before, and she wasn't sure if she ever wanted to feel them again. Throughout the years, especially after the death of her parents, Eva had placed emotional barriers around her heart. Now she felt wide open and exposed.

When they got to the brownstone that she had spent most of her teen years in, she felt the emotions threatening to spill over. Like she had been doing all morning, she breathed in deeply, willing the unshed tears away until she could get to the safety of her bedroom.

After Pearson stopped the car, he came around and opened the door for her. Eva stepped out and quickly pulled her coat tightly to her body. The air was brisk. The snow had stopped, but the breeze was enough to cause one's breath to catch. She and Pearson hurried toward the door. Before Pearson could open it, Frédérique pulled the door open. Pearson left the sisters alone as he walked toward the back of the house. For a time, they silently stared at each other.

Eva opened her mouth to say something, but she closed it because the tears started to fall, slowly at first, and then her face was awash with them. Frédérique's face immediately softened at the sight of her pain. Without a sound, she pulled Eva into her arms. They stood in the hallway and held each other for a while, then Frédérique gently pushed Eva away so they were looking at each other again.

"Hang up your coat," Frédérique said, sounding like she did when Eva was a little girl and had been out playing for too long. Eva complied. "Why, Eva?" Frédérique asked.

Eva didn't want to see the sadness and disappointment in her sister's face, so she made herself look away, but Frédérique turned Eva's face back so they were looking in each other's eyes. "Why would you do this to yourself? Why would you become intimate with a man you have no future with? I just don't understand."

Eva moved around her sister and went into the parlor. Frédérique followed and waited for Eva to speak. Finally, Eva found her voice.

"Frédérique, I know what I did the last few days doesn't make sense to you. I'm not proud of my choices, but I am not ashamed either," she said, trying to sound more confident and self-assured than she was actually feeling. "I am not Mother. I have no delusions that anything of substance will come of the last few days. I know that he will move on with his life, and I will too."

Frédérique moved to the edge of her seat where she could reach out for her sister's hands. She grasped them tightly. "But do you know that you will move on, Eva? From here on out, you will compare every other man to this one."

"Frédérique, I am not you," she said. "I love you, and I love the family you and Pearson are building together, but what you have is not what I want. Come tomorrow, I am meeting with a loan officer at Industrial Savings Bank, and hopefully in March I will be starting the process of opening a second restaurant. Boyfriends and husbands do not have a place in the dreams I have for myself."

"Eva, I can't say I understand this desire you have to be a businesswoman," Frédérique said. "But there are men who can live with your aspirations. Perhaps Wendell . . ."

Eva laughed out loud. "Wendell is the last man on earth who could live with not being the center of attention. Oh, he talks a good game, but all it would take would be for him to have a party to go to and I couldn't be on his arm, and everything would come crashing down."

"You don't know that," Frédérique insisted.

"Yes, I do," Eva said. "Freddie, I appreciate all of your concern, but I want to travel a different path than most women. Look at Mary McLeod Bethune and all she has accomplished. Both of her parents were slaves, yet she has started her own school, college, hospital, not to mention the activism work she has done. Heads of state listen to her every word. She is the woman I want to be like. I want a life where I make a name for myself. I'm totally fine if I don't end up being someone's Mrs."

Frédérique let her sister's hands go and sat back into the softness of the couch. The phone rang, but neither woman paid attention to it. Nine times out of ten it was for Pearson anyway. After a moment the ringing stopped.

"There is no shame in being someone's Mrs.," Frédérique said in a quiet voice. "Some of us count it as a blessing. I wouldn't trade one day of being Reverend Dr. Pearson Montgomery's wife."

Immediately, Eva saw that she had insulted her sister, and she felt terrible. This subject, like so many more, were sore subjects for them to talk about.

"I didn't mean it like that, Frédérique," Eva said. "Of course there is no shame in being a wife and mother, but there is also no shame in not wanting either of those things."

"So what are you saying, Eva?" Frédérique asked. "Do you just have relations with men when the mood strikes? Even if Mother didn't teach you any better, I thought I had."

Before Eva could respond, Pearson reentered the room carrying Daisy, whose eyes immediately went to Frédérique. She began to grunt loudly, reaching for Frédérique. Once Frédérique had her in her arms, Daisy let out a huge sigh. Eva was glad her sister had a child to dote on, but she knew Frédérique would never stop smothering her.

"Eva, Mary McLeod Bethune is on the phone for you," Pearson said. "You can take the call in my study."

"Thank you," Eva said and went into her brother-in-law's office. She picked up the phone, happy for the interruption. "Mrs. McLeod Bethune. Good morning. How are you?"

"I am fine, dear," she said. "Checking up on you, actually. I know the incident the other Sunday was difficult on you. How are you holding up?"

"I'm fine, ma'am," she said, although that wasn't entirely true, but considering all that Mrs. McLeod Bethune and the other leaders had witnessed, she was not going to complain. "I am doing fine. I will not allow a few rogue individuals to deter me."

"That is nice to hear. When they come for you like that, Eva, that means you are doing the righteous work. They don't come for those who are passively sitting by watching the rest of us do the hard labor," Mrs. McLeod Bethune said. "No. They come for those who are battle ready, and that is what you have been since I first met you."

"Thank you, Mrs. McLeod Bethune," Eva said with a smile.

"You're welcome," she said. "Now, do you remember I mentioned I was going to have a gathering of some ladies in the movement?"

"Yes, ma'am," Eva said, although it seemed like a long time ago.

"Well, I apologize for the short notice, but the meeting is tomorrow. Just a few ladies who are dedicated to the cause. I was hoping you could join us. We need your youth and energy."

"I would be honored," Eva said. "I have a meeting at the bank at 2:00 p.m. That shouldn't take longer than an hour or two."

"Perfect," Mrs. McLeod Bethune said. "My meeting doesn't start until 4:00 p.m. You can bring that sister of yours, if you like. It would be nice having Reverend Pearson Montgomery's wife in the midst."

Eva smiled. She couldn't count how many times she had tried to get Frédérique to go with her to a meeting of the NAACP or a neighborhood association meeting, but Frédérique always begged off, feigning church work or something she had to do at home. Eva knew now that her sister's excuse would be Daisy.

"I will ask, but my sister is more of the quiet type," Eva said in a diplomatic voice. "She much prefers working from the back. She and Pearson regularly donate to the United Negro College Fund and the NAACP. She just isn't as bold as I am when it comes to other things."

"We all must find our way. There is not one way to fight for freedom, but many. We are grateful for whatever Mrs. Montgomery is willing to do," Mrs. McLeod Bethune said. "I will see you tomorrow. Stay well."

After they both hung up, she went back to the front room where Frédérique and Pearson were waiting. Eva noticed Daisy was gone. Frédérique must have taken her to her room for a nap. Eva told them about the meeting.

Pearson shook his head. "The last thing you need to be doing is taking part in another meeting. Eva, you are going to have to tone things down. Second Street Baptist has tried to build up a relationship with the D.C. police department, but if they are planning and plotting against you and some of these others, well, that means not only are you at risk, but the entire community is also at risk."

"I'm not tucking my tail and running like some mangy animal," Eva said, trying to control the anger and frustration she was feeling. "I have done nothing wrong, and I will not kowtow to anyone, especially the D.C. police and whomever else is working with them."

"Then you are willing to put yourself and others at risk?" Frédérique said in an accusatory tone. "Is that what you're saying?"

"I don't want to put anyone at risk, but at the end of the day, Frédérique, aren't we already at risk? Don't Negroes have to look over our collective shoulders every single day, even when we do nothing to agitate anyone?" Eva asked.

Eva knew her sister and brother-in-law's mantra. *Be patient. Let God fix the unfixable. Pray.* Eva believed in all of those things too. But she also believed prayer without works, like the Bible said, was detrimental to everything the civil rights movement was about. Eva had to believe that the little she was doing was making a difference.

"The fact that we know we are in danger every single day is enough for us to practice caution," Pearson said. "As you know, I have seen a lynching, Eva. I know what some white folks are capable of doing. I will not stand idly by and watch my family get destroyed."

"I'm going to do what I can for as long as I can," Eva said in a careful voice, "but I don't want to put the people I love in danger. Perhaps I should move out."

There. She'd finally said the words she had been thinking about for a while. She loved living with her brother-in-law and sister, but she also wanted to take the next step toward being completely and totally independent. She couldn't live with them forever, nor did she want to. The time she had spent with Courtland had opened her eyes to a lot of things, including her need to begin figuring out what her life was going to look like—with or without a man in it. She was independent in everything else in her life. Living on her own seemed like the next natural step.

"Don't be ridiculous, Eva," Frédérique said. "The last thing you need to do is move out, especially with this added danger. People are watching you. Can't you see it?"

"Honey, we have never tried to stifle your growth or stand in the way of your ideals or goals, but you are stepping into uncharted waters. If they were willing to bomb your restaurant, they will not have any issues with killing you or the people you love," Pearson said forcefully.

"I'm going to the meeting," she said resolutely.

"Sweetie, maybe you could hold back a bit until we find out who all is involved in this mess," Pearson said, always the diplomat.

The phone interrupted their conversation once again. Pearson got up and went to the other room. Eva and Frédérique sat in silence. It wasn't long before he returned.

"Sister Lena Fenway is dying," Pearson said. Sister Lena was one of the church mothers. She had been a member of Second Street since she was a little girl. "I need to go. Eva, I know what we are saying seems conservative and overly cautious, but the times we are living in now are difficult. We just don't want to see anything bad happen to you or anyone else."

"I understand," Eva said, "but there are some things I have to follow my conscience on. Please give my sympathy to the Fenway family. I'm going upstairs."

Before either of them could say anything else to Eva, she hurriedly left the parlor and went up the stairs to her room, shutting the door behind her. She needed time to process everything she was feeling.

She knew someone out there had a vendetta against her—or if not her, against the company she kept. Processing that was not easy. And then on top of that, trying to fathom the enormity of what she and Courtland had said to each other. *I love you*. Eva's mind was twisted and torn. Who was she, and what did she want? Those were the questions that tormented her prayers every single day.

She went over to the window and knelt. Tears started to fall down her face. She had never felt so out of sync with her family and God. She felt like she was a terrible disappointment to all of them, and she wasn't entirely sure what to do to fix things. She looked up at the sky. There was no blue to be seen, just grayness and fluffy, angry-looking clouds. It looked like more snow might fall. The outside seemed to match Eva's insides. Troubled. Hazy.

Too exhausted to pray her rosary, she simply looked upward. "Help me," she said. "Help me to figure this out. Please."

TWENTY-SIX

Eva

"Thank you for coming by today, Miss Cardon. I have reviewed your financial statements and your business proposal, and everything seems to be in order for you to receive the business loan you have requested," said Mr. Childress, the loan officer at Industrial Savings Bank.

Eva smiled and took a deep breath. She knew everything was in order, but until she heard the older man tell her the good news, she wasn't sure. She knew her youth and her gender worked against her. When new vendors would come to the restaurant, they would always look past her as if she were not standing there, or they would ask her where her boss was. She was used to having to prove herself to everyone. It was nice that things had worked out the way she had hoped.

Eva smiled. "Thank you, Mr. Childress. I truly appreciate the confidence your bank is showing me. I am excited to move forward." She and Albert Cassell, her architect, had met that morning. They had gone over the renovation plans, and she had brought them with her to the bank for Mr. Childress to look over.

Signing the paperwork and going over the terms of the loan took another hour, so it was after four before she was ready to leave the bank. As she was walking toward the front door, Jesse H. Mitchell, the president of the bank, was walking into the building. He looked at her and smiled.

"Miss Eva," he said, offering her his hand. "I hope we treated you right today."

Eva shook his hand and returned his smile. "Yes, sir. I will be starting on the renovations of the building I just got approved to buy. Hopefully I will be opening my new restaurant by the summer."

Mr. Mitchell nodded in approval. "That's wonderful. We love seeing the entrepreneurial spirit alive and well in this part of D.C. Give my best to your sister and Reverend Dr. Montgomery."

"I will," Eva said and made her way outside to her car. As she pulled out of the lot, she noticed a police car pulling out at the same time. She was several turns away from Mrs. McLeod Bethune's home, but when she turned left, the police car turned left, and when she turned right, the police car turned right. When she got to Mrs. McLeod Bethune's neighborhood, the police car was still behind her. She pulled up behind one of the cars that was already parked, and slowly the policeman drove by. She only caught a quick glimpse of him, but his face looked ominous. For a moment, Eva wondered if she should go home instead of attending the meeting, but then she saw Mary Church Terrell. Eva immediately got out of the car and greeted Mrs. Terrell, who was in her eighties but still going strong.

Snow was beginning to fall just a little. Mrs. Terrell placed her hand on Eva's arm.

"Eva, darling," she said. "So nice to see you. I always love it when you young women show up for these meetings. We can't do it without you. Don't tell Mary McLeod Bethune I said this, but she's not getting any younger."

Eva laughed. "I am grateful to be included."

"Escort me in, dear," Mrs. Terrell said. "I don't want to fall."

The two women made their way into Mrs. McLeod Bethune's home where the room was filled with women known in Washington, D.C., for their charity work and their activism. Eva waved at Mrs. McLeod Bethune's close friend and executive secretary, Jeanetta Welch Brown, and Mrs. Jernigan, the wife of Reverend Jernigan from the Mount Carmel Baptist Church. She was also excited to see Sister Gloria Therese sitting beside another woman from St. Augustine; the two were talking animatedly to each other. Eva was surprised to see a couple of white women present. It wasn't long before Mrs. McLeod Bethune called the women to order. Eva sat beside Mrs. Terrell, but she noticed some of the other ladies seemed to be struggling to figure out where to sit.

"Sit anywhere, ladies," Mrs. McLeod Bethune said, waving her hand impatiently. "This isn't Thompson's Restaurant on 7th Street. There is no segregation in this room. Sit where you see a chair. We are all equals in this space. If anyone believes otherwise, we thank you for attending, but your efforts are not needed here. Now, some of you might wonder what the white women are doing here. We women, regardless of our skin color, all subscribe to the same moral code, and as a result of that fact, we are equals, so we all must join together in our fight against injustice."

Eva recognized several of the white women, and she knew that Mrs. McLeod Bethune was not just including them for their Christian charity. They were there to provide whatever financial support Mrs. McLeod Bethune felt was necessary to do the work that needed to be done. Eva smiled. Mrs. McLeod Bethune was all feminine grace until she needed to lay down the law. She didn't mind putting anyone in their place, regardless of their ethnicity or gender.

"You can tell when the new folks come around," Mrs. Terrell said in a loud whisper in Eva's ear. "How are you going to fight segregation out in the world if you can't figure it out right here in this room? Mary is much kinder with her words than I am."

Eva laughed and lightly patted Mrs. Terrell's hand. Once everyone was seated, Mrs. McLeod Bethune started sharing with the women about plans to reinforce their resolve to buy in the Negro community only.

"Ladies, it makes no sense for us to take our dollars down to the white stores if they do not treat us with the respect we deserve," she said. "Our Negro businesses depend on our support, and too many of us are taking our patronage to people who don't even think we are fit to walk on the same side of the road with them, yet they will willingly take our money."

"Exactly," Mrs. Terrell said. She turned toward Eva and said in a low voice, "We will integrate those white businesses—it is just a matter of time—but we must be careful that we don't undermine our own. They must be protected."

Eva agreed. As much as she thought segregation was wrong, she did worry what it would do to their community if schools and restaurants and department stores all became integrated. It was one thing for the white patrons to come to her restaurant, but she wondered what would happen when Negroes had the right to eat at any restaurant they wanted. Along with discussing strategies for promoting local Negro businesses, they also talked about voter registration and women's rights.

"Women are truly our future in our communities," Mrs. McLeod Bethune said. "Every day, women are leading the charge when it comes to education and community engagement. We must stay vigilant and encourage the men in our lives to fight for justice."

Once Mrs. McLeod Bethune was done speaking, she put the women into groups and tasked them all with focusing on one thing. Eva's group's purpose was to talk about helping Negro women become business leaders. The other group members were a local beauty shop owner, a seamstress/dressmaker, and a bookkeeper who handled the accounts of a number of businesses on U Street.

Desiree Lawson, the beauty shop owner, started the conversation. "We need more of our women going to college and studying business and finance. Too many of us are getting by with our God-given talent, but as time goes on, that is not going to be sufficient."

Eva nodded. "I agree. I was blessed to have a head for business, but now we need our girls to get business and finance degrees, like you said, but we also need them to get law degrees and study professions that we are often thought to be weak in, like mathematics and science."

"So true," Desiree said. "I have ideas for products that I would love to develop, but I don't have a chemistry background. It would be wonderful to work with a young Negro woman on my ideas."

Lettie Odom, the bookkeeper, interjected. "If we want our girls to get degrees in those areas, we need to provide them with scholarships. The United Negro College Fund is a good start, but they are trying to help Negroes all over the country. Everyone keeps talking about there being more than three hundred businesses on U Street . . . Well, we need to approach all of those businesses and tell them they need to help us provide scholarships for our young people, but especially our girls."

From there they continued to brainstorm different ideas for how they could achieve the goal to educate more girls and empower more women to start businesses. By the time Mrs. McLeod Bethune called time on their discussion, they had some detailed plans in place.

"Thank you all for coming today," Mrs. McLeod Bethune said, smiling at each of them, pride clearly etched on her face. "When women make plans, things happen. I know today is just the beginning. Before we leave, Sister Gloria Therese, would you mind leading us in prayer?"

Sister Gloria Therese came forward, and the Catholics in the room made the sign of the cross along with her, and then everyone bowed their head as she prayed, "Father, you have called us to serve others. Help us to serve with open hearts and minds. Cover us all with your blood, and watch over us as we leave here today—women with a stronger purpose and stronger servants of God. We pray this prayer in the name of the Father, the Son, and the Holy Spirit. Amen."

At this point, everyone began to disperse. Sister Gloria Therese came over and kissed Eva on both cheeks. "It is wonderful seeing you here today, Eva. This is the first time I have been to one of these meetings. It was nice seeing some familiar faces."

"Thank you, Sister Gloria Therese," Eva said.

"I will continue to pray for you, my dear," she said and made her way across the room. Mrs. McLeod Bethune came over next. She hugged Eva tightly.

"I am so happy you were able to attend today's meeting, Eva. I am hopeful you will allow me to host a fundraiser dinner at your restaurant in support of our Southern brothers' and sisters' efforts to register voters. Everyone's voice needs to be heard," she said to Eva.

"Yes, ma'am," Eva said. "I would be honored." She knew both Pearson and Frédérique were going to be livid, but she hoped by the time the event took place, whoever was responsible for the acts of violence against her restaurant would be behind bars.

"That is wonderful," she said. "I will have my secretary get in touch with you and make the necessary arrangements."

"That sounds wonderful," Eva said. It had gotten dark outside, and the snow was coming down again, so she wanted to get on the road toward home. Eva said good night to everyone and went out to her car. Once she started her car and pulled into the street, she noticed a car was driving extremely close to her. Scarily close. Eva tried to speed up a little to put some space between her and the car, but the driver behind her matched her speed.

Eva was frightened. She didn't know what was going on. She was going faster than she wanted to go in snow and ice, but the car behind her was not letting up, to the point where he tapped the back of her car with the front of his. Then he flashed his lights. It was a police car. Eva screamed. She was so focused on the police car behind her that she didn't pay attention to the fact that she was veering off into the other lane. She looked up just in time to see a city bus heading toward her. She jerked her steering wheel, and immediately the car started to spin out of control, hitting a patch of ice and then flying across the street into a tree, knocking Eva unconscious.

~

"Eva!" she heard a voice calling out to her, but it was so faint and sounded so far away that she didn't think she had enough strength to make the voice hear her response, so she didn't even try. *I'll just stay here*, she thought. *At least for a while. Anyway, this isn't so bad, wherever this is.*

"Eva!" she heard a sharp voice call, and this time it was close by. She immediately recognized it, even though it had been many years since she last heard it.

"Mother," she heard herself say, although she didn't move her lips—or at least she didn't think she did. It was like her voice was floating outside of her body. She tried to move something, but she couldn't feel anything. Not her legs, her feet, her hands . . . nothing. That scared her and caused the panic to rise again. *Got to go deeper into the darkness*, she thought. *It's safer there.*

"Eva Cardon, do not do that," she heard her mother say. "Go back. Go back now."

Eva didn't know what to do. She never disobeyed her mother when her mother was alive, but now that her mother was . . . Wait a minute. Dead. Was she dead too? Eva was confused.

"Mother?" she called out again, and this time her lips did move. She felt them. "Mother?"

"Eva," she heard a voice say with a sense of urgency. She

recognized that voice too. It was Frédérique. For a moment she was really confused. Was Frédérique dead as well? *No*, she thought. Wherever she had been, she knew she wasn't there anymore. She couldn't hear her mother's voice. Her mother had sent her back somehow. But back from where? That was what she didn't understand.

"Freddie," Eva mumbled, but it hurt to speak. Her throat felt raw, like it had blisters. And she still couldn't open her eyes for some reason, but she could hear. She felt like she was closer to where Freddie was than to where their mother was.

"Oh, thank you, Jesus!" she heard her sister cry out. "Thank you. Thank you. Open your eyes, Eva. Open your eyes, baby. Pearson, go get the doctor. Tell him she's awake. Eva, open your eyes."

"Can't," she said, barely above a whisper. Everything hurt. She just wanted to go back into the darkness. She didn't hurt there. *Go back*, she thought. *Go back to Mother.*

"Yes, you can open your eyes, my love," she heard Frédérique say. "Try. Try for me."

Eva tried, but it made her tired and in pain like she had never felt before. *Go back to the dark . . .*

"Eva," she heard a male voice say. "Eva, this is Dr. Overton, Dr. Felix Overton, and I want you to squeeze my hand. Can you do that?"

"No," she said, moaning.

"Sure you can, sweetheart. Squeeze," he said. "Doesn't have to be hard. Just a little squeeze."

Eva tried to do what the doctor said, if for no other reason than to make him stop talking. The talking made her head hurt worse, so she focused her attention on squeezing his hand like he asked. It wasn't easy. It was like her brain and her body had stopped communicating with each other, but after a moment or two, she was able to press his hand with her fingers.

"Good," he said. "That's good. Now, tell me your name."

She grimaced again. She wished the pounding in her head would stop. She could concentrate better if the pounding would just stop. She thought he would let her rest after his last command. "Eva," she finally croaked.

"Yes, Eva," he said. She could hear the happiness in his voice. Why would he be so happy over her knowing her name, of all things? He kept poking and prodding and tapping on her knees, elbows, and feet. Finally, he seemed satisfied with what he was finding. "Would you now try to open your eyes?"

She still didn't want to. She could already feel the light pressing against her eyeballs. She just wanted to return to the darkness—to go find her mother. To go where she didn't hurt.

"Eva, I need you to open your eyes," he said more forcefully. "You can do it. Just open them, even if just for a minute."

Eva groaned, but she attempted to open her eyes like he instructed her to do. It took a moment, but finally, she was able to squint. It hurt. She groaned even more, but she kept fighting to open her eyes wider until she was staring up at a Negro man in a white doctor's coat. He seemed familiar, but she couldn't quite place where she had seen him before. He had salt-and-pepper hair and a friendly smile. She looked around the room, trying to get her bearings. Trying to figure out where she was.

"Freddie," she moaned. Immediately her sister appeared and took her hand in hers.

"I'm right here, Eva," she said.

Tears were streaming down Frédérique's face. Seeing her sister in tears scared Eva.

"Why are you crying? Where am I?" Eva asked. "My head hurts."

"I'm crying because I thought . . . I'm crying because I'm happy," Frédérique said with a watery smile.

Eva squinted up at the doctor. She remembered him. He was Adam's friend.

"Where am I?" Eva asked again.

"You're at Freedmen's Hospital, Eva," Dr. Overton said. "Do you remember what happened?"

Eva closed her eyes as she pondered that question. Did she remember what happened? Seemed an easy enough question, but for some reason she was struggling with the details. She tried to make her mind take her back to her last memory. She remembered going to the bank and getting approved for a loan, but she didn't think that was her last memory. Then she remembered being at a meeting at Mrs. McLeod Bethune's house.

"I think I was on my way home after leaving Mrs. McLeod Bethune's house," she said slowly.

"It's okay if you don't remember everything today, sweetheart," Frédérique said, stroking Eva's hair.

Eva couldn't move her right arm, and she noticed it was in a sling. There was clearly a lot for her to remember.

Eva looked up at her sister with huge eyes that were filling up with tears. "A police car was following me. It was so close. I sped up. He hit me from behind, and my car slid on the ice. A bus was coming toward me and then . . . and then . . . I don't know what happened next. Did I hit something?"

"Yes. A tree," Frédérique said, the tears continuing to fall down her face, but she didn't stop to wipe them. She just kept holding Eva's hand like she was afraid to let it go. "Did you say a police car?"

Eva told them how the police car had followed her after she left the bank, and then, as she left the meeting at Mary McLeod Bethune's house, another police car, or maybe the same one, had pulled up behind her, even ramming the back of her car until she spun out.

Eva watched as Pearson came over and put his arms around Frédérique.

"Are you sure it was the police?" Pearson asked.

"Yes," Eva said. "I know it was."

"Okay," he said, his voice deep with emotion. "All that matters now is we got you back."

"Got me back from where?" she asked, looking from one solemn face to the other.

"You had a rough go of it, Eva," Pearson said, but he didn't explain what he meant by it.

"I don't remember anything after the accident," Eva said.

"You were very blessed," Dr. Overton said. "You broke your arm, bruised some ribs, and suffered a terrible concussion. You have been unconscious for a little over three days, Eva."

She looked at him with confusion. "That makes no sense," she said. "It seems like it was just today."

She didn't want to question the validity of the doctor's statement, but she just couldn't wrap her brain around the possibility that she had been unconscious for three days.

"I know, Eva. Unfortunately, we do not know enough about comas to adequately answer your questions, but thankfully you came out of it, seemingly unscathed," he said. "I will want to run a few tests, but it looks like you are on the mend, young lady."

Eva began to cry in earnest. She couldn't stop the tears, and before she knew it, she was hiccupping and having trouble breathing.

Dr. Overton put an oxygen mask on her face. "Take deep breaths," he said in a soothing and calm voice. "I know this is a lot, my dear. Try not to take in everything at once. We don't have to discuss anything else today."

Eva tried to take deep breaths and not focus on what she just learned, but then her mind instantly went to the bus filled with people. She reached up and pushed the oxygen mask away.

"Was anyone else hurt?" she asked.

"No, sweetheart. Just you," Frédérique answered.

Eva had more questions, but before she could ask anything else, someone knocked on the door to her room. Before anyone could say something, Courtland entered. Eva felt her heart begin to beat extra hard in her chest.

"Courtland," she whispered. "Courtland."

She barely heard the objections of her sister, brother-in-law, and doctor. Her only thoughts in that moment were about Courtland as he made his way over to her bed.

TWENTY-SEVEN

Courtland

"You shouldn't be here," Frédérique said angrily to Courtland. "She is not well enough for visitors."

Courtland heard the words Eva's sister was speaking, but he was completely focused on Eva. She looked so tiny and helpless in the bed. He was used to her being tall and bold with her every move. He desperately wanted to go to her and take her into his arms, but he didn't know what her brother-in-law, who was looking at him in a menacing way, would do if he tried to get any closer than he was. Even the doctor looked like he wanted a piece of Courtland's hide. He wasn't afraid of either man, but he didn't want to upset Eva.

"I'm sorry," Courtland said to all of them, but he made no move to leave. The only way he was leaving was if Eva ordered him to leave. "I don't want to upset anyone. It's just that Adam called me and told me what happened. If I had known, I would have been here sooner. I had to see her. I . . ."

"It's okay," Eva said in a soft voice. "Let him stay."

Frédérique looked at her sister. "Eva, you have been through a lot these last few days. You just woke up. This is not the time for you to deal with this," she said, waving her hand toward Courtland. "He can come back another day when you are stronger."

"Let him stay," Eva repeated.

"The police will be coming by soon, and they will want to talk to Eva about what happened," Pearson said. "I'm not even sure I want them to come in, considering what Eva shared with us. It would not be wise for you to be here, Senator. Your presence will only complicate matters."

"What did Eva share?" Courtland asked. Pearson hesitated but then filled him in on what she had told them about the police's involvement in her accident.

"Let me help. I'm a United States senator. That might carry some weight," Courtland said in a careful voice. He didn't want to be offensive to Eva's family or the doctor, but he also knew that his presence might make a difference in how the police behaved.

"You mean you are a white man with influence," Pearson said bitterly. "We don't need your help."

"Eva, what do you want?" Courtland asked, looking at her intently.

For a moment, it was as if no one was in the room but the two of them.

"I want you to stay," she said. "Please don't make him leave." Eva looked tearfully from her sister to her brother-in-law.

"He can stay," Frédérique said resolutely, "but he is here for your support only. Pearson will speak to the police. Having too many cooks in the kitchen is not a good thing."

Courtland went over and sat on the other side of Eva's bed near her good arm. Tears began to spill down her face in earnest. He reached into his pocket and took out a clean handkerchief. He gently wiped the tears away, and then he took her hand in his.

"You're okay," he said. "You're okay. We will figure this out. I'm so sorry," Courtland said and kissed Eva softly on her lips.

She still had a small lump on her forehead. He could kill the animal who did this to her. This was the second time she could have lost her life because of some maniac's act of hatred. For a second his mind drifted to his father. Could Nap have had something to do with this? Could his father be behind this particular incident? He needed answers, because whoever was responsible was clearly not going to give up until Eva was dead. He could not think of any reason someone would focus so much attention on Eva. She wasn't even one of the most prominent members of the civil rights movement. She was no Mary McLeod Bethune or Mary Church Terrell. This seemed extremely personal to whomever was doing it, and he wanted to know who and why.

"I know you probably shouldn't be here, so if you want to leave, I—"

"I am where I want to be, Eva Cardon," he interrupted. "I love you. I told you that already. I will be here as long as you want me to."

And Courtland meant every word. He didn't care if her family liked it or not. He loved this woman, and there was nothing he wouldn't do to protect her, even if that included going up against his father.

Lieutenant Stevens entered the room, his large frame filling up the door. Courtland knew he was the last person Eva wanted to see. It took all Courtland could do to remain silent and allow Pearson to handle things. He patted Eva's hand and mouthed, "It's going to be okay."

"I need to speak to Eva Cardon," the lieutenant said in a clipped tone. "You all can go out into the hallway."

"Eva has just awakened from three arduous days of being unconscious," Dr. Overton said. "I need to make sure she doesn't overtax herself, so I am not leaving the room."

"We are not leaving either," Pearson said forcefully. "You are lucky we are even allowing you to ask a few questions today."

The lieutenant's eyes met Courtland's, but neither he nor Lieutenant Stevens said anything to each other. Courtland could see the derision in his eyes. He knew that men like Lieutenant Stevens could not stand the idea of men like him being attracted to a Negro woman. Given the opportunity, Courtland imagined the middle-aged white man would have a few choice words to say about the two of them. Courtland hated the idea of Eva getting questioned by such an arrogant bigot. And now that she was sure it was a policeman who caused her wreck, he wondered if it was a good decision to allow her to speak to the police, particularly this policeman.

"You don't have to talk to him without a lawyer being present, Eva," Courtland said in a low voice so that only she heard him.

"I just want to get it over with," she said, closing her eyes wearily.

"Well, let's begin," Lieutenant Stevens said. "May I get closer to the . . . uh . . . complainant?"

Courtland looked back down at Eva. She was shivering, and he knew it was not from being cold. "No," he answered. "You're fine where you are."

Lieutenant Stevens looked at Pearson, who nodded in agreement. "She can hear you where you are. I am going to allow you to ask her some questions, but you do not have all afternoon. My sister-in-law needs rest, not an inquisition."

The lieutenant pulled out a notebook and a pencil. "State your name, miss," he said in a cryptic voice. He clearly was not going to do anything to make this interview relaxing for Eva. She looked up at Courtland, and he nodded with a smile, patting her hand encouragingly.

"Eva Cardon," she said in a hoarse voice, clearing it slightly.

"Miss Cardon, where were you at approximately 6:30 p.m. on Friday, March 12, 1948?" he asked.

"I was leaving Mrs. Mary McLeod Bethune's home," she said.

"And what were the driving conditions like that night?" he asked.

"It was sleeting and there was a bit of ice in places on the road," she said.

"Yes," he said. "It was a nasty night to be out. Do you frequently go out on social calls late in the day, but especially on days when there is inclement weather?"

"Water," she said.

Frédérique reached for the cup of water and gave Eva a few sips. She cleared her throat again before responding. "Sir, I am a business-woman. I often have late meetings. That is the nature of my life. But my being out during inclement weather has no bearing on the fact that one of your officers ran into me, causing me to almost hit a bus and ultimately run into a tree."

"Well, miss," he said, smiling at her condescendingly, "we spoke to an entire busload of people, and nary a one of them mentioned there being a police car involved in your accident. The bus driver said you were weaving all over the road, and then you must have realized you were heading toward a bus, so you spun out and then hit a tree. Fortunately, one of our officers was patrolling that area, and he was able to save you."

Courtland looked at Eva. He saw her confusion.

"That's not right," she said. "Surely some of the people who were at my meeting saw what happened."

"No need to question them when I have credible witnesses saying they saw no inciting incident as it pertained to your crash," he said.

"Have you looked at the back of her car?" Pearson asked. "The entire car is totaled, but there are clear marks on the back. I didn't know where they came from until Eva woke up and told us she was rear-ended by some policeman on your force."

"Our police officers are very skilled drivers," Lieutenant Stevens said. "They know how to drive in inclement weather. Were you drinking that night, Miss Cardon? Perhaps you were inebriated and got a bit disoriented as you drove."

Courtland watched as Eva began to cry. He'd had enough of Lieutenant Stevens. Before he could speak, Eva's sister stood.

"How dare you," Frédérique said. "Get out of this room now."

Pearson stepped toward the officer, stopping short of being in the man's face. "You heard my wife. It is time for you to go. You will not falsely accuse my sister-in-law of such behavior. We will be seeking the services of an attorney. Until then, you stay away."

Unperturbed, Lieutenant Stevens continued to talk to Eva. "You are a grown woman. Yes? I would suggest you answer my questions. The longer this rocks on, the guiltier you look. So were you drunk the night of the accident?"

This time Courtland stood and went to the officer with his fist ready to pound his face, but Pearson grabbed his arm. Lieutenant Stevens casually rested his hand on his firearm, which was still in its holster.

"No, Senator," Pearson said. "Not worth it."

For a moment, Courtland almost jerked his arm away so he could finish what he wanted to do, but he glanced back at Eva, who was crying silently in her sister's arms. He was not going to do anything to upset her more than she already was. He nodded at Pearson, who slowly let go of him. Courtland glared angrily at Lieutenant Stevens.

"If you ever talk to her that way again, you will rue the day you ever saw Eva Cardon's face. I will haunt you like your worst nightmare, Lieutenant Stevens," Courtland said. "And if I'm not mistaken, both Reverend Dr. Montgomery and I have a mutual friend, Attorney General Tom Clark. I would hate to have to see him get involved in this."

Lieutenant Stevens laughed. "Standard questions, Senator. I had no intentions of rattling the little lady. I didn't ask anything I wouldn't ask any other person. You contact the attorney general if you like. Better yet, why don't you contact my good friend J. Edgar Hoover over there with the FBI. Since we're calling friends and all."

"Get out," Courtland said.

Lieutenant Stevens laughed again but turned to exit the room. Before he did, he turned around once more. "If Miss Cardon continues to insist that she was run off the road by a member of the D.C. police department, I will be needing some medical records from you, Doctor. Just so we can corroborate the stories that are being told to us about her . . . condition that night." Before anyone could tell him to leave again, he slowly sauntered out of the room. At this point, Eva began to cry so hard she was hiccupping and then coughing. Courtland wanted to go to her, but Pearson, Frédérique, and the doctor were surrounding her bed. Eva's face was still pressed against her sister's shoulder.

"It's okay, love." Frédérique crooned like she was talking to a small child. "It's okay. It's okay. He's gone. You will never have to speak to that ugly bigoted man again. I promise. Just don't cry anymore. You will make yourself sick."

"My head hurts," she finally said.

"I will prescribe you something for the pain," the doctor said. "Right now, you just need to rest. Everyone, I need you to leave the room so I can help take care of any discomfort Eva is feeling. You can come back in shortly."

"Let my sister stay," Eva said, moaning. "Please."

The doctor nodded and turned toward Pearson and Courtland. "If you two gentlemen wouldn't mind, please leave for a time so I can tend to Eva."

"I'll be right outside," Courtland said. "I'm not going anywhere."

Pearson followed Courtland out into the hallway.

"There is a sitting area right around the corner," Pearson said gruffly.

It was clear to Courtland that Pearson wished he would disappear into the woodwork or the floor. Maybe that would be the expedient thing to do, but he could not imagine leaving right then, especially with Eva being so upset. Courtland followed Pearson to the waiting room. It was empty. Pearson motioned for Courtland to take the seat beside him.

"Senator . . ."

"Courtland," he said. "Just call me Courtland."

Pearson sighed but then continued. "Courtland, I am sure you are a good man. I didn't think that before because of some of the things written about you in the papers, but seeing how you act around my sister-in-law just in these last few minutes tells me you are a thoughtful and caring man."

"Thank you. I . . ."

Pearson raised his hand to stop Courtland. "But having said all of that, goodness alone is not enough to make a relationship work between you and my sister-in-law. Two people may love each other passionately, yet because of circumstances out of their control, their relationship is simply doomed before it can ever truly start."

Courtland looked at Pearson. "I can't argue with what you are saying, Reverend Dr. Montgomery. But I can say this: I am ready to walk away from everything so that I can be Eva's husband. Not her lover. Not her boyfriend. But her husband. I understand the world might not be ready for a relationship like ours, but this isn't about the world. It's about what Eva and I feel for each other."

Pearson made an angry sound. "If you truly love my sister-in-law, you will let her be. Walk away now, Senator."

Courtland stood. "This weekend, I am going home to tell my family about Eva. My grandmother left me a diamond-and-pearl engagement ring that I plan to give to Eva when I return. If she says yes, we will make the announcement about our wedding."

"Wait a minute," Pearson snapped, standing so he was facing

Courtland. "Man, are you crazy or something? This is 1948. Has your whiteness blinded you so much that you don't understand that these cops or whoever is behind all of this madness will kill my sister-in-law? They are trying to kill her now, for God knows what. Maybe because she speaks her mind. Maybe because she is rising too fast. Or maybe because someone saw you kiss her at her New Year's Eve party."

Courtland looked at Pearson with surprise. Pearson laughed harshly.

"Of course I know about that kiss," Pearson said. "Those two sisters are thick as thieves, and whatever my wife knows, I generally know. But my point is this, if you think you can protect her, you are truly out of your fool mind. As white as you are and as light skinned as my sister-in-law is, to the world, you will be a nigger lover, and she will be a Black whore. Is that what you want for our Eva?"

"You know it's not," Courtland said. "But Eva is an adult woman. Let her decide what she wants."

"Didn't she tell you she wants to pursue her career?" Pearson asked.

"Yes," Courtland said, "but she also told me she loved me."

"Just walk away, man," Pearson said. "Walk away and cause her some temporary pain. Stay, and you are condemning her to a lifetime of heartbreak. I know she had to have shared with you what she and Frédérique endured when they were children. They might not show it to everyone else, but from my vantage point, both of them are still broken up inside from what their parents did to them. My wife is the most loving person I know, but the hatred she holds in her heart for her father—and in some ways her mother—is heartbreaking for me to watch. Eva—well, until you came along—buried her heart deep within her chest and poured all of her love into her restaurant. She will say she holds no grudges against her parents, but I see it. I see it daily affecting both of them. Don't do this to her. Don't do this to your future children. Walk away."

"I need to talk to Eva," Courtland said.

"Talk to her about what?" Pearson snapped. "Are you deaf? Did you not just hear the words I said?"

"This conversation is one that needs to happen between Eva and me," Courtland said.

"Let me ask you this, Senator," Pearson said. "Have you noticed the one common denominator in all of this?"

"I'm not sure what you are talking about," Courtland said.

"What I am talking about is this: none of this violence started taking place until you were part of Eva's life," Pearson said angrily. "You, sir, are the common denominator. Eva's civil rights activities are well known, for sure. All any person would have to do is read about her philanthropy in the Negro papers, but she is by no means as radical as some. So there has to be something else that she has done to make someone or several someones in the D.C. police want to kill her. You are the only explanation."

Courtland didn't want to acknowledge any of the truth in what Pearson had just said. He was willing to give up everything to be with her, but was it fair to ask her to give up everything to be with him? If both of them gave up everything, then what would be left for them to give each other? And what if these hate crimes were a direct result of his friendship with Eva? What if someone, like his father, were pulling the strings?

The doctor came around the corner. "You can go back into the room. I ended up sedating her, so she is sound asleep. It's best that she is not upset any more today." He looked pointedly at Courtland.

"Thank you, Dr. Overton," Pearson said. "Please tell my wife I will be there shortly." The doctor looked from one man to the other, then reassured Pearson he would relay the message. Once he was gone, Pearson turned back to Courtland. "Be the bigger person that I believe you want to be. Use your whiteness for good instead of for conquest and ownership of my sister-in-law. Continue your work in the senate so that someday the laws concerning a relationship between you and my sister-in-law and others like you can happen."

"I can't let her think I don't love her," he said, feeling tortured inside. "I can't leave with her thinking I don't care enough about her to walk away from everything and be with her."

"She might not understand it today. She might not even understand it tomorrow, but eventually she will see that you did what is right for her and yourself," Pearson said. He put his hand on Courtland's shoulder. "The most loving thing you can do today is to walk out of the hospital and not look back."

"I'm leaving," Courtland said. "But I will be back. You tell her that. Once I figure out who is behind all of this, I will be back for her."

Pearson shook his head. "You might find out the one person responsible for this particular situation, but for every one bigot who hates my sister-in-law for being with a man like you, there are dozens more waiting in the wings to take their place. This is bigger than you and Eva, Senator Kingsley. It always has been."

"I'm not giving up on Eva and me," Courtland said. "I won't."

Courtland turned and walked out of the waiting room and out of the hospital to where his driver, Harold, was waiting for him.

"Where would you like to go, sir?" he asked.

"Take me home, Harold, and then take me to the airport," he said. "I'm on my way to Parsons. My father and I need to talk."

TWENTY-EIGHT

Courtland

Courtland made his way out of the train station where his friend Jimmy Earl was waiting to take him home. Courtland had called around and was able to charter a plane to get him to Atlanta. Once there, he took the train to McDonough. Jimmy Earl met him at the station.

"We weren't expecting you until next weekend. Good to see you," Jimmy Earl said.

"I wasn't planning to come home until then, but something happened that forced my hand," Courtland said as he put his bags into the trunk of Jimmy Earl's car.

"What's going on?" Jimmy Earl asked.

Once they were both settled in the car and heading down the road toward Parsons, Courtland filled Jimmy Earl in on everything. When Courtland was done, Jimmy Earl had an incredulous look.

"Come on, Courtland," Jimmy Earl said, glancing over at Courtland for a brief moment. "You can't possibly believe Mr. Nap would be involved in something like that. I mean, yes, he can be abrasive at times, but bomb this woman's business . . . get a policeman to run her into a tree? No, I can't see it. Now if we were talking about some of my backwoods relatives, I could believe it, but Mr. Nap? That just seems too far-fetched."

"That's why I came home," Courtland said. "I need to talk to him face-to-face. And I also came home to make the announcement that when Eva has had time to heal from her injuries, I am going to ask her to marry me."

Jimmy Earl abruptly pulled the car over to the side of the road and put it in park, turning toward his friend since childhood. "You're going to do what?"

Courtland had a grim look. This moment should be the most joyous of his life. He and Jimmy Earl should be discussing the fact that Courtland would want him to be his best man, just like Courtland was when Jimmy Earl married Lori Beth. But instead, Courtland knew he was going to have to defend his decision to his friend.

"I love her, Jimmy Earl," Courtland said, "and seeing her bruised and battered reminded me that I don't want to spend another second of my life without Eva in it."

"Courtland, have you thought this through at all, man?" Jimmy Earl demanded. "Due to the miscegenation laws, as you well know, you won't be able to bring her anywhere near Georgia, so that means your family can only see you in D.C. And we both know Mr. Nap will forbid that. So that means any children you have won't have your mother and sisters in their lives unless Mrs. Millicent and the girls decide to defy Mr. Nap's wishes, and that is not likely to happen."

"I know everything that you are saying, Jimmy Earl, but that changes nothing," he said. "If Eva will have me, then I am willing to take a chance on everything you are saying. I trust you and Lori Beth won't turn your back on me."

Jimmy Earl pulled the car back onto the road and started driving again. "Have you ever known me not to support you, Courtland? And as far as Lori Beth goes, if you say the sun rises in the west and sets in the east, she will believe it because she loves you and trusts your judgment that much. We aren't your problem."

"Thank you, old friend," Courtland said.

"What about your career, Courtland?" Jimmy Earl asked. "I can't imagine the senate won't try to expel you immediately upon hearing about your engagement to Eva. Oh, they won't say it is about that, but we all know even the most liberal of them will not look kindly on such a union. What will you do?"

"I have a law degree, so I can practice in D.C. She speaks French, and I can get by, so maybe we move to Paris. Thanks to my grandfather, if I never work again a day in my life, financially I can take care of my family," he said. "The options are endless."

"What does she want?" Jimmy Earl asked.

"She wants her career," Courtland admitted, "and I am not opposed to that at all. But I would be lying if I didn't admit that it will be difficult for her to be with me and run her restaurants in D.C."

Jimmy Earl shook his head. "I don't want to be a naysayer. You know I want nothing but happiness for you, Courtland, but nothing about this situation makes sense. You're asking for problems. Twice this woman has been attacked because of her race and/or her actions. Do you really want to have to live your lives looking over your shoulders?"

For a time Courtland was silent. He knew Jimmy Earl only wanted the best for him, and if he was being completely analytical about the situation, he would probably be agreeing with everything Jimmy Earl was saying, but for once in his life, he was truly listening to his heart.

"Listen, Jimmy Earl," Courtland said, "I know I am inside of a rowboat trying to cross an ocean without a paddle, but if you knew Eva . . . if you had met her . . . you would know why I am willing to fight so hard to be with her."

Jimmy Earl made the final turn that led up the long driveway to Courtland's family's home. Upon bringing the car to a stop, Jimmy Earl spoke. "You have been my best friend since we were in knee britches. You took up for me when others were busy tearing me down, and when my father committed murder, you stood by me when it would have been more expedient for you to distance yourself completely. I support you, Courtland, and I will be there by your side no matter what."

Courtland reached over and patted Jimmy Earl on his back. "You always give me so much credit for the things I did for you, but my friend, you pulled me through a lot of difficult days as well. I can't wait for you and Lori Beth to meet Eva. Assuming I can convince her to marry me," Courtland said with a dry laugh.

"Whatever is meant to be will be," Jimmy Earl said. "Give me a call later or stop by."

"I will," Courtland said, grabbing his walking cane and then exiting the car. Before he could get his bags out of the back of the car, Ezra Parsons, an elderly Negro man who had worked for the family since before Millicent was born, came over and took the bags from Courtland.

"Welcome home," Mr. Ezra said. "I'll take your bags upstairs."

"Thank you, Mr. Ezra," Courtland said. "I don't mind taking my . . ."

Mr. Ezra waved away Courtland's words and began walking toward the stairs.

"I'll give you a call later," Courtland said to Jimmy Earl.

"Absolutely," Jimmy Earl said. "Feel free to come over if you like."

"We'll see how things turn out here," Courtland said and waved as his friend took off.

Courtland went inside, the voices of his sisters and his father meeting him at the door. Courtland went to his father's study where Nap was sitting in a chair while Courtland's sisters preened and primped in front of him, each talking over the other. From what Courtland could glean it had to do with dresses.

"Good afternoon, family," Courtland said. The girls looked at him with total misery all over their faces, and Nap looked like he just wanted to be rescued. "Ladies, I need to talk to your father."

"But Courtland—" Violet started, but her father interrupted her.

"You heard your brother. Now scat," Nap said. "He and I need to talk."

Although they grumbled, Violet and Catherine kissed their brother on the cheek and then hurried up the stairs, still arguing over dresses. Some things never changed in the Kingsley household. Courtland went and sat in a chair across from his father.

"Pops, there is something I need to talk to you about," Courtland started, but Nap held up his hand.

"Let me talk first, son," Nap said. "I wanted to call you, but since you decided to come home, I figured this should be a conversation we have face-to-face."

"Okay," Courtland said. As much as he wanted to just confront his father, he knew listening was probably his best bet.

"This isn't your time, Courtland," Nap said.

"What are you talking about, Pops?" Courtland asked.

"You don't need to get messed up with Strom or those Dixiecrats. The more I've thought about it, the more I've come to the conclusion that this isn't the year for you to get mixed up in a presidential election, either as the vice-presidential candidate or the presidential candidate," Nap said, looking at his son intently.

"Pops, I don't understand," Courtland said. "A few days ago you were determined for me to run. Now . . . what's going on?"

"Courtland, I thought I was dying not too long ago. I was terrified that I would miss out on seeing your greatest success—you getting sworn in as President of the United States—but today I really thought about the chaos in the Democratic Party and the popularity of Truman. You were right, as much as I would like to believe otherwise. Truman will win, so let Strom and whomever he selects as his VP deal with the confusion the Southern Democrats are creating. You don't need to be mixed up in all of that."

Courtland looked at his father and shook his head. "You amaze me sometimes, Pops. I have been arguing this point since you first brought it up, and now, suddenly, you have had a change of heart. I don't understand."

"I know I've been a puzzle at times, including the other day, but son, what I realized was I want what is best for you. That's it. This season in your life is not about me. It's wonderful that you are including me in it, but this is your time, and you need to do what is best for you," Nap said, leaning back in his chair. "I've lived a good life—made some mistakes—but you and those girls were and are my testament to God that my time here was well spent."

Courtland was amazed. This didn't even sound like his father. Nap was a bulldog. He didn't let something go until he got what he wanted. Courtland wanted to believe this epiphany, but he had spent a lifetime watching his father play chess when everyone else was playing checkers. A part of him wanted to believe this kinder and gentler Nap was legitimate, but he wasn't sure. The advice made sense, but he just felt like there was another motive behind the words.

"Pops, to tell the truth, I had already made my decision about this run for the presidency," Courtland said. "In fact, I doubt I will be in the senate much longer."

"What are you talking about?" Nap asked, leaning forward in his chair, eyeing Courtland suspiciously.

"I'm in love with Eva Cardon," Courtland said. "She—"

"That niggra?" Nap spat out. "Is that why you came here, to tell me some cockamamie mess like that? Get out of my face. That's not possible."

"I'm going to ask her to marry me," Courtland said. "But before

I do, I need to know you have not been involved in some of the violence that has happened toward her."

"How am I supposed to do violence to her?" Nap asked. "You see this bum arm and leg? I can barely take a crap on my own, let alone do something toward another person. Stop letting those niggras cloud your brain."

"No one is clouding my brain, Pops," Courtland said carefully. "Look me in my eyes and tell me you had nothing to do with it."

"I'm not telling you a thing," Nap said, standing up abruptly. "I'm going upstairs to take a snooze. You think whatever you want to think. I wash my hands of all of this."

Courtland was about to follow his father, but something told him to stay back. Maybe the answers he was looking for were right there in the office. Courtland began to search his father's desk drawers, but nothing stood out to him. He saw his father's briefcase in the corner of the room, but when he opened it, there was only a piece of paper with some handwritten notes about a new piece of land his father was hoping to purchase. Finally, he went over to the filing cabinet by the window and opened it. He flipped through a few of the folders, but nothing caught his attention until he was about to close the drawer and he noticed a thick manila envelope way in the back. Courtland pulled out the envelope and went to the other side of his father's desk and sat down. He rubbed his leg.

Courtland hesitated to open the envelope, but then he decided if he planned on getting any information, he was going to have to dig for it. So Courtland opened it and pulled out a thick stack of papers. He scanned the first page and realized it was a report about Strom Thurmond. Most of it was harmless enough, just information about Thurmond's finances and some of his business endeavors— information that more than likely would have been public record. But once Courtland got to the third or fourth page, the information he found made him take a long pause. It read:

Strom Thurmond, at the age of twenty-two, became involved in a secret romantic relationship with his family's domestic servant, a Negro girl named Carrie Butler, who was fifteen or sixteen at the time. On October 12, 1925, Carrie gave birth to Thurmond's child, Essie Mae, who was raised by Carrie's older sister, Mary, and Mary's husband, John Henry Washington. Essie Mae first met Thurmond in 1941 when she was sixteen years old. Since then, the two have had a cordial relationship to include Thurmond funding Essie's education at South Carolina State College and providing her with regular financial stipends.

Courtland looked at the next page and saw a ledger that documented every amount given to Essie Mae Washington by Strom. There were also pictures of Strom in compromising positions with Carrie Butler, Essie Mae's mother, at his office, hotels, and what appeared to be a secluded house, and the dates on the photos clearly indicated that the relationship between the two continued even after both of them had married other people.

Courtland was honestly shocked by the information. Strom's rhetoric concerning Negroes was anything but conciliatory. He spoke loud and often about segregation and maintaining white power and control. The idea that Strom had an ongoing relationship with a Negro woman that led to them having a child whom he took care of was absolutely unbelievable, except the photos did not lie.

Courtland continued to look through the papers, and then he saw his name on several documents dating all the way back to when he was first elected. There were details about meetings he had been part of, specifically meetings with Adam and other leaders in the Negro community. There were details about his work in Congress and information about specific senators he had worked with and worked against in the senate, ranging from their business dealings all the way to individuals they had relationships with. The last bit of information was about Eva. There were pages of newspaper articles from the Negro papers that focused on her restaurant and her activism. There was a ledger that showed the donations she had made to the NAACP and the United Negro College Fund, as well as private donations she had made to individuals.

Then, on the final page, there were details about his and Eva's relationship. Most of the information was in the form of copious notes in his father's scrawling handwriting. At the top of the last paper was the name Lieutenant Gregory Stevens and a telephone number. Courtland opened a second, smaller envelope that had pictures of him and Eva at the New Year's Eve party, including the kiss. Clearly someone was following him and capturing moments he had thought were private. Then Courtland saw photos of the explosion at Eva's restaurant after the fact. He had seen enough.

Courtland shot up, the envelope still in his hand. He took the stairs as quickly as his leg would allow.

"Wake up, old man!" Courtland bellowed as he barreled into his father's bedroom—the rage almost consuming him.

Had Nap been anyone other than his father, he would have flung the man out of the bed and against the wall, and he still had not completely ruled that out. But instead of acting on his feelings, Courtland stood in front of Nap's bed, clenching and unclenching his fist, determined to get some answers.

Nap sat up in his bed, looking disoriented and disheveled. "Have you lost your fool mind? What is the meaning of this?"

Courtland threw the papers at his father. "Explain this. Now."

"You had no right looking through my personal papers," Nap said in a calm voice. "This paperwork was confidential."

"This paperwork is about me and Eva," Courtland said. "How dare you collect information like this and then try to act indignant. What is the meaning of this?"

"You weren't taking care of your career, so I didn't have any choice but to work around you," Nap said, looking at Courtland intently, matching him stare for stare. "Had you been left to your own devices, you very well might have destroyed your career forever."

Courtland moved closer to his father, so close that it would have taken nothing for him to begin beating him to a pulp.

"How dare you," Courtland said, trying to sound as calm as his father, but all he could think of was that Lieutenant Stevens and God knows who else were taking orders from his father to do harm to Eva. "How dare you entangle yourself in something as diabolical as this."

"Are you going to stop seeing that woman?" Nap asked.

"What I do is none of your business," Courtland said, his voice rising.

"Then my hands are tied because I have no intention of allowing you to ruin everything we have worked so hard to accomplish," Nap said calmly.

"This is my life. Not yours!" Courtland roared, balling his fist up to smash it into the older man's face. "It is taking everything I can do not to choke the very life out of you," Courtland said, moving even closer to his father, but before he could grab Nap, Violet and Catherine ran into the room.

"What's wrong? Why are you yelling?" Catherine cried.

Neither girl was used to hearing raised voices in their home. Their mother didn't allow it. Courtland knew his behavior was scaring them, but he did not have time to assuage their fears.

"Leave the room, girls," Courtland said, not taking his eyes off his father. "Now."

"Not until you—" Violet started.

"Leave the room!" Courtland roared, causing both girls to jump.

Catherine grabbed Violet's hand. "We're going to get Mother," she said, and they both ran out of the room.

Courtland walked over to the door, locked it, then walked back to the bed where his father was now sitting on the edge.

"Get on that phone, call that policeman, and stop anything else you might have in the works," Courtland said. "Because if Mother gets here before you make that call, I will spill all of this to her, and I do mean all of this."

"I am not going to be spoken to in this manner. I am still the father, and—"

"You are a lot of things to me right now, but father is not the first thing to come to mind," Courtland said with so much distaste it was difficult for him to even look at Nap. "Tell me what you are planning to do next."

"I believe what you read is pretty self-explanatory. Both you and Strom have crapped and fallen into it, but the only mess I am responsible for cleaning up is yours," Nap said in a cold voice. Colder than Courtland had ever witnessed before.

Courtland did not want to believe Nap was that evil, so he tried another tactic. "You could have killed Eva and dozens of others. You could have killed me!" Courtland yelled, his fist ready to pound the old man into the bed, but then he heard his mother and sisters screaming outside the door, knocking incessantly. Their cries were the only thing stopping him from killing his father in that moment.

"No one was intended to die," Nap said in a quiet, emotionless voice, even as the screams and pounding continued.

"Call off your bulldog or I will have the entire government raining down on your head, Stevens's head, and any other co-conspirators," Courtland said.

"Courtland, open the door this instant!" Courtland's mother yelled. "I do not allow doors to be locked in my home."

"I want this to stop," Courtland said, his anger rising as he moved closer to his father.

"Then stop seeing her," Nap said. "Stop seeing her, and all of this stops. For goodness' sake, Courtland. All you had to do was follow the map that was laid out for you. I even sent you a replacement. A beautiful blonde with a pedigree to rival all—"

"Wait a minute," Courtland said, interrupting his father. "Madeleine Gillibrand? Your friend's daughter? The woman from your birthday party and the D.C. party?"

"Worst investment I ever made," Nap said sullenly. "But yes. I gave you a beautiful, intelligent white woman who would have made a good armpiece for you. It's not too late if—"

Courtland reached down and pulled his father up by his collar. To the older man's credit, he did not flinch. He just stared at Courtland with empty eyes. "Call off your goons."

"Is your niggra still at the hospital?" Nap asked. "I'm sure she's safe there, don't you think?"

Before Courtland could say anything else, the door flew open. Mr. Ezra was standing there with a key in his hands. Millicent and the girls rushed into the room, and Millicent ran over to her husband, angrily pushing past Courtland.

"Stop it, Courtland," Millicent ordered. "Take your hands off your father this instant."

"What is happening?" Violet cried. "Why are you and Father quarreling?"

Courtland flung his father onto the bed. "I'm done," he said. "Do you hear me? I'm done." With that, Courtland stalked out of the room. If this was what power looked like, he wanted no part of it. If he hurried, he could get to Atlanta and book a flight back to D.C.

"What happened between you and your father, Courtland?" Millicent asked, walking hurriedly toward her son. "And where are you going? You just got home. Surely you and Nap can work through—"

"We can't," Courtland said. "And I don't have time to explain everything to you now." Courtland kissed his mother's cheek and attempted to walk around her, but she gently put her hand on his arm.

"He doesn't have many more years," Millicent said in a begging voice, and Millicent Parsons Kingsley did not beg. "Whatever he has done, forgive him. Life is too short for there to be division between you and your father. Nap is a lot of things, and many of them I pray about every day, but one thing I have never wondered about is his love for you, me, and those girls. He would die for all of us."

Courtland did not want to listen to this conversation. He didn't want to say anything to hurt his mother or even to cause her to have issues with Nap, but he was not going to stay just to humor her, the girls, or even Nap himself. This decision Nap had made to bargain with the devil was more than Courtland could ever fathom forgiving.

"I'm leaving, Mother," Courtland said and kissed her cheek again. "I will call you soon."

"Courtland!" she called, but Courtland hurried past her and down the stairs. He went to his father's office and called the hospital. Luckily, Pearson picked up the phone. Courtland quickly told him what he had just learned.

"I will dispatch some men from the church to help stand guard. Thank you for the warning," Pearson said in a cold voice.

"I'm about to be on my way, Pearson. I'll catch a plane and—"

"You stay away from my family," Pearson ordered. "I might be a man of God, but if anything happens to them—any of them—I will hunt down both you and your father. Believe me."

Courtland called the private company he had used to fly to Atlanta, and they said they could get him back to D.C. that night. He hated the idea of flying at night, but he didn't want to delay his return.

He was grateful he was able to fly out as soon as he could get to the airport. All he wanted was to be where Eva was so he could make sure his father never did any more harm to her again.

TWENTY-NINE

Eva

When Eva woke up, the room was dimly lit and it was dark outside. For a moment, she was a bit disoriented, but then she remembered she was in the hospital. She looked over at the chair beside her, and Frédérique was sitting in it, sound asleep and holding Daisy, who was also asleep. She wondered when her sister had left to pick up Daisy, who had been staying with a friend of Frédérique's from their church, or if someone had brought Daisy to her. The two of them seemed to be resting so well that she didn't want to wake them up. She looked over by the door, and Pearson and someone she didn't recognize were standing together talking in low, hushed voices.

"Pearson," she called out in a loud whisper.

He looked over at her and came toward her with long strides. "Hey, sweetie. Are you feeling better?" he asked in a quiet voice.

Eva's head was still throbbing, and her arm was feeling uncomfortable inside of the cast, but she was alive, and that fact alone was a huge blessing.

"I'm okay," she said. "Who is that?"

The man by the door walked over. "Hello, Miss Cardon. My name is Burtell Jefferson. I'm new to the D.C. police department.

Representative Adam Clayton Powell Jr. put me in contact with your brother-in-law. I'm just here to make sure you and your family are all safe and sound."

Eva looked at Pearson. "Are we in danger?"

Pearson took her good hand in his. "Don't you worry yourself about anything. You know me. I don't take any chances when it comes to my girls. I just want to make sure we know everything we need to know about the bombing and the wreck. Officer Jefferson is just a little bit of insurance. That's all."

Suddenly, Eva remembered that Courtland had been in the room earlier that day—or at least she thought he had—but she didn't see him anywhere now. She wondered if he had been a part of her dreams. She almost didn't want to ask because she knew Pearson didn't care for Courtland at all, but she needed to know.

"Pearson, was Courtland here before?" she asked tentatively.

For a moment he didn't answer, but then he finally responded. "Yes, honey. He was here earlier today. He had to leave. Knowing the senator, I'm sure he will return."

She wanted to ask more questions, but just the little bit of talking she had done had her feeling worn out, and her head would not stop pounding.

"Okay," she said, too tired and in too much pain to really process what he was saying, except for the part about Courtland having been here. "I'm just going to close my eyes for a few minutes," she mumbled, and before she could hear Pearson's response, she had drifted back off into a fitful sleep.

Her dreams were filled with the sounds of explosions going off in her restaurant and images of her being hit from behind by a faceless police officer. Eva found herself awakening with a start and a moan.

"Frédérique!" she called, feeling disoriented. "Frédérique."

"I'm here," she heard her sister call out.

Eva looked over by the door where her sister, Pearson, and the man from the night before were standing, talking together in whispered tones. Eva watched as her sister walked toward her.

"Where's Daisy?" Eva asked. "She was here, wasn't she?"

Eva felt so discombobulated. At this point, she wasn't sure what day it was or how long she had been in the hospital. Everything was starting to run together in her mind.

"She's at home," Frédérique said.

"By herself?" Eva asked, confused.

Frédérique smiled. "No. She's not home by herself. One of the ladies from church is looking after her," Frédérique said, sitting in the chair beside Eva. "How are you feeling? You were in a good deal of pain last night. Do you remember the nurse coming in around midnight with a shot?"

Eva shook her head slowly. "No. I don't remember that."

Frédérique kissed Eva on the forehead. "That's okay. Do you remember anything else from last night?"

Eva struggled to pull up a memory from the previous night, but nothing came to mind. "No," she said tearfully. "Did I do something wrong?"

"Oh no, honey, no," Frédérique said, stroking her sister's hair. "You absolutely did not do anything wrong. Everything is going to be okay. You just rest."

Eva felt herself drifting back off to sleep, but before she did, she heard bits and pieces of conversation between her sister and brother-in-law.

"Doesn't remember."

"For the best for now."

"We have to tell her."

"Not now. Let her get stronger."

"Tell me what?" she tried to say, but even to her ears, her words sounded garbled.

"What did you say, honey?" Frédérique asked, sounding like she was miles and miles away.

Eva tried to open her eyes, thinking maybe that would help her focus, but her eyelids felt so heavy.

"Tell me . . . ," she started, but sleep overtook her. When she awakened the next time, she felt a lot more like herself. This time Pearson and the Negro policeman were gone; it was just Frédérique and her in the room.

"Hey there, sleepyhead," her sister said, smiling down at her. "Are you in any pain?"

Eva thought about the question for a moment. Her headache was gone, for the most part. There was a little bit of throbbing, but nothing major. Although her arm felt tight, it wasn't aching. She tried moving her legs, and that didn't cause her any pain either. "I'm better," she finally said after completing her own self-assessment. "May I have some water?"

"Absolutely," Frédérique said, getting up and pouring her sister some water from a pitcher by the bed. She helped Eva lift her head so she could take a sip. "Don't drink too fast."

Eva nodded and took several sips before pushing the cup away with her good hand. "Thank you."

"You're welcome, honey," Frédérique said, sitting in the chair by Eva's bed.

Frederique looked tired to Eva. Her dress was wrinkled, and her hair was coming undone in places. Eva wanted to be brave enough to send her sister home, but the idea of being alone in the hospital without her sister was overwhelming. Eva was never a sickly person, so this was her first time ever being a patient in a hospital. The only other times she had been to one was when her mother died and when Frédérique had a miscarriage. As a result, hospitals had always been scary to her.

"Do you need anything? I can help you get cleaned up if you like," Frédérique said.

"Yes, please," Eva said.

She was fastidious when it came to her hygiene, and she felt all cruddy from top to bottom. "I know you don't like Courtland, Frédérique, but he might show up soon, and I don't want him to see me like this."

Eva watched as a look went across her sister's face. "What's wrong?"

"Nothing," Frédérique said, getting up and going across the room to a dresser. "Let me get your toiletries together and a clean hospital gown."

Eva watched as Frédérique gathered the items she needed to help Eva take a sponge bath. Eva desperately wanted a shower, but Frédérique said the doctor didn't want her up and about yet. Frédérique went to the bathroom and filled a metal tub with water. Once Frédérique had everything she needed on the table by Eva's bed, she began gently washing her sister, starting with her face.

"When we get home, I'll help you shampoo your hair. For now, let's just get you cleaned up everywhere else."

"Where's Pearson?" Eva asked after a while. She was enjoying the warm bath cloth on her face. It felt soothing and relaxing. If Eva tried, she could easily fall back to sleep.

"He had to run out and take care of some things," Frédérique said, not quite meeting her sister's eyes as she began to work her way from Eva's face to her neck and arms. "He'll be back soon."

"Sis, is everything okay?" Eva asked.

Eva knew her sister was worried about her, but Frédérique was acting funny. It was as if there was something she wanted to say but was afraid.

"Yes, honey," she said, this time looking directly into her sister's eyes. "Everything is fine. Let me get done with this, and then we can talk."

The bath was so relaxing that Eva gave herself over to the experience and let her sister take care of her. Tears began to trickle down Eva's face. "You are too good to me."

"You would do the same for me," Frédérique said, and then smiled. "Actually, you have done the same. Remember?"

Eva nodded. She knew her sister was referencing her last miscarriage. Eva had taken care of her sister's every need the days immediately following the miscarriage, including giving her sister a sponge bath.

Before Eva could say anything more to her sister, Dr. Overton came into the room. He walked over to the bed, first speaking to Frédérique.

"She's awake," he said with a smile.

"Yes, she is. We just got her cleaned up, and I am hoping you will let us take her home soon."

"We'll see," he said absently. "How are you feeling, Eva?"

"Better. I would like to go home," she said, repeating her sister's words. Now that she was awake, Eva wanted to be home. She also wanted to get back to work. She knew Chef du Passe would take care of everything, but she had a system, and she didn't want anyone else messing with the way she did things. And she had a ton of things to do if she hoped to open her new restaurant by the beginning of the summer. She needed to go home, but the look on the doctor's face told her it would not be today.

"I know you want to go home," he said, taking his stethoscope and listening to her chest. "Let me see how you do today. I want to see you walking around a bit and eating solid foods. I also want to make sure you can make it for at least forty-eight hours without the pain medication."

Eva couldn't stop the tears from falling. She was disappointed.

The longer she stayed, the longer she had to think about what happened to her. She just wanted to push all of that drama to the back of her mind and keep moving forward.

Dr. Overton patted her good hand. "Now, now. Don't go getting upset on me. This time tomorrow or the next day, God willing, you will be feeling even better than you are now, and I can let you go home. I just don't want to rush it. You suffered from a terrible concussion. We have to make sure you didn't do any lasting damage, alright?"

"Alright," she said, knowing she sounded like a sullen child. "You're right." This time she sounded more like herself. Getting upset was not going to make her departure from the hospital come any sooner. She knew she should just be grateful that she was alive. "I don't want to rush it and then have to come back. I understand."

"Good," Dr. Overton said with a smile. "Do you have any questions for me?"

"How long will I have to wear this cast on my arm?" she asked.

"You really did some major damage to this arm, so you will have it on for at least another five to six weeks," Dr. Overton said. "You are right-handed, aren't you?"

She nodded. "Yes."

"Good," he said. "At least you can still maneuver."

"When can I go back to work?" Eva asked.

Frédérique groaned. "Eva, the last thing you need to be thinking about is the restaurant."

"The restaurant is my baby, and I have no choice but to think about it," Eva said patiently. Then she looked at Dr. Overton again. "When can I start back working?"

"To be honest, Eva, not until the cast is removed. A restaurant is too dangerous of a place for you to be with a bad arm," he said.

Eva tried to rise up in the bed, but she felt a sharp pain in her head, and she fell back on the pillow. Dr. Overton looked at her with concern.

"Did that hurt?" he asked. "Trying to sit up? Did that hurt?"

Eva didn't want to tell him the truth, but she trusted Dr. Overton, and keeping information from him would only delay her departure from the hospital. "Yes," she admitted. "I felt a sharp pain when I sat up."

Dr. Overton nodded. "It will be that way for a while. Take small steps, and you will feel like yourself soon. As far as the restaurant goes, if you don't already have an assistant, you need to hire someone or promote someone you trust. You don't need to involve yourself in the day-to-day inner workings of your restaurant until you are more stable. Your brain needs time to heal, just like your arm."

Eva nodded, but she was overwhelmed at the idea of turning over her restaurant to someone else to run. She knew Chef du Passe could handle most everything, but he couldn't do it all. His responsibility was the back of the house. She always handled the front of the house and the office work.

Frédérique reached over and touched her sister's hand. "It's okay. You are not alone. We will figure this out. Together. Okay?"

Eva nodded.

"Let me finish checking you out," Dr. Overton said.

Eva agreed and patiently endured the poking and prodding. It wasn't long before he nodded.

"Everything seems to be healing properly. I promise you, in a day or two, you can go home. Okay?"

"Okay," she said.

Dr. Overton left the room, and for a time, everything was quiet. Eva looked at Frédérique, who was looking at her with a strange expression.

"What is it?" Eva asked.

Frédérique shook her head as tears began to flow.

"What is it?" Eva repeated. Frédérique was not a crier, and seeing her crying now immediately caused Eva to panic. "What's wrong? Where's Pearson? Has something happened to Pearson? Daisy?"

"No, sweetheart," Frédérique started, wiping away her tears. "It's just . . ."

Before Frédérique could finish, Pearson walked into the room carrying Daisy.

"There's my girls," he said with a huge smile, but he stopped smiling when he looked at Frédérique's face. "Did you . . ."

Eva watched as her sister shook her head. Daisy reached for Frédérique, and Frédérique took her from Pearson, who went and sat in the chair on the opposite side. Eva looked from Pearson to Frédérique and back to Pearson. She could tell they were trying to communicate something to each other, but finally Pearson spoke.

"Sweetie, we didn't want to tell you until we knew more, but . . ."

Terrified at what they were about to tell her, she felt her own tears beginning to fall. "Y'all are scaring me. What's wrong? What's happened?"

"It's Courtland," Pearson said. "Last night when he was flying back here from his home in Georgia, the plane he was on went down. There were no survivors, honey."

A wail came out of Eva's throat. "Nooo. Noooo. Noooo."

Pearson stood and took Daisy from Frédérique.

Frédérique climbed into the bed with her sister and rocked her, not saying anything, just allowing her sister to cry, and for a while that was how they stayed as the tears washed over Eva again and again and again.

THIRTY

Eva

Praying the rosary was all that brought Eva some semblance of peace. She had been home from the hospital for three days, and most of that time she had spent by herself in front of the window in her bedroom where she did her morning and evening prayers, except now, her prayers were constant. Over and over, she prayed the eternal rest prayer, thinking about the last time she had prayed it for her mother and her grandmother before her: *Accorde le repos éternel à Courtland, ô Seigneur, et que la lumière perpétuelle brille sur lui. Qu'il repose en paix. Amen. Eternal rest grant unto Courtland, O Lord, and let perpetual light shine upon him. May he rest in peace. Amen.*

She also asked God for her own peace of mind, but no peace came to her. Over and over, the words *There were no survivors* played in her mind. *No survivors. No survivors. No survivors.*

Eva had not felt this level of pain since the passing of her parents and grandmother. Her heart hurt. Whenever she would try to close her eyes to sleep, she would see the image of his plane going down right outside of the Shenandoah National Park. *The Washington Post* said it had gotten dark and foggy.

Trying to imagine Courtland dead was unfathomable. How

could that big personality with the magnificent smile be gone? How could death have overtaken someone as formidable as Courtland? None of it made sense to her.

The sunlight was shining bright outside her window. It was close to noon on a Tuesday. She knew her sister would be coming to the door soon to check on her and see if she wanted to eat. Eva had only taken a few bites of the eggs and oatmeal her sister had brought to her earlier. She didn't want to eat. She just wanted to stay in prayer with the hope that some part of her pain would lift, almost like a fog. Like the fog that had surely led to Courtland's death. She wondered what his final thoughts were. She prayed that death came swiftly and that he didn't know what happened until he got to experience what Father Anthony at the church she and Frédérique attended when they were girls called the Beatific Vision.

Eva remembered that Father Anthony had referenced the words of St. Cyprian of Carthage. Once Eva was able to learn the translation of his words that had been spoken in Latin, the meaning was even more significant considering the losses in life she had experienced: "How great will your glory and happiness be, to be allowed to see God . . ."

Eva prayed that experience for Courtland. Even as she knelt before her homemade altar, full of sadness and heartbreak, she prayed that Courtland was experiencing only the greatest of joy. She knew that possibility alone should give her great comfort, but it didn't. She just wanted Courtland back. She wanted another opportunity to say to him the words he had freely said to her, *I love you,* but she wanted to say them without reservation or concern that saying the words might end up hurting her.

She wanted to be able to say to him that she was not afraid of a relationship between the two of them. She wanted to say so much, and the fact that she would never get the chance to say what she felt for him left her in despair. Her despair was compounded by the fact that just like when her father died, there could be no closure. She couldn't call his mother and tell her how sorry she was for Courtland's passing. She couldn't send a note to his sisters telling them how much their brother adored them. She couldn't go visit his grave and lay a wreath on it or just lie down on top of it and wail until her grief was spent. She couldn't do any of the things a woman in love could do when the person they loved passed away. All she could do was hold her grief close to her and release bits of it one moment at a time.

As expected, the knock at her door came a few minutes after noon. Eva lay her rosary on top of her Bible and slowly got up from the floor where she had been kneeling. She was careful about standing because with only one good arm, her balance was off. Eva smoothed down the wrinkles in the blue housedress her sister had helped her put on earlier and went and sat in the rocker beside her bed.

"Eva, honey!" Frédérique called out. "May I come in?"

"Yes, come in," Eva said.

Frédérique opened the door gingerly. Both of them had always been mindful of each other's space. Their mother had taught them that there was nothing wrong with spending time alone, and a closed door meant they needed time with their own thoughts. Frédérique was carrying a tray, and she placed it on top of Eva's bedside table.

"I brought you some chicken soup and some homemade crackers," Frédérique said.

Whenever Eva and Frédérique were sick as children, their mother had made them their grandma Bettine's homemade chicken soup. Now that both women were gone, Frédérique would always make it for Eva if Eva was sick or just having a really bad day. It always seemed to make her rally. Eva knew Frédérique was trying to give her some space and help her heal from her injuries, physical and emotional.

"Thank you," Eva said. "I'm not hungry right now, sis, but I promise I will try to eat some of it a little later." Seeing the look on her sister's face, Eva tried to smile. "I know from the outside looking in I must seem a mess, but I promise I'm doing okay."

"I just worry about you," Frédérique said. "I came to check on you last night, and I heard you crying. I wanted to come in, but I also wanted to give you space and not hover. Tell me how I can help you through this time."

Eva shook her head. "I don't know, sis. I truly don't know what you or anyone can do. Courtland and I had such a strange relationship. It never got the chance to develop, but the love I feel for him seems like we were together forever. Isn't that ridiculous?"

Frédérique sat down on the bed facing Eva, and she reached out and took her sister's hand. "Feeling what you feel is never ridiculous. Eva, honey, I wish things would have been different for you. God knows I wish that for you." Frédérique got up from the bed, tears streaming down her face as she knelt in front of Eva. "My darling little sister, my heart, my best friend, I wish the two of you could have had a normal, spectacular courtship. I wish he could have brought you flowers and taken you to the finest restaurants in D.C. that weren't Chez Geneviève."

Eva smiled, but the tears started to lap underneath her chin. The wishes her sister had for her were the same ones she had, but too late.

The idea of walking away from her restaurant and being a wife to Courtland did not seem so ridiculous to her anymore. To have him alive, she would give it all up. Frédérique wiped the tears from her sister's eyes. "My dear sweet Eva, I wish that after some time, Courtland's family and our family could have gotten to know each other like future in-laws do, and I desperately wish the day could have come when he entered this house and said to Pearson, 'I need to talk to you,' and then, in the way fathers do, I wish Pearson could have listened to him ask for your hand in marriage, and in the way Pearson does, I wish he would have made Courtland sweat until he broke a smile and said, 'Of course.'" Eva laughed in spite of her tears. She listened as her sister continued. "And then, my love, I wish that on a beautiful, sunny June day, Pearson could have walked you up the aisle, and you and Courtland could have become one. I am so sorry the world was not ready for that."

Eva nodded. "Me too," she said, choking. "I wish for that with all my heart."

"I know you do," Frédérique said as she stroked her sister's hair. "Don't give up on love, Eva. I know your heart is breaking right now, but don't close it off for the future. You are such a wonderful young woman, and I know God has something special in the future for you. I just know that."

"I don't want to think about that," Eva said, shaking her head. "I don't think I could bear this pain again."

"Sweetheart, part of loving is saying goodbye," Frédérique said. "Granted, you and Courtland didn't get a proper goodbye, but you got to feel his love, and you got to experience what it means to love a man. Don't give up on that feeling."

"I don't know," Eva said. Right now, the only thing she wanted to do was to go back to work . . . to throw herself back into Chez Geneviève and the restaurant she planned on opening during the summer. She didn't ever want to risk feeling this way again. If this was what it meant to love someone, she couldn't fathom putting her heart out there to potentially get broken all over again.

"Sweetie, do you remember when Pearson preached about the true meaning of love?" Frédérique asked.

"I think so," Eva said slowly. "He called it the long goodbye. I think."

Frédérique smiled. "Yes. Pearson said, 'If God grants us a sound mind and any type of longevity, saying goodbye to those we love is the price we pay for being here. But what a powerful price to pay in order to feel love.' You didn't get to verbally say goodbye to Courtland, but the memories you did share will be with you forever, and that feels daunting right now, I know, but years from now, maybe not so much. You will always have your memories."

Eva had something she needed to tell her sister. Something she only realized the night before. She didn't know what she should be feeling at this point, but she had to say the words out loud.

"Frédérique, I didn't get my period on Saturday."

Frédérique looked at her sister quizzically. "What?"

"My period," Eva said. "I didn't get it."

"Well, considering all you've been through, it wouldn't surprise me if you were a few days late," Frédérique said slowly. "Your body and your mind have suffered an inhumane amount of trauma. It's no wonder your cycle is off. I wouldn't worry about it."

Eva nodded. "You are probably right, but I've never been late before. Not even one day. Every twenty-nine days I get a period. It has been that way since I was twelve. I get cramps the night before, and the next morning I'm bleeding. It lasts for three days, and then I am good until the next cycle. I can set my watch to my periods. I am never late."

"Oh my Lord," Frédérique said, her face finally showing the shock of Eva's words. "You couldn't be . . . I mean . . . You said you two used—"

"Protection," Eva said. "And you're probably right. It's probably way too soon for me to think I could be . . . well . . . but I'm never late. What am I going to do if I'm pregnant?"

"We'll figure things out as we go," Frédérique said, a resolute look on her face, "but for now you mustn't worry. You need to focus your energy on healing. Everything else will work itself out. Okay?"

"Okay," Eva said, but something told her that Courtland had left her with more than memories, and when Frédérique took Eva to see Dr. Overton the following week, she tentatively brought it up to him. She was terribly ashamed, and she just knew he would be judgmental, but he looked at her with kind eyes.

"Well, it is still a bit early, and you have been through a lot in the last couple of weeks," he said, echoing the words Frédérique had been saying to her since she first brought it up, "but since you say you have never been a day late, let alone a week late, pregnancy is a possibility. I say we continue to monitor you, and if you notice yourself getting sick to your stomach or just feeling an overall sense of malaise, then you might very well be pregnant. But for now, let's just watch and see."

Once Eva and Frédérique got done at the doctor's office, and before Frédérique could drive off, Eva turned to her sister. "Freddie, I need you to take me somewhere," Eva said, feeling both tentative and resolute.

"Okay," Frédérique said. "I hope you aren't worrying about the restaurant. We just went there yesterday, and everything was doing fine. Between Chef du Passe and the rest of your staff, the restaurant couldn't be better. And as far as the new restaurant—"

Eva interrupted her sister. "I want to go to St. Augustine."

Frédérique looked at her sister with confusion. "Are you sure you feel up to it?"

Eva took a deep breath. "Yes. If there is a baby growing inside of me, I want to release this terrible guilt I have been carrying."

"Then let's go," Frédérique said, turning the car around in the direction of St. Augustine Catholic Church. Once there, she turned to Eva. "Do you want me to go inside with you?"

Eva shook her head. "No. I'll be fine," she said.

Frédérique got out of the car and went to Eva's side and opened the door for her. She walked with Eva to the entrance and helped her into the building.

"I'll wait right here for you," Frédérique said, pointing to a chair in the hallway.

Once Eva entered the confessional, she felt the tears begin to fall even before a single word came out of her mouth or the mouth of the priest on the other side of the partition. She knelt and made the sign of the cross and proceeded to say, "Bless me, Father, for I have sinned. My last confession was three months ago."

She remembered this because she had gone to Mass and confession in the month of December right before her New Year's Eve party at Chez Geneviève just days before she met Courtland. It was hard for her to believe that only three months had gone by. Eva confessed her sins to the priest, he assigned her penance, and by the time the priest prayed the prayer of absolution, Eva felt her whole spirit in sync again. With a renewed spirit, Eva went back to the hallway where her sister was waiting for her. Frédérique looked at her with such tender eyes, Eva almost started weeping again.

"Better?" she asked.

Eva nodded. "Much better. No matter what, I am ready to face the future," she said, and on April 18, the day her period was supposed to start, not long after the cherry blossoms began to bloom, Eva's future was clear: she was, indeed, pregnant with Courtland's baby. She awoke that morning with a sick stomach and no period. She knew that the only thing left to do was to tell Pearson. She had talked to her sister about it when she first thought she might be pregnant, and Frédérique had said they would wait until they knew for certain. Now that she had missed her cycle twice, and the nausea had started, she knew she couldn't hide her secret anymore. Eva decided to tell him after they were done with supper. Eva had been feeling sick all day and hadn't eaten much of her food. Pearson had noticed.

"Are you okay, sweetie?" he asked, looking at her curiously.

Eva opened her mouth to speak, but she couldn't say the words out loud. Not to her brother-in-love as she called him sometimes because he was more than a brother-in-law. He was her brother in her heart, her stand-in father, her spiritual leader. She couldn't make herself say the words. Frédérique, who was holding Daisy, feeding her little pieces of chicken, must have understood Eva's hesitation, because she looked at Eva and nodded.

"Sweetheart, Eva is pregnant," Frédérique said.

"What did you say, Frédérique?" he asked.

Frédérique reached for his hand, but Pearson pulled away as if her hand was something powerfully hot to the touch.

"Eva is pregnant," Frédérique repeated.

"I can't believe this," Pearson snapped. "The selfishness of such a lustful deed is hard for me to even fathom, Eva. You know better. We raised you better than this."

Eva tried to hold back the tears, but she couldn't. She couldn't stand upsetting her sister, but making Pearson disappointed was almost more than she could bear.

"I'm sorry, Pearson," Eva said. "I know I am a huge disappointment to you right now."

"It's not my disappointment you should be concerned with," Pearson barked. "It's your Savior's disappointment you should be worrying about."

"Pearson, don't," Frédérique said.

"Don't what?" Pearson asked. "Don't tell her what thus sayeth the Lord?"

"Do you remember the lesson you recently taught about the woman caught in adultery, my love?" Frédérique asked in a hushed tone, glancing down at Daisy and then back to her husband.

"Of course I remember," Pearson said in a gruff voice. "I don't need to be reminded of my sermons."

"Well, then tell Eva the last part of that lesson. Tell her what you said about that woman," Frédérique said.

Pearson looked like he was going to argue further with his wife, but after a moment his face softened. "I said we should all wish to be like the woman caught in sin because she was the embodiment of what a contrite soul looked and acted like."

Frédérique smiled. "You finished your sermon by saying Jesus never focused on her sin, only on her, the sinner, and helping her to become whole again. 'Go and sin no more' were your final words to the congregation, I believe."

Pearson lightly touched Frédérique's hand. "Give me and Eva a moment," he said in a quiet voice.

"She has been through a lot," Frédérique said.

Frédérique got up, kissed Eva on the forehead, and then made her way out of the dining room carrying Daisy.

"I'm sorry," Eva said in a soft voice, the huskiness from her tears still evident.

"You were always enough for me, Eva," Pearson said. "I mean, and you can ask your sister, because I said it to her after every miscarriage, that you were the daughter I always wanted. I never dreamed about sons. Just girls. Girls that I could spoil and protect," Pearson said. "When Daisy came into our lives, thanks largely because of you, I thought, 'my cup runneth over. God has blessed me with two.'"

"I know I have disappointed you," Eva said. "I'm sor—"

Pearson held up his hand. "Let me finish. Whenever I would tell Frédérique that you were enough, she would always say, 'But I want my own baby. I want a baby that comes from me.'"

Pearson stood and walked toward the window. Eva watched but remained silent. She knew that Pearson was mulling things over, and whenever he went inward and became thoughtful, the best thing any of them could do was let him be. Finally, Pearson turned back around and returned to the table.

"Your sister and I will do whatever we can to help you with this baby. Just like we took care of you after Geneviève died, we will help you in any way with this baby. You will not be alone in this. Okay?"

Eva got up from her chair and wrapped her good arm around her brother-in-law. "I love you. Thank you," she said, grateful for the love of her family. Grateful that no matter what, she would not have to do this alone.

THIRTY-ONE

Eva

It was only seventy-five degrees outside, fairly cool for the second week of July in D.C., but Eva felt like it was twice that hot, especially in her back corner office. She had gone to work early to get some paperwork done, thinking it wouldn't be so hot, but her office at Chez Geneviève felt like an oven inside. She had fans on in two corners of the room, but she was still hot. Her sister had reassured her that she was just feeling the effects of her pregnancy.

"Your hormones are in turmoil right now," Frédérique had said. "I never got this far with any of my pregnancies, but even I felt the effects of being big with a child."

Eva had heard the wistfulness in her sister's voice. Every day, Eva felt guilty being the one pregnant. Frédérique had done everything right, and she couldn't carry a baby no matter what she did. Frédérique never said or did anything to try to make her feel bad about her choices or the outcome of them, but guilt continued to rise up in her every time she caught a glimpse of her sister eyeing her belly with a sadness that Eva couldn't begin to fathom.

Eva was now five months pregnant, and although she was still able to camouflage her belly, she knew the time was rapidly coming when that would not be possible, and at that point she would have to turn over the day-to-day operations of the restaurant to the new manager she had hired, Gordon Pew. Gordon was a close friend of Hal's, the owner of The Phoenix, and had come highly recommended. He was a soft-spoken man of about forty-five or fifty, but he understood every facet of the restaurant business, having worked in it at all levels, from bussing tables to managing the schedule and payroll for restaurants in Chicago, New York, and Philadelphia.

When Eva hired him, he had just moved to D.C. Eva suspected it was because he and Hal were involved, although neither man said so. Eva didn't care. Gordon was a hard worker, and Hal was her friend. Nothing else mattered to her. Gordon and Eva immediately built a rapport, and when she finally confided in him that she would not be working in person after July due to her pregnancy, he had not missed a beat.

"Then we better make sure we get all of our ducklings in a row before you have to be away," he had said, the kindness radiating from his eyes.

Eva had thanked him. Knowing she could trust him to help Chef du Passe in her absence gave her peace of mind, something she had not felt a whole lot of in the last few months since Courtland died and she found out she was pregnant.

Because her pregnancy was all-consuming at times—her morning sickness became day sickness, and her constant sadness that Courtland wasn't there to witness this pregnancy with her overwhelmed her. Once Eva knew for certain she was pregnant and the pregnancy appeared to be moving forward without a hitch, she decided to wait on her plans to open Bettine's Diner. The bank had reassured her that her loan was secure for as long as she needed to wait. She wanted to be able to give her all to the project, but she quickly realized that Chez Geneviève and her pregnancy were going to have to be her main focus.

Eva looked at her watch and saw that it was almost eight o'clock. She had been at the office working since six. Gordon and Chef du Passe would be in at any moment, and the rest of the staff would show up around ten. The only reason Pearson and Frédérique had been comfortable with her coming in early was because of what had been in the newspapers the previous day. Frédérique had burst into Eva's room without knocking, something she never did. She was excitedly waving a newspaper.

"They got them," Frédérique had said and handed the newspaper to Eva.

Since Courtland died, Eva had mostly stayed away from the newspapers. It hurt when she would get caught off guard by a headline talking about his accident or some legislation he had been working on. The last paper she had read that mentioned Courtland said that the state of Georgia had selected his friend, Jimmy Earl Ketchums, as his replacement in the senate. She imagined Courtland would like that. As much as it hurt to see Courtland mentioned, she knew it would hurt even more to see his friend mentioned in his place.

But yesterday morning Frédérique brought her the newspaper and demanded that she read it. The headline read, *Local Police Exposed: 13 Members of the DC Police Arrested.* Eva read the first sentence or two but then stopped. The article said the policemen were arrested for accepting bribes from people ranging from bookmakers to government officials. Eva noticed two things: one of the first names listed was Lieutenant Gregory Stevens, and there wasn't even a whisper of the violence against Negroes or, more specifically, the police's involvement in the bombing of her business or her nearly fatal wreck. Eva had nodded and handed the paper back to Frédérique without reading any more of it. She felt her eyes become flooded with tears.

"They got them, Eva. You should finish reading the article," her sister said.

Eva shook her head, wiping away the tears. "They got them, but not for the reasons they should have. And anyway, it won't change anything. It won't bring back Courtland. I'm happy for the arrests, but these arrests aren't even touching the surface. There will always be more hateful men like Lieutenant Stevens."

Eva knew Courtland's death was ruled an accident, and she believed it was an accident, but she also knew it wouldn't have happened had he not been responding to the threats that had been made against her. As far as she was concerned, Lieutenant Stevens and Courtland's father were as responsible for his death as the fog that had inhibited the pilot's vision.

Eva was thinking about these things when she heard a light knocking at her door.

"Yes, come in," she said. She knew it was someone with a key to the building because the alarm system had not gone off. Pearson had insisted that she add an alarm system to her windows and doors, especially since she liked to come in early and stay late.

The door opened, and Vernon Michaels, the young man Courtland had brought to her attention, came in. He was dressed in a black suit and tie and was clearly already in work mode. He had his trusty notebook and pencil in hand, something he always did when he came to her office. He said he always wanted to write down the important details she shared with him so that he wouldn't have to worry her with unnecessary questions. Eva had promoted Vernon to maître d' a couple of months ago. The knowledge he had brought from working as a Pullman porter had shown her that he was capable of so much more than bussing tables. So not long after Courtland passed away, she called him in and offered him the new position.

"I owe you so much. I owe him so much," Vernon had said, standing in her office that day with tears running down his face. Eva had shed tears with him.

"The only thing you have to do is continue to be great," she had said to him. "That is all Courtland ever wanted for you, and that is all I could ever want from you as well."

Since then, Vernon had spent every spare moment at the restaurant when he wasn't in class or studying. He was the ultimate time manager. She had a feeling he had a schedule that listed everything, including sleep.

"Good morning, Miss Eva," he said.

"Good morning, Vernon. How are you doing today?"

"Very well, Miss Eva," he said. "I wanted to let you know I was here. We have three new waiters starting today, and I wanted to get them into the restaurant early so I can properly train them and make sure they are prepared for the lunch crowd."

Eva nodded appreciatively. "That sounds good, Vernon. Feel free to bring them back at any point so they can get their paperwork done and I can meet them again."

"Yes, ma'am," he said, starting to leave, but then he stopped. "Miss Eva, I didn't want to say anything, but three times in the last week, there's been this white lady sitting in a car outside the restaurant. She doesn't get out or anything. She just sits there and stares at the front of the building. She usually arrives around noon, and she stays there for an hour or two. It might not mean anything, but I wanted you to know just in case."

Eva wasn't sure what to think. She didn't know anyone who would come and sit outside of her restaurant, least of all a white woman. It was puzzling, but she wasn't too alarmed considering it was a woman—not to say a woman couldn't prove to be a danger. She decided to take Vernon's concerns seriously.

"Thank you, Vernon," she said. "If you see her outside again today, come and let me know."

"Yes, ma'am. I surely will," he said and then exited the office. Eva didn't lose any time returning to her paperwork. She needed to do a huge food order because over the weekend, Mrs. McLeod Bethune was going to hold a gala at the restaurant to raise money to help with voter registration in the South and provide scholarships to young Negro women interested in careers in business, law, and science. Eva had volunteered to do most of the planning of the event, and Frédérique had even joined in.

"I can do more to support and encourage our people than I am doing," Frédérique had said, sitting at the dining room table one evening where Eva had all of her notes spread out pertaining to the event. "I must learn not to allow my fear to overtake me. Thank you, little sister, for being such a powerful example."

From that day in early May until the present, every day Frédérique had joined Eva in the planning of Mrs. McLeod Bethune's gala—from the invitations to the flowers to the musical guests, Count Basie, Ella Fitzgerald, and Hazel Scott. Frédérique's involvement made Eva feel even more strongly connected to her sister, mainly because it allowed Eva to get her mind off Courtland and the baby.

Today Eva was making sure she had enough food ordered to accommodate Chef du Passe's menu for Saturday, and she wanted to double-check the flower order she had placed with Lee's Flower Shop. She and the staff would close the restaurant at noon on Saturday and spend the rest of the day getting ready for the party, which would begin that evening at eight. Eva wanted the evening to be elegant and worthy of the illustrious guests who would be present. She had spoken to Mrs. McLeod Bethune the previous day, and she was extremely pleased with all of the work Eva and Frédérique had done.

"I could not have pulled this off without you and your sister's help, Eva," she had said. "I know you have been going through a lot. I want you to know your efforts are not taken for granted."

Eva wasn't sure if Mrs. McLeod Bethune was referring to the violence she had experienced from the bombing and the car crash, or if she somehow knew about Courtland and the baby. Either way, she simply thanked her.

Now, as Eva sat in her office, a feeling of melancholy came over her. She couldn't help but think about how much she was going to miss being there every day now that it was becoming more and more difficult to hide her ever-growing belly. So much of fashion right now was all about slim fit and cinched waists. She was wearing a short-sleeved, black, loose-fitting shift dress, but if someone caught a glimpse of her at just the right angle, they would see the protruding belly. That was why she mainly stayed in her office, but when Vernon came to her door once more and mentioned the white woman was back in front of the building, she got up and went to the front of the restaurant without giving thought to the fact that someone might notice the indentation of her belly against the cloth of her dress. Eva opened the door and went out, Vernon walking closely behind her. She went to the car window and knocked. The woman slowly lowered it. The car looked new and expensive, and the woman was fresh-faced and well-dressed.

"May I help you?" Eva asked in a tight voice. Even though she didn't think the woman was there to start trouble, she didn't want to assume anything.

"Oh no," the woman said. "I-I was just—"

"Are you waiting for someone? Do you need something?" Eva asked, suddenly becoming aware that people were stopping and listening to the exchange.

"I . . . well . . . I'm Courtland's first cousin, Lori Beth Parsons Ketchums," she said.

Eva was stunned. She didn't know what exactly to say. Why was this woman here spying on her restaurant? What did she want? Eva also didn't like the feeling washing over her. She was trying to find ways to distance herself from Courtland and his death, and now here was this woman who quite possibly saw him before he died.

She wanted to run, but she forced herself to stay and find out what Lori Beth wanted. Eva turned around and looked at Vernon, trying to smile.

"It's okay, Vernon," she said. "Everything is fine."

"Yes, ma'am," he said and went back into the restaurant. Eva turned her attention back to Lori Beth.

"I don't understand why you are here," Eva finally said. "What do you want?"

"Would you mind if I came inside to talk to you for just a moment?" the woman asked.

Eva wanted to say no. Her mouth even formed the word, but she didn't say it. She didn't want to have a conversation with this woman, but she also didn't want to be rude to someone she knew Courtland had cared deeply about, so she sighed and agreed.

"That's fine," Eva said, "but I don't have a lot of time. I have . . . Well, I don't have a lot of time."

Lori Beth exited her car and smiled sadly at Eva. "I promise I won't take up much of your time."

Eva caught Lori Beth glancing at her belly. Eva almost put a protective hand over it, but she didn't want to attract more attention to her stomach, which now suddenly felt huge. Eva led the woman to the back where her office was located. She could feel the eyes on them as they went through the dining area, but she forced herself not to pay the glances too much attention. Once both women were seated in her office, neither of them said anything at first. Eva was not interested in leading the conversation, mainly because she wasn't sure why the other woman was there.

"Eva, I appreciate you seeing me, and I want to apologize for sitting in front of your restaurant all of these days," she said. "I wanted to come inside, but my fear continued to overtake me, so instead I just sat there."

"I don't understand," Eva said simply.

"When my cousin was home the . . . well . . . the last time, he told my husband, Jimmy, that he was going to ask you to marry him," she said.

Eva closed her eyes. The pain of hearing the words threatened to overtake her. Some days she was able to push the pain away. Other days the pain was so debilitating that breathing became almost impossible. Her body would be wracked with tears, and all she would want to do was hide somewhere. The baby, of course, kept her going. She was still in shock over the fact that she was pregnant with Courtland's baby, but she made sure she went through the motions of trying to take care of the child growing inside her.

"Are you okay?" Lori Beth asked, looking at her with concerned eyes.

Eva nodded. "Yes. I'm fine."

"When Jimmy told me about Courtland's feelings for you, I didn't believe him at first," she said.

"You didn't think it possible for your cousin to fall in love with a Negro woman?" Eva asked angrily. She was seconds away from asking this woman to leave.

Lori Beth shook her head. "No. It's not that. Courtland was different when he returned home from the war. Jimmy was, too, but not in the same way. Courtland took every death of every man who served under him personally. I watched my cousin date a lot of women, but he never allowed them to get close. That is, until you."

Eva couldn't stop the tears from flowing, and seeing them, Lori Beth reached into her purse, took out a handkerchief, and handed it to Eva. Eva thanked her and wiped her eyes.

"Eva, I sat out there the last few days because I wasn't sure if my being here was the right thing," Lori Beth said. "I wasn't sure if you would want to hear anything from me, but after thinking about the loss you must be feeling and the lack of closure you were granted,

I wanted to come and share with you some of the things Courtland said to Jimmy about you."

"I don't know," Eva said.

"I understand," Lori Beth said and reached into her purse again and took out an envelope. "I understand that now might be too soon, but I wanted you to have the words for the future. My first husband, Beauregard, died at Pearl Harbor."

"I'm sorry to hear that," Eva said softly.

Lori Beth nodded. "Thank you. I think the worst part of it was I didn't have any letters from Beau. He wasn't an overly sentimental man. I knew he loved me, but he never said it, so his death was particularly difficult. And then I got that awful, cryptic letter from the military telling me he was gone. Well, I wanted more, and there was never going to be any more other than them shipping my husband's body home. But you didn't even get that, and I'm sorry. So I wrote down every good thing, every sweet thing, every loving thing Jimmy told me Courtland said about you. Courtland and I never discussed his relationship with you, but my husband was his best friend . . . more like his brother, and they shared everything with each other, and Jimmy shares everything with me, so here you go."

She handed the envelope to Eva, and Eva placed it on her desk. Lori Beth stood.

"I hope I didn't make things worse by coming here," she said, her Southern drawl reminding Eva of her sister's. "I truly was trying to do for you what I would have wanted someone to do for me. I would have felt such joy if some nice person in the military would have been able to recall some memories of my husband talking sweetly about me to them and then them taking the time to share those words with me."

Eva got up from her desk and went around and stood in front of Lori Beth, taking both of the woman's hands in hers. "This means a lot, Lori Beth," she said, tears still shining in her eyes. "I regretted not being able to go to Courtland's funeral or to speak to his sisters or his mother. Having you come here and give me such a kind and thoughtful gift . . . Well, thank you."

Before Eva knew what was happening, Lori Beth wrapped her arms around Eva's waist and hugged her tightly. But just as quickly as she embraced Eva, she backed away with a stunned look.

"Are you . . . Are you . . ."

"Yes," Eva said defensively. "It wasn't planned, and Courtland never knew."

"Oh my goodness," Lori Beth said, tears streaming down her face. "You are having Courtland's baby. My dear, dear cousin will live on after all."

"You aren't upset?" Eva asked tearfully.

This was not the kind of thing most people would see as good. Eva was very sensitive about the fact that being a pregnant, unmarried woman in 1948 was not something that was accepted. Had she been a poor Negro woman without a family to support her and the economic wherewithal to take care of herself and the baby, there was no telling where she or this child would have ended up.

"Eva, I will not stand in judgment of you," Lori Beth said. "I am just grateful that my sweet cousin will live on. I pray you will allow me to see the child when it is born."

Eva nodded slowly. It was hard for her to believe the words coming out of Lori Beth's mouth. "I guess so. I would prefer it if you did not tell the other members of his family. I imagine we both can agree that they won't see the silver lining that you have so graciously seen in this situation."

Lori Beth reached out and placed her hand on Eva's shoulder. "I won't tell anyone but Jimmy, and I promise you he will be gracious and will want to know this child just like me. But I will say this, Eva, Mrs. Millicent and Courtland's sisters might surprise you, especially

Courtland's sisters. They have been pining for their brother so. Knowing he has a child on the way might cause them some welcome relief from the sorrow, but I will not overstep my boundaries. I will leave it up to you to decide who to tell what."

"Thank you," Eva said.

"Well, I won't keep you any longer," she said, but then she stopped. "Let me give you my number. We are actually living in Courtland's old home. It was easier than trying to buy a new place, and it has more than enough room for my husband, myself, and our twin boys. You must come visit us sometime."

Eva shook her head. The very thought of going inside of Courtland's house again without him being there was more than her heart could fathom. She handed a piece of paper and a pen to Lori Beth.

"I don't think so."

Lori Beth seemed to understand. "It's okay. I apologize for not thinking about how uncomfortable and painful that might be for you. I am working on being a more sensitive person as I grow older, but I am still a work in progress. Take care, Eva," she said and walked out of Eva's office.

Eva wasn't sure what to do next. She went back and sat down, looking at the envelope on her desk with her name on it. The handwriting was elaborate and extremely feminine. Eva thought about opening the envelope, but the thought of even reading words Courtland had said was too much for her to bear at that moment. She wasn't sure when or if she would be ready to read what he had said. She felt a slight movement in her belly. The baby normally remained fairly quiet during the middle of the day, but by late afternoon, it was as if the baby was making up for the quiet of the early morning. Throughout the afternoon and the evening, she would feel the kicks and pokes. She always welcomed the movement. It reminded her that she did have a piece of immortality in her belly. It reminded her that no matter how much she missed Courtland, she would always have this child who was born out of their mutual love.

Eva opened her purse and pushed the envelope to the bottom. She would read the letter later.

"Thank you for loving me, Courtland Hardiman Kingsley IV," she whispered. "I will continue to love you and love this child of ours that is growing inside my belly."

Almost as if the baby heard her words, it lightly pushed against her stomach again, and she placed her hand there, closed her eyes, and silently wept for the both of them and the loss they would feel for the rest of their lives.

—

Eva stood off by herself the night of the gala, dressed in a powder-blue evening gown with a fitted empire bodice and puff sleeves. The delicate ivory lace overlaying the satin was breathtaking. The dress completely hid her pregnancy and allowed her to be comfortable as she moved behind the scenes, making sure everyone had plenty of food and beverages, both alcoholic and nonalcoholic.

Ella Fitzgerald, who was being backed by the Count Basie Orchestra, was singing "It Don't Mean a Thing (If It Ain't Got That Swing)," an old standard she normally sang with Duke Ellington. It didn't matter who accompanied her. Ella had the entire place crammed on the dance floor. Eva had even caught a glimpse of Pearson and Frédérique dancing earlier when Hazel Scott had wowed the crowd with "The Jeep Is Jumpin'" and "A Foggy Day." The night was a huge success, and it reminded Eva of her New Year's Eve party. She tried not to let the sadness overcome her as she thought about meeting Courtland for the first time. And of course she remembered that kiss.

"You okay, Eva?" she heard someone behind her ask. She turned and saw it was Adam Clayton Powell Jr.

She smiled. "Yes, I'm fine. Are you having a good time? Wasn't Hazel amazing?"

He nodded. "She is always the belle of the ball. My wife's talent never ceases to amaze me. I noticed you were looking a bit melancholy over here by yourself. Are you sure you're okay?"

She thought about lying to him but decided if there was anyone she could safely confide her thoughts in, it was her family friend Adam.

"I miss him," she said simply.

Adam lightly placed his hand on her arm. "I miss him too. The country boy was a good man and a good friend."

"How is his friend, Senator Ketchums, doing?" she asked tentatively.

She didn't want to let it out that his wife had been by to see her earlier in the week.

Adam shook his head. "He's no Courtland, that's for sure. I felt like Courtland was on his way to pushing a more progressive agenda, but I'm afraid this friend of his is content to let the white majority continue to rule in a much egregious way. He's not promoting a racist agenda, but he's not pushing any boundaries either. We'll see. Maybe with time we'll see a different side of him."

"Maybe," Eva said.

"Courtland would want you to live," Adam said. "He wouldn't want you to give up on love now that he is gone."

Eva nodded, willing the tears away. "It's too soon for me to think along those lines."

"I understand," he said, and then he whispered in her ear. "After the baby, perhaps?"

She looked at him, and he patted her cheek. "I'm pretty oblivious when it comes to some things, but I have noticed the changes in you over the last few months. This baby will have a village to love it and cherish it, just like we did with you."

This time, Eva did shed a tear. "Thank you, Adam."

"Absolutely," he said. "Let me go find Hazel Scott before some handsome young man whisks her away."

Eva laughed as she watched him leave. Not long afterward, Frédérique came over.

"The party is a huge success," she said, gently placing her hand on Eva's back. "You did it."

"We did it," Eva said with a smile.

"How are you feeling?" Frédérique asked.

"Tired," Eva replied, "but I am happy everyone is having a good time, and . . ."

Before she could finish, Mrs. McLeod Bethune came over to them. She was dressed in a long black evening gown with a white Peter Pan collar. She kissed both women on their cheeks.

"Ladies, you have put on an amazing event," she said. "I was just checking with our treasurer, Ernestine Meadows. She says, as of right now, we have raised enough to offer ten full scholarships to young Negro women interested in majoring in business, law, or science, not to mention to help support the efforts taking place in the South to register Negro voters. Thank you for your hard work and dedication."

Eva was pleased to hear the good news. It was nice knowing all of the work they had done had led to their goals being met. This was going to be her final outing until after the baby was born. She was happy to go out on a high note.

"Thank you, Mrs. McLeod Bethune," Eva said. "It was our honor to help."

"It's just nice knowing that the next generation is ready and willing to serve," Mrs. McLeod Bethune said and then made her way across the room.

For a time, Eva didn't say anything, and Frédérique didn't either.

"I don't know what I'm going to do with myself now that I am about to be homebound," Eva said, trying to keep the sadness out of her voice, but to no avail.

Frédérique took her hand in hers. "You will be fine. Daisy and I will keep you so occupied you won't know where the time has gone. I promise."

"I will hold you to it," Eva said and leaned her head against her sister, and for a time, this is where they stayed as they listened to the Count Basie Orchestra play "Pennies from Heaven" and watched Washington's Black aristocrats dressed in their finest attire dance the night away.

EPILOGUE

"Push, Eva. Push," the midwife urged as Frédérique wiped Eva's brow with a dampened bath cloth. In the corner of the room, Daisy lay on a pallet on the floor sound asleep. She had awakened when Frédérique came to Eva's room to check on her, and rather than force the clingy little one to leave, Frédérique had just made her comfortable in the corner, and almost immediately she had gone back to sleep.

Eva tried to be quiet so as not to awaken Daisy, but the contractions were coming so fast and so hard, each one nearly stole her breath. Eva clutched her grandmother's rosary, hoping to draw strength from it and the spirit of her grandmother. She breathed deeply and then pushed as hard as she could.

"Good girl," Miss Thomas, the midwife, said. "You keep doing that, and we're going to have a baby here in no time. Make sure you rest between pushes and take deep, cleansing breaths so you'll have more power the next time you have to push."

"Yes, ma'am," Eva said, even though she was exhausted.

Eva went into labor the first week of December, and just like her periods always started on the same exact day, her contractions started down to the letter on the day she was due.

Eva had never felt such pain as she was feeling. "I'm so tired," she said, moaning. She had been pushing for two hours, and the baby just would not come. Miss Thomas would say, "I see the crown," and then seconds later she would say, "This baby is content to stay put."

Eva wondered in between pushes if the baby knew it was entering into the world without its father. She prayed that wasn't why it seemed so reluctant to be born.

"Just a couple more pushes," Miss Thomas said in an encouraging voice.

As Eva pushed, she forced her mind to stay focused on the present. *Viens, petit,* she thought, willing her thoughts to reach her baby who was fighting the whole process of birth. *Come, little one. It's time for you to come out and meet the world.* As if in response to her encouragement, Eva felt another huge contraction.

"Oh my!" she cried. "It feels like the baby is coming out."

"Yes, my love," Miss Thomas said in a gruff voice. "One more good push, and we will have a baby. Now push with all of your might."

With all of the strength she had left in her, Eva bore down and pushed, grunting and then crying out as she felt the baby slide out into the capable hands of Miss Thomas.

"What is it?" Eva asked. "Is it okay?" But just as she said the words, she heard a loud, lusty cry.

"You have given birth to a baby girl," Miss Thomas said.

Eva watched as Miss Thomas wrapped the baby in a white cloth and laid it on her belly, wiping the tears from her eyes.

"No matter how many times I do this, I am still in awe of the beauty that is childbirth," Miss Thomas said, smiling broadly.

Meanwhile, Frédérique was crying and laughing.

"Oh, sissy," she said. "She looks exactly like you did when you were a baby. She is perfect."

Eva smiled through her own tears as she watched Miss Thomas cut the cord. For a time, Eva just basked in the love she was feeling for the tiny baby on her stomach. "Take her," Eva said, looking up at her sister with all the love in her heart.

"Oh, Eva, no," Frédérique said, talking over the baby's cries as she rubbed the newborn's back. "This is your time to bond with your daughter."

"This baby is ours. She belongs to you and Pearson just like she belongs to me. I can't do it without the two of you, so hold her," Eva said.

Frédérique looked at her sister questioningly. Eva nodded, and finally Frédérique lifted the crying baby from Eva's stomach.

"She is you all over again," Frédérique said, crying right along with the baby. "Look at those beautiful dark curls. There's more hair than there is baby. Oh, don't cry, little one. Don't cry," she kept cooing until finally, the baby quieted down.

"She knows you," Eva said.

As much as Eva's heart was broken that there was no Courtland to celebrate this moment with her, she was overjoyed that she could share this time with her sister.

Miss Thomas cleared her throat. "Let me go get some warm water for her bath, and you let me know when you feel like pushing again. That will be the placenta needing to come out. You did good, Eva. Real good."

Eva watched as Miss Thomas hurried out of the room. Eva's belly felt like it was cramping a bit, but she didn't have an urge to push.

"I'm going to go put Daisy back in her bed and wake up Pearson so he can see this new beautiful little girl," Frédérique said, kissing the forehead of her niece and then placing her back on Eva's stomach. Eva protectively placed a hand on the baby's back. "I don't have words to say how thankful I am for you and your pure and unselfish heart, Eva. Thank you for sharing this moment and this little girl with me. I will love this child as much as I love you and Daisy. She will never want for anything, especially love. I promise to be the best auntie I possibly can be to her."

Eva nodded. "I know. Go get Pearson."

Frédérique picked up Daisy and started to walk out the door, but then she stopped. "What will you name her?"

Eva smiled. "Her name will be Simone Frédérique Cardon."

At first Eva had felt saddened that her daughter couldn't carry her father's name, but the Cardon name had served generations of Cardon women—strong women who did not always have the genuine love and protection of a man, and yet they persevered. She prayed the same would be the case for little Simone.

Frédérique placed her hand to her heart. "That is beautiful. Thank you. Now let me go get Pearson," she said, the pure joy in her voice so evident that Eva could not help but smile.

Frédérique, holding Daisy close, quietly left the room. For the first time, Eva was alone with her baby girl. Eva looked down at the child, her heart feeling as if it might melt from the power of her love for this little human she had just met for the first time. Eva reached underneath her pillow and pulled out the envelope Lori Beth had given to her months ago. Eva had slept with it underneath her pillow ever since. She had tried several times to sit down and open the envelope, but she just couldn't. As much as she wanted to look at it now, she still didn't feel strong enough to do so, but it did bring her comfort knowing that at some point she would be able to open it and find words Courtland had spoken about her. Words of love and his commitment to her. She kissed the envelope lightly and placed it back underneath her pillow for safekeeping.

Eva gently lifted the baby up closer until she felt the baby's heart beating next to her own. "You will never know what it feels like to be unloved, little one," Eva whispered. "I cannot give you all that you deserve in life, like a father, but love, I can give you that for as long as I have breath in my body."

The baby made a soft cooing sound. Eva closed her eyes, allowing herself to feel all of the emotions she had kept bottled up inside since Courtland's death.

"Courtland, I so wish you were here," she whispered, the tears falling freely. *"Nous avons fait un bel ange."* We made a beautiful angel.

Eva looked toward the window as the morning light began to break. Night was lifting, and a new day was dawning. Eva closed her eyes, listening to the soft breathing of her baby girl, who was born out of love—a love Eva hoped would sustain them both for years to come.

Acknowledgments

My love of words was given to me by the maternal grandmother I never knew. Thank you, Ellena English, for unknowingly holding a space for me in your heart and bequeathing to me your love of writing. I hope I have done you proud. Your legacy lives on in me.

I am always grateful to my aunts who have shown me so much love and given me so much encouragement. Thank you, Aunties Yuvonne, Brenda, and Jean. We lost Mom way too soon, but you have filled a void that I thought could never be filled. I love you.

Thank you to the surviving matriarch of the Jackson family, Aunt Lenoria. You loved me and listened to me when no one else would. Memories of times in my childhood spent in your kitchen prepared me for this time when I get to bring our ancestors to life in the stories I tell. You and Big Mama were and are the mothers I needed.

Thank you, Paw Paw Joel and Kem, for believing in me and always showing pride in my work. Thank you, Renee and Art, Joeli, Eddress, Derrick, and Terry. We don't see each other enough, but when we do, it is always like no time has passed between us. Thank you to my cousins, nieces, and nephews, near and far. Your love and support mean a lot to me.

As always, thank you to my dear friends and constant first

readers, Lauren Bishop-Weidner and Libby Filiatreau. You always give me an honest assessment of my work, and I always know if you have blessed it, then it must be ready for public consumption.

Thank you to my teachers from Ariton, Alabama, who always made me believe I could be a writer, especially Ms. Dorothy Dolasky and Mrs. Theresa Jernigan.

I am grateful to my former teachers and colleagues in the Naslund-Mann School of Writing at Spalding University. I started out there as a student and now I am a member of the faculty. I can't imagine being a writer without the encouragement of the amazing people at Spalding.

Thank you to my Facebook and Instagram village. You are always ready to give me advice and share details I didn't know about certain topics. Thank you, Melissa Palmer and Michele Miller Baltrusaitis, for answering my questions about Catholicism. Any errors made in the book are completely my own. I felt very confident writing certain scenes because of you.

I appreciate those friends who are there for me no matter what: Anita and Joe, Kiesha, Emily, Adriena, Julia, Alita, Elaine, April, Ashyha and David, Crystal, Carrie, Colleen, Rikki, Kailyn, April, Mijiza, Dena, TaMara, Bebe, Elaine, Krista, Patsy W., Patricia V., Victoria N., and so many more. My circle is rich because you are in it.

This novel would not have been possible without all of the wonderful resources I was able to find that allowed me to confidently write about the vibrant Black community on the historic U Street in Washington, D.C., the 1948 presidential election, and the civil rights movement that was alive and thriving in the 1940s and before. Some of the resources I used were: Shellée M. Haynesworth and the Black Broadway on U Street website; the Harry S. Truman Presidential Library and Museum records; *Truman* by David McCullough; *Adam by Adam: The Autobiography of Adam Clayton Powell, Jr.* by Adam Clayton Powell Jr.; *Adam Clayton Powell, Jr.: The Political Biography of an*

American Dilemma by Charles V. Hamilton; *Mary McCleod Bethune* by Jeanette Lambert; *Women in the Civil Rights Movement: Trailblazers and Torchbearers, 1941–1965* by Vicki L. Crawford, Jacqueline Anne Rouse, and Barbara Woods; *Dear Senator: A Memoir by the Daughter of Strom Thurmond* by Essie Mae Washington-Williams and William Stadiem; and *Strom Thurmond's America: A History* by Joseph Crespino.

Thank you to my amazing editor, Kimberly Carlton, as well as the rest of the editorial, sales, and marketing team at Harper Muse, especially Amanda Bostic, Becky Monds, Jodi Hughes, Savannah Summers, Kerri Potts, Nekasha Pratt, LaChelle Washington, and Patrick Aprea.

I could not do any of this without the support and encouragement of my phenomenal agent, Alice Speilburg. As always, you are my friend and staunchest supporter. I look forward to working with you on all of the projects yet to be born.

Thank you to the readers and the booksellers. You keep me writing even when I worry that I don't have any more words to give. You truly are my muses and I thank you.

To my loving husband, Robert. I am the most luckiest girl in the world to have you as my husband and best friend. Thank you for listening to me read my stories to you first. When I can make you cry, I know I have found the right combination of words.

My dear, dear son, Justin. We have been on this writing journey since before you could walk. You have always been my biggest cheerleader. I love you. Thank you.

To my daddy, M. C. Jackson, you are never far from my thoughts. Thank you for telling me I was a writer even before I could put my thoughts into words on the page.

Discussion Questions

1. In what ways does this novel defy the traditional roles you think of when it comes to Black women in the 1940s?
2. Oftentimes when people think about the civil rights movement, they think about the 1960s, but this novel illustrates how vibrant the movement was even in the 1940s. What were some things you learned about the civil rights movement that you did not previously know?
3. Discuss how Eva and her sister, Frédérique, have suffered as a result of their mother's relationship with a white landowner from the South and how their mother's choices ended up affecting Eva's relationship with Courtland and Frédérique's relationship with her husband, Pearson.
4. In what ways does Courtland transcend his white, upper-class upbringing and in what ways does he follow in lockstep with his family's legacy?
5. So much of this novel follows the historical timeline of the 1948 presidential election when the Democratic Party split in two. Although this book is fiction, it still honors much of the historical past. How far is historical fiction allowed to veer off the path of truth?

6. Parties play a huge role in the lives of Eva and Courtland. What do these social events reveal about the protagonists and the historical characters portrayed in the novel?

7. Eva's faith plays a strong role in her life, but she has found ways to create her own version of religion. What are your thoughts about how she seems able to combine her Catholic upbringing with her brother-in-law's Baptist faith?

8. This novel explores loss on many different levels. How does loss affect both Courtland and Eva in the story?

About the Author

Angela Jackson-Brown is an award-winning writer, poet, and playwright who is a member of the graduate faculty of the Naslund-Mann Graduate School of Writing at Spalding University in Louisville, Kentucky. In the fall semester of 2022, she will be joining the creative writing program at Indiana University Bloomington as an associate professor.

Angela is a graduate of Troy University, Auburn University, and the Spalding low-residency MFA program in creative writing. She has published her short fiction, creative nonfiction, and poetry in journals like the Louisville *Courier Journal* and *Appalachian Review*. She is the author of *Drinking from a Bitter Cup, House Repairs,* and *When Stars Rain Down.*

~

angelajacksonbrown.com
Instagram: @angelajacksonbrownauthor
Twitter: @adjackson68